# COUNTRY AFFAIRS

# COUNTRY AFFAIRS

Jennifer Rennick

HEADLINE

First published in 1995 by
HEADLINE BOOK PUBLISHING

10 9 8 7 6 5 4 3 2 1



British Library Cataloguing in Publication Data

Rennick, Jennifer
Country Affairs
I. Title
823 [F]

ISBN 0-7472-1228-7

Typeset by
CBS, Felixstowe, Suffolk

Printed and bound in Great Britain by
Mackays of Chatham PLC, Chatham, Kent

HEADLINE BOOK PUBLISHING
A division of Hodder Headline PLC
338 Euston Road
London NW1 3BH

To Richard
with my love

# *Chapter 1*

The receptionist at the Imperial appraised the woman approaching the desk with the eye of a connoisseur. She was pretty in an out-of-doors kind of way, small and blonde and probably buxom beneath her all-enveloping mink. He allowed himself a tiny fantasy whereby she dropped the fur and stood before him naked. She might look rather good in the buff, he thought, better than she did in that old-fashioned fur which made her appear so dumpy. But there was nothing in his demeanour to hint at such rapacious thoughts as he inclined his head towards her with well-schooled impassivity. She leant across the reception desk, and he caught a delicious waft of expensive scent.

'Where's my husband?' she demanded, her blue eyes blazing. 'I know he's here somewhere. Which room is he in?'

The receptionist swiftly rearranged his thoughts. 'I'm sorry, madam,' he replied warily. 'I'm not sure what you mean.'

'My husband has booked himself into your hotel with some wretched tart,' she bellowed, 'and I don't intend to let him get away with it!'

'I'm sure there must be some mistake,' the man protested in his best, most soothing voice, endeavouring at the same time to look shocked at the very idea of ladies of the street in a hotel like the Imperial. 'What is the name, madam?'

'Smith – Bray-Smith, but he's probably dropped the Bray. I suppose you have dozens of Mr and Mrs Smiths checking in here for a bit on the side.'

'On the contrary, madam,' he retorted, nettled at the thought of London's most famous hotel filled with couples on one-night stands. She glared at him scornfully and he glanced down at the hotel register with calculated disdain. 'We only have one Mr and Mrs Smith booked in tonight, both well known to us, being old and valued clients.'

The woman leant further over the desk and peered at the register. 'There it is! I knew it,' she shrieked, jabbing at the book with a blood-red fingernail. 'Patrick Smith. It's his bloody handwriting.'

The receptionist shut the book with a snap, like a stable door after the horse has bolted, and cast an imploring glance at his superior, safe behind the glass of the office. The situation was beginning to get out of control. The head receptionist was busy telephoning, he hoped for the night duty manager. He turned to the angry woman at the desk. Better try to stall until help arrived.

'If you could give me your address, madam, we can check our records for you,' he offered, but the woman wasn't listening.

She had turned her back on him and was staring across the hall at the couple walking down the stairs from the American Bar arm in arm. They were a good-looking pair, a credit to the Imperial. The man was tall, thin and patrician, his dark pin-striped suit worn with the casual elegance of one born to dress in Savile Row. The woman with him was certainly no tart, of average height, slender, and dressed in a silk shirt and straight black skirt, with her hair tied back in a neat chignon. She had nice legs, he'd noticed earlier as he watched her climb the short flight of stairs directly across the hall from the reception desk. The skirt she wore had been just the right length to show them off to perfection. They were laughing now as they walked down the stairs together. It was Mr and Mrs Smith, all right, the receptionist thought with relief. Then the small blonde woman at the desk gave a cry like an eager hound scenting the fox.

'Patrick!' she screamed, sprinting across the lobby before the horrified receptionist could stop her. 'I've caught you! How dare you bring her here, of all places!'

The hall was suddenly very quiet; everyone turned to stare in eager anticipation at the small tableau at the foot of the stairs – at the man, frozen into immobility, guilt stamped all over his handsome face; at the slim woman still clinging to his arm, white as the silk shirt she wore; at the small, vengeful figure of the one who claimed to be the rightful wife, who suddenly lunged forward as if to strike. The man moved quickly, shaking off his companion and catching hold of the other woman's upraised arm.

'Deborah!' he exclaimed. 'Not here, for Christ's sake.'

Then, before the fascinated gaze of all, the accused mistress vomited copiously over the Imperial's immaculate marble and slid to the floor in a dead faint.

The night duty manager, arriving on the scene not a moment too soon, came quickly to the rescue. Taking firm hold of the blonde woman by the arm, he began pouring oil on troubled water.

'My dear Mrs Smith, please accept our deepest apologies,' he burbled. 'I can see there's been the most terrible mistake. All the fault of our young receptionist.'

Scooping up the bemused Mr Smith, he steered them away from the catastrophe at the foot of the stairs and began shepherding them across the hall, like a circus manager ushering in a new act. It was done with such swiftness, such easy confidence, the receptionist was lost in admiration. He guessed that it took years of training, night after night spent coping with all the hundreds of different dramas which might occur in a great hotel such as this, to acquire such unruffled poise. But although he was impressed by the duty manager's inspired quick thinking, his sympathy lay with the inert figure out cold on the marble floor.

Swiftly he darted from behind the reception counter and crossed the hall. She was showing no signs of returning to consciousness. Picking her up, he carried her down the steps to the powder room, breathing hard by the time he deposited her on the chaise longue therein. He left her in the charge of the motherly soul who presided over the Imperial's palatial ladies' sanctuary and returned to the hall, sadly aware that a life spent in reception did not equip a man for the task of knight errantry.

Two chambermaids were already busy with buckets and mops, removing all traces of the disaster. People were milling about the hall greeting each other, checking in, checking out, besieging the hall porter, climbing the stairs to the American Bar. The night duty manager was coming up the stairs from the river restaurant. He cast a quick appraising glance around the hall.

'What have you done with her?' he demanded.

'She's in the ladies' room. Elvira is taking care of her,' replied the receptionist.

'Well, bundle her into a taxi as soon as you can.' He was obviously pleased with himself now that everything seemed to be returning to normal. 'We can't have two Mrs Smiths sharing room 256.' He winked at the young man with ruthless cheerfulness. 'By the look of the one in the restaurant there'll be blood spilt before morning,' he added, chuckling as he glided away to keep the great hotel running on oiled wheels, its reputation unsullied, until morning.

So mesmerised had she been by the manager's charm, and so shocked at having had her suspicions confirmed so dramatically, Deborah Bray-Smith had allowed herself to be led away without protest. Which was perhaps just as well. It had given her the chance to marshal her forces for a renewed attack.

'Let me take your coat,' the manager had murmured persuasively. 'I'll have it taken up to your room.' She'd let him soothe and cosset her, aware of the need to maintain some sort of dignity but still shaking with anger. 'A river room – naturally no extra charge,' he'd babbled on while she gave him her mink. 'The table in the restaurant is ready. It's in the window, overlooking the river.' He paused and she supposed this was some very special favour, but she was not going to be easily placated. 'The cabaret tonight is really good,' he added beguilingly.

Before she knew it she'd found herself seated in the Imperial's pink, candlelit restaurant, overlooking the river, at the table Patrick must have reserved for his mistress. The thought now fuelled her anger. As soon as the manager, heaping apologies upon her head, had bowed himself away, she flew into the attack.

'How dare you bring her here! It's so tawdry, so obvious.' She was suddenly so angry she hardly knew what she was saying. 'If you had to be unfaithful to me couldn't you have been a bit more . . . subtl

'It's not as bad as it looks,' he said, eyeing her warily.

'It couldn't look worse! Are you fucking her or aren't you?'

'Yes and no,' he replied, grinning at her sheepishly.

'Don't tell me. You felt sorry for her, I suppose.'

He gave her his little-boy-lost look and she wanted to hit him. 'No didn't. Yes . . . Deborah, for God's sake, if you want to make a scen can't you wait until we're upstairs in our room?'

'The room you booked for your mistress!' She might have hit him then, only a waiter appeared bearing a large bucket of ice out of which protruded the golden crest of a champagne bottle.

'With the management's compliments,' he said, setting about the business of opening the champagne with elaborate ceremony. Impatiently Deborah waited for him to whip off the wire and pop the cork. Her husband was taking an exaggerated interest in the whole performance, engaging the waiter in knowing discourse about the wine, while Deborah seethed in silence. With great reverence the waiter poured a stream of liquid gold into a fluted glass which he handed to Patrick to taste. More talk ensued about the business of wine, as if the two of them were in league against her. Deborah watched him fill a second glass for her, clinging to her anger like a shield as she took a gulp of her champagne. The cold bubbles broke against the back of her throat and she swallowed, letting the delicious liquid slide tingling down. Then she fixed the waiter with a malevolent stare. He whisked himself away.

'How long has it been going on – this affair?' she demanded.

'It's not an affair – that's what I'm trying to tell you,' Patrick insisted. 'We knew each other years ago when I was in London, before I started farming. We just went to bed together for old times' sake – that's all. She's happily married.' He stretched out a hand and gripped Deborah's across the table. 'As we are.' She tried to pull away from him, but he held on tightly.

'What were you doing with her here tonight, then?' she flung at him. He dropped her hand.

Another waiter appeared with menus. Patrick seized his like a drowning man.

'There's tournedos Rossini – your favourite,' he said, his nose buried in the menu. 'Shall we have that?' She stared at the large printed placard uncomprehendingly, unable to bear the false note of reassurance in his voice. It was the way he spoke to the horses when he was trying to calm them.

'I don't care what I have so long as it is the most expensive thing on the menu,' she said, staring at his bent head defiantly. 'Tonight is going to be very, very expensive for you, Patrick.' She took a long refreshing sip of champagne and caught the waiter's impassive eye. 'What would you recommend?' she asked.

'Tournedos Rossini is on the set menu,' he replied without blinking. 'But we have lobster on the à la carte.'

'Lobster will do nicely,' she said triumphantly, 'and I'll have some oysters to start with. Can you stuff them with caviar?'

The waiter was well trained. 'I'll ask the chef, madam,' he replied imperturbably. 'Sir?'

'I'll have the same,' Patrick mumbled, 'and you'd better bring another bottle of champagne.'

Still the waiter hovered. 'The lobster, madam? How would you like it cooked, thermidor or plain grilled, or cold with sauce hollandaise, or mayonnaise?'

'Patrick,' Deborah growled, 'do you want your bloody lobster hot or cold?'

He looked up startled. 'Thermidor for me. What about you, darling?'

'The same,' she said through gritted teeth. The waiter took himself off and the Bray-Smiths fell into an uneasy silence. Deborah scrutinised her husband, lounging in his chair looking so lean and fit and handsome. Despite it all, she couldn't help feeling proud to be here with him. She supposed it wasn't surprising other women wanted him. The only thing that was surprising, she had to admit, was that he'd never seemed to want other women – not until now.

He caught her eye at last and looked so woebegone and contrite she began almost to feel sorry for him. 'We only did it once, darling. It didn't mean anything.'

'Then why did the young man at the reception desk assure me that you were both well known to them, as husband and wife?'

Patrick's startled expression would have made her laugh if she hadn't felt so miserable. 'Once a year,' he said. 'We met once a year for old times' sake – that's all, I swear it.' The waiter was back, fussing about the table, laying knives and forks, placing a warm roll reverently on each side plate. His face was blank, but she was sure his ears were twitching. Deborah waited impatiently, while the implications of Patrick's excuses sank in. The waiter cleared his throat discreetly.

'Well?' She gave him another black look, hoping he would take himself off.

'The chef says he is unable to stuff the oysters with caviar, madam,' he said in the kind of hushed voice undertakers use with bereaved relatives.

'I thought the Imperial always boasted it could do anything,' she challenged him.

'Debs, for Christ's sake,' Patrick muttered.

'Not can't – won't,' said the waiter. She regarded him thoughtfully.

'The chef has suggested that he does a special seafood platter – oysters, caviar, giant prawns, some smoked salmon stuffed with scallop mousse perhaps.'

'Yes,' she said, nodding brightly at Patrick, 'that all sounds very expensive.' The waiter departed, looking relieved, and Deborah drank deeply from her champagne before turning to her husband again.

'How long?' she demanded. 'How long, Patrick, has this annual fucking reunion been going on?'

'Five years.'

'Five years!' He knew without even having to work it out. 'Oh Patrick.' The champagne was beginning to do its work and her temper, which had so far kept the pain at bay, was cooling. 'I thought we were happy. I thought you loved me.'

'We are happy. I do love you.' He stretched across the table, tried to take her hand, but she clung defiantly to her glass with both hands. 'It was only once a year. It was nothing. Don't cry Deborah, for Christ's sake.'

She shook her head furiously. 'I'm not bloody crying, the champagne's got up my nose.'

'I've been to bed with the woman five times – that's all. It's no big deal. It won't happen again.'

She looked out of the window – at the lights twinkling across the River Thames. It was one of the most romantic views in London.

She couldn't believe she was sitting here, being wined and dined by her husband in his mistress's place. She didn't want to believe he had a mistress. From that terrible moment when she'd first found the letter, stuffed into a drawer with a sheaf of bills in the farm office, she'd been sure it was all a mistake. She'd been looking for a telephone number and found the letter instead. It had been from the Imperial, offering Patrick a river room instead of his usual double, at no extra charge. The words 'you and your wife', 'esteemed and regular custom over the years' had leapt off the page at her but she'd been sure it was all some silly mistake. Patrick was at a livery dinner. It was men only. He went every year in September, had been going for years now. She'd never thought anything about it. She dropped the letter as if it had been some piece of nuclear waste and rushed upstairs to Patrick's dressing room to search feverishly for evidence that he had indeed gone to this dinner. But his tail coat was hanging in the wardrobe, his starched white shirt, tie and waistcoat still immaculately wrapped in cellophane from their last encounter with the cleaners. Deborah stood in the middle of the room and stared about her in miserable disbelief. This isn't happening to me, she thought, this is what happens to other people, not to me. Patrick can't be having an affair. I've got to prove it's all a mistake. Without stopping to think, she'd leapt into her tidy town clothes and her car and driven up to London. Now here she was and her worst fears had been proved all too horribly true.

She became aware of music in the restaurant, of couples dancing. The tune the band were playing was 'As Time Goes By'. She could not believe she could hurt so much.

'Why?' she said. 'Why did you do it?'

He shrugged apologetically.

'Why does any man do it? I don't know. She was part of my youth, I suppose, and I was feeling my age.'

'But you brought her to the Imperial. You never brought me here.'

'You're always too busy with the horses or the children or the garden. You never wanted to come to London.' He reached across the table. This time she let him take her hand. 'But we're here now and it's costing me a small fortune. Let's enjoy it, shall we?'

She hadn't the heart to pull away. The champagne on an empty stomach was making her head swim. Dimly in the back of her mind she knew it was important to forgive him, to pretend that everything was all right between them, to believe that what he had told her was the truth.

'Come and dance,' said Patrick.

She didn't want to dance, she wasn't much of a dancer. What she wanted was to go to bed. But not in the plushly luxurious, artificially contrived romance of the Imperial's river-view bedchamber. She wanted to be back home in the country, in their own cosy comfortable king-sized bed, making love to her husband in her own way, unchallenged by thoughts of what he might have chosen to do with his mistress. Patrick was watching her expectantly. Her temper had gone. Now all she wanted was her husband back – on her terms.

'You're right – let's dance,' she said, getting to her feet unsteadily. By the time they got back to their table she was beginning to giggle.

'You have to hand it to the Imperial,' she said, collapsing into her seat, 'they made the most of that débâcle. Do you think they have terrified females throwing up all over the front lobby every night of the week?'

'Poor girl, I wonder what they've done with her,' he said.

'Chucked her in the river, I hope,' said his wife. 'And bloody good riddance to her too.'

# *Chapter 2*

Kate Hopegood huddled in the back of the taxi still in a state of shock. The staff of the Imperial, who had welcomed her into the hotel with so much deferential warmth, had bundled her out of it as if she had been a piece of left luggage, which she supposed she was.

'Where to, lady?' demanded the taxi driver.

Where to indeed? She couldn't go home. Her husband thought she was staying the night with an old school friend somewhere out of town.

'I don't know,' she whispered.

'Well, we can't sit here all night,' he muttered. 'We're blocking the traffic.'

She peered out of the window at the narrow street with its queue of taxis and limousines waiting to disgorge their glamorous occupants. The hotel's uniformed doormen were leaping from one to the other, opening doors and ushering people into the Imperial's warm, expensive embrace. One of them had done that for Kate when she had arrived such a short time ago, and she had floated in through the revolving door filled with as much excitement and happy anticipation as Cinderella on the way to find her Prince Charming. The same man had now slammed the taxi door shut without even bothering to give instructions to the driver. Midnight for this poor Cinderella had come sooner than expected, thought Kate ruefully, and she'd been turned into a proper pumpkin.

'Look, lady, if you don't have anywhere you want me to go there's plenty of others that do.' The taxi driver was becoming angry with her and so, from the sound of the vociferous honking all around, were all the others.

'Could you just drive me around a little?' stammered Kate. Her head was throbbing and her teeth beginning to chatter. 'It doesn't much matter where.'

'OK.' He put the cab in gear and began to ease out of the narrow lane into the Strand.

Where could she go? She ought to marshal her scattered wits, think of something, get a grip on herself, but her mind refused to be marshalled. She kept thinking of the horrifying moment when that woman had appeared in front of them, screaming that she was Patrick's wife. If only she had been able to make a dignified exit, if only she hadn't been so frightened, if only she had fainted dead away without first being sick all over the Imperial's immaculate marble floor. Patrick must have been so ashamed of her.

Patrick. He'd been the first big love of Kate's life. She'd met him at a New Year's Eve party six months after she had come to London. He was standing in the window surrounded by a bevy of beautiful girls, wearing a flowing white shirt open at the neck and tucked into tight black velvet trousers which showed off his long lean figure to perfection. With his chiselled features and dark straight hair flopping over his forehead, he looked a bit like a modern Hamlet she thought, except that he had an air of too much suppressed vigour about him for Hamlet. He was so handsome she couldn't stop staring at him, until he'd looked across the room and caught her eye. She'd blushed then and looked down at her feet, fervently wishing she was half as beautiful as any one of the girls clustered around him. But then to her amazement he'd come and asked her to dance. He had been a brilliant dancer and she loved dancing. They'd danced all night together, then he'd walked back with her to the flat she shared in Chelsea. It had been a wonderful walk. The streets were filled with people wishing Happy New Year to complete strangers. The air was bright and frosty, the sky filled with a million stars.

When they got back to Kate's flat the place was like a railway station from an old war weepie. Two of Kate's flatmates were entwined with their boyfriends in opposite corners of the sitting room, while the third was snogging on the stairs, effectively blocking the wide smooth path to temptation in the bedroom. Muttering something about coffee, Kate dragged Patrick into the kitchen. When he kissed her it was as if someone had touched off a firework inside her. She seemed to explode into a shower of brilliant stars. Kissing him back fervently she didn't care that the kitchen smelt of stale beer and frying, or that the bright bare bulb of the light above her head was shining unromantically down on a pile of dirty dishes in the sink. All she knew, as she stood there uncomfortably poised above the draining board with the moisture of desire running down her legs just from kissing him, was that she was in love. He was the most wonderful, exciting, magical thing that had ever happened to her. The man she had left home and come to London to find.

Home was in the Scottish borders where her father was a country doctor. Kate's childhood had been protected, happy and uneventful. Like most children with loving, undemanding parents she had taken all the security for granted and chaffed at being stuck in such a boring backwater where nothing at all exciting ever happened. As soon as she left school she'd persuaded her tolerant parents to allow her to go to London to do a secretarial course. She was eighteen, romantic, idealistic and ready for any adventure. And once she'd met Patrick she was lost.

She went to bed with him on their second meeting as blindly as a moth flying into a candle flame, losing her virginity without a trace of regret, hardly able to believe that a man so gloriously attractive as Patrick could actually want to make love to her. The miracle of it was that he did, not just once but all the time. It lasted for seven glorious, golden, heady months. He was in the City learning about money, she was at secretarial college learning to type. Together they explored London – eating in bistros, drinking in pubs, dancing at the Chelsea Arts Club, making love wherever and whenever they could. At weekends he disappeared to Gloucestershire to hunt. But when spring came he occasionally spent a weekend with Kate in London. There were long walks among the daffodils in Hyde Park, lazy breakfasts in bed together on Sunday mornings when his flatmates were away, picnics by the river. It never seemed to rain that summer. The London season was in full swing. They gatecrashed coming-out dances, spent a wonderful day at Henley, got seats for the rehearsal of the Trooping the Colour, watched the marines beating the retreat in St James's Park.

Then in July Patrick's father had died suddenly. He went home for the funeral, told Kate he was staying to help with the harvest and never came back. She did not hear from him again. She waited and she waited for him to telephone or write, but he never did. She swallowed her pride and went to his flat and asked his flatmates for his address, but they fobbed her off with excuses. Her heart was broken. She failed her secretarial exams time after time. In the end she left the college without a diploma and got a job as a receptionist in an advertising agency, but she wasn't much good at it. It was the day after she got the sack from there that she met Alan.

It was November, dark and foggy and dismal. One of Kate's flatmates had dragged her off to an ice rink in Bayswater to get some exercise and take her out of herself. Only it wasn't very successful as Kate wasn't much good on skates either. She was wobbling miserably around the edge, wishing she hadn't come and feeling a terminal failure, when she'd felt a hand beneath her elbow.

'Here, why don't you let go of the rail and relax a little?' she heard a reassuring voice in her ear. 'You'll find it easier than you think.' She tried to look at him but began wobbling dangerously. 'It's all right,' he said. 'I've got you.' He had a nice voice, she thought, deep and dependable, rather like a St Bernard's if a dog could talk. He held her up and guided her around the ice until she got her balance. 'I think you've got the hang of it now,' he said. 'Want to try it on your own?' She nodded and he released her, skating along beside her, ready to catch her if she needed him. She didn't.

'I can do it!' she cried, absurdly pleased with herself and grateful to him for showing her how. He stayed with her, remaining within easy reach, and she was grateful for that too, as they skated another careful circuit of the rink.

Afterwards she let him buy her a drink and he wrote down her telephone number. He wasn't handsome – just middling. Middling height, middling build, his hair middling brown. Nothing to get excited about. It wasn't love at first sight, although Alan said it was for him.

From the moment he came into her life, Alan took charge. When he took her out to dinner he chose what she was going to eat and she was enormously impressed that he seemed to know just what it was she wanted. It made her feel wonderfully cherished. He found her a job and made her put up her hair and lengthen her skirts. She changed from a starry-eyed lovesick teenager into a chic child of the seventies. With Alan she felt safe. What she liked about him was his competence, his masterfulness, the way he always wanted to protect her all the time. Everything Alan did he seemed to get right. She admired him enormously. When she took him home to Scotland to meet her parents they loved him. When he asked her to marry him she accepted with gratitude. Love had come later, with the children, with shared triumphs and disasters, with respect and dependence and understanding.

She was brought back to her present predicament with a jolt by the taxi driver wanting to know how much longer he was to drive around wasting petrol. Belatedly Kate thought of money. How much did she have in her purse? She fumbled in her handbag. Fifteen pounds and a few bits and pieces. She peered at the meter. Seven pounds already. She must think of something. If only Alan were here, he would know what to do. She began to laugh. Poor dear Alan, what was she doing being unfaithful to him in this ridiculous way after so many years of happy married life? What was it one of her flatmates had said when Alan started taking Kate out? 'He may not be what you want, but he's what you need. Someone to look after you.' Shirley was right.

Suddenly Kate sat up straight in the taxi. Shirley, of course! Why hadn't she thought of Shirley before? Shirley was a career woman. She had a good job and a smart flat and her love life was in permanent turmoil. She often said she envied Kate her wonderful safe married life, which may have been why Kate kept in touch – in a desultory sort of way. Perhaps she could go to Shirley's for the night? Kate began fumbling in her handbag again, searching for the small pocket address book Alan had given her, making sure she copied all her addresses into it. He was so thoughtful, so good at looking after her. How could she have been so utterly foolish?

'The Salvation Army has a hostel for the homeless,' the taxi driver offered, and she wasn't sure whether he meant it kindly or not.

'It's all right,' she told him hastily. 'I've thought of somewhere. Could you take me to 13 Beverley Gardens, please?' He muttered something under his breath but it was plain he was relieved he had a definite goal at last.

As the taxi wove its way through the evening traffic towards Knightsbridge Kate wondered what Patrick was telling his wife. The truth perhaps. Patrick never had been much good at lying. At least he'd never bothered to lie to her. Because he knew she wouldn't create a scene or because she wasn't worth deceiving? A depressing thought. But that wife of his would be giving him hell. And Patrick, poor lamb, did so hate scenes and rows.

'Here we are, miss,' said the taxi driver. 'Beverley Gardens.'

Kate felt utterly discredited. The driver didn't even think she was married. But maybe he'd have thought worse of her if he'd realised she was. She stumbled out of the cab dragging her overnight bag awkwardly behind her, dropping her handbag as she fumbled to find the money to pay him with. He didn't make any attempt to get out and help her, just counted out her change with deliberate carefulness as if to imply she should have tipped him more generously.

As he drove off Kate wished she'd had the courage to ask him to wait, to see if Shirley answered the door, but it was too late now. Suppose Shirley was out or, worse, in and entertaining a man? Suppose they were already in bed? She peered at her watch but it was too dark to read the time. It must be quite late by now. The forlorn sound of the taxi receding into the distance made Kate feel utterly desolate. Anxiously she peered about the secluded square. It was very quiet, lonely and deserted, not the place for females to be wandering all alone and unprotected.

'Please, God, let Shirley be at home,' Kate prayed as she rang the bell. 'Dear God, if you let Shirley be in I'll never see Patrick Bray-Smith again, I swear it as long as I live.' She waited shivering on the doorstep with her heart pounding and her mind suddenly filled with anger towards Patrick, who had lured her to the Imperial and then abandoned her without any attempt to discover what had become of her. After what seemed like an age the intercom squawked.

'Shirley,' she shouted into the wall. 'It's Kate, Kate Hopegood. Can I come in?' She heard an unintelligible squawk from a voice that sounded like Shirley's. The door buzzed, she pushed quickly and it opened. She crossed the red-carpeted lobby and up the three steps to Shirley's front door.

'Good God, it *is* you!' Shirley stood in the doorway staring at Kate in amazement. She was in her dressing gown. Kate's heart sank.

'Have I come at a bad moment?' Shirley stared at her blankly. 'You aren't entertaining? Have you anyone with you?'

Shirley laughed. 'Good God no, not in this dressing gown. I'm having a maintenance night.' She flung open the door. 'Come in.' Kate let out her breath in a long sigh of relief. It seemed as if she'd been holding it ever since she entered the building.

'What the hell are you doing here?' Shirley demanded, staring at Kate's overnight case. 'You haven't had a row with Alan, have you? I thought you two never rowed.' Shirley dragged Kate into her flat. 'Alan hasn't thrown you out, has he?'

'Oh no – it's not like that. It's worse, much worse. I went to the Imperial to meet a man and, coming out of the American Bar, we bumped into his wife.'

'Wow!' Shirley slammed the door shut and leant against it, staring at Kate. 'Whatever did you do?'

'I made an utter fool of myself as usual,' Kate told her.

Picking up Kate's case, Shirley led the way to her small single bedroom off the hall, whilst Kate filled her in on every pitiful detail of the evening, 'But I thought you and Alan were happily married,' Shirley said, putting the case down by the bed and fixing her with a troubled frown.

Kate collapsed wearily on to the bare duvet. 'We are. I only saw Patrick once a year. It didn't mean anything.' She paused, aware she was blushing. 'It was for sex, that's all.'

'Good heavens, don't you get all the sex you want from your husband?' Shirley demanded. 'I thought the one good point about being married is that you could have sex whenever you wanted it.'

Kate shrugged. 'Well, yes, you can and of course like everything you can have when you want it – it's not so exciting.'

'Maybe not, but I wouldn't have thought you were cut out for leading a double life,' said Shirley a little scornfully. 'You haven't the bottle.'

Kate sighed. 'I know that, especially after tonight.'

Shirley tut-tutted sympathetically and Kate, relaxing a little, looked at her properly for the first time. She was deathly pale and there was something strangely immobile about her face.

'Are you all right, Shirley?' she asked. 'You look a bit white.'

'Never better,' said Shirley, rushing to the dressing table and peering at herself in the mirror. 'My God, the face pack. It's time it came off. Make yourself at home. I won't be a mo. Pour yourself a drink.' She disappeared and Kate lay back on the bed despondently.

Presently Shirley came back carrying some bright blue and yellow sheets, her face scrubbed and healthily pink. Kate roused herself to help.

'You of all people,' Shirley said, stripping back the duvet. 'I always thought you were the good one, Kate.'

'Well, I was,' Kate seized hold of the fitted sheet, 'until I bumped into

Patrick one day outside Harrods. I hadn't seen him since he dumped me all those years ago. I forgot about him after I married Alan – or at least if I did think about him I thought he'd probably become a red-faced farmer with a paunch and tweeds. But when I saw him he'd changed so little. The only difference was that he seemed to have grown into himself. Before he'd been, well, a bundle of coiled up nerves ready to spring into life. Now he was stronger, more powerful, full of laid-back charm. Oh, he was still lean and fit, but he'd matured. He was wearing a perfectly cut dark grey flannel suit and looked more attractive than ever. I can tell you, Shirley, I was glad I'd just come out of the hairdressers.'

'Patrick?' Shirley frowned. 'I don't remember him – there were so many men in and out of the flat in those days.'

'You must remember Patrick Bray-Smith. I was madly in love with him.'

'He wasn't the one with the sports car who kept disappearing to the country to kill things and leaving you stranded at weekends?' Shirley grabbed hold of the sheet Kate was holding and started covering the mattress with it. 'The one you were always waiting by the phone for? Kate, you haven't been unfaithful to Alan with that shit, have you?'

'The funny thing is I never really felt as if I was being unfaithful to Alan,' Kate said. 'It started quite innocently – with a cup of coffee.'

'It always does,' said Shirley, deftly stuffing a pillow into a bright blue pillowcase. Kate turned away feeling foolish. 'There now.' Shirley put her arm round Kate and gave her shoulder a sympathetic squeeze. 'There's no need to be so downhearted. You've only broken one of the Ten Commandments.' She laughed rather feebly, but Kate wasn't amused.

'I still love Alan,' she said determinedly. 'It didn't feel as if I was being unfaithful – not with Patrick.'

'I suppose it must get boring doing it with the same man all the time,' said Shirley, replacing the duvet. 'Even if you are still in love. I've never managed to hang on to them long enough to find out.'

Kate glanced at Shirley, surprised. She was very attractive, a blonde, with a splendid bosom and slim hips, the sort of woman men made straight for at parties, not the sort who got dumped.

Shirley smiled at Kate a little wistfully. 'Come on,' she said, leading the way out of the bedroom. 'You'd better tell me the whole sordid tale.'

'It wasn't sordid, that's the point,' said Kate, following her into Shirley's spacious sitting room, 'at least not until tonight.'

'From the beginning,' pleaded Shirley, walking over to the drinks cabinet.

'Well, we had coffee at a place round the corner from Harrods and we talked and talked. It was all quite innocent and friendly – what we'd been doing with our lives since we'd split up, our children, that sort of thing. Then he asked me to have lunch with him at the Imperial. I wasn't doing anything much that day and it seemed quite harmless. I knew Alan wouldn't have minded. He's never been the jealous type.'

'No harm in having lunch with an old boyfriend,' commented Shirley, busy pouring drinks. 'I do it all the time. It's very good for the ego, especially in a wonderfully smart restaurant like the Imperial. You'd have been mad to have turned it down.'

'I'm afraid it was completely wasted on me,' confessed Kate. 'I could hardly eat I was so nervous. The trouble was I couldn't help feeling the most terrific urge for him. I was terrified he might guess and be embarrassed.' Kate paused, remembering how she'd knocked over her wine at one stage, spilling it on her dress. Patrick had helped her mop it up. The feel of his hand against her breast had been almost more than she could bear. He'd caught her eye and they'd just gazed helplessly at each other. That was when she'd known that he felt the same.

Shirley set down a glass filled with dark brown liquid in front of Kate. 'How did he manage to overcome your natural reluctance to rush upstairs?'

'At the end of the meal he just said, "It's no good. All I can do is think of going to bed with you – you feel it too. I can tell. I'm well aware of all the reasons why we shouldn't, but it's not stopping me from wanting to."'

'Oh dear, oh dear, oh dear, and you fell for it, Kate.'

'It was all so unexpected, so sudden,' she protested. 'I had no time to prepare myself, bumping into him like that in the street. I was taken completely unawares.'

'I suppose he gave you some incredible spiel about his wife not understanding him, or being frigid, or some other such rubbish,' said Shirley, throwing herself into a chair.

'No he didn't.' Kate was indignant. 'You think Patrick has lots of women on the side but he doesn't. I know that.' She couldn't bear the way Shirley was looking at her so pityingly. 'You don't understand anything, Shirley. He isn't like that at all.'

'Don't try and hoodwink me, Kate. This is Shirley – you know, the basking shark who lies in wait for all these sex-starved husbands up from the country. I know what it's about, believe you me.'

Kate looked at Shirley curled up in the squashy black leather armchair, in her fluffy white towelling robe and thought how very sexy she looked. She was the only one of the four of them who'd shared the flat together who'd never married. Perhaps she was too clever and frightened men off, or maybe she was just spoilt for choice. She took a long drink from the glass Shirley had put in front of her and coughed. It was neat brandy.

'The thing about temptation,' she said when she'd recovered, 'is that it just creeps up on you unawares.'

This time Shirley didn't mock, just smiled understandingly.

'I suppose I could have said no,' Kate went on, encouraged. 'But I wasn't conscious of being given a choice. One moment we were staring at each other across the table, the next walking into his room upstairs.' With painful clarity she remembered the moment of panic when she'd found herself standing in that plush bedroom in the Imperial, of not daring to look at the huge double bed, of being overawed by the enormous bathroom, of feeling that she'd somehow strayed into a Hollywood movie. Then he'd started kissing her and all the old magic came rushing back. Not many men knew how to kiss well, she'd found, but Patrick was one of the ones who did. In bed together the magic had continued only he'd been more tender, more considerate and she, a little tense at first, had felt wonderfully relaxed.

Shirley got up, fetched the bottle of brandy from the cabinet, refilled their glasses. 'So you made love, the earth moved and then what?' she asked.

'When it was all over we lay in each other's arms talking about what to do.' Kate sipped her brandy carefully. 'He said he was happily married to Deborah and I think I said it might be better if we didn't see each other again. But he said he couldn't bear the thought of losing contact and promised to write.' She glanced at Shirley who merely looked resigned. 'Of course I didn't believe him. Patrick never was much of a writer, even in the old days. I went home and tried to forget about him. The awful thing was that that night Alan insisted on making love. I didn't want to do it and that scared me. I tried hard to put a little extra effort into our marriage and Alan seemed pleased.' It was important to make Shirley understand. 'The thing is, it made our marriage better. Our sex life more exciting. I know it sounds crazy but that's the way it was.'

'Not crazy at all,' said Shirley, sinking back in her chair and cradling her brandy. 'A lot of people say that.'

'I heard nothing from Patrick until December,' Kate went on, ignoring her. Once launched into her confession it seemed impossible to stop. 'Then I received a brief, rather formal letter from him, saying he was coming to London for the Smithfield Show and suggesting we might meet for lunch or dinner. Of course I didn't reply.'

'Of course.' Shirley swirled the brandy round and round her glass.

Kate glanced at her imploringly. 'I managed to ignore the letter. It wasn't easy. I was thrilled that he hadn't forgotten all about me but I knew it must stop. He didn't write again. I thought that was that. Then at the end of September, exactly a year since we'd met, I received a telephone call. "Let's do it again, please," he said. I was angry at him for having taken the risk of telephoning me at home. Was he deliberately trying to wreck my marriage? But it was one thing to ignore a letter, quite another to refuse him on the phone. He suggested dinner this time, not lunch, and rang off before I had time to protest.'

'And you went,' said Shirley with a sigh, 'because you couldn't bear to think of letting him down.'

Kate drank quickly, unable to bear Shirley's cynical gaze. 'For a while I did think of standing him up,' she said, determined to make a clean breast of it. 'I thought how angry Alan would be if he found out. I told myself that I was thirty-six years old with two teenage children and quite old enough to know better. But in the end I went because I couldn't bear not to.'

Shirley got up, came and sat on the arm of Kate's chair and put her hand on her shoulder. 'It's all right, Kate. We've all done that. It's called chemistry. It's what makes the world go round. Or go on – I'm not sure. Anyway, there's not much you can do about it.'

Kate sighed. Whenever she thought of Patrick she began to tremble inside. Nothing remotely like that had ever happened with Alan.

'So you invented the school friend in Farnham,' said Shirley. 'And Alan, dear trusting soul that he was, believed you. It always amazes me the way married people never seem to believe that others won't find their other half attractive.'

But Kate wasn't listening. She was remembering walking into the Imperial that first time, what a terrible ordeal it had been. There'd been no sign of Patrick. She had no idea where the ladies' room was and she didn't know what to do with her little overnight bag. The hall seemed to be filled with flunkies all hovering about with the express purpose of making her feel ill at ease. Suppose he had decided to stand her up? Suppose she was left standing there like some sort of Paddington Bear without the luggage label? Then he'd come rushing through the revolving door, full of apologies. The look on his face when he saw her there made everything worth while. They had gone straight upstairs to the bedroom and made love before dinner. Afterwards everything had been wonderfully relaxed and romantic. They sat at a discreet table in the river restaurant tucked away in the corner. When Patrick asked her to dance, Kate had demurred in case they might be seen by any of Patrick's friends. But he said people who lived in Gloucestershire didn't come to the river restaurant in the evenings and certainly not on Fridays. Kate didn't think anyone she knew was likely to be in the Imperial at all. And so they had danced the night away just like that first time they'd met, and then gone back upstairs and made mad passionate love again.

'Whose idea was it to meet only once a year?' Shirley asked.

'Over dinner that first time Patrick asked if we could carry on doing this – meeting once a year for as long as we both wanted to. To me it made a lot of sense. It seemed the only way of having an affair without hurting anyone. So that was what we agreed to do. I don't want to mess up my life. Without Alan and the children I'd be nothing.'

'Are you sure you and Patrick were only doing it for the sex?'

'Of course I'm sure. I love Alan. Right from the start I made it a condition of our continuing that Patrick never rang me or wrote. The fact that I did that must mean that my marriage and children are the important things in my life.'

'And he accepted your conditions, of course?'

'Of course. Neither of us wanted a proper affair. We didn't want to risk our marriages. After the second time he didn't even call to arrange the meetings. He said the uncertainty made it all more exciting. It did too. Each year I went to the Imperial never really sure if Patrick would turn up. But there he always was, waiting for me, with a big grin on his face. It was all such fun, and hoodwinking all the staff of the Imperial made it even more so. They treated us like an old married couple. They thought it was our wedding anniversary.' She sighed, remembering with horror how tonight the whole pantomime had ended in farce. The staff had shown themselves in their true colours then – she thought. Professionals, that's all they were. Creating magic certainly, but it was a fragile illusion.

'If you ask me, Kate, you were in danger of building a little bit more into this safe, once-a-year romp than you think. You've had your hair done, that's a smart little black skirt you've got on which didn't come from Marks and Spencer and you stink of Oscar de la Renta. You're not looking for more from this little bit on the side than you'll admit?'

Kate shook her head ferociously. 'That's not true.'

Shirley grinned at her with infuriating scepticism. 'The trouble with you, Kate, is that you're too romantic. It was a great little arrangement you had, very sensible, plenty of damage limitation. But you're not a sensible girl, Kate, and damage limitation isn't something you know how to do. You're a no-holds-barred, cap-over-the-windmill, disaster-waiting-to-happen person.'

'No I'm not,' said Kate, laughing. 'Oh, I might have been once upon a time all those years ago, but marriage to Alan has changed all that. I'm really very much in control nowadays.'

'OK – so what are you going to do?' asked Shirley, not looking at all convinced.

'Well, of course I can't see him again – not after this. I always knew our meetings would have to stop eventually. It used to depress me more than anything, the thought that one day Patrick wouldn't fancy me any more because I'd be too wrinkly or flabby. Perhaps it's better to end like this. No fantasy can last for ever.'

'Don't you think you ought to get even with him for abandoning you like that? Fancy just walking away with his wife and leaving you out for the count on the hotel floor. He's behaved like a shit.'

Kate shivered. 'It's not his fault. I dare say I'd have done the same. His marriage comes first – just like mine. I can forgive him but I can't forgive myself for making such a fool of myself.'

'Oh, I suppose you had too many of those famous cocktails on an empty stomach. You get a sudden fright – the blood rushes to your heart or whatever – and up it all comes. It happens to us all.'

'I bet it never happened to you, Shirley,' said Kate, pulling a face.

'Well, I've had more practice in living dangerously. You're too nice. Perhaps it's time you learnt how to put the boot in occasionally. Nice people always come last while the race goes to the strong or the shits.'

'But I'm not trying to win a race,' said Kate.

'You're lucky you don't have to,' Shirley told her. 'That wonderful husband of yours keeps you wrapped in cotton wool. You're a lucky woman – you've had a little fling and singed your wings a trifle, but no harm's done and you can go back to Alan tomorrow morning and everything'll be the same as before.'

'I wonder,' said Kate. 'I've learnt something about myself tonight. I'm a poor little shrinking violet. If that's what twenty years of happy marriage has done to me I'm not sure I care for it very much.'

Shirley got up and came round to stand in front of her friend. 'Don't look so sad. You're tired and hungry and you've had a horrid shock. I'm going to find you something to eat. Then later, if you want a shoulder to cry on, you can cry on mine. I know what it's like, I've been there often enough.' She disappeared into the kitchen and Kate thought how very kind and understanding she had been. Shirley may have been a little hard on her but it was necessary to be cruel to be kind sometimes. To inflict pain to obtain relief. Rather like going to the dentist and having a tooth out. But she wished she could feel more relieved now that Patrick was out of her life once and for all.

# *Chapter 3*

Kate returned home next morning to Fulham. As she walked from Parsons Green tube station carrying her small overnight case, she wondered what she would do if Alan was still in the house. She didn't yet feel ready to lie to him, she felt she had guilt writ large all over her face. She put down her case and looked at her watch. It was almost ten o'clock. Alan would have left ages ago. She turned into her own quiet shady street thinking that with the way her luck was running at the moment, some malign quirk of fate might perhaps have delayed Alan this morning. Her heart thumping, she walked along the row of identical terraced houses until she reached their own little wrought-iron front gate. Her hand was shaking as she put her key in the lock. Shirley's right, she thought apprehensively as she unlocked the door. I'm really not cut out for sinning.

She walked into the house and stood in the narrow hall, listening to the silence. Alan had left for work as usual. She was safe. She picked up her overnight bag and began slowly to mount the stairs. The house, which had been her home for so long, welcomed her. Alan had bought it with every penny he could scrape together all those years ago when the children were getting too big for their small cramped flat. Kate remembered how excited she had been about having a proper house to live in. Of course it had been terribly dilapidated, and they had only been able to put it right one step at a time. Alan's salary had to go on so many things, the mortgage, the children's school fees, the family car, holidays. Somehow he'd managed to find the money when they needed it and gradually the house had blossomed and grown like the children. Kate had put everything of herself into her home and family, struggling with the children's homework and their extracurricular activities, and providing huge meals for constantly fluctuating numbers when they brought their friends home. There were times when she had felt tied down, cramped, invisible sometimes. But mostly she had been happy and fulfilled. The children were her reward, Naomi was at Edinburgh University and Matt, now working his way around the world for a year, was going to Cambridge. Alan too was doing well.

Kate entered the bedroom. It was a woman's room, pink and chintzy, with fitted cupboards down one wall and a built-in dressing table. Alan had his own dressing room next door, with his clothes and books, and a leather-covered armchair, where he could be by himself when he wanted. Kate dumped her overnight bag on the big comfortable bed and began hastily unpacking. The staff at the Imperial had been very efficient. Nothing was missing, not even the little scrap of silk which was an apology for knickers. She'd bought them for Patrick's benefit. Each year she treated herself to one tiny silly little sexy indulgence. A wave of something approaching despair swept over her. How much she had cherished that annual one-night stand. It was the only thing she had which was her very own – a little piece of wicked self-indulgence in a life which was otherwise almost entirely spent looking after other people. Now she had nothing to look forward to.

She carried her washing things into the bathroom and paused in front of the mirror. Not much to get excited about there, she thought, examining her reflection critically. Eyes brown, nose straight, cheeks pale, hair an undistinguished shade of brown, scraped back and pinned into a neat chignon, a style which was easy to maintain and Alan thought elegant, but maybe her face was too small and pinched and unremarkable for such a severe style. What she needed were sweeping cheekbones or a *retroussé* nose or huge soulful eyes. Patrick said she had a wonderful body and it wasn't bad, she knew. She'd kept her figure and she'd always had good legs. She sighed, feeling deeply depressed. What did it matter now anyway?

A ring on the doorbell made her jump and run into the bedroom to look apprehensively out of the window. Double-parked and blocking the street outside was a florist's van. She ran downstairs and opened the door.

'Mrs Hopegood?' The van driver grinned at her as she nodded in surprise. 'Somebody loves you.' He thrust a large bunch of red roses at her and scurried back to his van. With her heart beating a little faster Kate shut the door and carried the flowers into the kitchen. Her hands were shaking as she tore the little white card out of its envelope. There were just two words. 'Forgive me.'

Kate dropped the card and stared at the beautiful long-stemmed roses wrapped in Cellophane and tied with a huge red bow.

He's got a nerve, she thought, sending them to my home. What if Alan had been here? Furious with Patrick and at the same time with herself for the quick thrill of pleasure those two little words in his handwriting had given her, she seized the flowers, marched outside, and dumped them unceremoniously in the dustbin. She was finished with Patrick for ever.

Back in the kitchen she set about making herself coffee. Her kitchen was small and narrow but so cleverly designed that it had everything she wanted in it. She pulled out the small shelf which acted as a table, and sat down with her coffee and the newspaper propped up in front of her. She read an entire paragraph without taking in any of the words. All she could think of were a dozen long-stemmed red roses hiding their light under a bushel in the dustbin. Kate sighed and looked out of the window wistfully. Fancy Patrick sending roses. Shirley would probably say only shits sent flowers and she was probably right. Kate returned to the paper and tried to read the same paragraph all over again, but the roses were calling to her from outside, like little boys shrieking trick or treat on All-Hallows Eve.

'I'm weak,' Kate said, downing her coffee and pushing back her stool. 'Weak, weak, weak,' she muttered as she marched outside and retrieved the red roses from the dustbin. 'But damn it, I don't care what he is – I'm not going to waste a dozen red roses.' She arranged the roses carefully, in a tall white vase, feeling defiant and guilty. When she had finished she carried them into the dining room and set them in the middle of the table. The effect was wonderful. But what could she tell Alan? Suddenly she had a brilliant idea. Tonight she would have candlelight and all Alan's favourite food to go with the roses. She was going to overcome evil with good. The roses would be a start. From now on she was going to make a big effort to put some romance into her marriage. If the Imperial could conjure up magic so could she. Then maybe she and Alan could recapture some of the sparkle they'd lost over the years.

Alan came home half an hour late and said scarcely a word. He didn't seem angry – he never got angry – but he was clearly infuriatingly preoccupied. Too preoccupied, Kate thought, to notice the flowers, or the candles or her little black dress with the long slit up the side. She bit back her disappointment and said nothing. It wasn't until Alan had eaten his way through smoked salmon and beef Stroganoff that he suddenly looked at her across the candlelit dinner table and asked: 'So you know then? Who's told you?'

She froze. 'Know what?' She gasped, fork suspended in midair, her mind racing in guilty, confused panic. Had he found out about Patrick? Was he leaving her? Was that what she was supposed to know?

'All this celebration? I thought you must have heard about our move.'

'Move! What move?' She was totally bewildered.

'We're going to Saudi for six months. We've got to be ready to leave in three weeks.'

'Saudi! Three weeks!' Her fork fell from her nerveless fingers, and bounced off her plate with a clatter spraying white creamy sauce over her best dress, but she was too stunned to notice.

'Yes, they need some help setting up a new computer system, the firm's seconded me to the Saudi Government to advise them. It's a great challenge, of course, and a terrific compliment. We get a house with its own swimming pool and tennis court and servants and a car and everything. You'll love it.' He scraped up the last of the beef Stroganoff appreciatively. 'I thought that was what all this was about.'

'I'm coming too?'

'Yes. Now that the children are both away you should come with me for once, instead of being left behind to cope on your own at home.'

'I've always been quite happy coping on my own before,' she said stiffly, trying to gather her scattered wits.

'I know, darling, you've been wonderfully uncomplaining, but this time there's no need. You can come with me. Think of it as a holiday – a six-month break. I think you deserve it after all you've done looking after the kids – and me.' He smiled lovingly at her and she knew she ought to be grateful. But she wasn't. She felt more desperate with every word he uttered.

'I'm not sure a holiday is what I need.' She got up quickly. 'I think what I need is time on my own. To discover who I am.' Even to her ears her statement sounded like something out of *Cosmopolitan*, but it was the only way she could express the sense of panic she felt.

Alan stared at her in astonishment. 'You know who you are. You're my wife and the mother of our children.'

She scooped up the empty plates and carried them into the kitchen. 'I think I'm having a bit of an identity crisis,' she shouted nervously through the hatch. She'd never had this kind of conversation before with Alan and she wasn't at all sure she was tackling it in the right way. But she *had* to explain to him somehow why she didn't want to be dragged off to Saudi Arabia!

'All you need is a good long rest,' he insisted. 'Time to take stock, rediscover yourself, get things in perspective.'

'In Saudi Arabia, where women are shut away behind closed doors and not allowed to be seen in public unless they're masked? I don't think I'm going to find my own identity in Saudi.' She opened the fridge and stared at the *crème brûlée* sitting there so smug and triumphant. She had been pleased when it had worked so beautifully, now she hated the very thought of any more food. Alan came into the kitchen.

'Kate, darling,' he said, putting his arms around her waist and pulling her towards him. 'This isn't like you. You're not starting to get menopausal on me, are you?'

'Of course not, I'm only forty, for God's sake.' She pushed him away and grabbed the *crème brûlée*, stalking back into the dining room. He followed her and sat down at the table again with his tolerant, I'm-not-going-to-be-provoked expression. She struggled to remain calm.

'Alan, please try to understand,' she said. 'You've been protecting me all these years. Now the kids are grown up I can't just decide the one job I did is over and follow you around the world.' She could see from his face that that was exactly what he thought she should do. She tried again. 'I've got to go out and do something for myself by myself before it's too late.' It didn't sound very convincing. 'Otherwise I shall become one of those terrible women always moaning because you're late home or something, too dependent on you,' she finished desperately.

'But I like coming home to you, I like seeing that you've spent the day getting everything looking so beautiful and it's been for me. The trouble you've taken tonight, all my favourite food.' He tried to take her hand, but she was still holding the dish with the *crème brûlée* in it. 'It makes everything I do seem worthwhile,' he added, smiling up at her.

'It's not enough for me any more,' Kate said more vehemently than she intended, as she dumped the pudding in front of him. He looked shocked and not a little hurt. Belatedly she remembered all her good intentions for this evening. How tonight was to be the start of a new, more sparkling marriage for them both. 'Why don't I enrol for a course in something while you're away?' she added lamely.

'You can't stay here,' he said baldly, 'I've let the house.'

She sank like a collapsed soufflé into her chair. 'Without consulting me?' she exclaimed.

'It was all done by the firm.' He didn't even look guilty. 'There wasn't much time – you know these relocation people. They arrange everything for us in Saudi and then – surprise, surprise – there's a family living in Saudi who are coming to London who need somewhere to live until they find something permanent.'

'Not Arabs – I'm not having Arabs living in my house!'

'No, no, of course they're not Arabs – they're Brits who work in the oil business. Darling, you'll have to stop being so prejudiced about Arabs. They're not savages, you know. The Arabs have a much more ancient civilisation than we do.'

'I'm not coming with you, Alan,' she said. 'I've made up my mind.'

'Don't be silly, darling, of course you are. It's my fault for bouncing it on you like this – but I only knew myself today that it was all signed and sealed. You'll feel better when you've slept on it.'

He began helping himself to *crème brûlée* with obvious pleasure and she watched him in exasperation. Alan was impossible to have a row with. He was always so calm and understanding and reasonable. She wondered what he would do it if she picked up the *crème brûlée* and threw it at him. Probably take it as evidence that she was truly becoming menopausal. She sipped her wine, unable to face anything more to eat. Alan was now placidly spooning up *crème brûlée,* churning it around his plate with extravagant, unnecessary strokes in the way he always attacked his puddings. She got up, unable to sit watching him any longer, and went into the kitchen to make coffee. I'm only forty, she thought angrily. My hormones are in better working order than they've ever been. I know that and Patrick's proved it.

Until last night the thought of Patrick had always produced a small secretive glow of happiness, but now when she thought of Patrick she could not help remembering Patrick's wife screaming abuse. She began grinding coffee beans with grim determination. Deborah Bray-Smith wouldn't let her husband take all the decisions, she thought, her anger rising. The machine growled in noisy support.

She peered through the hatch at Alan sitting at the dining room table, sipping his wine in the candlelight. He looked what he was, dependable. His suit was crumpled, somehow no matter how diligently Kate looked after Alan's clothes they always appeared as if he'd slept in them two minutes after he'd put them on. He got up, switched on the electric light, and began to clear the table, extinguishing the candles and putting the dirty dishes through the hatch. Then he looked at his watch.

'Time for the news,' he said. 'Do you want me to take the coffee through, darling?'

'It's all right,' replied Kate. 'I'll bring it with me when I've done the dishes.' So much for her attempts to stand up for herself, so much for her romantic evening, she thought sadly.

But Alan wasn't entirely immune to all her special effects. When they were in bed he wanted to make love, which was, Kate supposed, victory of a kind, except that she found she had to make a supreme effort to appear keen. As he worked hard to bring her to climax she kept thinking of Patrick, no matter how hard she tried to push him out of her mind. When it was over, Alan turned to her full of loving solicitude.

'How was it for you?' he asked, as he always did.

'Brilliant,' she replied, as she always did.

'Mmm,' he murmured, kissing her tenderly. 'Me too.' Then he fell asleep almost immediately.

Kate lay awake for a long time, wishing she didn't have to pretend, that she could be more courageous, that she dared suggest some ways of making their love-making more exciting. If she was such a wimp in bed how could she be anything other than a wimp elsewhere? But I'm not really like that, she thought, tortured by memories of Patrick. With Patrick she had been as amorous and adventurous as a Jackie Collins heroine. Resolutely she pushed rebellious thoughts of Patrick away and tried to concentrate on her immediate future.

It seemed to her that she had reached a turning point in her life. The woman who had disgraced herself in the Imperial was the sort of wife who would tamely follow her husband to spend six months in a country where women were totally subservient. But the girl who had left Scotland to come to London in search of adventure hadn't been a wimp. What had happened to that girl in the intervening years? Kate wondered. I've become a non-person, she thought miserably. One thing she was determined about:

she would not go with Alan to Saudi Arabia, however much he swept her objections under the carpet.

Next morning Kate rang Shirley and asked if they could meet for lunch. Shirley sounded surprised.

'I'm up to my eyes today,' she said. 'But if it's a crisis I could squeeze an hour. Has Alan found out?'

'No, no, nothing like that, thank God,' said Kate. 'But it is a crisis.'

'OK, but you'll have to come to the office. I can't possibly get out. Bring some sandwiches and we'll talk here.' Meekly Kate agreed. It's strange, she thought as she hung up, Shirley wasn't a close friend now, although she had been once when they shared a flat together all those years ago. Friendship was forged out of propinquity, out of triumphs and disasters shared, it needed common interests and common difficulties to keep it alive and kicking. While the other three girls in the flat were finding themselves husbands, Shirley was training to become a lawyer. While Kate and the others were busy getting pregnant, Shirley had got herself qualified. They had drifted apart, each of them driven by a new set of pressures and priorities. But last night Shirley had come to the rescue in Kate's hour of need and now she was the only person Kate could turn to for help and advice. It was almost like being twenty again.

Shirley was a partner in a smart firm of City solicitors specialising in property. Her office was on the wrong side of the river but in a high modern block with a liveried attendant on guard in the entrance hall, and lots of plate glass and swift lifts, one of which shot Kate heavenwards, leaving her stomach chasing from several floors behind. Shirley was on the telephone when Kate was shown into the office. Kate looked around her at the large desk, the window overlooking the river, the pretty watercolours on the walls and was very impressed. She'd never been in Shirley's office before. Shirley mouthed at Kate to sit down and went on talking a stream of incomprehensible legal jargon into the telephone. Kate settled herself on a small sofa and carefully deposited her sandwiches and bottle of wine on a coffee table beside a pile of magazines. Idly she glanced at the magazine on the top of the pile.

'Whatever are you doing with *Horse and Hound*?' she asked, picking it up and waving it at Shirley as she came off the telephone. 'I didn't think you were the horsey type.'

'Oh that,' Shirley grinned. 'One of our clients bought a horse advertised in there which hasn't been sound since the day he bought him. We're trying to get his money back for him. The dealer has an identical advert in this week.' She fished in a cupboard behind her and came round from behind the desk carrying two long-stemmed wine glasses. 'Now then – where's the fire? I hope you haven't come to me for a divorce.' She produced a bottle opener and began expertly removing the cork from the bottle.

Kate tried to laugh but it sounded a little forced. 'Of course not! Alan's been sent to Saudi Arabia for six months, he's let our house without consulting me and expects me to go with him. We're off in three weeks.'

Shirley poured some wine into a glass. 'This isn't bad,' she said, tasting it.

'I don't want to go with him, Shirley.'

'Don't then.'

Kate squirmed around on the sofa. Shirley in her short black skirt and long tailored jacket was quite different from the voluptuous sister in crime of last night. How could Kate expect a woman like Shirley, with her executive office and her designer clothes to understand the helplessness she was feeling. 'The thing is,' she began, 'I don't have any money of my own. We've always pooled our resources. Alan is generosity itself. He's always given me whatever I've asked for. Somehow I just don't feel I can ask him to finance me if I refuse to go with him.' My God, Shirley was looking embarrassed, she must think she was asking for a loan. 'So I've got to find somewhere to live and some means of supporting myself and I've only got three weeks to do it in,' Kate finished in a rush.

The telephone began ringing again and Shirley snatched it up, looking relieved.

Kate took a gulp of wine and wished she hadn't come. Shirley was perched on the edge of her desk, the telephone cradled beneath her chin, scribbling busily on a pad. She looked as if she might be there for quite some time. Kate picked up *Horse and Hound* and began studying the pages of the classified advertisements, trying to look as engrossed as Shirley. There were so many things for sale – horses, trailers, lurcher puppies. Kate wondered if all the horses were as good as they sounded how their owners could bear to part with them. Then suddenly one particular advertisement caught her eye.

*Girl Friday wanted to look after independent, active old gentleman in Gloucestershire. Light duties of a supervisory and companionable nature, other staff employed. Self-contained flat, own horse welcome, opportunity to hunt with the Blazers.*

Quickly Kate whipped out her pen and scribbled down the telephone number.

'What have you got there?' Shirley was off the telephone.

'It's a job – a residential job. It might solve all my difficulties.'

'My God, I can see we have got a crisis on our hands. I'd better get them to hold my calls.' Kate sipped her wine nervously while Shirley gave orders to some minion in another room, then studied the advertisement.

'You haven't got a horse,' she said, throwing the magazine back on the table. 'You don't hunt.'

'I know that,' said Kate, picking it up and reading it over again. 'It's just added bait, an indication of their attitude. They want someone who's an equal. I think it sounds rather interesting.'

'What they're looking for is a willing slave who's horse mad,' said Shirley crushingly.

'Well, of course it's not perhaps what I had in mind but three weeks isn't very long to conjure up the perfect solution and unless I have somewhere to go by the time Alan leaves I'll find myself on the plane to Saudi Arabia.'

Shirley was looking embarrassed again and Kate wondered whether she was afraid she ought to offer to share the comfortable flat in Beverley Gardens with her. If she was honest about it, she'd come here with some such idea in her mind, but she realised now that had been a mistake.

'Gloucestershire,' said Shirley, chewing absently on a sandwich. 'Doesn't Patrick live in Gloucestershire? I thought you were going to forget him.'

'What if he does? There must be hundreds of thousands of people in Gloucestershire – it's a big county.'

Shirley looked unimpressed. 'Subconsciously I think you're trying to cling to Patrick,' she said. 'Don't do it, Kate. All right, so maybe Alan's been a bit high-handed. But at least he's thinking of you, looking after you. You don't know what the big, bad world is like. It's tough. It's competitive.' She looked Kate up and down in a rather unnervingly professional way. 'You're unqualified, too old, and you've been out of the job market for far too long. You're unemployable, Kate.'

'Thank you,' said Kate with as much dignity as she could muster. 'I thought you were supposed to be my friend.'

'I am your friend. What are friends for if they can't tell you the truth? Hang on to Alan, Kate, you don't know how lucky you are to have him.'

As Kate left the shiny building half an hour later, her mind was made up. Until then she hadn't seriously thought of finding a job. She had come for sympathy and some friendly advice. Well, she had got no sympathy and the advice was pretty unfriendly. Now she was full of chablis and a determination to prove Shirley wrong. Just for fun she would answer the advertisement. If Shirley was right she wouldn't get the job. But at least she would have tried.

She rang the number as soon as she got home, before she had time to sober up, convincing herself that she was sure to be too late. There must be hundreds of horse-mad girl Fridays ready to jump at the chance.

'I'm afraid I don't hunt,' she told the woman who answered the telephone. 'But I've kept house and cooked for my husband for twenty years and brought up two children.' It sounded so lame. She wasn't going to get very far if she couldn't sell herself better than that.

'You sound marvellous,' the woman said, much to Kate's surprise. 'Much better that you don't hunt. The previous girl broke her back in a bad fall out cub-hunting and that's put paid to her, I'm afraid. How soon could you come?'

'In about three weeks,' Kate stammered, stifling a pang for the poor crippled wretch she was to replace.

'You're not anti-hunting, are you?' the woman demanded. 'My father was Joint Master of the Blazers for many years, until he had to give up riding.'

'No, I'm not anti,' Kate said, and then felt compelled to add for honesty's sake, 'I've never given the matter much thought.'

'That's all right then. I expect you'd like to know more about us before you make up your mind. Could you come and see me tomorrow morning about twelve?'

Breathlessly Kate agreed. The woman gave her name – Caroline Kindersby – and an address in Arlington Crescent, and hung up. Kate danced a jig round the bedroom, filled with jubilation. She had an interview for the very first job she'd applied for. She twirled to a halt in front of the mirror. What should she wear? Should she try to look smart or cosily capable?

'I certainly can't look horsey,' she told her reflection severely. 'Perhaps I'd better just be myself. Oh dear.' In the end she settled for the sort of thing she used to wear to parent-teacher association meetings – a grey coat and skirt with a bright pink shirt and low pumps. She comforted herself with the thought that if it was wet she could cut more of a dash with her new simulated-silk raincoat.

It wasn't wet. It was one of those warm September days evoking mists and memories of late summer evenings. Kate thought with excitement of how beautiful the country would look on a day such as this with the sun shining down on the yellowing trees, the hedgerows a cornucopia of blackberries, sloes and bright red hips. She got off the bus at South Kensington with her spirits soaring. What an adventure. If she got the job it would be a miracle, of course, but she hadn't felt so exhilarated since – well, since she bumped into Patrick that fatal day five years ago.

Arlington Crescent was a row of terraced houses, but not the sort that Kate lived in. These were tall, stately triumphs of Georgian architecture sparkling in the sunshine as white as the icing on a wedding cake. Each house was identical with little wrought-iron balconies on the first floor and railings protecting the ground floor from the street. Some of them had window boxes filled with colourful and exotic flowers, or unusual miniature trees in large pots by the front door, which Kate supposed were tended regularly by expensive garden contractors. It was a beautiful crescent curving in a graceful sweep out of Old Brompton Road and screened from its commercial clutter by a small secluded garden filled with shrubs and leafy trees. Only seriously rich people could manage to live in such perfection, thought Kate, wonderingly.

Her heart was beating uncomfortably fast as she climbed the steps to the pillared portico of number 44 and rang the bell. An oriental manservant in a short white jacket opened the door and ushered her inside. She gave him her name and he bowed politely. She followed him through a light and airy hall with little time to notice anything save that the patterned carpet which matched the flower arrangement on a marble-topped table was the kind only very superior interior decorators used. The manservant opened a door and she followed him into a room which, with its silk-covered walls, festooned curtains and highly polished antique furniture, was like something straight out of *House and Garden*, right down to the elegant fawn-coloured whippet posing in front of the French marble fireplace.

Caroline Kindersby wasn't at all what Kate had expected. From her voice on the telephone Kate had anticipated a butch-looking woman in well-cut tweeds and a face bright with broken veins. Instead she was tall and very elegant, in a straight black skirt and expensive designer jacket in scarlet cashmere, and lots of chunky gold jewellery.

'Come and sit down and tell me all about yourself,' she said, getting up from the gilt-edged desk in the middle of the room. Kate was struck dumb. What did the woman want to know? she wondered. Luckily Caroline didn't wait for an answer.

'Of course, Daddy thinks he's perfectly able to look after himself,' Caroline said. 'But he's lonely and he's old, and left to himself he lets things slide. Mrs Murphy, who comes in every day, is terribly loyal but her food's horrible and she's not up to dealing with a real crisis if anything should happen to him. Sherry?' She picked up a decanter of pale dry sherry and began pouring it into a glass without waiting for Kate's answer. 'It was such bad luck that girl breaking her back just when she was fitting in so well,' she continued, handing the glass of sherry to Kate. 'Now everybody seems fixed up for the season and we're desperate.' Kate felt she ought to play a little hard to get. She didn't want this woman to think she was their last straw.

'I can't come permanently,' she said, taking a great gulp of sherry and trying hard not to be intimidated. 'I can only come for six months.'

'Six months will get us through the hunting season,' Caroline said, visibly relieved, 'and give us plenty of time to find someone else.' Kate tried to think of probing questions to ask, but she was too overawed by the room, the disdainful dog and this brisk businesslike woman. She sipped her sherry feeling uncomfortable and tongue-tied. The elegant whippet stretched, letting out a quite audible fart.

'Do you like cooking?' Caroline Kindersby broke the silence so suddenly Kate jumped.

'Yes, I do.' Kate took another quick sip of her sherry. 'I find it therapeutic. I didn't until I married Alan – my husband – but he's very fond of food and his interest and encouragement made me into not a bad cook. We've been abroad for holidays in places like France and Italy quite a lot and it gives me ideas.' Heavens, Kate, she thought, don't go on so, the woman will think you're a female Robert Carrier. But she didn't want Caroline to think she was just a suburban housewife.

'I'm afraid you might find poor Daddy rather boring to cook for – he only really likes mince and chops and overdone roast beef. But perhaps you can persuade him to entertain a bit more. It would do him good. The people he's had looking after him in the past have always been too busy in the stables to worry about cooking. It would be so much easier if he would just get married again.' She looked hard at Kate.

'My husband's been sent abroad at a moment's notice,' Kate explained hastily, wondering whether she were being interviewed for a prospective stepmother, 'and I wanted to have something to do while he's away. It's not that I don't love my husband, I do. We're very happy together. It's just that I need a breathing space.' She paused, appalled that in her nervousness she had said too much.

'The work's not hard, which is why we're not offering much in the way of wages.' Caroline Kindersby didn't seem to want to know about Kate's problems. 'But you have your food and drink and your own little flat above the stables. It's small and fairly basic, I'm afraid, but it's quite self-contained.' She smiled at Kate reassuringly. 'You needn't worry about privacy.'

'Oh, I'm not at all worried about that,' Kate reassured her hastily. 'I've never had much of that. There's not much privacy with a husband and two children in a little house like ours.' She smiled timidly and Caroline smiled back. Kate warmed to her. She was not nearly as formidable when she smiled.

'You'll do,' Caroline said. 'I'm sure Daddy will love you, you're just the person we've been looking for.'

Without really knowing how, Kate accepted the job and a second glass of sherry and found herself promising to set out for Gloucestershire the day after her husband left for Saudi. Caroline Kindersby wrote down her father's name and address and started giving directions of how to find it. Kate, gulping sherry and trying desperately to concentrate on what Caroline Kindersby was telling her, was filled with tremendous elation. I've done it, she kept thinking, I've got the first job I've applied for in twenty years all on my own. I'm not unemployable, I'm just what they're looking for. Just wait until I tell Shirley.

It wasn't until she was outside in the street again, her head swimming from all that sherry on an empty stomach, that Kate realised she wasn't going to meet her employer or see where she was going to live until it was too late. My God, what have I done, she thought, in sudden panic. She took out the piece of paper Caroline had given her. Colonel Beamish, The Court, Little Riddleton. It sounded really quite romantic. She began to feel a bit like a heroine in a Jane Austen novel. Or like Jane Eyre on her way to meet Mr Rochester . . .

Alan was stunned when Kate told him what she'd done.

'I'm not having my wife going off into the depths of the country to wait hand and foot on some impossible old buffer!' he exclaimed. 'You must be mad.'

'Please, Alan, try and understand,' she begged. 'I'm not mad, I'm just trying to prove to myself that I can do something on my own. That I'm still a person in my own right.'

'Why, Kate? Why this sudden urge for self-fulfilment?'

How she longed to tell him the whole awful truth – I've been unfaithful to you, I got caught out, and I made the most absolute fool of myself, that's why I have to get back some self-respect. Only she couldn't. The unwritten rule of any affair, however harmless, was never to confess. She'd read enough agony columns in enough women's magazines to know that.

'I don't know,' she said, avoiding his gaze. 'Perhaps it's because the children don't need me any more. Perhaps I've lost confidence in myself. All I know is that when Caroline Kindersby offered me the job it gave me the most tremendous boost.'

'Kate, don't be a fool. I think you've got some snobbish idea in your head that you're going to live in some grand country house and meet lots of exciting new people, whereas all you're going to be is a servant. You'll be used, Kate. You know what you're like, they'll all take advantage of you—'

'Caroline Kindersby didn't treat me like a servant,' Kate interrupted indignantly. 'She was very kind and friendly.' He wasn't at all impressed, she could see, and she wanted him to be proud of her. 'There's a daily body called Mrs Murphy who does a lot of the work. All I have to do is keep the old man company and deal with any emergencies. Caroline Kindersby said I was just the person they were looking for.'

'Why doesn't this daughter supervise her father's house for him herself if it's so easy?' he asked. 'The trouble with all these country house swanks is that they're too busy killing things to look after their own relations.'

It was no good, she thought, depressed. He was determined not to give her any credit at all for her little triumph. That was the trouble being married to a high-achieving husband. Nothing she could do would ever begin to match Alan's success.

'Why don't you want to come with me?' he said, taking both her hands in his and peering anxiously into her face. 'Kate, am I missing something?' He looked so loving and concerned, she nearly gave in then, only she knew that if she did she would have failed in her one small bid to assert herself. Instead she said, 'It's not your fault, Alan, it's nothing you've done or not done. It's me. I've been walking in your shadow all our married life. I just want to see whether I exist at all as a person in my own right. Can't you understand?'

'I understand my wife doesn't love me enough to want to come to Saudi with me,' he said almost petulantly.

'Oh, Alan. It's not that. Of course I love you, you know I do.' She put her arms round his neck and would have kissed him on the mouth but he turned his head away. 'You've been away on your own before,' she whispered cajolingly, into his ear. 'Six months isn't long.' She tried another kiss, but he didn't respond. 'I can't understand why you're making such a fuss about it,' she said, giving up.

'I don't want you making a fool of yourself,' he told her.

'That's just it,' she said miserably. 'I don't like being a burden to you. I have to learn how to stand on my own two feet and I can't do that with you there protecting me all the time.'

'Oh, Kate, don't be so absurd,' he sniffed dismissively. 'There's nothing I want more than for you to be yourself. It's just that you always seem to get into such a muddle when you're on your own.'

It was hopeless she thought. He had such a bad opinion of her, how could she possibly win?

Desperate for reassurance, Kate telephoned her daughter, Naomi, in Edinburgh.

'You're suffering from the empty nest syndrome, Mum,' she said with a laugh. 'I suppose you want something to look after now we've both left home.'

'Your father thinks I should be looking after him,' confessed Kate. 'He's taking it very personally. But you know how protective he is. He doesn't seem to think I'm capable of doing anything on my own.'

'It's not Daddy's fault, you know.' Naomi always was the intuitive one. 'It can't be much fun working so hard to be the breadwinner all the time. Don't blame him for your identity crisis. But couldn't you do something a little less demeaning than being a housekeeper to some old fart in the depths of rural Gloucestershire? You're a brilliant cook – couldn't you open a restaurant or do something stylish?'

The trouble with the young was that they were so confident in their own superiority, thought Kate as she listened to her daughter's idea of what her mother should do with herself. But wasn't that what she had striven so hard to give them? She should be pleased, not demoralised, when they trampled all over her.

'Perhaps I will, darling, one day, once I learn to spread my wings a little. I've got to learn to walk before I can run. It seems I've led such a sheltered life looking after you all, I'm unfit for any decent employment.'

'Go off and look after this old buffer in darkest Gloucestershire then, if you must,' said Naomi, laughing. 'It'll probably cure you for good. Then when Daddy's back from Saudi you and he can go off on a second honeymoon somewhere romantic and get it all together again.'

Kate hung up, not in the least reassured. If Naomi thought their marriage had gone a little stale then maybe Alan did too, only of course he was far too kind to say so. Suppose he was bored with her being so useless. Perhaps in taking her to Saudi he was trying to break out of the rut they had got into. Only it wouldn't work, thought Kate. What was wrong with their marriage was that it was too one-sided. Alan was trying to do it all, to take responsibility for her happiness as well as her material welfare. Nobody can ensure another person's happiness. I'm the one who's the problem, she told herself firmly. I'm the one who's got to change.

It was this thought which enabled her to stick to her guns, and once Alan realised that she wasn't going to give in he refused to mention the subject again. Kate received a letter from Caroline Kindersby confirming the job and the date she was expected to arrive, with precise instructions how to find Colonel Beamish's house. After that she didn't really have time for regrets or arguments. Alan was working long hours at the office, getting ready to leave, and coming home tired and preoccupied. But Kate was galvanised by enormous energy which kept her going all day, packing up the house ready for the incoming tenants, locking away what few valuables they had, turning out the children's bedrooms, ruthlessly chucking out stuff hoarded for years. Each night she flopped into bed exhausted and Alan did the same.

On the night before he left, Kate tried to wring some sort of reconciliation from him. But he wasn't having any. When she snuggled up to him in bed he pushed her away, saying he was too tired, but then lay awake beside her tense and silent for quite some time. She knew that what he wanted was for her to give in, even at this eleventh hour and deep down she knew that if he took her in his arms she might do so. At that moment she was feeling guilty enough and frightened too at the thought of what she was letting herself in for. But he lay with his back to her, exuding disapproval, and she simply was too tired and too disappointed in him to make another attempt.

Next morning, however, as Kate drove him to the airport, Alan behaved with infuriating magnanimity, showering her with last-minute instructions about the house, advice on how to behave with her new employer, what to take to the country. There were no recriminations or remonstrations, but nor was there encouragement either. Only when they were saying goodbye in the departure lounge did he offer her an olive branch.

'Remember, darling, if it doesn't work out you don't have to stay. You just book yourself on the first flight to Saudi and I'll be there waiting for you.' She thanked him tearfully, but she wished he'd had a little more faith in her. It was almost as if he wanted her to fail.

Driving back into London, she felt almost certain she was going to oblige him. It was only mid-morning. She had a whole afternoon and evening and night to get through before she had to hand in the keys of the house to the relocation agency tomorrow and set out for Gloucestershire. What have I done? she thought. She peered at her face reflected in the driving mirror as she waited at some traffic lights. It looked small and pinched and frightened. She couldn't bear to go back to the empty house, stripped and clean all ready for the new tenants. What she needed was something to give her confidence. An expensive new dress for instance. But she didn't think she was likely to need new dresses in the country. Her hair! That was it. Feeling excitedly reckless she took herself off to the most fashionable hairdresser in Bond Street, where she told the camp young man who was assigned to her that today she was embarking on a new life and wanted to look completely different. Emerging hours later with her long brown hair shorn and highlighted, clinging to her head like a small blonde cap she could barely recognise herself. But she was pleased.

'I feel pretty,' she sang as she set off home. And for once she almost believed herself!

# *Chapter 4*

Little Riddleton was one of those villages so buried in countryside it was impossible to find. The pouring rain didn't help. Caroline Kindersby's instructions had been clear enough and Kate thought she had followed them to the letter. She had taken the M4 out of London, left it at exit 15 as instructed, and driven on until she reached the town of Bratchester without difficulty. According to her instructions Little Riddleton was less than fifteen miles away. She found the gravel-pits-turned-into-water-parks, which in the gloom of the wet autumn afternoon was something of a triumph, but after that nothing seemed to match her instructions. She drove about for over half an hour, round and round various stretches of man-made lake, and up and down a maze of identical country lanes, peering through her steamed up windows but the village simply didn't seem to be where it was supposed to be. Perhaps it's like Brigadoon, thought Kate in exasperation, it only appears once every hundred years.

And the trouble with getting lost in the country was that there was nobody about to ask. She had tried to stop a bicyclist. 'Excuse me!' she'd shouted, braking sharply as he came towards her. He paused and she struggled to wind down her window but by the time she'd got it open he'd ridden on past and was fifty yards away peddling furiously, head down, into the rain. 'I thought people who lived in the country were supposed to be friendly,' she muttered, engaging the gears with a protesting squeal. But when at last she did find Little Riddleton she was glad it was hidden away so well for it was a rapacious estate agent's dream. It had everything a country village ought to have – an ancient grey stone church with a little stumpy tower, a whitewashed pub called The Cat and the Mustard Pot, a row of Cotswold stone cottages, even a village pond with ducks frolicking in the downpour.

Leaving the village pond on her left according to her instructions, Kate drove on through the village, noticing one or two quite substantial houses, their walls covered in brilliant red creeper, lurking behind stone walls or overgrown yew hedges. Her spirits soared. She was going to live in one of these for six whole months. A mile up the narrow road she came to a T-junction. The Court should be a hundred yards further on to the left. With heart beating faster she peered through the steady rain and saw a derelict gateway. She drove in and slowed to a crawl. At the end of the long winding drive was a large Victorian stone pile, surrounded by dripping yews and laurels, as dark and gloomy as the fading day. Kate pulled up in front of the house and tried not to feel disappointed. She'd come to do a job, she told herself firmly, not to buy the place. She sat in the car listening to the rain drumming on the roof, dripping from the sad evergreens all around her. There was no sign of life and the house had a unwelcoming, secretive air about it. This is my choice, she told herself firmly. I'm here because I wanted to prove myself. Now's the time to start. Feeling a little like the heroine in some gothic melodrama she quickly got out of the car and dashed through the relentless rain to the front door, before her courage deserted her completely.

Timidly she pulled the old-fashioned iron bell pull beside the door and waited while the rain beat down on her new hairdo. Nothing happened. Perhaps she'd come to the wrong house. She yanked more vigorously. A bell jangled discordantly within and was instantly acknowledged by vociferous barking. How stupid, she hadn't thought about dogs. But of course the Colonel was bound to have dogs. Nervously she wondered what breed. From the sound of them they were descended from the Hound of the Baskervilles.

It seemed a very long time before she heard the sound of bolts being drawn and a key being turned with difficulty. Colonel Beamish must be very old and frail and frightened, she thought, to barricade himself in in a quiet secluded spot such as this. Never mind, help was on hand. She'd come to keep him company and make things more comfortable for him. She began to feel better, more confident again. A light came on above her head. The door opened and two dark hairy creatures bounded out to leap at Kate.

'It's all right,' a voice shouted as she shrank back in alarm. 'They only want to be friendly! Down Fred! Here Spot! Whatderyerthinkyerdoing? Leave the poor girl alone!' The dogs crept back past Kate into the house, tails tucked in, and she felt like doing the same. The man she'd come to look after certainly didn't sound either frail or frightened. With a mighty effort she pulled herself together to face her employer with what dignity she could muster. The man standing in the doorway was long and thin and must have been very tall once, but now he was bent and, like the house and the dogs, had seen better days.

'Colonel Beamish?' she asked. 'I'm Kate Hopegood.'

'So I supposed,' he growled. 'You're late. I've been expecting you this last hour – can't stand unpunctuality,' If he'd been expecting her there wasn't much sign of a welcome, Kate thought as she eyed the dogs nervously.

'Well, come in, come in,' he muttered impatiently. 'Don't mind the dogs – they'll leave you alone in a minute. I expect you'd like a cup of tea?' He turned and went back into the house, setting off down a long dark passage without waiting for her to close the door. She scurried after him, questions chasing through her head, wondering whether she should have first locked the car; if he had taken an instant dislike to her or if he was like this with everyone; if she could bear to spend a whole winter in a place as huge and dark and cold as this one.

'We'll have tea in the kitchen,' he announced, when they reached the back of the house. 'It's the warmest room.'

The kitchen had obviously been designed to accommodate a lot of servants but now resembled a bedsit. At one end there was a huge green thing which Kate took to be the cooker. It was draped with various articles of clothing drying on it. At the other was a sofa, a television set, and a dresser littered with letters, newspapers and a telephone. There were no labour-saving devices in sight. As if to confirm the need for many hands, a row of bells hung above the dresser and Kate eyed them warily. She did not trust her autocratic employer not to put them to good use if they were still in working order.

'I've got old Mrs Murphy to do a shepherd's pie for tonight,' he said, taking two mugs from their hooks on the dresser. 'You can take over the kitchen tomorrow.' He set the mugs down on the large stripped pine table which filled the middle of the room. 'When we've had tea I'll show you to your little flat. It's above the stables.' Kate opened her mouth to thank him. 'Caroline said you hadn't got a horse,' he said accusingly, before she could speak. 'Pity. We've got damned fine stables here – better than the house – more comfortable. Are you sure you don't ride?'

'No,' she stammered. 'I'm afraid I don't.' He looked so displeased she braced herself for another withering attack but was saved by the telephone which began to ring.

The old man waved her in the direction of the stove and shouted, 'Put the kettle on!' as he answered the telephone. She took the kettle over to the sink, filled it and returned it to the side of the stove, which didn't seem very warm. But then, she thought, nothing in this house seemed warm. While he shouted into the telephone at some poor unfortunate she took the opportunity to study him more closely. He was dressed in ancient tweeds of immaculate cut with a green sleeveless Husky over the top. He had a fine head of almost white hair and a bristling moustache. His face was strong and craggy like a mountain peak, prominent nose, beetling eyebrows, beneath which faded blue eyes flashed piercingly. His cheeks were bright beacons of red, and his mouth, although sunken by age, had a very tough line to it. Kate wondered how old he was.

'Bloody fool,' said the old man, hanging up the phone. 'What's the point of him being on the Council if he doesn't do what he's told? I campaigned to get him on, he wouldn't have got elected if I hadn't put everything I had behind him and now he says he's waiting for the recommendation of his Planning Department before he makes up his mind.' He glared at Kate so furiously she felt compelled to say something.

'The tea,' she said, since she had absolutely no idea what he was talking about. 'Where might I find it?'

He rummaged about inside a wooden cupboard and produced a tea caddy. 'Milk's in there.'

She opened the fridge and almost recoiled from the smell. It was filled with what appeared to be the remains of countless different meals since the last poor girl Friday had been carried off to hospital.

'Bloody holiday village. What do we want with holiday villages in a place like Riddleton?' Kate had no idea so she grabbed a fresh milk bottle and shut the fridge door hastily. 'Not that bottle – that's unopened,' he said, taking the milk out of her hand and putting it back in the fridge. 'There ought to be a jug in here somewhere – yes, here it is.' He set down on the table a jug covered with a little muslin top edged with beads like a miniature bedspread. 'Now what's wrong with the damned kettle? Why's it taking so long to boil?' He looked at the stove, then rounded on her angrily. 'Christ, girl, you haven't put the kettle on yet.'

'I'm sorry,' stammered Kate, petrified. 'I'm afraid I've never seen a stove like this one before.'

'It's an Aga,' he informed her witheringly. 'God Almighty, and you're supposed to be the cook.' She felt tears coming to her eyes and longed to be able to creep beneath the table and hide there like the dogs. Her first test and here she was already behaving like a wimp. 'Just as well I got old Mrs Murphy to do me a shepherd's pie tonight. I told that damn fool daughter of mine I could manage quite well enough on my own. I don't need you.' He glowered at her fiercely.

'I'm sorry. I didn't know. Your daughter didn't say anything about an Aga,' Kate whimpered, wishing she had never come, that she was back at home in safe, familiar Fulham, or with her dear darling Alan a million miles away in Saudi.

'Lesson number one.' The Colonel seized the kettle and poured half the water away into the sink. 'Never fill the bloody thing up to the top with cold water, it takes too much energy to heat it all up. Lesson number two: to boil a kettle you have to lift this cover here and put the kettle on the hot plate underneath.' He looked at her as if she were a very small worm on the end of a hook. 'Not very difficult, is it?' She shook her head miserably. 'Well, is it?' he barked.

'No,' she stammered. 'I expect I'll get the hang of it in no time.'

He seemed mollified. 'Mrs Murphy'll put you right – damn good woman, Mrs Murphy, married to the stud groom. He's been with me since he joined the army – my batman. Not a bad chap – bit of an old scrounger at times like they all are, but his stable management's first class. Hopeless with machinery, of course – no use in the garden in the summertime. Mrs Murphy knows this house better than anyone, every nook and cranny, been with me since before the children were born.' Kate looked forward grimly to meeting this modern Mrs Danvers.

'Where do they live, Mr and Mrs Murphy?' she asked, praying it wasn't on the premises.

'They've got a cottage just by the gate, used to live over the stables until they had too many children and there wasn't room for them all. The under groom lived there then. That was when we had a full yard. Now we've just got one hunter – Caroline's.' He broke off and stared at her resentfully.

'It's a pretty village,' Kate said hastily, afraid he was going to upbraid her again for not having a horse. 'I couldn't see much of it through the rain but it seems very traditional and unspoilt.'

He glared at her more fiercely than ever, his face getting redder by the minute.

'It's all going to be ruined if the developers have their way.'

She had hoped to divert him into calmer waters, but all she seemed to have achieved was a retreat into dangerous rapids. The kettle began to boil at last and she got up thankfully and busied herself making tea.

'It appears we've got a bit of a crisis on,' he said when she sat down again. 'Some big development company has crept up like a thief in the night and proposes to turn our neighbourhood into a mini Butlins. There's an application for outline planning permission for a holiday village to be built here just outside Little Riddleton. We've got to stop them. But the buggers have done their homework well and got it all over bar the shouting before any of us locals knew a damn thing about it. Now we've only got two weeks before the date of the planning application. If the District Council mutinies we're done for.' His moustache was twitching alarmingly and Kate began to tremble.

'Can't you fight it?' she said. The Colonel was obviously spoiling for a fight with someone and she was afraid that for want of anything better he had chosen her.

'I could, perhaps, if I had someone to help me,' he said, eyeing her challengingly.

'I'll do what I can, of course,' she stammered. 'We ought to be able to rally local opinion against it.'

'How?' he demanded. Kate's mind went blank. She couldn't possibly think with him scowling at her so fiercely. She longed to suggest that he might try a little gentle persuasion instead of bullying everybody, but of course she didn't dare. So she finished her tea in silence, wondering what she could possibly do to retrieve the incredibly bad impression she had made.

'Now I expect you'll want to see your quarters,' he said, getting to his feet. He led the way out of the kitchen down another passage, past a room that Kate saw contained rows of riding boots and wellingtons and various ancient garments designed to keep out the rain. As they went he proceeded to cross-question her. She told him that her husband had been sent abroad on a six-month assignment.

'Husband in the army then?' he asked almost eagerly. She was tempted to give him something to cling to but rejected it in favour of honesty.

'No, he's in computers.'

The Colonel scowled. 'He'd have done better if he'd gone in the army. At least the army knows how to look after people.' He led her into another room which seemed to be some sort of wash house with a washing machine and some old-fashioned pulleys as well as two large deep freezes. It was so damp and cold that Kate couldn't believe anything ever dried there.

'So he's had to put you out to work, has he?' the Colonel said, pausing to look her up and down unnervingly.

'My daughter's at university and my son's going to Cambridge next year – he's working his way round the world at the moment,' she said. 'There didn't seem much point my sitting at home idle.'

He nodded sympathetically. 'I know how it is – education's a bugger. Bleeds you dry. But you've got to do it.' Just for a moment he seemed almost human. 'If you send them to the local comprehensive they come out hardly able to read or write.'

She decided it was better to let him suppose that she was working for financial necessity. She was sure he would not begin to understand her need for self-discovery. She wasn't even sure she did herself. 'We had this marvellous opportunity for letting the house and so here I am,' she said confidently, and left it at that.

He opened a door and the two dogs loped past, nearly knocking Kate off her feet in their eagerness to get out into the rain.

She could feel her smart town loafers filling with water as she splashed through puddles towards the stables which formed three sides of a quadrangle behind the house. Ruefully she thought of the new wellingtons she'd bought, resting in the boot of her car. She hadn't expected to need them quite so soon.

The stables were the old-fashioned indoor kind with a splendid arch in the middle leading out into the road. On either side of the arch a corridor led past a row of loose boxes with iron grilles and cobbled floors. The Colonel was right, thought Kate looking around her impressed, they were comfortable, large and roomy and dry. It was such a shame they were nearly all empty. She began to see why he was so disappointed she hadn't brought a horse. A light was on in the end box and from it came the sound of tuneless humming.

'Is that you, Murphy?' shouted the Colonel, setting off down the corridor.

A gnome appeared out of the box. He was small and bandy-legged, his weatherbeaten face wrinkled as a pickled walnut. He could have been any age from sixty to ninety.

'Just settling the mare down for the night, Colonel,' he said. The Colonel introduced Kate and then went into the box to talk to the horse. She was big and black and most of her was covered with a rug. She nuzzled the Colonel with what Kate thought rather alarming familiarity, poking her soft nose about him, inquisitively blowing at his hand while he murmured endearments and fished in the pocket of his tweed coat beneath the Husky.

'What's her name?' asked Kate.

'Bella,' he said, producing a packet of Polos. She watched anxiously as he fumbled with stiff arthritic fingers while the mare nudged him impatiently. 'Because she's a black beauty aren't you, my darlin'?' The mare's velvety lips were practically over his hand. 'Now don't you be in such a hurry,' he said caressingly as he pushed the soft nose away. 'You'll get it all in good time.'

'I'm glad you're here, madam,' said Murphy, and Kate warmed to him. It was the first word of welcome she had received. 'I don't like the poor old girl being all alone here at night. I always likes to have someone living above the horse in case she gets cast in her box.'

The Colonel had at last succeeded in getting a Polo mint on to the palm of his hand. 'Mrs Hopegood doesn't ride,' he snapped, as the horse sucked it up greedily. 'I doubt very much she could do anything about a cast horse.' Murphy looked shocked, Kate didn't know whether at her lack of horsemanship or the Colonel's rudeness. But she didn't want to lose her only ally.

'I can at least come and call you, if there's an emergency,' she said smiling at him.

'That would be very good of you, madam,' he said. 'Mrs Murphy'll show you our cottage tomorrow. No doubt you'll want to take a look round the village.'

The Colonel gave the mare a final pat. 'Mrs Hopegood wants to see her flat now,' he said, coming out of the box. 'Take her up there, Murphy, will you? Show her where everything is.' He stumped off out of the stables, leaving Kate with Murphy and the distinct feeling that she was nothing but a bloody nuisance.

Kate fetched her car round and Murphy helped carry her luggage up to the flat above the stables. It was a large bedsit with a tiny kitchen and bathroom, and had clearly been converted from what had once been a hay loft. The roof was low and raftered, the floorboards creaked. The bed tucked away in one corner was small and narrow and chaste. But it was snug. It had character. Kate would have been delighted with it if she had not been so overwhelmed by a sense of her own inadequacy.

After Murphy had gone she sat down on the bed feeling utterly useless. Nothing was what she had expected. She was totally unsuited to this sort of life. Why, she couldn't even rescue a cast horse – whatever that might be. The whole idea was an unmitigated disaster. If she could she would have jumped into her car and driven straight back to London, but she couldn't. Her home was possessed by strangers. Her loving husband was in Saudi sorting out the Arabs' communications problems. In the past she had always been able to turn to Alan for help, but she had deliberately cut herself off from him and his protection. I'm weak, she told herself, getting off the bed and peering out of the window at their family saloon now parked in the stable yard. I'm weak and the Colonel knows it. He'll take advantage of me, has already taken advantage of me. Alan was so right.

She looked at her two suitcases waiting to be unpacked. To run away was accepting defeat. It was too early to give in. She threw open one of the cases and began to hang up her clothes in the lean-to wardrobe under the eaves. This is what she'd come for, to learn not to be a wimp, and it looked as if she'd picked the right school.

Kate took her washing things into the bathroom, and groaned as she looked at herself in the mirror, appalled at how wet and bedraggled she appeared. She ran the tap and there was a great deal of hissing and gurgling from an old-fashioned geyser attached to the bath. Eventually a stream of near-boiling water shot into the basin. Thank God, instant hot water. At least she didn't have to struggle with a temperamental boiler. She longed to have a bath, to lie and let the hot water soothe her battered spirit, but suspected that the ancient geyser would take far too long to produce enough water to fill it and there would not be time. She ought to be getting back to the house to do battle with that terrible Aga and get the Colonel's supper. She washed her face. Towelled her hair vigorously. It went back into shape surprisingly well, as if the genius who had cut it had designed it for a drip-dry life. It was extraordinary how a change of hairstyle could alter the shape of one's face, thought Kate, now pleased with what she saw. Her face was no longer small and pinched but heart-shaped. If only she'd had a *retroussé* nose she could have tried for a part as Peter Pan. Feeling better, she left the bathroom, changed her wet tights and fished out a pair of dry shoes. He's an old man, helpless and alone, she told herself resolutely. He can't eat you. The worst that can happen is that you'll be sent packing and then you can go and join Alan in Saudi. With this thought to cling to, she put on her new wellingtons and, carrying her dry shoes, returned to the house.

The kitchen was empty. Relieved Kate pottered about looking for the shepherd's pie, which wasn't in the fridge. Eventually she found a larder about the size of a single bedroom. It was well stocked with tins and jars and quite a number of platefuls of food in various stages of decay, and the shepherd's pie. Kate sniffed it dubiously. It was fresh enough but didn't look very appetising. She went back to the Aga and examined its four ovens, cautiously. The top right was too hot, the bottom left was too cool. Feeling a bit like Goldilocks she thrust the pie into the bottom right and let it take its chance. What else? She wondered if there were any frozen peas to be had. Somewhere in the back premises Kate remembered seeing a freezer. She found it two rooms away alongside the washing machine. It was full of dog meat and unplucked game and lots of unidentifiable bundles of what she thought might be frozen vegetables from the garden but which she wasn't at all sure about. She found a packet of Birds Eye frozen peas and decided to play safe with that. She put their water on to boil and wondered what to do next. Where was this meal to be eaten and did the Colonel expect her to join him? Once again her spirit quailed. Everything was so much more difficult than she'd imagined it would be. Still, she couldn't skulk in the kitchen. She must carry the battle into the enemy's camp, which meant finding the Colonel.

Kate opened the kitchen door and crept along the passage towards the centre of the house. A light was coming from a room across the hall. The door was ajar and the news was being read in the plummy tones of a Radio Four announcer. Surely nobody listened to the news on the radio any more? thought Kate. Didn't the Colonel have television? She took a deep breath and tiptoed across the hall. Outside the door she paused. The newsreader went on reading. Kate slid into the room.

The Colonel was sitting in a high-backed, winged armchair, a glass of whisky by his side. He didn't appear to notice her. Kate wasn't surprised, it wasn't much of an entrance. She looked about her. It was the sort of room people described as a snuggery, only it wasn't at all snug. A quite inadequate fire was smoking in a fireplace too small to heat the spacious room. The faded heavy curtains were pulled tight over long tall windows but were moving in the draught. A small gate-legged table stood in front of the fire – laid for one. One of the dogs was stretched out by the fire. He got up, padded across to Kate and put his nose up her skirt. The Colonel looked up.

'Got the supper ready?'

'I've just popped it in the oven,' she said, pushing the dog's head away. 'It won't take long.'

'I usually have my supper at half-past seven,' he said, taking a swig of whisky.

The implication was plain. Kate was expected to vanish back to the kitchen and return with his supper when it was ready. But she couldn't do that. Mindful of Alan's warning about being treated like a servant she knew she had to make a stand tonight. She took a few tentative steps forward. He ignored her. She couldn't believe that anyone could be so deliberately unpleasant and began to wonder whether the last girl really did have a riding accident or whether she'd fled in the night. I must say something, she thought, do something to attract his attention. The dog had lost interest and gone back to the fire. Kate noticed a round table on the far side of the room, covered with photos.

'Are these your family?' she asked, walking across the room to examine them. It worked. He switched off the radio and got up from his chair to show her the photos. One was of a handsome man in uniform, himself in his youth. Another was of an elegant woman riding side-saddle.

'My first wife,' he said. 'Killed out hunting, didn't breed.' Another faded wedding photo was of the Colonel and his second wife, the mother of his children. There were other more recent wedding photographs. Kate recognised a younger, softer Caroline Kindersby, looking radiant in tiara and tulle and billowing taffeta. Then Kate's heart suddenly gave a great lurch as she found herself staring down at a handsome young man whose picture she had once kept beside her bed for over a year and still had hidden in a drawer. Patrick!

He was in morning coat, just as in her dreams she had once tried to imagine him. Gazing up at him adoringly was a pretty blonde girl in full bridal attire. Kate felt herself going hot and cold; she could almost hear the girl in the photograph screaming at her as that woman had screamed at them in the Imperial; she remembered with an awful clarity the floor rushing up to meet her. Dear God, not that. It couldn't be. But the Colonel's voice behind her confirmed it.

'That's my younger daughter, Deborah.' His voice was full of pride. 'She married a local farmer – Patrick Bray-Smith. Good chap to hounds. Field Master on Saturdays.'

All Kate's ideas of asserting herself were totally dissipated by the shock. She bolted from the room too stunned to do anything except serve the Colonel his shepherd's pie alone in his study and, having done the washing up, creep away supperless to bed.

# *Chapter 5*

Of course Kate didn't sleep a wink. She lay in her narrow little bed under the eaves tormented by thoughts of Patrick, of what she was to say to him when they met, as surely sooner or later they must. What would he think of her? Would he think she was chasing after him? Was she? Had she really come to Gloucestershire to find herself or was she looking for her lost love? She tried to examine her conscience honestly and in the process fell at last into an uneasy sleep. But she dreamt of Patrick and his wife both screaming at her and throwing her out of the house.

She woke up suddenly and became aware that the screaming was not part of her dream but of the unfriendly night. She lay listening in terror, wondering what it was. Had the horse got cast? Should she do something? While she was still trying to decide, it stopped. Not daring to move, holding her breath as she huddled beneath the bedclothes, Kate listened to the silence. No familiar traffic noises, no friendly church clock chiming the hours, not even the wailing of a nice police siren to reassure her. Nothing but deathly silence. Even the rain had stopped. Then she heard it again – an eerie high-pitched cry. At least it didn't seem to be coming from the stable below, but from somewhere outside in the fields. She pulled the covers over her head and tried to go back to sleep, but without success. The noise seemed to have stopped. She got up, turned on the light, stood by the window peering out into the dark night. All was quiet and very still. Whatever it was had either died or perhaps managed to kill something.

She looked at her watch. It was only four o'clock. She wandered about the little flat, confused, frightened, appalled at what she'd let herself in for. What was she doing here in this unfriendly place? Perhaps she should creep out now, get into her car and be off? All it would take was one telephone call to Alan and he would fix everything. She stood in front of the coin-operated telephone just inside the door of the flat and thought about escape. She could ring Alan, he would be overjoyed. Perhaps if it had been an ordinary telephone she might have done it. But the thought of trying to ring Alan in Saudi from a coin box was too much.

This panic was ridiculous, it was mere pre-dawn blues. Everything would seem much better in the morning. She turned out the light and got back into bed, drifting into sleep at last, only to be woken again at dawn by the sound of the horse shouting for her breakfast from the stable below. Well, at least that's one animal that doesn't seem to have expired in the night, thought Kate, getting out of bed and going to investigate the tiny kitchen.

Somebody had cleaned it out since the last poor inhabitant had had her accident. The fridge was empty and had been turned off, but there was a jar of Nescafé, some sugar, a tin of baked beans and a packet of cornflakes in one of the cupboards. Kate made herself a cup of black coffee, added sugar and took it back to bed. From there she could see out of the window which ran from the low ceiling to the floor. The view of uninterrupted countryside was breathtaking, a patchwork of green and brown stretching to the far horizon, broken only by grey stone walls, trees and the occasional church spire. Sipping her coffee, Kate felt her panic in the dark hours before dawn receding. Here was peace and tranquillity. Here was space unlimited. The sound of rooks arguing nearby reminded her of the autumns of her childhood. She had taken country things and her parents for granted then, but now, with the unmistakable sounds and smells of autumn wafting through the open window, she was overwhelmed with nostalgia.

Happy memories are one of the most priceless legacies one can leave to one's children, she thought, far more enriching than material possessions. If my parents had bullied me or subjected me to persistent cruelty then the sound of that rook calling and the smell of manure from the stables below would make me tremble with fear instead of feel all warm inside. Filled with a sense of peace and gratitude to her parents, both now dead, Kate sipped her coffee and gazed out of the window in wonder. The light was so soft and gentle, like a Turner painting. A faint mist hung in the hollows where the sun hadn't yet penetrated. In the middle distance she could see a church spire with a huddle of houses surrounding it. Greater Riddleton perhaps? She could see why the Colonel was so incensed at the idea of the holiday village.

The thought of the Colonel brought her back to earth with a bump.

Somehow she had to retrieve the bad impression she had made on him yesterday. Perhaps if she were to offer to help him fight the holiday village scheme he might be able to forgive her for not having a horse. It would be a cause well worth fighting. Full of good resolutions she threw back the covers and leapt out of bed. It was only seven o'clock, but she would make a good impression by being early on the job.

Half an hour later, dressed in black trousers and brightly coloured sweater, her sleek new urchin cut framing her face becomingly, Kate ran down the stairs into the stables ready to face a new day with all its challenges.

Murphy was coming down the corridor leading Bella, who was saddled and bridled and almost prancing in her eagerness to reach the door.

'Good morning, Murphy,' said Kate, flattening herself against the stable wall to let them pass. 'She looks very big and bouncy today.'

'Ah, the old girl knows she's going hunting,' he said, slapping the mare's neck proudly. 'There's a spring in her step this morning.'

He led his impatient charger out into the yard and Kate followed, feeling slightly bemused. Surely people didn't go hunting at this hour in the morning? She was even more surprised to see Caroline Kindersby waiting outside, dressed in a tweed coat, bowler hat and brown boots. Kate looked anxiously up at the stable clock. Was her watch wrong? Had she overslept after her disturbed night? But the stable clock too said seven thirty. What was Caroline doing dressed as if going for a ride in Rotten Row but here in the country so early?

'I see you've arrived safely, Kate,' said Caroline, climbing up on to an old stone mounting-block. 'Is everything all right? I told Mrs Murphy to clean the flat out for you.'

'Oh yes, the flat's fine, very comfortable,' stammered Kate.

Kate wondered if she dare enlist Caroline's help with some of her problems but Murphy was leading the mare up to the mounting-block and Caroline was climbing on. After that Caroline seemed very busy with Murphy, far too busy to be able to pay any attention to Kate. First the girth had to be tightened, then the stirrup leathers shortened, then some bit of the bridle wasn't quite right. Bella was growing impatient, fidgeting, throwing up her head and chewing at her bit. She looked bigger and more dangerous than the much-petted creature who had been so loving and patient with the Colonel the evening before. Caroline too seemed different, rather pale and strained and preoccupied. It occurred to Kate that she was not the assured woman who had interviewed her in London. She wondered if Caroline really enjoyed hunting. She certainly didn't look as happy to be going as the mare.

'Be off with you then.' Murphy gave the horse a final pat. 'You don't want to be late for the meet.'

'Heavens no!' Caroline gathered up her reins anxiously. 'Daddy can't stand it if any of us are late.' Murphy released the bridle and the horse surged forward. 'Make sure you have his breakfast ready for when he comes back, Kate.' Kate was too busy leaping out of the way of those huge hooves to think of asking what time that would be.

'Is the meet far away?' Kate asked Murphy as Caroline rode under the arch and out on to the road.

'About four mile. She'll do it easy,' he said. He picked up a broom and began sweeping a few wisps of straw from the immaculate cobbles.

'Do they always go hunting this early in the morning?' she asked him.

'No, madam, they don't,' he said, looking at her pityingly.

'I'm sorry,' she said, smiling at him shyly. 'You see, I'm not at all horsey and so I don't know these things.'

'Well, it's like this, see,' he said, putting down the broom. 'Hunting starts first Saturday in November or thereabouts and the Blazers meet then at a quarter to eleven. But before hunting can start you've got to teach the young hounds their job and cull the fox population to keep the farmers happy and teach some young horses good manners. So we start in August, soon as the harvest is in, but it's too hot during the day for there to be any sort of a scent so we meet at first light – six in the morning. Then as the mornings get darker we meets later. This week the meet's eight o'clock, next week it'll be nine until we gets to November, see, when the leaf is off the trees and the cattle are all in and the wire's all down. Then we go hunting proper.'

Kate wasn't at all sure that she did see, but she was reluctant to shock him with the depths of her ignorance. 'The Colonel's gone to the meet this morning, I suppose?' she asked.

'Of course. The Colonel never misses a meet. But he'll be home for his breakfast as soon as hounds move off – then he'll be back out following until they goes home.' Murphy winked at her. 'Better go in and have yours while the going's good.' She thanked him and he grinned. 'That's all right, madam,' he said, picking up the broom again. 'Anything you want to know, just ask old Murphy – I'll be more than glad to help if I can.'

Greatly encouraged Kate walked off to the house.

In the kitchen she found a small wiry woman with a weatherbeaten face and frizz of startlingly black hair, busily frying bacon in a pan full of grease.

'Ah, you must be Mrs Murphy,' said Kate. 'I've heard so much about you.' The woman glared at Kate suspiciously over her shoulder. 'What a wonderful help you are,' Kate tried to explain. The woman glowered at the spitting bacon. Oh dear, thought Kate, she probably thinks I'm patronising her. 'He said he couldn't possibly manage without you,' she added and knew too late that she had only made matters worse.

'That's as maybe,' the woman muttered, breaking an egg into the pan. 'We'll manage well enough without you – that's for sure.'

Dear God, thought Kate, her heart plummeting once more. She noticed that the table was laid for one and she longed to retreat to her flat and have hers there. But she knew that if she let herself be put out of the kitchen now she would never be allowed into it except on this woman's terms.

'I came over early this morning because I don't know what time the Colonel has his breakfast,' she said in what she hoped was a firm but friendly tone.

'I always get the Colonel his breakfast,' said Mrs Murphy. 'Eight o'clock he has it, regular as clockwork. When he's not gone hunting.' She scooped a piece of bacon out of the pan and laid it on top of the fried bread keeping hot at the side of the Aga. 'Then while he eats his breakfast in here I does the sitting-room out, lays and lights the fire, and when he's finished here I'm finished there. He reads his paper until the post comes, then he opens his letters.' She turned round to gaze at Kate defiantly.

'The Colonel said that you would be able to show me how everything works,' Kate said, going to the dresser and fetching a plate, cup and saucer. She set them down on the table opposite the place laid for the Colonel and cut a slice of bread for herself. The woman ignored her, pouring hot water into the teapot and setting it on the table while Kate searched in vain for something in which to make the toast. Mrs Murphy watched expressionless.

'I don't seem to be able to find the toaster,' Kate said, pouring herself a cup of tea.

'There isn't one.' Mrs Murphy sounded triumphant.

'You don't have a toaster?' Did they toast bread on the end of a fork, thought Kate, dismayed. Surely things weren't as primitive as that.

Mrs Murphy suddenly produced a hinged metal implement like a giant double-sided fly swatter, clamped Kate's bread it in, put in on the hot plate of the Aga and slammed the hood down.

'I'm afraid I've never cooked on an Aga,' said Kate, 'but I'm sure if you show me how I'll soon get the hang of it.'

The woman eyed her balefully but then suddenly cocked her head on one side like an alert sparrow. Kate heard tyres crunching on the gravel outside.

'The Colonel,' Mrs Murphy said, 'that's him back now.' She scooped the egg out of the pan and added it to the bacon and fried bread swimming in its own grease, dumping the plate down on the table. Then she trotted out of the kitchen leaving Kate in possession. Kate wasn't sure whether to sit down at the table and pretend to be getting on with her breakfast or to stand to attention and wait for the Colonel. She was saved from having to decide by a smell of burning coming from the Aga. She lifted the hood and found her toast in its metal container reduced to a black cinder stuck to the hot plate.

'Good morning, Mrs Hopegood,' said the Colonel, breezing into the kitchen, with the two dogs running in front of him. 'You've burnt the toast.'

'I know that,' said Kate through gritted teeth. 'What I don't know is how you can cook anything on a medieval machine such as this. It ought to be in the Science Museum.'

Much to her surprise he roared with laughter. 'Here, let me do it for you,' he said, prising the burnt pieces off the rack and dropping them on the floor for the dogs. 'Don't you want something cooked?'

'No, thank you.'

He put a fresh piece of bread in the implement and left it under the hood. 'Quite right – it's perfectly filthy but I can't upset Mrs Murphy.' He put the plate Mrs Murphy had filled with such possessive pride on the floor, and sat down. Kate watched the two dogs lick it clean within minutes and wondered what the Murphy woman would think if she knew. It seemed a shame that she should go to such trouble every morning just for the dogs.

'The toast,' said the Colonel, waving his teacup at her. 'Turn it over.'

Kate did as he told her and a few minutes later it was ready. He watched her bring it to the table with proprietory interest and she supposed that, as he'd given his own breakfast away, he was expecting to eat hers. Determined to get off to a better start today, she gave it to him with a smile and made some more. He accepted the toast without comment and ate it while reading the morning paper. Kate was relieved to be able to enjoy hers in silence. The toast was excellent, far better than anything produced in an electric toaster. She looked at the Aga with new respect, as she wondered what she should do next. She longed to make a start on the fridge, turning out all the unsavoury leftovers, but it was difficult to begin with the Colonel sitting there at the table absorbed in his newspaper. Suddenly he looked up and demanded if she was coming with him to watch the hounds working.

'I don't think so,' she replied nervously. 'I'd like to get the kitchen straight.' He looked so disappointed she felt compelled to add, 'Another day I'd love to come with you.'

'No need to worry about the kitchen – Mrs Murphy'll see to it,' he said.

'Yes, but I must go through things, see what's missing, go shopping.' He didn't look pleased. 'I really do need time to find my feet,' she declared firmly.

'Right then,' he capitulated with alarming suddenness. 'You just give me a list of things you need and I'll get them in Bratchester on my way back this morning. There's a Waitrose there and I've got the girls well trained. They all know me.'

Kate got up and took her cup and saucer over to the sink. This was not at all how she wanted it to be. She wondered whether she should insist on doing her own shopping, but felt inhibited by her lack of experience of working in a private home. Besides, she didn't know how she was supposed to pay for it. She ought to have asked Caroline what to do about housekeeping money. She didn't dare ask the Colonel. Perhaps all jobs were like this at the beginning. Shirley was right, she thought miserably. It was so long since she'd worked for anybody she'd forgotten what it was like.

'Right,' said the Colonel, producing pen and pencil. 'Fire away.'

Kate's mind went blank. She began to clear the rest of the things from the table to give herself time to think, but his moustache began to twitch alarmingly and so she sat down and asked for chops.

'They don't do decent chops in Waitrose,' he said almost triumphantly. 'If I want those I go to the butcher in Greater Riddleton.' Kate racked her brain trying to think what Caroline had said he liked – mince and chops and overdone roast beef, wasn't it? She opened her mouth to suggest mince but was forestalled by the Colonel. 'They do a decent corn-fed chicken. I'll get one of those. What else?'

'Vegetables,' Kate said faintly. 'Carrots, a cauliflower perhaps, a bit of salad, potatoes?' At home she was accustomed to getting her inspiration while out shopping. Yet here she was expected to know what she was going to need without even having had time to go through the cupboards.

'There's plenty of vegetables from the garden, the deep freeze is stacked with them,' he said. 'I can't begin to eat everything we produce all on my own.'

'Just bring whatever you think best,' she said, giving up. Was he being contrary deliberately, or was it second nature?

'You're the cook,' he said with a distinct gleam in his eye, and it occurred to her that it was just a game he was playing, and rather a childish one at that. 'Are you sure there's nothing else you want?'

'Not until I've had time to go through the fridge and the cupboards and the larder and the deep freeze,' she said, trying to sound businesslike. 'Some bread perhaps.' He wrote it down.

'Good,' he said, getting with a little difficulty to his feet. 'Then I'll see you at lunch.'

As soon as he'd gone, Kate set to work to introduce a little hygiene into the kitchen. She began with the larder, throwing out everything that smelt bad or had mould on it, then she tackled the fridge, emptying everything on to the kitchen table and filling the sink with anything that could be washed. Of course what it really needed was defrosting but she would do that when she had more time. She had just got the kitchen into the maximum state of chaos, when Caroline arrived back from hunting.

'Good heavens, Kate, you really are getting stuck in,' she said, sauntering into the kitchen and staring about her in amazement.

'I'm sorry, Mrs Kindersby, everything's a bit of a mess,' said Kate, taking her head out of the fridge, which she was busy washing down with warm soapy water. 'But I wasn't really expecting you back so soon.'

'Soon! It's eleven o'clock.' Caroline sank down into a chair. 'I've been in the saddle over three hours, quite long enough this early in the season. My old bones aren't used to it.'

'Can I get you anything – a cup of coffee?' asked Kate, drying her hands on her apron. Caroline looked round the cluttered kitchen and Kate thought she repressed a shudder.

'Don't bother about me, I only came to see how you were getting on.' She seemed more relaxed, more approachable again. Was she relieved, Kate wondered, to have got home in one piece? And why did she do it, if it frightened her?

'Any problems?' Caroline asked. Kate took a deep breath and leant against the draining board wondering where to start.

'The Aga,' she said. 'I'm afraid I've never seen one before and it's taking me a little time to get used to it.'

'There ought to be an Aga cookbook somewhere about,' said Caroline, wincing as she got up. 'They're marvellous things, Agas, once you get the hang of them. I really miss not having one in London.'

'It's just that I wanted to make all these odd bits and pieces of cheese into a soufflé for the Colonel's lunch but I wasn't sure if I dared,' explained Kate, trying to impress.

'A soufflé!' exclaimed Caroline, delving through the drawers of the dresser. 'He hasn't had anything like that since poor Mum died. What a find you are! I can see you're going to be terribly good for him.'

'I'm not sure your father would agree with you,' Kate said nervously. 'I don't seem to have got off to a very good start.'

'Don't let him bully you,' Caroline told her. 'He can be sweetness itself if you handle him right. But you've got to stand up to him otherwise he'll pick on you endlessly.' She gave a cry of triumph as she dragged something out from the back of the drawer. 'I knew it was here somewhere.' She presented Kate with a well-thumbed, much-stained paperback. 'I think you'll find everything you want to know is in there.'

Kate seized it gratefully. 'Oh thank you, Mrs Kindersby. I'm sure it'll be a great help.'

Caroline smiled somewhat graciously. 'Call me Caroline, do.'

'Thank you,' Kate said again, and inwardly winced. She sounded exactly like a servant. Whatever would Alan say if he could hear her now?

'Are you sure you wouldn't like some breakfast?' she asked pushing all thoughts of Alan from her mind. 'It won't take me long to make some.'

'No thanks, Kate, I must dash. I'll be late for a meeting in London. I'll get breakfast on the motorway. It's the only meal the service stations do passably well.'

It wasn't until Caroline had gone that Kate realised she ought to have asked about the housekeeping money. Oh dear, there seemed so much she didn't know. Still, at least she now had a book to tell her about the Aga.

Mrs Murphy appeared when Kate was studying the cookery book over a cup of coffee. Kate offered her one but Mrs Murphy refused, saying she hadn't time to dawdle all morning over coffee. She then retired with an audible sniff and Kate felt a small sense of triumph. She had taken possession of the kitchen and Mrs Murphy knew it. By twelve she had her empire restored to order, and was feeling confident enough to risk the soufflé. It was time she showed the Colonel that she could cook. In the larder she found a packet of flour for the roux, but when she picked it up a stream of white poured on to the floor.

'That's mice, that is,' said Mrs Murphy, appearing like an evil genie at the door. 'Ever since the old cat died the mice have been having a field day. Can't seem to keep them out of the larder, greedy little buggers.'

Kate longed to throw the almost new packet of flour into the dustbin, but Mrs Murphy was watching her with a gleam in her eye. Kate was sure she wouldn't approve of wasting a perfectly good packet of flour just because the mice had got at it. So she shut the larder door hurriedly and went back to the kitchen with the flour cradled in her apron like a baby. Shortly afterwards Mrs Murphy took herself off home and Kate was left to get on with lunch undisturbed.

The Colonel returned at five minutes to one, by which time Kate was ready, with the table in the kitchen laid for two, some French beans she found in the freezer cooked and keeping hot in the warming oven. As soon as she heard his car she beat up the egg whites and folded them into the cheese sauce. Then with a quick prayer she slid the soufflé into the hottest oven just as the Colonel came into the kitchen with his purchases. Feeling pleased with herself she told him that lunch would be ready in twenty minutes. Just time for him to have a drink while she put his purchases away.

'Why isn't it on the table, Mrs Hopegood?' he demanded. 'It's not as if you've had anything else to do all morning.'

'It isn't on the table because I've made a cheese soufflé and a soufflé will spoil if it's kept waiting,' she explained, then remembering Caroline's advice added more tartly, 'just like you, Colonel Beamish.'

'I always have luncheon at one o'clock sharp,' he said growing perceptibly redder in the face. 'And I never keep anybody waiting.'

Kate drew a deep breath. It was now or never. Either stand up for yourself or be bullied for evermore. 'Look,' she said, 'I think we'd better get this straight. I didn't come here as a full-time cook and you're certainly not paying for one. What I came here to do was duties of a light and companionable nature.'

The Colonel glared. 'If this is about wages I'm afraid I can't afford to pay you any more than you're getting,' he said quickly.

'It's not about wages,' she retorted, indignation giving her courage. 'It's about attitude.' He seemed startled. 'I am not a servant and I didn't expect to be treated as one. When your daughter interviewed me she led me to believe that what you wanted was someone to keep you company and make things more comfortable for you. Instead of which ever since I arrived you've made it perfectly plain that I'm not wanted here, aided and abetted by Mrs Murphy.' She paused, rather frightened that she might have gone too far. If he took offence now she would have no alternative but to pack her bags and walk out.

There was a taut silence which finally the Colonel broke. 'What I resent,' he said, his moustache twitching fiercely, 'is people trying to arrange my life for me. I like to think I'm still perfectly capable of doing everything myself.' He shrugged defiantly. 'I'm not, of course, that's the worst part of getting old; the fact that I can't seem to manage as well as I did infuriates me. I don't like having to depend on perfect strangers.' He glared at Kate and her heart sank. In spite of everything she did not want to be thrown out – not yet. 'Unfortunately I need you, Kate – I think I'd better call you Kate. You're far too pretty to be called Mrs Hopegood all the time.' Kate was stunned. It was such an unexpected capitulation. Suddenly he smiled. 'I'm awfully sorry,' he went on. 'It appears I've been guilty of the most shocking bad manners. Will you forgive me? Now, let me pour you out a drink and we'll start all over again, shall we? What's it to be? Sherry – gin – whisky?'

'I'll have a gin and tonic,' she said. He disappeared and she leant against the Aga feeling weak with shock. She had stood up to him and it had worked, but her nerves were jangling like an untuned piano.

The Colonel came back with two glasses on a silver salver. Kate took the one he offered her and drank quickly. It was so strong she nearly choked. At home she and Alan always drank wine. The Colonel was looking at her questioningly.

'Do you think I could have some more tonic?' she asked, determined to stand her ground. 'Your drinks are rather too strong for me, I'm afraid.'

'Are they? Good God! I'll get the bottle, then you can put in as much as you like. Can't have the cook getting drunk when there's a soufflé in the oven.' He winked at her and disappeared to fetch the tonic. She took another sip of her drink, marvelling at the change in him. The old rascal had plenty of charm when he wanted to use it.

The soufflé when Kate took it out of the oven was a great puffball of cheesy perfection, brown on the top and runny in the middle. The Colonel pulled out her chair for her when she sat down and she felt wonderfully warmed by this small sign of gallantry. He praised the soufflé and they seemed to be getting on so much better that she decided to tackle him about having something done about the mice in the larder.

'What do you want me to do, send for the Pest Control Officer?' he scoffed. Since that was precisely what she had had in mind, Kate was silent. 'You don't want to worry about the odd little mouse,' he assured her. 'They're only fieldmice; they tend to come indoors at this time of year when the weather gets colder. You're not one of those women who jump on a chair every time they see a mouse, I hope?'

'No, of course not,' Kate lied. 'But they're in the larder creating havoc. Something's got to be done about them.'

'Well, set a trap for them. Good God, girl, haven't you ever caught a mouse before?' His moustache was twitching and she could see he was beginning to get angry with her again.

'Perhaps you could lay one for me,' she said, smiling up at him beguilingly. 'There's quite an art to laying traps, so I've heard.'

'Now don't try to flummox me, young woman,' he said, but he looked pleased. 'I'll set it for you if you want, there's nothing to it.'

She thanked him, relieved that she had managed to placate him so easily. What he really wanted was to feel useful, she decided. Everybody was so busy trying to protect him from the effects of growing old they were taking away his self-respect. He's like me, she thought with a flash of insight. He only wants to stand on his own two feet.

Over coffee the Colonel raised the subject of the holiday village scheme.

'You said yesterday you'd help me fight the damned thing. Where do we start, Kate?'

Kate had no idea, and she certainly couldn't think with him scowling at her so fiercely.

'I thought you said you knew how to organise protests,' he persisted.

'Did I? I don't remember.' His scowl deepened and she realised that she was in danger of letting him bully her again. Properly handled he may have been all sweetness and light but it was rather like trying to ride the big dipper: every time you got to the top of a hill there was another stomach-lurching drop on the other side.

Feverishly she racked her brains for some intelligent suggestion. 'Who decides on the application?' she asked. 'Is it the people who sit on the Council or is it the people who do the work behind the scenes?'

'It's the Planning Department who recommends to the Council whether they should approve or refuse the application,' he said, spooning sugar into his cup. 'The Chief Planning Officer's a proper little Caesar. He's got too much power for a man like that and the trouble with our councillors is they won't stand up to him.'

'Couldn't we take an advertisement in the local paper spelling out the application and what it will mean locally. It would help to rally local opinion against the scheme.'

'I can't see what good that'll do.'

'We could ask people to write to their local councillors, put some pressure on them.'

He stirred his coffee impatiently. 'No time for that claptrap. I'll have to get a list of councillors and decide who I can coerce. Pick 'em off individually. Bring a bit of pressure in the right places. All this getting up of petitions is a waste of time.' He stared at her challengingly but she was saved from having to disagree with him by the telephone.

Kate couldn't help being aware that the Colonel was talking to Patrick. She sat drinking her coffee, her cheeks burning. Suppose the Colonel were to mention her name? What would Patrick say? Would he expose her? After a few minutes the Colonel hung up.

'I've got to go out. My son-in-law says some cattle got loose this morning. They put them back but they're not sure they didn't get mixed up in the process. The old farmer's a bit tricky at times, but he's a friend of mine so I'd better go and have a word, see if I can smooth things over. You able to amuse yourself for the rest of the day?' Kate assured him she could. 'Don't forget dinner at seven thirty sharp,' he said with a wicked twinkle, 'and if you want a drink be in the study by seven fifteen.' With which parting shot he left her to worry anew about Patrick.

# *Chapter 6*

Deborah Bray-Smith was also worried about Patrick. She had been brought up not to cry or show pain – to kick on, button up, show the flag. But ever since she'd caught Patrick red-handed at the Imperial she had been suffering from a terrible sense of inferiority. It didn't matter that Patrick seemed anxious to make it up to her. She wanted to believe him when he said that it was all over, that it had never been anything except a silly blunder. He said he loved her as much as ever, but she was plagued with the most absurd self-doubts. She would lie in the bath and gaze at her body with dislike, noticing things which had never bothered her before – like her thighs which were bigger than they used to be and dimpled in places. She wondered if Patrick's old girlfriend had thighs pitted with cellulite. When they made love she couldn't help wondering if he'd done the same things with that woman, and she had to force herself not to ask him. She had read enough advice in women's agony columns about what to do when you discover your husband's having an affair. Men – so these experts seemed to believe – did not want to be plagued by whining wives. If you wanted to keep your husband you had to be twice as sexy, twice as amusing, twice as understanding and accommodating as the mistress and then he would come back to you. Of course, what they never told you was how to do it, when you felt about as attractive and accommodating as a fifty-year-old spinster long past her sell-by date.

It didn't help that Deborah was finding it difficult this season to keep up with Patrick in the hunting field. Usually at this time of year morale was at its highest; the horses sound and bouncing with health, all their battle scars healed after a summer at grass. It was in October when the hounds were beginning to run, and the horses to gallop, and the fences not tackled since last spring loomed so large and challenging, it was then that the heart began to pound and the adrenalin to pump and the blood to sing. But not for Deborah, not this October. Saturday, 15 October, only two weeks away from the opening meet, and here I am dreading it, thought Deborah bleakly.

She watched Patrick leading an eager field towards a line of inviting hedges, as the Blazers at last let a fox out of the covert they had been holding up all morning. Patrick was Field Master on Saturdays and his job was to lead the way and control the rest of the field, and the only way a field master could do that with the Blazers was by setting a cracking pace. Patrick was well mounted and he sat down and rode at the first hedge, giving the horse no chance for second thoughts, holding his head tight and whacking him a couple of times with his hunting crop to remind him what was expected of him. Deborah was proud of both of them as she watched the chestnut rise to the occasion. It was a great deal to ask of a horse to set sail over a sizeable obstacle alone and out in front after standing still for so long. She checked her own horse to let the first wave of impatient thrusters hurl themselves at the fence in Patrick's wake and sure enough there were refusers and empty saddles as horses and riders still not properly prepared for heroics so early in the season were caught out. She caught a loose horse she recognised and helped the chagrined young farmer back on board, then cantered her own reliable Hercules at the obstacle. He cleared it neatly and she went on to clear two more obstacles before catching up with the rest of the field who were halted in a lane not much further on.

'Thanks for the lead, Deborah,' said the farmer as they stood knee to knee in the narrow lane. 'Just what we needed to get us going after that stupid fall.'

'Oh Hercules is a real star,' she said. 'He never stops unless it's an outright emergency. But I wish he wasn't blowing so hard already.'

'Bit short of a gallop, I expect,' the farmer said sympathetically.

'I wish that was all, Jim,' said Deborah anxiously. 'But I'm afraid he's got emphysema and it's getting much worse. I have to pull him up to get his breath back before he jumps anything big and he does hate it so not being able to keep up. He's completely unstoppable down hills now, he's so desperate to catch up.'

'Sounds dangerous.' Jim Farrell looked concerned. 'You ought to be thinking of replacing him.'

'I know, but he's been such a wonderful hunter I can't bring myself to do it.'

'That new chap who's taken the Duchess's yard – he's got a very nice five-year-old for sale.'

'Has he?' Deborah put a hand on her horse's flank – it was still heaving. 'What's he like?'

'Ned Jones? Got plenty of cheek. Good horseman though, and he knows a bit about horses, I'd say.'

'That's not all he knows about, so I heard tell,' put in a man ahead of them, turning round with a grin.

'Really, George, like what?' Deborah demanded mischievously.

'Bit of a ladies' man.' George gave an embarrassed smirk. 'Know what I mean?'

'No, George, I don't know what you mean,' Deborah told him all wide-eyed and innocent. 'Anyway, I don't want to think about nice five-year-olds, not just yet.'

Jim Farrell looked relieved to be on safe ground again. 'Don't forget,' he urged, 'it's only two weeks till the opening meet. You don't want to waste too much time.'

They were slow moving out of the lane and Deborah could see horses queueing to jump a small wall into a field with a fairish drop down. It was an awkward place because there was no room for more than two or three strides in approaching the wall. Several riders thought better of it and rode on down the lane, which only helped to discourage those horses whose riders expected them to take the plunge. Deborah sat watching the confusion in front of her impatiently, knowing that all the time they were kept waiting in the lane the hounds would be getting further and further away. At last it was her turn; Hercules threw up his head and bounded into the wall jumping off his hocks and landing well out in the field below. He set off at a determined gallop, maintaining his pace across the stubble and sailing over a timber rail into the next field which was ploughed. Deborah tried to spare him as he struggled round the edge of the field but he was breathing hard by the time they came out on to the road. Galloping down the tarmac he recovered a little but as soon as they left the road and had to tackle a short, quite steep hill he was reduced to a trot and blowing horribly. Deborah's heart sank when she reached the top of the hill and saw them disappearing over the far horizon. She knew it was useless. The poor old fellow wanted so badly to stay with them but he just couldn't find the breath. She'd never catch them now. She reined Hercules in and watched the stragglers coming up behind. One of them was her sister, Caroline, whom Deborah suspected had chickened out of the drop wall further back and had had to make a detour all the way round by the road.

'It's hopeless,' Deborah said. 'They're running like stink – we'll never catch them now.'

'It doesn't matter,' said Caroline. 'Foxes never travel far at this time of the year. We'll catch up with them again if we follow along quietly.'

'It's no fun creeping about at the back away from all the action,' Deborah said crossly. 'I'm going home. If you're going on will you tell Patrick? If he can't get a lift later he can ring me, and I'll come out and fetch him.'

'You'll have to be looking for a new horse,' Caroline said. 'If you can't keep up with them now, you'll never stay with them once proper hunting starts.'

It was on the tip of Deborah's tongue to point out that Caroline wasn't doing much better on Bella, but she knew it was pointless. Caroline didn't want to be up in front, her chief concern seemed to be to stay out of trouble.

'Maybe I'll stop off at the Duchess's yard on my way home,' she said instead. 'Apparently that new chap has a good young horse for sale. I might have a look at him.'

'The horse – or Ned Jones?' Caroline asked. 'They say he's the Duchess's lover. Can't think what she sees in him.'

'Perhaps he's very good in bed – you know what these horsey men can be like,' said Deborah. Caroline raised her eyebrows and Deborah couldn't resist adding: 'But of course, you wouldn't know, you're far too snobbish. You'd only ever go to bed with a duke.'

'Don't be ridiculous, Debs,' Caroline looked genuinely shocked. 'I hope I'd only ever go to bed with John.' Immediately Deborah felt contrite. It was mean of her to take out her low spirits on Caroline, but she felt so unsure of herself these days. Patrick had taken away all her self-confidence.

The Duchess of Blazeborough was separated from the Duke and lived in a splendid mansion overlooking a lush green valley with a river running through it. The Duchess never went hunting before the Opening Meet and so might well have been at home but Deborah knew there was no danger of disturbing her in the middle of the morning; the stable yard was far enough away from the house to be completely separate. Deborah drove her lorry in through the back gates and parked in the wide open space in front of the stables. A man appeared and walked towards her. He wasn't good-looking like Patrick, she thought, aware of disappointment. Stocky, slightly bandy legs, mousy hair, square weatherbeaten face. The Duchess must be pretty desperate – what *did* she see in him?

'Hello,' he said. 'What can I do for you, madam?' An innocuous greeting certainly, but accompanied by a cheeky grin which made Deborah feel more light-hearted.

'I hear you've got a young horse for sale,' she said, as she jumped down from the lorry. 'I'm on my way back from hunting and I thought I'd just have a look at him.'

'I've got several horses for sale,' he said. 'What are you looking for?'

'I'm not sure I'm looking for anything,' she said loftily. 'But I heard you'd taken over the yard and I thought I'd call in and introduce myself. I'm Deborah Bray-Smith.'

'The Field Master's wife, I know.' He had very blue eyes, she thought, mischievous eyes, and he was looking at her with far too much interest for a man who was someone else's lover. 'You'll need a good horse to keep up with that husband of yours on a Saturday. Wait here.'

He turned and strode off back into the stables. She sauntered across the cobbled yard and sat down on the mounting-block. It had turned into quite a warm sunny day and she began to relax, basking in the sunshine, glad she'd come.

Presently Ned Jones brought a horse out. Deborah felt her pulse quicken. It was a very nice grey. Ned walked the horse around the cobbled yard, while Deborah sat on the mounting-block watching critically. He trotted the horse up and down a couple of times and she knew that she was looking at quality. Then he led the horse up to Deborah and she tried to keep the excitement she felt from showing.

'He's a straight mover anyway,' she said, reaching up to stroke his silky neck. Ned shouted over his shoulder and a girl groom came running.

'Tack up the grey horse,' he said. 'Mrs Bray-Smith wants to see him put through his paces.' The girl took the horse away and Deborah suddenly felt unusually self-conscious alone with Ned Jones grinning at her in the sunshine.

'I really don't know that I've got time to see him ridden,' she began to prevaricate. 'I ought to be getting poor old Hercules home. I'd like to get him cleaned up and fed before I have to go out again for my husband.'

'We'll get your horse cleaned up for you,' he brushed her excuses aside. 'The hounds'll be out for hours yet.' Before she could stop him he had the back of the lorry down and was leading Hercules down the ramp. The groom had reappeared with the grey horse saddled and bridled.

'Tell that lazy bitch Janie to get her fat arse over here and clean Mrs Bray-Smith's hunter up,' he said, taking the grey from the girl. 'Then you can come back and ride the young horse for us.' Deborah wondered why he didn't ride the horse himself. 'That's a useful sort of a horse,' he said in approval as the girl led Hercules away.

'I've had five wonderful seasons with him and he's never put a foot wrong,' she said, feeling miserable again. 'But he's got emphysema and it's so bad now I don't think I can go on hunting him much longer.'

'That's a shame.' The blue eyes were full of sympathy and she warmed to him. 'I might be able to help you find a good home for him. I had someone in here the other day looking for a good hack to ride with the children.' He was standing holding the grey horse looking at her appraisingly. To hide her confusion she bent and ran her hand down the horse's legs.

'Good clean limbs,' said Ned, 'apart from a couple of honourable scars. He's bold but he looks after himself.' The groom came back and Ned legged her up. The grey pricked his ears, head up, alert but attentive, and the groom began walking him round the cobbled yard, while Deborah watched, impressed.

'He's got a good active walk,' she said approvingly as she and Ned followed the horse across the yard to a small fenced paddock behind the stables.

'I'll tell you something – I haven't seen a better horse come out of Ireland in the last two years.'

'Irish, is he?' Better and better. 'Has he been hunted there?'

'Last season – as a four-year-old.'

'So he can jump?'

'Like a stag.' The girl was cantering the horse in small circles and he was moving easily, not fighting her, changing legs when she asked him. There were one or two small show jumps in the paddock and she put him over them. The horse cleared them disdainfully as if barely aware that they were there.

'I can see he's been well schooled,' said Deborah. Ned ducked under the rails and raised the jumps to twice their height.

'Right, Molly,' he said to the girl, 'show Mrs Bray-Smith, what he can do.'

The horse pricked his ears and flew into the jumps, standing off and clearing them all with a foot to spare.

'You see, he likes jumping,' said Ned grinning at Deborah.

'Easy enough in there,' she said, determined to show him she wasn't easily taken in. 'You've probably schooled him over those things every day. He must know his way blindfold. What's he like over natural fences?'

'Take him down to the big field, Molly,' Ned shouted. Then he seized Deborah by the hand and led her in their wake.

Walking across the grass with her hand in his, Deborah felt terribly self-conscious again. She wanted to pull her hand away but if she did she thought it might make too much of an issue of it. She wanted just to let her hand lie there naturally as if it meant nothing, as it probably did to him. But the trouble was that it didn't mean nothing to her. It felt surprisingly comforting. Just as she realised this he released her. They came to a wooden post-and-rail fence. The grey horse jumped it effortlessly. Deborah suppressed the rising excitement within her, determined not to seem too eager.

'I'm not sure if he's up to my weight,' she said to Ned Jones and immediately realised she'd blundered as he eyed her speculatively. Before she knew what he was about he picked her up in his arms. 'He'll carry you all right,' he told her, looking down into her eyes with far too much amusement for comfort. Then he lifted her over the fence and deposited her on the other side.

'What about my husband?' she said, struggling for calm. 'I sometimes have to let him have my horse if his goes lame in the middle of a run or anything.'

'I know.' He vaulted over the rail and the amusement in his eyes was replaced by a kind of knowing sympathy. 'Field mastering's a demanding job for a horse, especially with the Blazers. But this chap'll do it, when he's matured a bit.'

Deborah couldn't help feeling drawn to the man. He was so understanding. Confused, excited, conscious that she was not quite in control of anything that was happening, she tried to concentrate on watching the grey horse jumping the hedge at the bottom of the field but she was far too aware of the man standing at her side. The girl put the horse at the gate in the corner of the field. The horse cleared it effortlessly. She jumped him back and rode him slowly across the field to stand in front of them.

'Do you want to have a sit on him?' asked Ned.

'No thanks, not today.' Somehow she must get back in control, show him she didn't really care. 'I should be getting home in case my husband rings. I'll talk to him about the horse and come back and ride him another time.'

'OK, but don't leave it too late. Mrs Snodgrass is very interested in him and I've got a chap from the Quorn coming to look at him tomorrow.'

God, she thought, what if the horse was sold before she had time to persuade Patrick to buy him? If he was all that Ned said he was, the man from the Quorn was bound to snap him up. Of course, this was exactly what all dealers wanted you to feel, but she couldn't resist asking Ned what time the man from the Quorn was coming.

'In the afternoon,' he said. 'Why don't you hop up now and just ride him back to the yard. Get the feel of him. He's got a great feel to him.' Before Deborah had time to say no, the girl was out of the saddle and Ned had a hold of Deborah's right leg by the ankle.

'No please,' she said. 'I'm no good at being given a leg up. I'll manage on my own, if you'll hold the horse still.' But he just grinned.

'Afraid of shooting over the top of the horse and landing in a heap on the other side?' he said laughing. 'Don't worry, madam, I'll not let you fall.'

It was said with such confidence she trusted him. He hefted her up with surprising ease and she landed in the saddle as if propelled from a catapult. The horse arched his back in protest at her sudden arrival. 'It's all right, easy boy,' she said, gathering up the reins quickly. The horse relaxed and she began to walk him quietly through the field. She squeezed with her legs and he broke into a trot. Her spirits soared, she felt right on him. She eyed the post-and-rail longingly but she mustn't give Ned Jones too much encouragement. She knew the horse could jump, she knew she wanted him. What she didn't know was how she was going to persuade Patrick.

'I'll come tomorrow morning,' she told Ned, dismounting in the stable yard. 'Promise you won't let anybody else have him before then?'

'I'll be waiting for you,' he said. It was a simple enough remark. But the cheeky grin with which he said it and the way his eyes sparkled made Deborah feel warm all over. Bugger Caroline. Deborah knew what the Duchess saw in him all right.

Driving home Deborah tried to suppress the excitement bubbling within her. Today a man had made it quite plain that he fancied her and she felt better than she'd done in weeks. Of course it didn't mean anything. He probably did it to all the women who came looking at his horses. He had the reputation of being a ladies' man, he was the Duchess's lover, for Christ's sake. She told herself that it was his horse which made her feel like this. It wasn't often one found a horse for sale that was everything one could wish for. Somehow she had to persuade Patrick to let her have him. Was he feeling guilty enough, she wondered, to indulge her in this? The trouble was Patrick never felt guilty. He didn't seem to think he could ever be in the wrong. It was a wonderful philosophy to have. Bugger Patrick.

There was no sign of Patrick when she got home although it was well after three.

'Has he rung?' she asked Jenny, the groom, who was drinking coffee in the kitchen.

'No – there's been no call.' Jenny got up and dumped her half-finished coffee in the sink. 'Did you get left again?' she asked sympathetically.

Deborah told the girl all about the new horse she'd been to look at as they got Hercules out of the lorry. 'Don't say anything to the boss until I've had time to talk him round,' she warned. Jenny promised and went off to get Hercules his hot mash.

The telephone started ringing and Deborah ran back into the house expecting it to be Patrick. But it was someone from the village asking her if she'd forgotten the church flowers.

'Oh my God! Did I say I'd do them?'

'It's the third Sunday in October,' the woman said accusingly. 'You always do them the third Sunday in the month.'

'Do I?' asked Deborah, deliberately vague.

Jane Evering had lived in the village for fifteen years but Deborah still liked to regard her as an interloper. Every stick and stone in Puddleworth had belonged to Patrick's father at one time, with the exception of the church, the school, the rectory and the glebe land. Occasionally, when the family got short of cash, they'd sold a cottage or two. When Patrick's parents died some fields and what was now the pub had paid the death duty. When Deborah had bullied Patrick into letting her have a new kitchen, he had paid for it by selling three cottages overlooking the village green to the Everings. Jane and her husband had converted the cottages into an attractive retirement home. Mr Evering had died and Jane, with too much time on her hands, had become a village stalwart. Deborah valued the work she did, at the same time resenting Jane for trying to usurp her as lady of the manor.

'I've cleared away all the Harvest Festival stuff,' Jane said with what Deborah felt was maddening smugness. 'It was all very dead, I'm afraid, so you'll have to start again from scratch.'

Bugger, thought Deborah, it'll take me hours.

'Would you like me to see if I can find someone else, or I could come and give you a hand?'

'No, no, I'll manage, Jane, thank you,' said Deborah. She was damned if she was going to have Jane Evering making a simple task twice as time-consuming with her elaborate flower club ideas. She hung up and made herself a quick cup of coffee, praying that Patrick wouldn't ring and summon her to fetch him from the opposite end of the country. If he did she would just have to take the silk flower arrangement out of the dining room and stick it in the church. It wouldn't be the first time. But she would have to forgo morning service; she wouldn't be able to face Jane Evering's disapproving expression.

She drank her coffee standing up and wolfed two chocolate biscuits left over from the children's last weekend out. Then she dashed to the stables to tell Jenny to listen for the telephone and come and get her from the church if Patrick should ring. Jenny looked a bit glum. She lived in a cottage in the village and was obviously hoping that she could slip away home until summoned out by Patrick. Deborah pretended not to notice.

Instead she looked pointedly at the tack the girl was just finishing as if to imply that it wasn't nearly clean enough, and went.

The dogs, two terriers and a lurcher bitch, chased after her enthusiastically, under the mistaken impression she was taking them for a longed-for walk. As she ran about the garden, tearing scarlet creeper off the walls and uprooting the last of the dahlias, the dogs leapt up and down and got under her feet, instinctively aware that the walk was not going to materialise and trying to persuade her that this was a terrible mistake. In desperation she let them come with her to the church, which was all of two hundred yards away, and left them in the churchyard, chasing each other round the tombstones, praying that some unsuspecting cat didn't choose to take it into its head to walk by.

In a great hurry she began sticking the dahlias into a vase without getting it properly wired first, but then the whole thing collapsed when she started adding the greenery and creeper and she realised that unless she calmed down she'd never get the job done. After that things went much better. The peace and quiet of the ancient church had a soothing influence on her ruffled spirit; the bright pink of the dahlias and the brilliant red of the trailing creeper looked marvellous against the grey stone walls; by the time she'd finished she was feeling quite holy, holy enough to kneel at the altar and talk to God.

'Dear God, let me find a good home for Hercules,' she prayed. 'And if it be Your will, please, God, let me get the grey horse and he be a success. Amen.'

Patrick was home when she got back to the house. He'd had a late breakfast at teatime with one of the farmers who'd then brought him and his horse home. He was on the telephone in the kitchen conferring with the hunt secretary. Deborah knew he'd be there for an hour sorting out the various things which had gone wrong, apologising and placating and chatting up the farmers whose land the hunt had ridden over that day. Now was not the time to tell him about the new horse. So she fed the dogs, then went and ran a hot bath and lay in it, soaking the ache out of her weary limbs, worrying about what to wear.

She and Patrick were dining with the Duke tonight. There would doubtless be at least twenty people to dinner, all of whom Deborah had probably dined with many times and always in evening dress. She lay and tried to remember what she had worn the last time she'd been to

Blazeborough. But all she could think about was what to wear for Ned Jones when she went back to look at the horse. Today Ned Jones had seen her in her muddy breeches and tweed coat. Tomorrow she'd have to be in riding things, of course, but she could wear a clinging sweater over her tightest breeches. That would make those naughty eyes of his fairly pop out of his head. She thought of the beautiful grey horse and the way he had responded to the least little squeeze of her legs. She wondered if he had a name. Probably not. At least Ned Jones wouldn't care if he had. Dealers never bothered with horses' names. I shall call him Ajax, she thought, if I get him. Her father had once owned a grey called Ajax, the best hunter he'd ever had. She was drifting off to sleep when Patrick finally came up.

'Come on, Debs, for heaven's sake,' he said, barging into the bathroom and jerking her back into reality. 'We're going to be late if you don't get a move on.' Guiltily she leapt out of the bath and into her towelling dressing gown. He clambered into the scented water and lay back. Sitting on the edge of the bath and adding more hot water, she told him about the horse.

'Darling, you know I can't buy you a new horse,' he said gruffly when she'd finished, 'not when I've had to buy Fiona a new pony, and a combine harvester this summer.'

She began to pick up the discarded hunting clothes, wishing she'd waited until he'd had a drink or two to mellow him before bringing up the subject.

'What about the school fees?' he demanded, laying out the facts of their finances as if she didn't know them already. 'There'll be another lot upon us after Christmas. The bank manager won't up the overdraft any more until the next grain cheque comes in – he told me last week. You'll just have to make do with Hercules a bit longer. You don't need a horse that can gallop if you know the country as well as you do, and he can still jump his way to the front.' He caught her eye and slid beneath the foaming bubbles. 'How much does the fellow want for it?' he muttered.

'I don't know,' she retorted. 'I never asked.'

'There you are, you see, you've not even stopped to think it through. If the horse is as good as you say, it'll be five grand at the very least, anything less and there's something wrong with it.' He lay frowning pensively at his toes just peeking above the bubbles. 'You don't need an expensive animal like that, Debs. You don't need a weight carrier and you ride well enough to make your own hunter. From what you say this one's had a lot of time spent on him already.'

She took the dirty clothes down to the kitchen and stuffed the breeches into the washing machine with the horses' saddlecloths and string girths Jenny had brought in from the stables. Then she poured a stiff whisky and took it up to Patrick in his bath.

'I may not need an expensive animal but you do, Patrick,' she told him, thrusting the drink at him. 'We could share him.'

He lay sipping whisky thoughtfully for a while. 'Perhaps you could get your father to buy it for you,' he said, setting the glass down at the side of the bath and looking rather pleased with himself. 'I tell you what, why don't you invite him for lunch tomorrow? We haven't seen the old boy for ages. After a good lunch and some of my best port, I'm sure to be able to talk him round.'

'Daddy doesn't drink port any more,' she said, slapping make-up on her face.

'Well then, you ask him to go with you and see you try it.' He sat up and took another sip of whisky. 'AB's a good judge of horse flesh and he'd love to help. Give him something to do.'

'I don't think that's a very good idea,' she said. 'It'll be too late then. The man from the Quorn is coming in the afternoon.'

'If the man from the Quorn exists,' Patrick retorted, sliding down into the water again. 'The horse won't be sold before then. These dealers always want to hustle you. There's plenty of good horses about this time of year. It's after Christmas, when they all start breaking down, that the market gets short. Let the fellow sweat – it doesn't do to show you're too keen.'

She started brushing her hair, thinking Patrick might be right, only she had been looking forward to seeing Ned Jones tomorrow. She wondered if he would be disappointed too.

'Go on – ring your father now.' Patrick lay back in the bath and closed his eyes. 'Ask him to lunch. We're not doing anything tomorrow. It's high time you showed some filial duty.'

Deborah studied his lean, muscular body, which she was well used to admiring, and wondered what Ned Jones looked like in the bath. It might be fun to find out, she thought, and serve Patrick right.

She left her husband lying in the bath and riffled through her wardrobe for something to wear. She dragged out a black velvet skirt and white silk shirt. Both had been horribly expensive but they were now old and she had worn them many times before. Never mind, she thought, nobody will remember, certainly not Patrick. He never noticed what she wore. Without bothering to look in the mirror she ran downstairs and rang Ned Jones.

'It's Deborah Bray-Smith,' she said.

'I know.' Her heart skipped a beat. How did he know? Had he been thinking about her?

'About the horse – I'm afraid I shan't be able to come and see him tomorrow. We're a bit tied up.'

'No problem.'

She ought to have left it there. Hung up – kept him guessing. 'If the man from the Quorn doesn't buy him, perhaps you'd let me know and I'll come and look at him sometime next week.'

'I'll do better than that,' he said. 'You can have half a day's hunting on Monday – if he's still for sale, that is. Then if you like him he's yours.'

She knew well enough the unwritten etiquette of trying a horse in the hunting field. Before you tried him you had to be a buyer. It wasn't fair to take a horse out and hunt him and then turn him down just because of price. People would think it was because he couldn't do the business. The horse got a bad reputation and the dealer lost face. She didn't want to do that to Ned Jones.

'We never discussed the matter of price,' she said. 'How much do you want for him?'

'Five grand – he's a bargain at that price. You know it and I know it. Now the man from the Quorn I'll ask six.' Even on the telephone the magnetism was compelling, burning up the wires.

'Why?' she asked, feeling reckless. 'Why do you want me to have him cheap?'

'You're the Field Master's wife. I've just come into the Blazers' country. I'm counting on you to make my reputation.'

God, she thought, he'd got an answer for everything. She could hear Patrick coming downstairs.

'Ring me tomorrow night,' she said. 'Let me know if he's still for sale.'

She rang her father as Patrick walked into the kitchen, impeccable in his claret-coloured smoking jacket and black bow tie. The Colonel sounded pleased, but to Deborah's surprise insisted that they come to lunch with him.

'I've got this wonderful new cook – she's dying to show off her culinary talents. I'll expect you at twelve forty-five – don't be late.'

'That's a turn-up for the books,' she said to Patrick as she hung up. 'Daddy's asked us there. Caroline's found some nice motherly type to look after him and he wants to show off her cooking he says.'

'Well, I hope it's better than the last one. Her cooking was terrible.'

'If we're going there for lunch, I'd have time to go and look at the horse in the morning,' she said longingly.

'Deborah – don't be a fool. It doesn't do to seem too keen – I've told you. If your father likes the horse he's much more likely to pay for it if you take him with you to look at it. You know what he's like – it has to be his idea.'

She sighed. 'I suppose you're right.'

'Of course I'm right. Aren't I always?'

Not always, she thought as she went upstairs to finish dressing. In fact, not even very often. The thought shocked her.

# *Chapter 7*

When the Colonel came into the kitchen and told Kate that Patrick and Deborah were coming for lunch she panicked.

'What are we going to give them to eat?' she said, putting the clean plates she'd just dried back into the sink full of soapy water. 'It's Saturday night and I wasn't expecting visitors for lunch tomorrow.' She knew it sounded feeble but the thought of coming face to face with Patrick and that woman made her feel like a terminal coward. The Colonel just stared at her. 'I mean the country's not like London, is it? There's no little Asian store just around the corner open to midnight. There's not even a shop in the village any more.' She was babbling hysterically. 'Couldn't you take them out to a pub for lunch?' she pleaded trying for calm.

He looked so shocked she realised he'd probably never been to a pub for Sunday lunch in his life.

'I think if your family is coming for lunch I'll have mine in the kitchen,' she said, accepting the inevitable, but trying for an orderly retreat. 'It'll be nicer for you to be on your own with them.'

'Not at all,' he replied gallantly. You're not a servant – as you keep reminding me – and I'd like you to meet them.'

It was useless. Her chickens were coming home to roost with a vengeance and tomorrow it looked as if she was going to be served up as the bread sauce. She stared down miserably at the soapy water in the sink. It was a pity that her new adventure was going to come to an end just when she was starting to enjoy it. She seized a Brillo pad and started scouring a perfectly clean saucepan vigorously, desperately searching for a way out. If only she could stay out of sight perhaps she might be able to get away with it.

'There's plenty of pheasants in the deep freeze,' said the Colonel, grappling with the problem of food.

'I've never cooked a pheasant,' Kate said absently, still grappling with the problem of Patrick.

'There's apples in the orchard,' the Colonel went on, ignoring her. 'I'll go out early tomorrow morning and pick some blackberries. They should be all right still – we haven't had much of a frost yet. You can make a blackberry and apple pie, I suppose?'

She nodded quickly as he was beginning to scowl. 'What about cream?' she murmured faintly.

'I'll get cream from old Joe at Gorse Farm. He's still got a milking herd, thank God.'

It was turning into quite a banquet, thought Kate, impressed by his resourcefulness. It was not surprising there were no little corner shops open till midnight in the country when you could live off the land so successfully. Then she had a brilliant idea.

'If we're going to all this trouble, why don't we go to town and make a proper party of it?' she suggested. 'You could ask some of the Planning Committee and their wives to lunch as well. Then you could get your daughter and her husband to help you talk them round.' The Colonel stopped scowling at her. 'You know how much easier it is to persuade people when they're in a minority, especially if they're feeling warm and relaxed and well cherished,' she added, inspired.

'I'll do better than that,' he said positively beaming. 'I'll ask the Chief Planning Officer. If we can get the measure of the little Caesar we can use him to bring some pressure to bear on that ass the Chairman.'

He was so delighted he didn't attempt to argue with her when she stressed that if she was to cook for such a large party she would have to remain in the kitchen. He went off to his study in great spirits to start telephoning, and Kate sank down at the kitchen table with the Aga cookbook, frenziedly searching for instructions on how to cook pheasants.

The Colonel found her half an hour later with her head in the deep freeze. 'I've got Derek Evans, that's the little Caesar, coming with his wife, Gladys. And I've persuaded Jean and Tony Manton to bat for us. They're dyed-in-the-wool supporters but Manton's on the bench and a tax commissioner so the little Caesar will want to keep in with him.'

'You don't think the Planning Officer is tax evading, do you?' said Kate, pretending to be shocked.

'No, I shouldn't think so but like all bureaucrats he's bound to be impressed by a representative of authority. What I'm counting on more is Jean. She's something big in the WVS and Gladys has aspirations in that department apparently. Get at him through the women,' he winked at her mischievously, 'that's the way we'll do it, Kate.'

Kate wondered how he came by such useful inside information. Beneath that brusque façade of simple bigotry there lurked quite a Machiavellian cunning, she thought, surprised.

'How many pheasants do you think you'll need?' he asked, peering into the deep freeze.

Kate eyed the stiff feathered corpses dubiously. She had no idea how many they would feed, nor how she was going to cook them. 'What am I going to do with them?' she asked. 'They're not even plucked and cleaned.' The Colonel was undaunted.

'The Murphys will dress them for you. We'd better have four to be on the safe side. I'll take them round now and I'll ask Mrs Murphy to come in and help tomorrow. She can do the waiting at table.'

Kate still looked dubious.

'First I'll give Caroline a ring and ask her to talk to you. She cooks the damned birds all the time. John's always shooting them.'

He was in his element, thought Kate, appalled at what she'd let herself in for. What had begun as a mere diversion to avoid having to meet Patrick and his wife, had turned into a full-scale military operation. And she was in the firing line. She shut the lid of the deep freeze with a bang. Kate, you've done it again, she told herself. You've gone and promised more than you can deliver. Will you never learn not to rush into trouble with your eyes shut? She could almost hear Alan's voice full of tender exasperation as he rescued her from her folly. But Alan wasn't here and he couldn't rescue her from this piece of stupidity. Somehow she had to get through tomorrow on her own.

By the Grace of God Caroline was at home and her instructions for roast pheasant were explicit. Kate wrote them all down carefully and spent a sleepless night worrying about how she was going to get everything done.

What to wear? She wanted to look good just in case she encountered Patrick, but of course she couldn't dress up, not if she were hiding in the kitchen disguised as the cook. She got up early, bathed and washed her hair, dressed in a short black skirt and clinging jumper, which she immediately discarded again. If she should bump into Deborah, God forfend, she didn't want to arouse her suspicions. In the end she settled for a flared wool skirt and flowered blouse with a wide belt cinched around her waist and a liberal dousing of scent. Twirling about in front of the small mirror in her flat she thought she looked demure but, she hoped, still beddable. Thrusting such a rebellious thought deep into her jangling subconscious she set out for the house to do battle.

The morning raced by so fast Kate hardly had time to be scared. Mrs Murphy was to lay the table in the dining room but when Kate saw the state of the silver she had to help her clean it all first. Then the apples had to be peeled and the pie made. The Colonel kept popping in and out of the kitchen. First he brought the blackberries he'd picked and then he took her away from peeling the potatoes to help him set up his drinks tray. By half-past twelve she was feeling distinctly dishevelled, her hair no longer bouncing about her head becomingly but clinging to her hot brow in wispy tendrils, her white chef's apron stained with blackberry juice, and her feet in her high-heeled shoes mocking her vanity achingly. It didn't help that the Colonel had now taken up residence in the kitchen and was offering helpful advice on making the bread into crumbs for the fried breadcrumbs and the bread sauce. Kate said nothing but thought longingly of her own labour-saving machine at home which could whizz up breadcrumbs at a flick of a switch. Silently she cursed herself for not having thought of bringing such essentials with her, instead of worrying about clothes. It was almost a relief when she heard the scrunch of tyres on the gravel outside and the Colonel took himself off to greet his first visitors. At least she could finish getting the lunch in peace.

She was just checking the pheasants one last time when Deborah Bray-Smith came into the kitchen.

'Have you got any more ice? I'm afraid we've run out,' she said.

Kate thrust the pheasants back into the oven, and took a deep breath. This was it. Her moment of discovery. Quickly she straightened up and went to the fridge, not daring to look at Deborah. Her hands were trembling so much she could hardly get the ice out.

'Here, let me do that for you,' said Deborah. She grabbed the tray from Kate and began breaking ice into the bucket. Kate let out her breath slowly, relief, resentment, shock, rendering her helpless. Deborah glanced at her impatiently. 'You get on with the lunch,' she said.

She hasn't noticed me, thought Kate, stunned. I'm a servant so I'm invisible. But wasn't that what she wanted? Perversely she found it wasn't.

'I wonder if your husband would be able to carve for me?' she asked, prompted by some demon of mischief as anger swept away all sense of self-preservation.

'He's not much of a carver,' said Deborah, scarcely glancing at Kate. 'I'd better do it for you if you can't manage on your own. I'll do it in here in the kitchen, where it won't make so much mess.'

Kate dished up the pheasants and Deborah carved, mercilessly dismembering the birds with quick decisive strokes of the knife, laying the slices in a neat pile in the dish Kate provided.

I'm letting this woman ride roughshod all over me, Kate thought resentfully, making gravy. Surreptitiously she studied Deborah. She was quite pretty, in an uncared for sort of way. Her blonde hair was long and straight and pulled back from her face by an old-fashioned padded Alice band. She wore very little make-up and a somewhat sulky expression. She was dressed in the country woman's uniform of pleated navy skirt, which was a little too tight for her, a frilled shirt and pretty patterned jumper, flattish shoes with brass chains and navy-coloured tights. Her legs, Kate noticed with relish, were too strong to be shapely and definitely thick round the ankles.

'Right, I'll go and call them,' Deborah said as soon as she'd finished carving. She grabbed the ice bucket and bore it away like a trophy, leaving Kate feeling a little sorry for Patrick. Deborah was the tough one in that marriage, she guessed.

Kate dished up and Mrs Murphy took it all into the dining room, beaming with pride. She was no longer so antagonistic towards Kate – in fact she now seemed to regard Kate as an ally, someone who could be relied upon in the battle to protect the Colonel from domestic anarchy and the persistent terrorist attacks of old age. Kate had felt proud of her victory but Deborah had spoilt all that. It was one thing to be accepted by Mrs Murphy as an equal. Quite another to be treated by Patrick's wife as no better than Mrs Murphy.

Kate piled all the pots and pans in the sink and turned the water on, trying to ignore the snatches of laughter and animated talk wafting down the passage. In vain she told herself not to be so stupid. It didn't matter what Patrick's wife thought of her. She ought to be pleased. She ought to be relieved. But she wasn't. She felt ashamed. She knew that Alan would be furious if he could see her now, with a chef's apron swathing her from neck to knees, and up to her elbows in washing up. This was not what she had broken away from a loving husband for. She applied herself to the pile of dirty dishes in the sink and told herself that she was here hiding behind the green baize door because she had chosen to be here in order to avoid a confrontation with Patrick.

Suddenly she was filled with a completely new feeling of animosity towards her former lover. It was his fault that she had to accept the role of servant. It was to avoid embarrassing him that she was skulking here instead of taking her part in the conversation round the dinner table.

When Mrs Murphy brought out the dirty meat dishes she was full of triumph at how well everything was going. But Kate wasn't in the least consoled. Ever since Deborah had come in for the ice she had wondered what she would do if Patrick came into the kitchen. Certainly not kiss and make up! What would he do, she wondered more and more nervously, if he found her here? She reminded herself that this time she would have the advantage of surprise and determined to make full use of it. When Mrs Murphy was in the dining room clearing away the pudding plates, her chance came. She heard footsteps in the corridor. Patrick? Her stomach gave a lurch and her heart began to thump like a Walt Disney rabbit sounding the alarm. She went over to the dresser and busied herself putting out coffee cups on a silver tray. Patrick came into the kitchen.

'I say, that was a damned good lunch. The Colonel was right, you are a wonderful cook,' he said heartily.

Keeping her back to him, Kate filled the coffeepot and dumped it down on the tray. Then she turned round.

'Remember me?' she said softly, thrusting the tray into his hands.

The effect on him was everything she could have possibly hoped for. He leapt back, startled. The coffeepot began to wobble, and the cups to slide, but Patrick was too busy staring at her in astonishment to notice. The coffee cups leapt off the tray and fell upon the stone flagged floor with a most satisfactory crash while the coffeepot toppled over and spilt its scalding contents all over his champagne-coloured moleksin trousers.

'God!' he yelled, hopping from foot to foot in agony, while Kate lunged for the coffeepot and caught it before it too hit the floor.

'You'll have to take your trousers off, Patrick,' she said, desperately trying not to laugh, 'if you don't want to ruin your best asset.'

'I'll be buggered if I will,' he muttered through clenched teeth just as Mrs Murphy came running into the kitchen.

'Whatever's the matter?' she cried. 'Oh my gawd, just look at the Colonel's best china smashed all to pieces!'

Kate dragged Patrick over to the sink and started soaking his trousers with cold water.

'Much better take them off,' Mrs Murphy supported Kate. 'You'll never get that there coffee out if you don't give it a proper soaking.'

'Leave me alone, both of you,' he shouted, grabbing the tea towel from Kate and rubbing ineffectively at his crotch. 'Just let me get the damned things dried a bit; they can go to the cleaners later.' Mrs Murphy started sweeping broken china into the dustbin, muttering and shaking her head dolefully, while Kate set about finding the second-best cups and making more coffee. By the time she had it ready Patrick had calmed down a little.

'What the devil are you doing here anyway?' he hissed as Mrs Murphy set off with the tray for the dining room. 'Are you trying to wreck my marriage, or what?'

'Don't be stupid,' she hissed back. 'I didn't know you were married to the Colonel's daughter. But it's all right, she didn't even recognise me. I won't say anything and as long as you don't go throwing any more coffeepots around she won't find out.'

'She didn't recognise you?' He was like a small boy caught raiding the larder. 'You're not going to expose me?' She shook her head solemnly. He looked relieved. 'What did you come here for then?'

'Oh, it's a long story, but it's nothing to do with us, I promise you.'

He was gazing at her, still perplexed. 'I don't suppose she would recognise you, she hardly saw you, after all, and you've done something different to your hair.' He grinned at her suddenly, his old mischievous smile. 'You're quite changed – prettier than ever.'

Until that moment she had thought she was cured, by ridicule, by humiliation, by his inability to protect her. 'I owed you one for leaving me lying on the floor of the Imperial,' she said, trying to stay cross with him. 'It wasn't a very chivalrous way to treat me, was it?' she demanded. He caught her eye sheepishly and she noticed with satisfaction that he didn't look quite so debonair twisting the dripping tea towel nervously in his hands.

'I know you think I'm a frightful shit,' he said ruefully, 'but I'm not as bad as you think I am, truly, Kate.'

'I did think badly of you, Patrick, at the time. But not now. We're all square now.'

'All square,' he agreed. Before she realised what he was up to, he had swiftly kissed her on the mouth. 'No hard feelings?' he said.

'No hard feelings,' she said unsteadily. 'You'd better go and explain to the Colonel what's happened to his best Crown Derby coffee cups.'

'Oh my God!' His face fell. Once again he was the little boy with his finger in the jam pot. She found it strangely endearing. 'Now the fat's really in the fire.'

'Why – you're not afraid of the Colonel, surely?' she mocked, turning back to begin the washing up. 'He's sweetness itself if you don't let him bully you. At least so Caroline tells me.'

He stared at her blankly. 'You couldn't put a word in for me, could you?'

'What do you want me to do? Tell him it was all my fault?' she joked, but the relief on his face was far from comical. It gave her a shock. Did he really expect her to pull his chestnuts out of the fire for him?

'Don't worry,' she found herself saying. 'I'll tell him it was me if you like. He doesn't have a very high opinion of me anyway, so I haven't got much to lose.'

'No, no, I couldn't let you. That would be a shit's trick.' She raised her eyebrows trying for scorn, but he just grinned at her apologetically. 'You see, Deborah is probably even at this moment trying to persuade him to buy her a new horse and he's not very likely to pay for it after he hears that I've broken all his best coffee cups.'

Kate wanted to tell him that it served him right, that if Deborah couldn't have a new horse it was too bad, we all have to do without things. Just for a moment she thought that it would be nice to be even with Deborah as well as Patrick, only he was looking at her with such beguiling helplessness that she couldn't.

'Best to say nothing about it for now,' she said. 'Time enough to tell him after he's seen the horse.'

'Kate, you're a real trooper,' he said, slipping his arm around her waist and giving her a quick squeeze. 'I'm glad you're here.'

'Ssh,' she said, wriggling free. 'I can hear Mrs Murphy coming. You'd better get back to the dining room, they'll be wondering what's happened to you.'

When he'd gone she set about clearing up the rest of the kitchen with Mrs Murphy. Now the dreaded encounter with Patrick was over she felt strangely deflated. Blearily, she listened to Mrs Murphy chatter on about the holiday village project.

'I couldn't help hearing what they was saying while I was handing round,' she said, dumping a tray of glasses on the kitchen table. 'About the new village. Bring a bit of life back to Little Riddleton, that will. There's nowhere to buy nothing now the shop's closed and the pub's empty half the time. It'll be the next to go. The heart's gone out of the place. It's dead, that's why all the young people move away. No work, no transport, nowhere for them to live that they can afford.' She began washing the Colonel's crystal glasses without changing the washing up water. 'It'll all be different when this new holiday village comes. More like the old days.'

'I think we'd better wash these glasses later,' said Kate, trying to be tactful.

''Course, you never knew this village in the old days,' Mrs Murphy went on, ignoring her. 'There were plenty of children here then, the school was full, there were men in the pub, we had the best darts team for miles around, nobody had to go to Bratchester for their weekly shop in them days, the village shop got all they wanted. Now it's all gone.' She turned round to face Kate, a glass in each hand. 'The Colonel now, he's against it but he's not going to win. He couldn't keep the gravel pits from coming and he'll not stop this new village. He's wasting his time.' She banged the glasses down on the draining board. Kate winced. 'Mind you, it'll keep him happy fighting the Council. Nothing the Colonel enjoys more than a good set-to. But you can't keep progress back. Good and bad, it's got to come and there's nothing any of us can do to stop it.'

Suddenly Kate couldn't stand the woman's chatter any longer. 'You get off home now, Mrs Murphy,' she said, taking over at the sink. 'I can manage the rest. It's been a long morning for you and I expect Murphy will be waiting for his dinner.'

To Kate's relief Mrs Murphy didn't need much urging. 'Well, I could do with a sit-down I don't mind admitting,' she said, stripping off her apron. 'You'll be all right then, Kate, will you?'

'Of course, I'll be fine.'

Left alone, Kate sat down at the kitchen table and poured herself a cup of coffee. She didn't feel hungry. She was too tired and too emotionally drained to be able to eat. She could see even from where she was sitting that the glasses Mrs Murphy had washed were all smeared. They would all have to be done again. Still, it didn't matter. She had the rest of the day to do it.

She was surprised when, a little later, the Colonel came into the kitchen.

'I'm off to look at a horse with m'daughter Deborah,' he said in a conspiratorial whisper. 'See what you can do to convince the Planning chappie.'

'You're not going out now!' she exclaimed. 'You're not leaving your guests in the middle of a lunch party to go and look at a horse!'

'Of course I am.' He didn't even have the grace to look ashamed. 'It'll be too dark to try the horse properly if we wait any longer, and I've got to have a look at him today if she's to hunt him tomorrow.'

Kate got up. Suddenly she'd had enough. 'After all the trouble I've taken. You're going to run away and leave us all in the lurch. What will your guests think? All this effort to make this Planning Officer and his wife feel at home and you have to spoil it by walking out and leaving them on their own.'

He wasn't the least bit abashed. 'They're not on their own. They've got Patrick and the Mantons and soon they'll have you. I've done my bit and I think he's coming round. They're all in the drawing room drinking coffee and port, happy as sandboys. The women are going great guns. All it needs now is an outside opinion – that's where you come in. You don't belong here. You can give an unbiased judgement.' He untied her apron and pulled it off over her head. 'It was your idea, Kate, after all.' He tossed the apron aside and propelled her towards the door. 'Now get in there and help Patrick entertain them until we get back.'

He was quite unscrupulous, Kate thought as she walked down the passage to the drawing room. With a total lack of regard for other people. So why am I helping him? she asked herself, pausing in front of the mirror in the hall. Is it because I want to belong? To do my little bit for the conservation of rural England? She studied her reflection anxiously, smoothing down her ruffled hair, wishing she had time to powder her nose, redo her lipstick. Pulling a face at herself she hurried on towards the drawing room.

It was a large room, well proportioned, high ceilinged and very, very cold. The curtains and carpets had seen better days, as had the faded chintz sofa covers, but the room was filled with good antique furniture. The contrast with the warmth of the kitchen made Kate shiver as she paused awkwardly at the doorway. She could see Patrick lounging in an armchair, a large brandy glass cupped in his hands, looking as desirable as ever with his dark hair and aquiline features, unconsciously elegant in sports coat and open-necked checked shirt; even the coffee stains on his tight-fitting moleskins couldn't entirely spoil the effect. When he saw her he got to his feet. She entered the room feeling self-conscious and shy. The other men were standing too. Patrick introduced Kate to Tony Manton and Derek Evans, and to the two women sitting side by side on the sofa. Jean Manton congratulated Kate on the lunch and Gladys Evans wanted to know how she made the pastry for the pie. They were friendly, interested and undemanding. Before long Kate was perched on the leather fender in front of the fire drinking coffee and port and beginning to relax. It wasn't long before the subject of the holiday village came up and Kate did her best to convince Derek Evans that he could not possibly allow such a blot on such an unspoilt landscape.

'It would solve a lot of problems in the vicinity,' he said. 'Local unemployment for one, improve roads, bring money and life to the region.'

Kate thought of what Mrs Murphy had been telling her in the kitchen and wondered with a pang whether perhaps she was on the wrong side.

Derek Evans came and sat down rather too close beside her. 'Isn't it being selfish wanting to keep the countryside pure and unsullied so that you can sit and look at it in silence?' he asked, breathing alcoholic fumes all over her.

'Isn't that what all these holiday villagers want?' she retorted. 'Why they come here in the first place – for the peace and the solitude and the beautiful scenery? But if you let them build their dreadful holiday camps all over everything, it'll all be spoilt and then they'll only be disappointed.'

'That's why we have planning authorities to keep it all in proportion,' he told her, patting her knee indulgently. She glanced at Patrick but he only winked and refilled Derek Evans' empty glass with more port.

'Of course if he loses, Alex Beamish could always sell,' Derek said. 'The house and fifteen acres of land are ideally situated to tie in with the scheme.'

Patrick was horrified. 'AB would never agree. It would ruin the hunting.' Kate looked at Derek anxiously. If he wasn't a supporter of hunting he might not think much of Patrick's line of argument.

'It's just a thought.' Derek said affably, far too full of the Colonel's port to be upset about anything. 'If there's going to be a holiday village anyway it's better to have it on your land than on your next-door neighbour's. Make the money yourself. Isn't that right, Kate?'

'I'm not sure that I can agree with you there,' she said, smiling at him and trying to ignore the hand on her knee. 'I think that's a lot more selfish than trying to keep the countryside pure and unsullied.'

They argued amicably until the port was finished. Kate began to enjoy herself, encouraged by these people who wanted to know what she thought. Maybe it was only because, as the Colonel had made plain, she didn't belong here. Or because she was a new face, somebody different. But she didn't feel as if she didn't belong. She felt valued. It was a new and heady experience being the centre of attention. When they got up to go Kate couldn't believe it was five o'clock. Derek kissed her on the cheek as he took his leave and promised to think very seriously before making his recommendations to the Council. Gladys pressed her hand warmly and urged her to join the WVS.

'Well, I must say I think you did a marvellous job with our Derek from the Council,' Patrick declared, coming back into the room having seen them off. 'You had the little fellow fairly slavering after you.' He was standing smiling down at Kate almost proudly. A strange feeling of unreality came over her. It was as if the years had slid away and she was seeing him for the first time at that party on New Year's Eve. She realised she must have drunk more than she thought, and on an empty stomach. He pulled her towards him and she knew he was going to kiss her but was powerless to stop him. She leant against him weakly, no will, no legs, just a wonderfully dizzy feeling.

'Shall we nip across to your flat?' he whispered.

'Don't be silly – they'll be back any moment.'

'You're right. God, Kate, you make me feel sexy. Why do I fancy you so much?'

'I don't know. Perhaps it's the brandy.' She giggled. Then she took an enormous pull on herself and pushed him away. 'But it's got to stop, Patrick. We can't possibly carry on an affair right under your wife's nose – not to mention her father's.'

He looked down on her, shaking his head sadly.

'I know, I know, I know. But why did you come here, Kate – if it wasn't because of me?'

'God,' she murmured, 'the arrogance of men. Do you really think I wanted to see you again after what you did to me in the Imperial?'

He pulled her back into his arms. She could feel him hard against her. 'You may not have wanted to see me then – but you want me now, just as I want you, Kate, very much. What are we going to do about it?'

'Nothing,' she said, struggling free. 'We're going to do nothing about it at all.' Her hands were shaking, her legs were like jelly. There was a cigarette box on the table beside her and it was filled, surprisingly, with cigarettes. Thank God for the Colonel's old-fashioned ideas of hospitality. She fumbled about in the box, extracted a cigarette with difficulty. Everything about her seemed to be trembling like a leaf. Patrick had flung himself into a chair with his legs stretched out in front of him and was watching her with an infuriatingly self-satisfied air.

'I thought you'd given up smoking when you married Alan,' he said as she started frantically searching for a light.

'I have, I did. I only smoke under extreme provocation,' she said.

'I'm glad to hear it,' he said, getting to his feet and taking the cigarette from her. 'That I provoke you that much, I mean.' He lit the cigarette and handed it to her, just as he always used to do when they had gone out together.

She inhaled deeply and then wished she hadn't. Her head spun alarmingly. 'No good will come of it,' he teased, flinging himself down in the chair again. 'Now stop trying to be sensible and come and sit on my knee.'

Kate took a desperate drag of the cigarette. 'Patrick, for God's sake don't be so irresponsible. Can't you see it's madness? And,' she added determinedly, 'it's not what I want.'

'What do you want? What are you doing here, Kate?'

'I came to try to find what had happened to the real me – the girl you knew in London all those years ago. My husband was going to Saudi Arabia, my children were away from home for the first time. I could be free – I wanted to be free to . . . find myself.'

'You haven't left your husband?' He looked genuinely alarmed.

'No – he's on six months' secondment to the Saudi Government. *I'm* having a sabbatical.'

'I thought it was only college professors had those,' he scoffed, but before she had time to answer him back Kate heard the sound of a car in the drive. She didn't know whether to be glad or sorry.

'I think I'd better go. The sight of us together having a little tête-à-tête might trigger something in Deborah's memory.' He didn't disagree and she made good her escape.

In her flat that evening Kate tried to sort out her disturbed emotions. It was strange how she was a different person with Patrick, more alive, more self-assertive, more combative. Was it because Patrick was such an overgrown schoolboy at times? His helplessness made her feel strong. With Alan it was always he who was the strong one, the brilliant conversationist, the decision maker. She was over-shadowed by him.

Unhappy about where her thoughts were leading her, Kate got up and made herself a piece of toasted cheese. She loved Alan and he loved her. They had a very successful marriage and two well-adjusted, happy, high-achieving children. So what was she doing here, yearning after Patrick? she asked herself. She was supposed to be finished with Patrick for good. Perhaps she should leave now, before there was any harm done. But what could she tell the Colonel? She couldn't just up and abandon him. She wouldn't do that to him. They'd never find another girl to come in the middle of the hunting season. She laughed at herself. They'd got her thinking hunting priorities now. She finished her toasted cheese, drank some tea and began to feel more sensible. What harm could possibly come of it after all? Patrick and Deborah lived miles away. It was very unlikely that she would find herself alone with Patrick again. And, she told herself firmly, that was all for the best.

# *Chapter 8*

Deborah was delighted with the way Sunday had gone, and even more so with Ned Jones when she'd taken her father to look at the horse. She'd been afraid Ned might try to hustle her father into having the horse, the way he had done with her, or be too familiar. But Ned had behaved impeccably. He just stood holding the horse's head, or leading him up and down, answering the Colonel's questions and not speaking unless spoken to. Short of actually pulling his forelock he could not have been more respectful, and apart from one swift appraising glance at Deborah, when she'd wished she'd been wearing something more sexy, he had ignored her completely. But the most important thing was that the Colonel had liked the horse.

'He's a bloody good sort,' he'd confided to Deborah on the way home. 'I don't think that fellow Jones realises just how good he is. If he can do the business, and I'm sure he can, he's worth every penny of what the fellow's asking for him.'

'He knows. He just wants to do us a favour, that's all,' Deborah said, rushing to Ned's defence without thinking. 'He could have sold him to the man from the Quorn for another thousand. He told me so.'

'He would,' scoffed the Colonel. 'I don't believe the man from the Quorn exists – figment of his imagination.' Deborah didn't care whether the man from the Quorn existed or not. What mattered was that she was going to hunt the horse tomorrow. The Colonel had arranged it with Ned Jones.

'The thing is,' she said, slowing down to pass a horsebox coming towards her, 'Patrick's feeling pretty broke at the moment. I'm not sure where we're going to get the five thousand from.'

'If he goes well tomorrow and you like him, I'll buy him for you,' said the Colonel, patting her knee fondly. 'He can be your Christmas present.'

She stopped the car and threw her arms around his neck.

'Oh, Daddy, thank you, thank you. You're the best father in the whole wide world.'

'Better to have it now than to wait until I'm gone,' the Colonel muttered, giving her a rather embarrassed hug. 'And I'll get a lot of pleasure watching you ride him.'

'I just know he's right for me. I could feel it as soon as I sat on him. Oh, Daddy, it's so kind and generous of you.'

'Subject to vet, of course,' the Colonel struck a note of caution. 'Better get Tom Hicks to come and do it after tomorrow. Just you go carefully. We don't want the horse failing the vet and that fellow saying we've crocked him up. After all, we don't know anything about this chap Ned Jones. He's new in the country.'

'All the more reason why he's not going to try and sell us a dud,' Deborah retorted, driving on. 'He wants to make his reputation. He told me so.'

'And so he will,' said the Colonel. 'With you riding him, that grey horse will do the fellow proud.'

Ned brought the horse to the meet on Monday morning. It had rained in the night and was still drizzling steadily. But the forecast was for brighter, colder weather later.

'It should be a good scenting day,' Deborah said, trying to appear cool as Ned led the horse down the ramp.

'You never can tell with scent,' said Ned. 'But let's hope you're right, Mrs Bray-Smith.' He was very businesslike this morning, she thought, whipping off the tail bandage, tightening the girths, holding the horse at the bottom of the ramp so she could use it as a mounting-block. He didn't offer to give her a leg up, perhaps because Patrick had arrived on his big chestnut and was watching her mount.

Ned adjusted her stirrup leathers for her, checked the girths again. 'Right you are, madam,' he said, giving the horse a slap. 'Enjoy yourself. Stay out as long as you like.'

'Will you be coming out too?' she asked him.

'Sure, I've got the Duchess's bay today. I'm getting him settled before the Opening Meet. I'll be there if you need me.' He grinned at her and she glanced at Patrick to see if he'd heard. But Patrick was looking impatient.

'Hurry up, Debs,' he said. 'We haven't got all day.' They rode out of the farmyard side by side. The grey walked out well, his ears pricked, his toes pointed, chewing excitedly at his bit.

'All right, Debs?' asked Patrick as they entered the field where the meet was.

'I think so,' she said as the grey gave a little bounce when his feet touched the grass. She sat still and ran her hand down his silky neck. 'I don't know what all the hurry was about,' she said as the horse relaxed a little. 'The hounds aren't even here yet.'

The Colonel had arrived, though. She could see his battered old Land Rover parked in the middle of the field and her father leaning on the bonnet talking to some of his cronies. He'd brought Kate with him. She was wearing a tightly belted raincoat, too long, too pale and far too smart, which looked more suitable for a stroll down Bond Street than standing about in a muddy field with a lot of dogs and horses. Feeling magnanimous Deborah rode over.

'You look just fine,' the Colonel said, studying her approvingly. 'You'll not get left behind on that fellow, that's for sure.' He fished in his pocket and produced a packet of Polos.

'Let me try,' said Kate, swiftly taking the packet from his hand and extracting a mint. 'He's been teaching me how to do it with Bella,' she explained to Deborah.

She held out her hand to the grey horse with the Polo sitting on the palm, but the horse wasn't interested in food. The Duke was bringing his hounds into the field. It was a sight as picturesque as any Christmas card and one that never failed to make Deborah tingle all over. The grey horse froze, standing absolutely still, tense as a drawn bow. Deborah talked to him soothingly.

'They don't look savage,' said Kate, gazing at where the Duke had the hounds drawn up in a well-disciplined pack under the authoritative eyes of the two whips. Some were sitting, some lying, others standing about, tails wagging, enjoying the attention of the spectators.

'Of course they're not savage,' said the Colonel, winking at Deborah. 'They wouldn't hurt a fly.'

'I wonder if the fox would agree with you,' retorted Kate.

'I dare say he wouldn't,' Deborah scoffed. 'But then nor would the chickens the fox killed last night. Not everything in the country is quite as nice and soft and cuddly as you might like to think.' Kate looked suitably chastened and Deborah thought it a shame that poor Daddy was stuck with such a wet goose of a girl who hadn't got a clue about hunting. Still, that wasn't her problem today, thank God. Her main concern today was the animal beneath her, now beginning to tremble with excitement. 'I'd better go and say good morning to the Master,' she said, preparing to join the stream of people riding past the great man and shouting 'Morning, Master' at him.

'I thought Patrick was the Master,' Kate said in surprise, gazing at Patrick who was deep in conversation with the Duke.

'The Duke of Blazeborough hunts the hounds,' the Colonel told her. 'Patrick leads the field.'

'Don't they have a huntsman?' Kate asked, putting out her hand tentatively to stroke the grey horse on the nose.

'Not here,' said Deborah. Really the girl knew nothing, it appeared. 'In some hunts they have professional huntsmen and the Master controls the field.' A horse nearby made a sudden unexpected movement, frightening the grey, who threw up his head and snorted in alarm. Kate leapt back, startled.

'Sit tight,' said the Colonel, grinning as Deborah steadied him.

'Don't worry, he's not going to do anything much,' Deborah said for Kate's benefit. 'He's got good manners for a five-year-old.'

'Better get on,' said the Colonel, slapping the horse on the neck. 'He's getting restive. He may explode if you hold him up much longer. It don't do to ask too much of a young horse.'

Kate looked terrified and Deborah laughed.

The hounds were moving off. Suddenly the whole field was in motion. Horses which until that moment had been dozing in the sunshine suddenly became all flashing feet and swishing tails. Deborah, trying to keep the grey horse moving forward calmly, nearly trampled on Kate who was running for cover.

'Stand still,' commanded the Colonel. 'They can't avoid you if you keep bobbing about like that.'

'I'm not going to stand still and be kicked to death by some uncontrollable maniac,' said Kate as an over-excited horse leapt sideways and then stood up in the air with both front feet off the ground.

'Probably first time out – young fool should have got it settled down at home before bringing it out in public,' muttered the Colonel as the horse went bounding off across the grass with the rider still miraculously in the saddle. 'Ah, here's Caroline, late as usual. No fear of her being carried away by too much enthusiasm.'

'I'll ring you tonight – let you know how I get on,' Deborah promised over her shoulder as she rode away.

'Have fun,' the Colonel shouted after her as she rode away.

The grey horse was keen but no trouble as they hacked down the road to the first draw. It was a big dense covert which took a long time to draw, and Deborah knew from experience they might have a long time to wait for a fox. She cantered her horse slowly across the field and he obeyed her, head tucked in, moving like flowing water. She was pleased. She saw Caroline come cantering up on Bella and felt a qualm of pity for her sister. It must be terrible to have lost one's nerve and not be able to admit it to oneself. If I lost my nerve, Deborah thought, I'd give up hunting tomorrow.

'I heard you were trying a new horse today,' Caroline greeted her. 'Looks a bit of a handful – are you sure you can hold him?'

'Patrick says if you can hold your horse you ought to sell him,' laughed Deborah, full of bravado. 'There's a lot of power there. I'm assured he's a brilliant jumper.'

Caroline studied the horse with narrowed eyes. 'He's certainly handsome,' she conceded. 'It was clever to get Daddy to buy him for you. I thought he didn't have any money – at least that's what he's always telling John.'

'Daddy's always got money for horses.' Deborah cocked her head listening hopefully. 'Was that a halloa?'

'I think it was a cow.'

'No?' Deborah was disappointed. 'Perhaps you're right. Awfully important to get a good start from here.' Caroline, she knew, didn't mind where she started from. She just wanted to be able to stay out of trouble and get home in one piece.

'Do you think that woman Daddy's got looking after him has designs on him, Caroline?' Deborah asked to change the subject.

'What, Kate?' Caroline looked surprised. 'Don't be ridiculous, she's young enough to be his daughter – and besides, she's got a husband in

Saudi on a temporary assignment. She's quite happily married I'm sure.'

'If she's so happily married why didn't she go to Saudi with him?' demanded Debs.

'She's suffering from the empty nest syndrome. She wants to decide what to do with the rest of her life.' Caroline frowned thoughtfully. 'I can sympathise with her in a way.'

'I suppose it's difficult if you don't hunt,' said Deborah, gathering up her reins as the grey horse pricked his ears and began fidgeting. Caroline moved Bella away nervously. 'Listen, the hounds are running.'

'Only in the covert,' Caroline said. 'They'll be messing about in there for ages. You know how difficult it is to get a fox out of Blackthorn Break.' Deborah let the reins lie slack again and the grey horse relaxed.

'Kate can only stay until March when her husband comes home,' Caroline said. 'We can't go on like this forever with one stopgap after another. We ought to find a permanent solution.'

'Only death's a permanent solution,' Deborah replied cheerfully. 'Daddy seems happy enough, why can't you just leave it? Something'll always turn up.'

'All very well for you,' retorted Caroline bitterly. 'It's me who has to find the something. I'm the only one that does anything for him. I keep my horse there to make him feel happy and to give poor old Murphy something to do. I'm the one who has to leave at least half an hour earlier on hunting mornings and put up with Mrs Murphy's moans. But as soon as *you* need a new horse you're round having lunch with him and he's parted with £5,000. It's not fair.'

Oh dear, oh dear, oh dear, thought Deborah. What does she want me to do?

A hound appeared at the edge of the wood – his nose to the ground, tail wagging enthusiastically. Deborah began to move away.

'This holiday village thing,' Caroline said, following, 'John thinks it might be a golden opportunity.'

'What for? It'll ruin the hunting in that part of the country.' Deborah wasn't really listening, she was watching the hound who'd started to give tongue.

'John thinks we might be able to sell The Court – to the holiday village consortium. It'd be worth a lot of money.'

'He wouldn't, would he?' Debs said, ignoring the noise of hounds giving tongue in the covert. 'Sell, I mean?' The grey horse began sidling uneasily.

'He might if the planning application goes through. He wouldn't want a mini Butlins on his doorstep.' The Duke came thundering round the top end of the wood blowing his horn. Hounds began pouring out of the covert.

'We'll talk about it later,' shouted Deborah, taking firm hold of the grey as he bounded forward. 'We'll have to wait and see what happens about the planning thing.' The cry of the hounds deepened as they came hurrying out of the covert and settled to the line. Deborah's heart began to thump with a mixture of fear and excitement as the field set off in a great cavalry charge down the field.

'Do you think you could persuade him?' Caroline shouted as they cantered side by side. 'You got him to buy you that nice new horse, after all.'

But Deborah wasn't listening any more, she was scanning the view ahead, looking for a way out of the field. She saw Patrick setting sail over a big hedge. One or two of the bolder riders were following him. Caroline was already making for a corner of the field where an impatient crowd of horses were huddled together queueing for a small rail. It's now or never, thought Deborah, sitting down and giving the grey his head. Let's see what you're made of. The grey pricked his ears and surged forward, gathered himself together, and took off effortlessly.

'Clever boy,' sang Deborah as they cleared the hedge easily. The hounds were running well and they galloped on towards a wooden fence. Deborah tried to check her horse as they approached. Park rails needed accuracy. But the grey horse had the bit between his teeth. He had been behaving impeccably for a very long time that morning and now his blood was up. Realising she had lost control, Deborah sat down and rode at the rails praying that the riders on either side of her would hold straight. The grey horse stood off and floated over the rail. The reins slipped through Deborah's fingers as she landed back in the saddle, taken unawares by such a huge jump. Quickly she gathered them up again. Patrick was wheeling left. There was a fairish stone wall there, she knew. She checked her horse, and this time he listened to her; he saw the wall, pricked his ears and bounded forward. She got him on his hocks and he flew over. In the field beyond, the hounds were checking, feathering about trying to find the lost scent. Patrick was shouting at the riders out of control to hold hard. Deborah sat down in the saddle and reined her horse back. He obeyed her. Good, he was beginning to settle. A halloa from up on the top of a hill got the hounds back on the line and soon, with a great cry, they were off again. Deborah and the grey jumped a wall, a tiger trap, then a drop wall on to the road. Deborah arrived in the road a bit sooner than she'd expected, for the grey had definitely taken charge again. But she was still up in front and going nicely. Then they were on grass again, galloping towards a line of hedges. Patrick ahead was sitting down and riding hard. There must be a big ditch on the other side, she thought. But it wasn't, the big ditch was on the takeoff. The horse to her right saw it and swerved, breaking their rhythm. The grey hesitated, Deborah caught sight of a gleam of water, then the horse sprang, changing legs lightly on top of the hedge and landing safely well out on the other side.

'You're an Irishman all right,' said Deborah rather breathlessly as they sped on.

But now the hounds were running into a big wood, and Patrick was pulling up. Those who were still with him did likewise, while from inside the covert came the long, winding sound of the horn that meant the fox had gone to ground.

'All right, Deborah?' said Patrick, coming up alongside. 'How's he gone?'

'He's brilliant,' she said, panting. 'Gives a great feel.'

The leaders sat on their blowing horses, grinning at each other smugly while the rest of the field began to catch up. Deborah saw Ned Jones riding a big rangy bay, which looked far too lively for a lady's hunter. Her respect for the Duchess increased.

'You look happy, Mrs Bray-Smith,' he said, grinning at her. 'Didn't I say he could jump?'

'He's everything you said he was and more,' she replied, excited, full of adrenaline, made reckless by the sheer fact of having successfully negotiated so many obstacles, and by his eyes wickedly encouraging her. 'He gives me a great feel. Better than a new lover, any day,' she told him.

'You don't need a lover,' he said, quick as a flash. 'Not when you've got such a dashing and devoted husband.'

'Yes, of course,' she laughed gaily. 'Only joking.' He didn't grin or rake her with his eyes any more, just studied her gravely.

'You were right,' he said. 'The scent seems to be good today. I shouldn't be surprised if we don't get a good run later.'

She wondered what he called the last exciting fifteen minutes and would have liked to ask him, only he moved away. She was disappointed. He was so unpredictable – one moment flirting with her outrageously, the next treating her with a deference which put a chasm between them bigger than anything even his grey horse could jump. It really was quite bewildering.

It was an hour before they found another fox and when they did he ran straight across a sea of corn. Deborah was at the back. Her heart sank as she saw hounds streaming away towards the far horizon with horses spread out nose to tail in single file in front of her zig-zagging their way around the edge of the fields like the four and twenty tailors climbing the hill after the snail. Next they were on roads, and when they finally got back on to grass it was down a steep and slippery bank. The grey horse plunged impetuously down – too impetuously. Halfway, he slipped, tried to right himself but his back legs seemed to be going faster than his front ones. Deborah thought he was coming over backwards with her and bailed out over the tail, by which time he was up and away. She leapt up quickly, none the worse, to see her horse disappearing over a set of rails at the bottom. She began to run after him, making slow progress in her riding boots, cursing silently under her breath as she saw him jump out over a low wall where he was caught trying to barge through a crowded gateway. There was no way back except over the two fences he'd jumped and she supposed she would just have to clamber over them. It would take ages and she'd lose them now for sure.

'Here, hop up,' a voice shouted behind her. 'I'll give you a lift.' It was Ned Jones.

'I can't.' Surely he didn't expect her to ride pillion like a medieval damsel in distress.

'Of course you can. Don't be wet. Do you want to miss the run of the season? Here, put your boot there.' He stuck out his foot. There was no denying him. 'Give me your hand.' Somehow she found she was doing what he told her. She gave him her hand and put her boot on top of his. He yanked her up with extraordinary strength and she found herself perched precariously in front of him with his arms around her waist. 'Now hold on tight,' he said, and rode towards the set of rails.

'Oh no!' She closed her eyes and clung to the martingale as the horse took off over the rails.

'There you are – it's easy,' he murmured in her ear. 'Are you OK?'

The horse was cantering smoothly towards the low wall, and Deborah leant against Ned, trying not to bounce about too much on the horse's withers.

'I'm OK,' she said.

'Right, here we go again.' Somehow he managed to hang on to her and still steady the horse going into the wall. 'Get on with you,' he shouted. The horse jumped so smoothly she hardly felt him leave the ground.

'No problem,' said Ned as they caught up with her horse. 'Wasn't that a lot quicker than doing it on your own two feet?'

The young stockbroker who had caught the grey stared at them in amazement. 'Bring him up close alongside, sir,' commanded Ned. 'Then she can slide over.' But the grey was impatiently sidling about, aware that horses were galloping in pursuit of the hounds and that he was missing out. He didn't want to stand still a moment longer.

'Go on, jump, woman!' shouted Ned.

'How can I? I'm not a bloody circus act,' she said.

'All right then, I suppose I'll have to lift you off.' He leapt nimbly down and seized hold of her. 'Women!' he muttered, pulling her off. 'Always want to be waited on hand and foot.'

'I do not,' she said, running round to the side of the grey horse and trying to get her boot in the stirrup. But her boots were slippery with mud and the horse was dancing about excitedly.

'Keep still and give me your leg, you silly bitch. You're all the same, happy to be rescued but quick to run off without a word of thanks. Now, one – two – up you go.' He heaved and she fell into the saddle like a sack of corn. The horse took off and she was too busy clutching at the reins and clinging to the pommel while she tried to find the stirrups to be able to reply.

When at last she had her breath back, her horse under control and her feet in the stirrups, she was able to see that they were miles behind.

'They're swinging right-handed, like as not,' said Ned, staring at the far horizon. 'We'll maybe cut them off if we go through here. Follow me.'

Deborah followed, aghast but excited as he led her a hell of a dance, jumping things she would never have thought of doing. He rode well, giving her the perfect lead, shouting at her to kick on, or hold steady, whichever was necessary. When they finally caught up she was breathless, exhilarated, amazed at herself.

'He's marvellous – the best horse I've ever ridden,' she panted. 'Thank you for allowing me to try him.'

'There's nothing so bold as a young horse,' he said, grinning at her, 'but it takes guts to ride one. I'm glad you've got him, Deborah. You'll do me proud, the pair of you.'

She was far too pleased and breathless and over-excited to care that he had helped himself to her Christian name without leave.

Of course it was all round the Blazers within twenty-four hours and the story lost nothing in the telling. The new man who had taken the Duchess's yard had jumped several fences with the Field Master's wife in his arms and she'd been so carried away by the experience she had bought the horse he was trying to sell her. By the time it reached Patrick's ears late the following evening, he was not amused.

'I can't think what you thought you were doing, Deborah,' he said coming into the bathroom as she was getting ready for bed. 'Encouraging that fellow. He's a frightful show-off when all's said and done, and he'll screw anything, I'm told. You'd better be careful or you'll be the laughing stock of the whole county.'

'I don't know what you mean, Patrick,' she retorted, furious that he should be so disparaging about Ned. 'All he was doing was getting me reunited with my horse in the quickest possible way. You're just jealous. I bet you couldn't jump two obstacles in quick succession with me sitting in front of you.'

'Jealous!' He stared at her in total disbelief. 'I'm not jealous of a jumped-up horse coper. I just don't want you to make a fool of yourself. He's the Duchess's lover, everybody knows that. It's why she's set him up in that yard, and he's having it off with his head girl as well – so they tell me at the Kennels. I just don't want my wife to be one of the also-rans.'

She got out of the bath and grabbed a towel, incandescent with rage. How dare he?

'That's bloody insulting,' she shouted at him. 'You're the one who's been having it off all over the place – don't think I've forgotten.'

'Well, if you're thinking of using Ned Jones to get even you'd better forget it.' He was glaring at her scornfully and she felt suddenly flattened.

She could match his anger, but she couldn't cope with his condescension.

'It's not true,' she said gathering her dignity and the towel around her. 'Ned Jones means nothing to me. He's a good horseman, that's all.' He was looking a little less like a suspicious husband, but all the same, she didn't want him putting two and two together and making trouble. She dropped the towel and wound her arms around his neck. 'Come on, darling,' she said. 'What's happening to us? Ever since I caught you with that girl in the Imperial we've been bickering away like anything. Let's not fight over this, shall we, it's silly.'

Patrick sulked a bit at first but as soon as she got him into bed he was happy to be won round. They made love rather desperately.

# *Chapter 9*

For the next two weeks the sun shone out of a cloudless sky and the autumn colours were at their best. The Colonel went about complaining that the hounds would never be ready in time for the Opening Meet unless the hunting improved, but Kate was thrilled. It mattered not to her that the ground was too hard and the scent nonexistent in such unseasonable weather. In her spare time, and she had plenty of it, she wandered the countryside, enchanted by the fiery reds and brilliant burnt oranges and yellowing greens all around her. It was as if nature was putting on a special show to welcome her and it made her feel exhilarated, as if she'd won an unexpected prize.

She also felt that the Colonel was beginning to accept her at last. Not that he was any less combative, or more considerate of her wishes. He guarded his independence fiercely and she respected him for it, which was why she gave in to him over the question of the shopping, realising that he enjoyed his sorties into Bratchester to do battle in Waitrose. It gave him something to do.

To please him she also endeavoured to conquer her fear of the horse Bella and succeeded so well she was even brave enough to slip into Bella's box occasionally on her own. The Colonel had been surprised to discover her there talking to the animal while the mare nosed about her pockets looking for titbits. He pretended to be jealous that the horse was being unfaithful, especially when Kate claimed that Bella had taken to greeting her with a nicker of recognition when she came downstairs from her flat in the mornings. Of course he wouldn't admit it outright but she knew he was secretly pleased that she was becoming fond of the horse. He certainly wasn't easy, but there were times when she detected an element almost of teasing in their verbal skirmishes, or perhaps it was just that she was getting used to having to stand up for herself all the time.

At the beginning of December the District Council turned down the holiday village planning application.

'We've done it, Kate,' cried the Colonel, his moustache bristling with triumph. 'I knew we'd get the better of them this time.'

Kate felt a wonderful glow of satisfaction, although she didn't feel she deserved any of the credit. It gave her a new belief in herself, something to cling to when she felt guilty at having cut herself off from Alan so wantonly; she had written to him regularly but his replies had been few and uncommunicative; the knowledge that in her own small way she was making a success of her new life comforted her a little.

Her only failure was the mouse in the larder. The Colonel's attempts at setting traps were not very successful, probably because his fingers were too stiff with arthritis to bait the traps effectively. The mouse always succeeded in making off with the cheese without getting caught. Kate had tried boarding up the hole he came in through, but he managed to gnaw his way back through the thickest obstruction. The Colonel raised no objection when she tried setting the traps herself, but still the mouse defied her.

'Haven't you caught that bugger yet?' he asked with obvious delight when he saw her putting the bag of flour into a biscuit tin for safety.

He often came and watched her when she was cooking. Kate had found it unnerving at first. Her own kitchen in London wasn't big enough for more than one person at a time and she was used to having it to herself. But the kitchen at The Court was the warmest room in the house as well as being comfortably roomy. She got used to the Colonel sitting in the big armchair at the side of the Aga, reading bits of the newspaper out to her and trying to entice her into an argument.

'I don't think it's a mouse, I think it's a monster,' she said, busy rubbing flour and butter together. 'There's nothing he can't eat his way through. He's got the jaws of a shark.' Before the Colonel could come back with a scathing retort, the telephone rang. She wiped her hands on her apron and seized it quickly to save him getting out of his chair. 'It's someone from the council,' she said.

He began to lever himself up, while she exchanged pleasantries with the Assistant Planning Officer, to give the Colonel time to get out of his chair. She pretended not to notice the difficulty he was having, knowing that he would manage in the end and hated to be helped. He was somewhat out of breath when he took the telephone from her. She went back to making pastry but she could see from his rapidly reddening countenance that the news was not good.

'Now the fat's in the fire,' he said, banging down the receiver at last. 'The developers have appealed the decision and there's to be a public inquiry.'

'I suppose it was good of him to let us know,' she said, dusting a wooden board with flour.

'I wouldn't put it past him not to have put them up to it,' muttered the Colonel. 'Derek Evans' assistant has always been keen on the scheme. He sounded quite pleased about it. We'll have to watch that bugger. He says we'll have to prepare a case to present at the inquiry. Bloody waste of everybody's time and money. Why can't the Department of Environment just listen to what the local authority advises, instead of stirring up a lot of pother with their stupid inquiries? It's jobs for the boys, that's what it is. Bloody parasites.'

'Do you mean to fight it then?' asked Kate, fetching the rolling pin from the dresser.

'Of course I mean to fight it, and you're going to help me. You said you would – remember?'

'Did I? I don't remember saying any such thing.' He scowled at her and she waggled the rolling pin at him. 'I haven't the least idea how to get up a case for a public inquiry.'

'Of course you haven't,' he agreed with her. 'We'll have to get some professional advice.'

Suddenly Kate remembered Shirley. 'I do have this friend – she's a red-hot solicitor in London. She's bound to know what to do.'

'Splendid. Get her on the telephone at once.' She went off to find Shirley's number and telephoned her from the Colonel's study while he was out in the stables.

'Kate, what have you promised now?' said Shirley when Kate managed to get through to her. 'Will you never learn?'

'I haven't promised anything; not this time,' said Kate. 'At least I don't think I did. But I'd like to help him if I could. It's such a pretty village and you've no idea how beautiful the countryside is around it. You must come down some weekend, Shirley, and see for yourself. It would be a terrible shame if it was all to be spoilt.'

'It'll cost you,' warned Shirley.

'How much?' asked Kate.

'To fight your case at a public inquiry? It all depends on the length of the inquiry. You'll need a good planning solicitor and then you'll need special witnesses. People like ecology experts, and traffic consultants, don't come cheap.'

'Whatever do we need them for?' Kate was bewildered.

'To prove that the volume of traffic created by the holiday village is more than the existing roads can bear,' explained Shirley patiently. 'Just as you'll need hydrological consultants to look at things like what the development might do to the local water levels. Then there's the QC to lead the case. His fees will be about £1,000 a day. But if the District Council's turned down the application you may get them to share the costs of the inquiry.'

Kate's heart quailed as she realised the Colonel had no idea what he would be letting himself in for. It was no longer just a matter of his twisting a few arms to get his own way.

'It'll be five figures at the very least. Do you think you can raise that sort of money, Kate?' Shirley's voice on the telephone sounded very businesslike. Kate pictured her sitting in her sumptuous office, perched on the edge of her important desk, and thought of all the money it took to keep her there.

'Of course we can,' she heard herself saying. 'No trouble.'

'Well, of course I know there's plenty of money about in that part of the world.' Shirley sounded rather impressed and Kate wondered what she would say if she could see The Court. She'd probably think the whole place was terribly run-down. 'Country houses are like gold dust down there,' Shirley went on, 'but not if there's a mini Butlins on the doorstep. People will put up quite a lot of money to preserve the value of their property. You want to appeal to their self-interest.'

'We thought we'd done that when we got the District Council to turn it down,' murmured Kate.

'Let me know when you've got the first £10,000 in the bag.' Shirley sounded bracing. 'I'll see whether we can take on the case for you for a flat fee. That should save you a bit if it runs on a long time. Who's the developer?'

'Meccarda,' said Kate, feeling slightly bemused. 'They're big in the leisure industry.'

'Aren't they about to be bought by ABC?'

'I don't know. I've never heard of ABC – they sound like a children's reading book,' said Kate, trying to get back on terra firma.

'Allied Brownstone Conglomerates,' Shirley swept on relentlessly. 'I'm sure they're trying to take over Meccarda. I wouldn't mind taking on ABC and winning. It'd be very good for our reputation. You get the begging bowl out, Kate, and see what you can do.'

Kate hung up, realising that Shirley was right: she had definitely rushed in way over her head this time. Her only hope was that the Colonel would think so too. But when she told him what Shirley had said, he was filled with enthusiasm for the fight.

'Right,' he said. 'Let's get cracking straight away. We'll start with the hunt. We'll write to everyone in the hunt book asking them to subscribe.'

'Do you think they will?' He scowled at her. 'No, don't tell me,' she said hastily. 'Some of the best of the Monday country is threatened – all grass and hedges. Of course they will.'

His eyes twinkled. 'Who told you?'

'Patrick. At least Patrick told Derek Evans.' She didn't tell him what Derek Evans had said, about selling The Court.

'We've almost 500 names in the hunt book,' he said. 'If they each give a tenner that's £5,000. Of course some'll give much more, some nothing. I don't think £10 average is expecting too much.'

She opened her mouth to protest that even if they did all give a tenner, which she thought unlikely, £5,000 was a mere drop in the bucket.

'Can you type?' He shot the question at her so fiercely she said yes before she had time to think better of it.

'Good girl.' He was smiling at her proudly and she felt as if she'd just completed an army cross-country course in one bound. 'We'll make a start tomorrow.'

'Have you got a typewriter?' she asked faintly. It hardly seemed the time to tell him that she hadn't used a typewriter since the day she left college.

'No, but someone in the village is bound to have one. I'll start with the ex-post mistress. She used to know everything that went on in the village before she had to give up the post office. All the bloody Council's fault, raising the business rate. Put her out of business. Got to go out charring now. Still, I might just catch her – if I pop round straight away. If there's a typewriter in Little Riddleton, Marian Bell will know where to run it to earth.'

He stumped off and Kate sank down into the armchair, trying to resist the feeling that a huge steamroller was about to iron her flat. The big dog, Spot, came and laid his head on her lap.

'What have I gone and done now?' said Kate, pulling his soft, velvety ears. 'Just when everything seemed to be going so well. I thought people came to the countryside for a bit of peace and quiet.' Spot gave a great big doggy sigh gazing at her sorrowfully with his expressive brown eyes in silent sympathy.

The Colonel came back from the village triumphantly bearing an ancient portable typewriter. Kate's heart sank. It was ridiculous what they were taking on. How could an old man, bent and arthritic and anachronistic, together with an unemployable housewife with no office skills, hope to raise the sort of money Shirley was talking about, with nothing more than an ancient machine such as that? It was like Don Quixote and Sancho Panza tilting at windmills. Tentatively she tried to suggest that the task was too big for the two of them unaided.

'Nonsense,' he brushed her protestations aside. 'You've got to expect to fail a little if you want to succeed. Aim for the ceiling and you may land on the mantelpiece, but if you only aim for the mantelpiece you might end up on the floor. Once we get this ball rolling you'll be surprised at how the money'll come in.'

She hoped he was right. He was so confident, perhaps he could indeed do it. Maybe his confidence would rub off on her.

Caroline didn't seem to think it such a good idea when she came down to hunt a few days later.

'What are you doing, Kate?' she asked when she came into the kitchen and found Kate busy typing at the table. Kate explained and Caroline looked concerned.

'You don't have to do it, you know,' she said. 'You weren't hired as a secretary, just as a companion for Daddy. You're working too hard.'

'No, no, I enjoy it, truly, Caroline,' Kate assured her. 'And your father is in his element. It's given him something to do.'

'I'd have thought he'd got enough to do already,' Caroline said, getting into her hunting coat.

'But nothing as challenging as this. He loves organising his troops for battle and he's very good at it. We've got the first meeting of the Amenity Society tomorrow night, and we're getting a letter printed which we're going to send out to all the hunt subscribers.' Kate got up and started searching through the pile of papers at the other end of the kitchen table. 'I've got a copy of it here somewhere. Would you like to read it?'

'No, I can't stop now, I'm late already,' Caroline said, rushing out of the kitchen in her stockinged feet. 'Perhaps when I get back this afternoon,' she called over her shoulder.

'Where's Caroline?' demanded the Colonel, coming into the kitchen from outside, with traces of rain on his wellingtons, flat hat and green Barbour jacket.

'In the boot room putting on her boots, I expect,' said Kate.

'Late as usual. Lucky for her I've sent Murphy on to the meet with the mare. She wouldn't have had a hope of getting there on time if she'd ridden over herself.'

'It's all right, Daddy, I'm here now.' Caroline reappeared booted and spurred and carrying her hunting whip. 'Kate's been telling me all about this public inquiry thing. You don't really think you can take on someone like Meccarda and win, do you?'

'Why not?' he replied chirpily. 'The money's coming in already. We aim to have ten thousand by Christmas, then we can brief this hot-shot lawyer friend of Kate's.' Caroline looked flabbergasted. 'Right, if you're ready we'll be off to the meet. Keep up the good work, Kate, and don't worry about lunch. As it's a lawn meet I'll tuck into the sausage rolls and cake and follow the hounds until Caroline wants to come home.'

He breezed out of the kitchen, pushing his daughter before him, and Kate was relieved that for once he didn't want her to go with him. She quite enjoyed following the hounds by car and the Colonel's enthusiasm was infectious. He was incredibly knowledgeable about the whole art of venery and Kate was learning a lot from him, not just about killing foxes but about the countryside and the balance of nature and farming and all its problems. All the same, it took up a great deal of the day and now she needed some time just to get all these envelopes addressed.

Kate finished typing the agenda for the Amenity Society and switched on the radio as she settled down to address envelopes. Outside the wind was blowing quite hard and flinging the rain against the windows. The weather had broken in time for the Opening Meet and it had been pretty wet and dismal ever since. Kate seemed to live in wellingtons and several layers of jumpers, but at least it was quite cosy in the kitchen. She felt quite sorry for poor Caroline, exposed to the elements and the dangers of the chase, while here in the kitchen, with the radio playing cheerfully in the background, it was wonderfully cosy and safe. Certainly Kate didn't feel she was hard worked. She became aware that the 'crafty cook' on Radio Two was giving a recipe for Christmas pudding. It brought Kate up sharp. Not Christmas already! Only two weeks into December and already Christmas had started popping up all over the place. Now it was on the radio. Why do they have to keep hammering it home? she thought, feeling guilty. Christmas this, Christmas that. We all know it's coming. Why does Christmas have to be spoilt before it gets here?

'Only twelve more shopping days to Christmas,' the radio presenter announced cheerfully when the Christmas pudding recipe was finished.

Kate stared at the rain hammering against the window. Alan hadn't asked her to come out to Saudi for Christmas, although she knew that both Naomi and Matt were going there. Alan, she suspected, was sulking. He tended to bear grudges if crossed, which is why she had always been at pains not to cross him. She used to hate scenes and atmospheres. She wondered if she should swallow her pride and invite herself to Saudi to be with the family. But she was damned if she would. That would just be giving in to him as she always had done. It was what Alan was expecting her to do. She wondered if that was why Alan's letters were so lacklustre. Was he waiting for some sort of sign from her that she had made a mistake? She looked around her at the comfortable, slightly dishevelled kitchen, at the table littered with papers, the battered old typewriter, the pile of envelopes waiting to be addressed. She hadn't made a mistake. She was enjoying every minute of her new life.

Caroline came back at about half-past two, covered in mud and soaked to the skin, and for once accepted Kate's offer of tea. She took herself upstairs for a bath while Kate set about clearing the table a little, wondering what people had for tea at three o'clock in the afternoon when they'd had no lunch and probably no breakfast either. She got out bread, a cake, which by good fortune she'd made the day before, put the kettle on and waited until Caroline came back, revived by the bath and looking more herself again in her London clothes. She settled for cake and lots of tea, informing Kate that it was the only way she kept her figure, not eating on hunting days. She said nothing about the campaign against the holiday village scheme and Kate was relieved. She suspected that Caroline was not much impressed by their efforts so far. She was, however, very friendly and encouraging, complimenting Kate on her cooking and the way she had fitted into country life so well. Kate wasn't sure whether Caroline wasn't being a little patronising but told herself not to be over-sensitive. She should be glad that for once she seemed to be making a success of things.

When the Colonel came in, Caroline raised the subject of Christmas.

'John and I are hoping very much that you will be able to come and spend Christmas with us, Daddy,' she said, pouring herself another cup of tea.

The Colonel sat down at the table and accepted a cup of tea and a piece of cake from Kate before replying. 'Well, that's very good of you both,' he said winking at Kate, 'but I think I'll be quite all right here at The Court with Kate to look after me.'

'Surely Kate will want to spend Christmas with her husband and family in Saudi?' said Caroline in surprise.

Kate became aware that both the Colonel and his daughter were staring at her questioningly.

'I don't have any plans for Christmas,' she stammered, covered in confusion.

'Good,' said the Colonel. 'That's all settled then.'

Oh dear, what am I to do now? thought Kate. Caroline was looking so hurt – more than hurt, angry. Surely she knew her father was just being selfish? He didn't want to leave his old familiar surroundings and fit in with other people's ways – only Kate couldn't tell his daughter that, not with him sitting there drinking tea and looking so smug. Was it wrong to give in to the Colonel? Would it have been better to give in to Alan, who was her husband after all? But she was not going to let Alan think he just had to snap his fingers and she'd come running. She had her pride and she was wanted here. Guiltily she wondered if Alan would think she was being useful or just used? Damn Christmas, she thought. It's asking some nasty questions I don't want answered.

* * *

Caroline, doing a hundred down the motorway a little later, felt that she'd had a nasty answer to the Christmas question. Christmas was always a problem if you had no children and a workaholic for a husband. Even if you escaped somewhere like the Caribbean, pretending Christmas didn't exist, they got you feeling guilty long before you could get away. The only way Caroline could get through it was to fill her house with tremendously sophisticated decorations and serve ever so original Christmas fare at as many parties as she could manage for the singles, the childless, the unloved and the unlovable. But it was all an empty, elaborate charade, especially the buying of her own present, then giving it to one of the staff to wrap for John to give her on Christmas morning.

She leant forward and switched on the radio. Some inane pop music began blaring out a repetitive, tuneless cry of pain. What was she going to tell John?

'I know I can rely on you, Caroline,' he'd said, as she'd driven off this morning. John wasn't going to be at all pleased with her. She jabbed the keys of the car radio to find another station. It was impossible to get anything worth listening to; she only had the radio on for the traffic warnings and the weather forecast.

It had been John's idea to ask the Colonel for Christmas. Caroline had been against the idea from the start. Christmas, which was difficult enough already, would be even more so if her father was staying in the house. Particularly as John wanted to persuade poor old Daddy to see things his way over the holiday village thing. She supposed she should be relieved that her father had turned down her invitation. But she wasn't. John would be very put out. He could be very determined once he got hold of an idea. She knew it was one of the reasons for his success. He never left anything to chance, but kept on and on and on, leaving no stone unturned until he achieved his objective. All their married life she had supported and helped him. She liked to think of herself as the even greater woman behind the great man, and now she had failed him.

She heard the six o'clock news and the weather forecast, which wasn't good. With an impatient sigh, Caroline switched off the radio. John would be furious when he heard what Daddy and Kate were up to, and Debs would no doubt refuse to do anything. Debs refused to face up to the fact that their father was getting old and frail. She liked to think that there was life in the old dog yet, that he might marry someone like Kate and start an exciting new life somewhere else. It was a ridiculous idea – just one of Debs' silly fantasies.

Caroline slowed a little and fished about for a cassette. A car behind started flashing at her. God, not the police! She pulled over, heart pounding. An angry Jaguar purred past. Thank heavens for that. Could Debs perhaps be right about Kate? Did she really have designs on Daddy? Caroline didn't think it possible. Kate was too nice, too normal, to want to marry a man old enough to be her father, and for what? It wasn't as if Daddy had any proper money. No, Kate wasn't a schemer. She was far too pliable for that. She had fitted in remarkably well considering what a little town mouse she was. Daddy seemed terribly happy with her, that was the whole trouble really. She was looking after him well and keeping him occupied. But how to make John understand?

Caroline pulled out into the fast lane again, keeping the needle at a hundred. The trouble with John was he was so single-minded. Once he got an idea in his head he would never give up. John couldn't accept failure. Caroline sighed, wishing that there were people for dinner tonight. But just for once they were on their own and not going out anywhere. She would have to tell him tonight that Daddy wasn't coming for Christmas after all, and she didn't relish dinner alone with him after that.

# *Chapter 10*

Kate sat at the kitchen table and tried to concentrate on typing up the minutes of the first Amenity Society meeting. But it was difficult with the Colonel peering over her shoulder, trying to alter everything that went into them.

'I can't say that,' she objected. 'It wouldn't be a fair record of what was said.'

'Don't be so difficult, Kate,' he retorted. 'Most of what was said last night was pure waffle. You want to write down there what we want to happen, not what all those well-meaning fools think. No one ever remembers what is said at these meetings.' He glowered at her fiercely.

'They do, you know.' She shook her head, smiling at him. 'What I'm putting down here is an acceptable account for you to read out at the next meeting, so that we don't spend half an hour arguing over it before we can get on to something else.'

'All right, have it your own way,' he gave in grudgingly. 'But I hope you're not going to be so damned obstinate about the accounts.'

'Oh there's no need. You can't fiddle those because the bank manager keeps them and he's not afraid of you, like I am.'

He laughed. 'You know, Kate, you're not such a timid little thing as I thought you were when you first came. You may look like a helpless blonde, but underneath you're every bit as tough as a good serjeant major.'

She went on typing demurely, knowing that it was the greatest compliment he could pay her and amused that he was trying to distract her with his considerable charm.

'Well, if I'm being a nuisance, I'll take myself off,' he said after a while. 'I don't suppose you'd like to come with me to the meet, would you?'

'I thought I might do some Christmas shopping later,' she said.

'Plenty of time for that. There's ten more shopping days until Christmas. They keep telling us on the wireless. Anybody would think one couldn't count.' She deigned to look up from her typewriter. He was watching her with such hopeful expectancy she hadn't the heart to disappoint him.

'If you take yourself off, I might get this finished in time to come with you,' she promised. He went out muttering about bossy females putting him out of his own kitchen, but Kate wasn't worried. The Colonel gave no quarter but she wasn't frightened of him any longer. He made no allowances, unlike Alan. Alan was always making allowances, expecting her to fail. Maybe that was why she had allowed herself to become so dependent. The Colonel expected her to conjure success out of thin air. He rubbed her up the wrong way just like Aladdin with his lamp and she found herself delivering the goods in some miraculous way. Kate wasn't sure whether she was slave or genius but at least she had achieved a little on her own. She'd even caught the mouse in the larder.

They drove to the meet in the Colonel's ancient Land Rover, with the dogs in the back, their heads hanging out over the tailboard. The Colonel was a terrifying driver. He drove in the middle of the road at a steady thirty miles an hour, a speed which he never varied. He made no concessions for blind corners, oncoming traffic or roundabouts. When he came to the main Bratchester Road, however, he did stop, twisted awkwardly round in his seat to see if there was anything coming and pulled out in the mistaken belief that the road was clear. An approaching car hooted angrily but the Colonel drove on in happy ignorance, and Kate wasn't sure whether he was too deaf to hear or just arrogant.

By the time they arrived at the meet, Kate was shivering from fear as well as cold. She had declined one of the Colonel's many ancient green waterproofs in favour of her fawn trench coat which looked fetching enough over her thickest jumper and well-cut gaberdine trousers. Patrick, she knew, would be at the meet in all his glory and so would Deborah. Even though she wasn't going to have anything to do with Patrick ever again, if he did chance to see her, Kate didn't want him not to have a pang of regret.

As it was Saturday there was a great crowd assembling. For the last mile or so they drove past boxes parked on every available spare bit of grass verge, with horses emerging from them dressed up like medieval destriers in fancy rugs and brightly coloured tail bandages. The meet was in a field in the middle of nowhere but the Colonel drove into it with a great crashing of gears, taking the muddy gateway with his hand on the horn and his foot flat down on the accelerator. They bounced and slid through the mud, startling the horses nearest to them into leaping in the air, so that a very elegant blonde who was trying to light a cigarette was nearly catapulted over her horse's head. The Colonel didn't even notice. He drove over the grass and parked close to where the Duke of Blazeborough was sitting with his hounds, talking to Patrick. The Colonel got out and walked up to talk to the Duke, and Kate followed, not knowing what else to do. The Colonel introduced Kate to the Duke of Blazeborough, who acknowledged the introduction with a brief nod, but was too busy doing the same to all the people coming up on horses and shouting, 'Morning, Master,' to do more. At the same time he seemed deep in conversation with Patrick and Kate wondered if there was really much point in all those people circling around in front of him trying to catch his eye. Hunting etiquette, she supposed. A hound jumped up, put two friendly paws on Kate's shoulders and tried to lick her face.

'Down, Whisper,' growled the Colonel sternly. 'Leave the girl alone.' The hound lay down, tail wagging apologetically.

'Do you know all the dogs by name?' Kate asked him.

'Hounds, girl, hounds,' he muttered, horrified. 'No, I don't know them all – just the good, the bad and the ugly.' He winked at her and took himself off to mingle with the crowd. Patrick didn't seem to have noticed her, so Kate trailed after the Colonel, keeping an anxious eye on the great prancing animals which all these people sat on with such apparent ease, chatting and laughing as if they were at some sort of cocktail party without the drink. One of them was Deborah, riding the beautiful big grey the Colonel had bought for her. On a horse Deborah no longer looked dumpy or discontented. In her polished black boots and tight yellow breeches it didn't matter that her legs weren't shapely. The well-cut blue coat made her look more streamlined and her profile was quite fetching with her blonde hair tied back in a neat bun beneath her velvet cap. No, on a horse, Kate had to admit, Deborah looked superb.

'Hello, Kate,' said Deborah, looking down her nose at her. 'You've got mud on that smart raincoat – what a shame.'

'I know,' said Kate, brushing half-heartedly at the imprint of the hound's large feet, stamped all over her shoulders. 'It'll wash off I expect.'

'You'd better invest in a Barbour. You'll never survive the winter in that thing.' Determined not to be upset by anything Deborah might say, Kate put out a hand to stroke the grey horse's silky neck.

'What's his name?' she asked.

'I've decided to call him Ajax, after a wonderful hunter Daddy had.' The horse began pawing the ground impatiently and Kate backed away. 'Careful,' warned Deborah, 'that horse behind you has a red ribbon on his tail.'

'Does it matter?' asked Kate nervously.

'Red for danger – means he kicks,' Deborah told her succinctly. 'Green ribbon means a young horse – might do anything.'

It all sounded quite horribly unpredictable, thought Kate, making good her escape. She didn't want to be caught in the middle of the field when all these uncontrollable animals started making for the gate.

A little ashamed of herself, Deborah watched Kate scuttling for the Land Rover. It wasn't fair really to bait the poor girl. She couldn't help it if she was terrified if a mouse farted. She was just so easy to frighten it was a wonder Daddy hadn't reduced her to a gibbering wreck.

She forgot Kate and looked about her in vain for a glimpse of Ned's black coat and black velvet cap, but Ned didn't seem to be out. She ought to have been thankful, since she was having a great deal of trouble resisting temptation in the shape of Ned Jones. The days when Patrick wasn't Field Master weren't so bad, because Deborah stuck by him. Patrick was a brave horseman, with a good sense of country. What he lacked was authority with the field. Like most good-looking, easy-going men, Patrick liked people to like him and he hated telling people off. Not like Ned, thought Deborah. Ned would make a brilliant master of hounds. He had the horsemanship, the eye for the country, the flair for knowing which way the fox might run and most of all he had a forcefulness which was truly compelling. All he lacked was money. It was on Saturdays when Patrick was busy trying to control the field that Deborah was most sorely tempted. It wasn't that Ned made passes at her. He didn't. That was part of the trouble. But she was so terribly aware of him on the hunting field, daring her to do things, egging her on, and if Ned wasn't out her day was robbed of its magic. Once she had committed the unpardonable folly of driving into the Duchess's yard in the hope of seeing Ned. The Duchess had been there, in the stables, and Deborah had had to invent a most implausible story which she feared the Duchess hadn't believed one word of. Every time she went hunting she was in such a state of feverish excitement, she could barely contain herself and she was terrified that Patrick might begin to suspect. But Patrick noticed nothing and Deborah told herself that once the children were home there would be no time or opportunity for her to get into trouble.

The day began well. The hounds picked up a fox almost immediately they left the meet. Deborah got away to a good start, riding in front with the rest of the thrusters, Ajax pulling hard. But in no time the scent petered out, the hounds running about aimlessly while the rest of the field came streaming up behind. The hounds drifted slowly across fields of plough, and the field followed strung out in a long tail, the horses struggling through the heavy going. Deborah was relieved when they left the plough for a narrow lane, although here there wasn't room for more than two abreast. But at least she was in a good position in the front. Then there was a halloa from behind. Ajax pricked his ears intelligently and tried to swing round.

'Just wait, boy,' Deborah murmured. 'All in good time.'

The Duke, cursing volubly, brought his hounds back, and in the lane all was turmoil as the field struggled to make room for him.

'And the last shall be first and the first last,' murmured Deborah, backing the grey horse up against a tree to let Patrick pass. It happened all the time in hunting and she was used to it. Not so Ajax. He took exception to his sudden relegation to the back of the field. As the horses in front of them made way for the Field Master struggling to get to the front, he tried to follow suit. But the horses in front closed ranks again behind Patrick and Deborah found herself running slap bang into a horse with a red ribbon on its tail.

'Don't be stupid,' she muttered, yanking Ajax back, which was her mistake. It gave the kicker room to express himself, which he did with a vicious backward thrust of his hind leg. There was a crack like a pistol shot. Ajax snorted and leapt about nervously.

'Oh God, my leg, my leg,' moaned Deborah, a searing pain in her left leg making her senses swim and sickness nearly engulf her.

The grey horse was dancing up and down in the narrow lane, thoroughly upset and eager to get on. Unable to put any weight on the injured leg, Deborah could do nothing to control him. Helplessly she clung to the pommel and tried to take the weight off her left leg. Dimly she was aware of people taking hold of the horse, of his prancing ceasing. But she felt so sick and dizzy from the pain she was unable to concentrate on anything else. She suspected her leg was broken – from the knife burning and twisting every time the horse moved. They led her into a farm yard but she was unable to get off. To dismount she had to swing the leg over the saddle which she was quite incapable of doing, it hurt so much. Either that or put her weight on it while she swung the other leg which would be worse. Ajax wouldn't stand still. Every restless movement was torture. None of the anxious faces around her seemed to understand what her predicament was. The man whose horse had kicked her kept apologising. She thought she would faint. She knew she was going to be sick.

'All right – I've got you, just relax.' A face swam in front of her eyes. It was Ned Jones. 'I'll have you off in a jiffy.' He lifted her off the horse and deposited her gently on a bed of straw.

'They're telephoning for an ambulance – it won't be long,' he said. 'Lucky we were in that lane and not back in those heavy ploughed fields.'

The poor man whose horse had done so much damage was on his knees beside her, still apologising. He produced a flask, his hands shaking. 'Here, have a swig of this.' Deborah snatched the flask gratefully but Ned grabbed it from her.

'Don't be stupid,' he said. 'If that leg's broken they'll have to operate. She needs an empty stomach. What we ought to do is get that boot off before it's too late.'

'Oh God,' she groaned, trying desperately not to burst into tears.

'The leg's probably swollen too much already,' someone objected.

'The boot'll help to keep the bones in place,' someone else said.

Deborah closed her eyes, trying not to listen to their arguments which were hardly calculated to console and comfort.

'They'll have to cut that boot off in the hospital.'

Deborah opened her eyes. 'Cut my best leather boots!' she exclaimed. 'Never!' She fixed Ned with a brave stare. 'Pull it off now. You can use my tie to keep the leg together.' But he shook his head.

'Better not. We'll leave it to the professionals. We don't want to move that leg about more than we can help.'

It seemed an age waiting for the ambulance. Deborah lay on the ground shivering with cold and shock, her leg hurting abominably, trying not to cry in front of Ned, who was holding her hand.

'I thought you weren't out today,' she said.

'I came out late. Had a flat on the lorry. But I'm here now, that's all that matters.' She wasn't quite sure what he meant by that, but she was comforted by his hand and she squeezed it gratefully.

When at last the ambulance came, the paramedics were very efficient. They produced a stretcher.

'Good luck sweetheart,' said Ned as she was laid on the stretcher, giving her the courage to bear the agony as they put her into the ambulance.

'Aren't you coming with me to the hospital?' she asked, desperate to keep him with her.

'I'll come later,' he promised. 'Somebody's got to take your horse home. You'll be all right – you've got all the pluck in the world.' She felt panic sweeping over her. She had only managed to be brave so far because she was determined not to break down in front of Ned. She didn't feel at all plucky.

'We'll get a message to your husband. He'll be at the hospital before you, I expect,' Ned reassured her as one of the ambulance men climbed in beside her. She tried to smile. She couldn't tell him that she didn't want Patrick, she wanted him.

When Patrick arrived at the hospital, Deborah was lying on a bed, still in her hunting clothes and still shivering. They had removed her boots, cut the one off her injured leg despite her protests, and taken her down to be X-rayed, but nobody would give her anything until the doctor had made up his mind whether she had to be operated on.

'The good news is that you're not going to have an operation,' Patrick told her, sitting down on the edge of the bed and holding her hand. 'They'll be giving you a jab in a minute which'll make you feel better.'

She clung to his hand gratefully. 'Then it's not broken? I don't believe it.'

'I'm afraid it's broken all right, a compound fracture. The bad news is that the doctor says you're to have a fortnight's traction before they can put it in plaster.'

'Traction! Oh, Patrick, no, not for a fortnight!' she wailed, bursting into tears. 'That means I've to stay in hospital.' He patted her hand, looking uncomfortable. 'Oh, Patrick, I'll be in hospital for Christmas.'

'Hush, Debs. It's all right really.' He looked around him anxiously. 'Poor darling. You've been very brave.'

A nurse came bearing down on them and he relinquished her hand with obvious relief. If she hadn't been in such pain she might have told him to bugger off, she could manage on her own, and watch the nurse's shocked face. But she was feeling too weak and sorry for herself. She needed a warm sympathetic hand to cling to. As the nurse stuck a needle into her, Deborah thought of Ned Jones. He had promised he would come later.

'If I'm not to have an operation do you think you could find me a nice hot cup of sweet tea?' she asked Patrick. 'It's supposed to be good for shock and I can't stop shaking.' He went off, glad to be useful, and she gritted her teeth while the nurse got her out of her clothes and properly into bed.

By the time Patrick came back with the tea, the effect of the painkiller had enabled her to think of things apart from the agony in her leg.

'Patrick, what are we going to do about the children's holidays?' she asked, sipping tea. 'They're due home next week.'

'We'll manage somehow,' said Patrick, but he didn't look very certain how. 'You're not to worry.'

'They're going to have a terrible Christmas,' she said. He didn't disagree with her, nor did he have any suggestions to make. He just sat beside her, trying to look sympathetic and, she had to admit, handsome. He had discarded his pink coat and hunting boots and put on a green Husky over his hunting shirt and breeches. He was muddy and his dark hair was plastered to his head in places where his cap had been. But he was so long and lean and graceful lounging on the end of her bed that several of the nurses stopped to take a second look as they passed.

'What are we going to do, Patrick?' she asked. 'About Christmas?'

'I don't know,' he said.

'Christ, can't you ever use your initiative?' she demanded, annoyed with him, with herself, with the pain in her leg, with this crisis which had fallen upon them out of the blue.

'God, Debs give me time.' He got up off the end of the bed. 'What do you expect me to do? Conjure Mary Poppins out of the sky?'

'Oh, Patrick, please don't be cross,' she moaned. 'Not now. It's all my own silly fault for being so stupid, I know.'

'There now, Debs, you mustn't blame yourself.' He stroked her face awkwardly. 'It's all been a bit of a shock, and I was too worried about you to think of anything else, but I'll come up with something, I promise you.'

If only she could believe him, she thought, moving restlessly to try to ease the aching leg. The nurse came and shooed him away. They were going to set up the traction. Patrick looked relieved to be going. He was no good at hospitals and emotions, thought Deborah wistfully, wishing that just for once Patrick might show a little more resourcefulness.

It was a long, long night for Deborah, lying on her back with her leg suspended by pulleys, reliving the accident and cursing herself for having been so careless. She slept fitfully until the painkilling injections wore off, then she lay awake worrying about her leg, about the children, about Christmas.

There was so much to do. She had hardly started getting ready. Patrick was hopeless. He couldn't possibly manage on his own. What he needed was somebody living in. But who? Not Jenny. She was too young and would have her hands full anyway with the horses and the children's ponies. Besides, she had a boyfriend of her own. She wouldn't want to spend Christmas looking after Patrick and the children. Caroline? For a moment in her desperation Deborah considered asking her sister to come to the rescue. But Caroline was a delegator, not someone you could leave to cope on her own. Besides, the children would never stand for it. Caroline, never having had children to disrupt her life and spoil the best laid plans, was far too well organised. Who then? Someone who knew how to look after children who was free at Christmas? The trouble with Christmas was that everybody would be busy with their own families. Sometime in the grey light of dawn Deborah had a brilliant idea. Kate! Kate had children of her own; she would know how to cope with them all at Christmas; she was a good cook. Caroline could have Daddy to stay – she wanted him anyway – and Kate would be free to look after them all at home. Deborah drifted off to sleep feeling slightly less desperate. She would telephone Kate first thing in the morning.

When Kate got the telephone call she almost laughed, the tables had been turned so completely. If she had wanted revenge she had it now, she thought, as Deborah pleaded with her to go and live with Patrick for Christmas. She was tempted, but her better self told her to refuse.

'I couldn't possibly,' she said.

'Why not? You're not doing anything for Christmas.' Deborah's voice was weak but insistent. 'You're not going to Saudi, are you?' The pips went. 'Damn these hospital call box things.'

The line went dead and Kate tried to collect her scattered wits. She ought to run away to Saudi, she thought, before it was too late. Invite herself, force herself on Alan if need be. The telephone began to ring again. She picked it up.

'Kate, you've got to help me out,' Deborah begged. 'The children are due home next week.'

'What about your father? Who's going to look after him over Christmas?' She was trying to think, to be sensible, to produce some plausible excuse, while all the time her rebellious mischievous self was leaping for joy.

'Daddy can go to Caroline. She's longing to have him, and he'd hate it with us, without regular meals bang on time, and the children always making so much noise. Kate, please will you do it? Patrick can't possibly manage on his own and I'm going to be on this horrible traction thing for a whole fortnight. The children will have such a miserable Christmas.'

'I don't know,' said Kate. Oh God, lead me not into temptation. 'I'll have to think about it.'

The Colonel came into the kitchen. 'Is that Debs?' he said. 'I want to speak to her.' Thankfully Kate relinquished the telephone, her mind in a whirl.

'How's the horse?' he demanded brusquely. 'The horse all right? Thank God for that. Your leg will mend but if it had been the horse they'd have had to shoot him . . .'

Kate fled, leaving him to commiserate with his daughter. She walked out of the house, across the yard to the stables, with some idea of hiding in her flat. The Colonel never came to her flat. He respected her right to privacy. Bella gave a nicker of welcome as she entered the stables. Kate was touched. She went to the mare's box and stroked the soft nose, while her mind darted about in ever-decreasing circles. How could she possibly go? It would be madness. How could she not? What excuse could she give? Bella poked about her pockets hopefully but Kate had no Polos to give her this morning. Then the mare pricked her ears and nickered again, as the Colonel appeared.

'Well, that's all settled,' he said, beaming at Kate. 'I've said you can go and look after them all.'

'What about you?' she asked.

'It's better I go to Caroline and John. I don't want to but I'll do it to help poor old Debs out.'

For once Kate didn't feel exasperated at the way he took decisions without regard to any other people's feelings. But she had to make one last attempt to square her conscience. 'Why don't you come with me too? Help me look after Patrick and the children?'

He shook his head, smiling at her. 'No, no, you'll have enough on your hands. Much better that I go to Caroline's. She was quite put out the other day when I said I'd rather stay at home here with you.'

He wasn't entirely selfish, she thought, pleased to discover a chink in his armour.

Deborah watched the nurse wheel away the telephone contraption, relief flooding through her. Christmas was Kate's problem now. Patrick and the children were taken care of. She lay back on the pillows, exhausted by the effort of struggling with the hospital's antiquated telephone system, strung up as she was by the leg like some poor turkey ready for Christmas. All she had to do was lie back and let the drugs and the nurses help her through the pain.

When Patrick came to see her he seemed completely stunned when she told him what she'd arranged.

'Kate didn't want to come at first,' she explained. 'But Daddy said not to worry. He'll fix everything.'

'I've brought you a nightie and things,' he said, dumping a small holdall on the bed.

She winced. He was looking so strange she wondered for a moment whether he'd surpassed himself and made other arrangements already. 'What's the matter, Patrick? Don't you think I've been clever getting Kate? Or have you come up with a better plan?'

'No I haven't, and yes you've been clever.' He was busy stuffing the contents of the bag into the locker beside her bed. She couldn't see his face and so she didn't know whether he was pleased or not. 'When's she coming?'

'I don't know. Daddy's bringing her in today to see me so I can give her her instructions.'

'Kate's not a servant, Debs,' he said, straightening up.

'She's Daddy's housekeeper, isn't she?'

'I don't know what her relationship with your father is,' he said. 'But she's certainly no ordinary housekeeper.'

'Well, maybe not,' she admitted grudgingly, 'and I'm not at all sure she doesn't have designs on him. It doesn't much matter. Daddy's prepared to spare her over Christmas and that's all I care about.' He was looking rather grim she thought. 'You will be nice to her, won't you, Patrick?'

He laughed. 'Oh yes, darling I'll be nice to her.'

Deborah had a sudden qualm. Was she being a complete fool? She tried to remember whether Kate was pretty, but she couldn't visualise her at all. She was sure she'd have noticed if she'd been pretty. She consoled herself with the thought that Kate would be kept far too busy to have time for any of that sort of nonsense and that three boisterous children were the best chaperones in the world.

Kate and the Colonel arrived later on that morning. Kate sat down on a chair beside the bed and produced a pencil and paper. She'd nice legs, thought Deborah. Damn. Kate scribbled down all Deborah's instructions in a most efficient manner and hardly asked any questions at all. When Deborah asked her how soon she could come she seemed worried about having to leave the Colonel before he went to London. They argued it out between them, Kate sitting on one side of the bed and the Colonel standing shouting at her on the other. Deborah lay back and studied Kate carefully. No bosoms. Patrick was a bosoms man. She was pretty in a way, though, but her face lacked any remarkable features, and her hair would soon need restreaking. Deborah could see quite a bit of root and it could do with another cut. She was beginning to show signs of having been away from London for too long. Definitely too fragile and towny to be Patrick's type. Deborah stirred restlessly. Kate and her father were behaving the way people always did when they visited the sick, talking to each other and ignoring the poor corpse they'd come to visit lying in the bed.

Did Patrick *have* a type? Deborah wondered. He didn't really go for other women except, she remembered with a pang, that old flame from his youth. Kate and Daddy seemed to be on very familiar terms with each other, Deborah thought, watching them with aggrieved detachment. Maybe there was something going on between them after all?

'Right then,' said the Colonel, when he and Kate had come to the end of their discussion, 'it's agreed. Kate comes to you the Friday before Christmas and I'll go back to London with Caroline on the Saturday after hunting. So now we'll be off. No good wearing out the patient. I always believe in keeping hospital visits to half an hour at the very maximum. You got anything more you want to ask, Kate?'

'No, I don't think so,' Kate replied, getting quickly to her feet.

She seems ill at ease, thought Deborah. I wonder why. Is it Daddy? As she waved them off, Deborah felt very alone and miserable. It would be perfectly horrible if Daddy was to fall in love with Kate. Caroline thought it impossible but Deborah wasn't so sure. Perhaps it was just as well Kate was going to be working her butt off at home and not alone with Daddy. Christmas was a very special time, it had a magic all of its own. It could go to a girl's head. Suddenly Deborah began to wonder what Ned Jones did at Christmas. He had promised to come but he hadn't done a thing – neither visited nor telephoned to find out how she was. Deborah felt more miserable than ever.

A nurse was coming down the ward.

'Do you think you could bring back that telephone thing again?' Deborah asked. She had to speak to Ned. At least thank him for what he did for her yesterday.

It took some time to get through to him and when she did all she could think of was her disappointment.

'You didn't come yesterday,' she reproached him. 'You promised.'

'Of course I didn't come.' His voice, vibrant and at the same time comforting, made her tingle. 'I didn't want to run into your husband. I was waiting for you to tell me when the coast was clear.' Immediately she felt better. He hadn't forgotten all about her. He was anxious to see her but worried about meeting Patrick. He wouldn't be worried about that if he didn't fancy her.

'I know,' she said. 'It's difficult. I'll try and find out when he means to come again and then I'll ring you.'

The pips went before he could reply. Damn National Health hospitals, she thought, but perhaps it was just as well. Already her relationship with Ned Jones had entered a new phase. They were conspiring together to deceive her husband, always the first step towards having an affair. A delicious shiver of excitement ran through her. What am I thinking about?

she reproached herself. I can't have an affair with him. Of course she couldn't. Certainly not with a broken leg. She sank back on to her bed of nails with a sigh. There's no earthly way I can get up to anything while I'm like this, she thought disconsolately.

# *Chapter 11*

'Poor old Deborah,' said the Colonel, taking Kate's arm as they left the hospital. 'It's a wretched thing to have happened to her just before Christmas.' He was leaning on her as if she'd been a thumbstick, as they walked across to the car park. He wanted to be courteous but he couldn't help it that he was old. He escorted her round to the passenger side of his old Volvo estate and opened the door for her.

'Are you sure you wouldn't like me to drive?' she asked.

'No thank you, Kate,' he said, and she knew there was nothing she could say that would persuade him. The only time he let her drive him was if he'd had a drink. She slid in and he closed the door for her.

They drove home in silence; it was impossible to have a conversation with the Colonel when he was driving. He was too deaf to hear above the noise of the engine and tended to turn round and take his eyes off the road in order to concentrate on what his passenger was saying. With her hands clenched on the door handle ready for a quick exit, and her feet pressed permanently on imaginary pedals, Kate tried to forget the Colonel's driving and think instead about the problems that lay ahead.

She too had felt sorry for Deborah lying in bed with her leg trussed up like that. But as she sat there scribbling down Deborah's instructions, she had been too overwhelmed by the sheer unreality of it all to be able to concentrate on what Deborah was saying. She realised now that there were all sorts of questions she hadn't had the wit to ask at the time. She didn't even know if there was a Christmas pudding or where the turkey was to come from. Let's hope Patrick knows some of the answers, she thought, and felt a huge surge of guilt and excitement. Patrick should never have agreed to such a mad scheme. It was totally irresponsible. But that was what made him so irresistible. He was mad, he was irresponsible and he was terribly, terribly attractive. She didn't know how on earth she was going to keep him at arm's length all over Christmas. She became aware that the Colonel was looking at her questioningly.

'I'm sorry,' she said. 'What did you say?'

'I said how are you going to get your Christmas things out to Saudi in time? Do you want me to see if John can get them sent out in the Diplomatic Bag? John's got a lot of friends in high places. I could get him to lean on a Foreign Office minister.'

'Yes!' she shouted, desperate for him to stop turning round to peer at her and concentrate on his driving. 'That would be kind.' She realised with another pang of guilt that she hadn't even bought presents yet for Alan and the children. Alan had remained obstinately silent and she supposed that subconsciously she wanted to punish him for sulking by being late with his Christmas present. But of course it wasn't fair to punish the children too. She had had some half-hearted idea of going up to London to catch her daughter at the airport as she flew out to Saudi. She thought it would be so much easier to explain to Naomi face to face why she couldn't come to Saudi for Christmas. But now that was out of the question. She would just have to ring her instead.

When Kate rang her daughter in Edinburgh later on that day and broke the news that she wouldn't be with them for Christmas, Naomi sounded every bit as disappointed as Kate had feared.

'Christmas won't be Christmas without you, Mum,' she said.

'I know, darling, and I shall miss you too.' Kate felt warmed. It was good to be wanted by one's children at Christmas. 'Colonel Beamish is trying to arrange for your presents to be sent out in the Diplomatic Bag. Is there anything special you want? I'm going shopping tomorrow.'

'Goodness, Mum, you are moving in smart circles. Are you sure you're not getting too grand for us? Is that why you don't want to come for Christmas?'

'Of course not, darling. It isn't that I don't want to come – I do – but it's just I've got to help these people out. The children are much younger than you are and they'll be missing their mother too.'

'And Dad, you'll miss Dad too – won't you?' Naomi persisted.

'Of course I'll miss Daddy, darling. I miss him all the time – be sure and tell him that, won't you?'

'Mum, you and Dad are all right?' The uncertainty in her daughter's voice made Kate feel terrible. 'You haven't had a row or anything?'

'Don't be silly, darling, of course we haven't had a row. Be sure and tell him that I would have come for Christmas if I could.'

She wondered what Alan would make of that. Would he take it as an admission of defeat or an olive branch? Naomi now seemed reassured and Kate listened to her happy chatter, glad that she had settled into university, that she was so well adjusted and positive. She doesn't really need me any more, she thought, and was not sad but proud.

'Get Daddy to ring me on Christmas Day,' she said, and gave her the Bray-Smiths' number. Would Alan do it, she wondered, or would it be too much for his pride? If he doesn't, I'll have to ring him, she thought. I've made my point. I can afford to be conciliatory now. But she hoped Alan would ring first. It was important that Patrick knew her husband cared.

Kate spent the best part of the next day in the spa town of Speenleham doing her Christmas shopping. The town was decked out with Christmas lights and little trees and very tasteful decorations. Every shop had 'O Come All Ye Faithful' *sotto voce* in the background. Kate wondered just how many unfaithful spouses were spending too much money on Christmas presents to assuage their uneasy consciences. By the time she returned to the peace and tranquillity of The Court she was laden down with parcels, feeling decidedly frayed around the edges and a great deal poorer.

'You're trying to buy your way out of trouble, Kate my girl,' she told herself ruefully, spreading all the presents out on her bed and wondering what Alan would make of the beautiful silk dressing gown she had bought him. It was wildly extravagant and Noël Cowardish and quite unlike the sort of thing he usually wore. Alan was astute enough to guess that she was in trouble with her conscience. Would it do him good, she wondered, and, if so, would he come rushing back from Saudi to see what she was up to? Was that what she wanted? I don't know, she thought, wrapping up the dressing gown carefully in Christmas paper. I don't know. She wrote a loving message and tied it to the parcel.

Was Patrick the symptom of something wrong in her marriage or was he the disease itself? God, she thought, I mustn't let him trample all over me. I've learnt to stand up to the Colonel, surely I can stand up to his son-in-law too?

With some such thought in mind she refused to let the Colonel bundle her off early on the day she was to go to look after Patrick and the children. Always in the past Patrick had kept her waiting anxiously by the telephone for his call. Now she wanted to keep him waiting for once. She wanted him to be wondering where she'd got to, to be worried in case she'd changed her mind and decided not to come. So she told the Colonel that she would give him lunch before she left and made him his favourite mince and mashed potatoes and swede, followed by baked custard. He was pleased, she could tell, although he kept looking at his watch and saying that she ought to be getting off. He had wanted to come with her to show her the way but she had dissuaded him. Things would be difficult enough meeting Patrick in his own home without having to worry about her self-assertive employer. So he gave her instructions how to find Puddleworth.

'The Manor, Patrick's house, is the biggest in the village, you can't miss it,' he told her.

As she was getting into her car he fished inside his coat pocket and produced a small package. 'For you,' he said. 'Happy Christmas, Kate.'

She thanked him, enormously moved and touched. She hadn't expected him to give her anything.

'I was hoping to be able to give it to you on Christmas Day, but it's not to be. You look after those grandchildren of mine and don't stand any nonsense from any of them.'

'I'll do my best, I promise.' Then, because he was looking a little sad and she was afraid he might make some embarrassing confession of need in a moment of weakness, she said: 'You'll be kind to Caroline, won't you? Don't bite her head off just because she does things differently. Remember it means a lot to her having you for Christmas.'

'No need to tell me how to behave with my own children.' He glared at her with the customary challenge back in his eyes. 'Now be off with you. If you hang about here much longer it'll be dark before you get to Puddleworth and knowing you you'll never find it.'

She jumped into her car, glad that he was his usual commanding self again. As she drove away from The Court, with the dogs bounding down the drive after her in token pursuit, she felt a glow of quite unexpected pride. Only two months ago he had terrified the life out of her that first day. Now he thought enough of her to give her a Christmas present and he'd looked really sorry to see her leave. Of course, he was outrageously opinionated and tremendously selfish, but selfishness was a form of survival in the old and the Colonel was nothing if not a great survivor. She respected him for that and for the fact that he was interested in people. Although he ordered them about quite mercilessly, he treated everybody the same and was as concerned for the Murphys and others in the village as he was for his own family. She suspected that beneath his brusqueness there lurked quite a kind, thoughtful streak. In spite of everything she had grown very fond of the old rascal.

Puddleworth was a small village nestling in a tiny hollow almost surrounded by a sea of ploughed fields. Driving slowly through it, looking for the largest house, Kate espied a church with a little stumpy tower, opposite which was what looked like the old village school. She drove on past a triangular village green overlooked by a pub, and a timbered shack which looked a bit like an ancient air-raid shelter, but which purported to be a village hall. She came to a row of Cotswold stone terraced cottages, one of which appeared to be the post office. She was about to get out and ask for The Manor when she espied a set of important-looking white gates leaning open against an ivy-covered wall. She drove up a sweeping drive, at the end of which was a Georgian mansion in honey-coloured stone, whose perfect proportions quite took Kate's breath away.

She parked outside the front door, her heart beating a little quicker, got out and rang the doorbell. But there was no answer, no sign of life anywhere, not even the sound of dogs barking. Perhaps it was the wrong house. Well, there was only one way to find out. She tried the handle and found the door wasn't locked. Greatly daring, she went in and found herself in a large stone-flagged hall littered with school trunks, their half-unpacked contents spilling everywhere. It was the right house, she guessed, only where were they all? She stood in the hall wondering what to do, not wanting just to barge in and start snooping about. Perhaps the groom was somewhere around. Deborah had said that Jenny lived in a cottage in the village, but with a bit of luck she might still be at work in the stables.

Kate went outside and started wandering about. The garden was very old and manorial and well established. There was something which looked like wisteria all over the front of the house, some mature laurel bushes and a lovely magnolia tree. She glimpsed a kitchen garden and beyond it an orchard. The stables she found behind the house, a row of half-doors with several heads hanging over them watching her curiously. A large horsebox was parked in one corner and beside it a horse-trailer. From a box at the end came the sound of pop music. Kate felt relieved. Jenny must still be at work.

Two terriers and a long black lurcher came bounding out of the tack room and Kate stood still to let them investigate her. They seemed very friendly and she patted them, relieved that they had accepted her so easily. She hoped that Patrick's children would do likewise. She found Jenny in the tack room busy cleaning a pile of dirty saddles and bridles.

'They've all gone to visit Mrs Bray-Smith,' she said, when Kate had explained who she was. 'But the house is open. Why don't you just make yourself at home? They'll be back soon, I dare say. I'd come with you and show you round only I've got so much to do here, I haven't the time.' Kate thanked her and walked back into the beautiful silent house. So much for keeping Patrick waiting. Once again here she was hanging around, not knowing when he was going to put in an appearance. She stood in the big cluttered hall gazing about her curiously. Often she had longed to see where Patrick lived. When they were going out together all those years ago he had never once taken her home. Now she was here, at his wife's request to look after him over Christmas. She was going to have to be very, very careful, she thought, to remember that she was happily married to Alan and here because the Colonel wouldn't take no for an answer.

Where to start? she wondered, averting her eyes from the school trunks so obviously in need of attention. In a corner of the hall a Christmas tree stood all naked and forlorn, waiting to be magically transformed into the spirit of Christmas. It made Kate feel nervous. Christmas was such a time of tradition – every family had its different way of doing things. She didn't want to upset them when their mother's accident must have upset them already. Oh dear, it was all going to be so very, very difficult. The deep chimes of a grandfather clock made her jump. Perhaps the kitchen was the safest place to begin, and probably the most important. When Patrick and the children came back from the hospital they would want tea.

Kate began opening doors at random, looking for the kitchen, which she found leading out of the dining room. It had plainly been designed for family living. It had wall-to-wall fitted cupboards, an electric hob and oven as well as an Aga, a round table covered with a check oilcloth in a corner by the window and a cork floor, much warmer than the stone-floored kitchen at The Court. Prowling further, Kate discovered the inevitable row of hunting boots and hard hats, wellingtons, Barbours, dog baskets and deep freezes, washing machines and pulleys, housed in two big rooms off the kitchen, with a large bunker entirely filled with logs. How wonderful, she thought, to have so much space. She opened one of the deep freezes and found it stuffed with the contents of the kitchen garden, soft fruit, home-made ice cream, frozen vegetables. She opened the other deep freeze. Game, all plucked and cleaned and neatly labelled. Dog meat, bread – why did Deborah keep so much bread in the freezer? Kate prowled about opening cupboards and doors, getting increasingly curious. She found a larder well stocked with tinned food of every sort, and innumerable bottles of different sauces, sweet, sour and spiced. It was extraordinary what you could learn about someone from the contents of their kitchen. Obviously Deborah was a keen gardener – she looked a keen gardener – the sort of person who was content to spend all summer growing things and all autumn harvesting them. But not much of a cook. She relied on tinned food and bottled sauces to add instant flavour if her larder was anything to go by.

Enough of this, Kate told herself. Concentrate on the job in hand. What to give them all for supper tonight? Perhaps Patrick had bought something and left it in the fridge. She went back into the kitchen and opened the fridge but it looked as if a plague of locusts had been through it. There was nothing left worth eating. It was too late to defrost anything substantial for dinner. It would have to be fish. She rushed back to the freezer and rummaged through the various packages and found some frozen haddock and some prawns. A fish pie would do, there was a sack of potatoes in the larder. Eggs shouldn't be difficult. Patrick was a farmer, he must have eggs and milk presumably. She looked at her watch. It was five o'clock already. Forget supper – what about tea? She wondered if there was such a thing as a cake in the house. Was it too soon to start the Christmas cake? Where did Deborah say the Christmas cake was? She pulled out her notebook. The Christmas cake was with someone in the village called Sue, being iced. Definitely too soon to eat the Christmas cake. Kate hurried back to the larder remembering a cake tin she'd not investigated, feeling like a burglar. But, she reminded herself, she wasn't here to steal Deborah's husband. She was here because she couldn't get out of it. But if she'd known this would happen, would she have refused to go to Saudi with Alan? Was she trying to find herself or Patrick? She stood still in the middle of the kitchen clutching the cake tin, trying for the truth. Whatever it was, she didn't seem to be making much progress. Instead of finding herself, she seemed to be doing nothing but find her way around other people's kitchens in a hurry.

The tin contained the remains of a sponge going mouldy. It would have to be sandwiches. She got a loaf of bread out of the freezer and put it in the bottom of the Aga with a packet of butter. Then she sat down at the kitchen table and waited for them to thaw. Tomorrow she would do a mammoth shop in Waitrose. She would take the children and they could tell her what they liked to eat. No doubt they would have Christmas shopping to do as well. Then she could take them to see their mother in hospital and she could ask Deborah all the questions she'd forgotten to ask before. The children would make it all come right. She was going to make this Christmas work for them. It wasn't the children's fault that their mother was in hospital and their father had been unfaithful. It was up to her to see that they didn't suffer.

When Patrick arrived Kate had a pile of two kinds of sandwiches stacked up and the kettle just coming to the boil.

'What wonderful timing,' she said, avoiding his eye. 'Tea's ready.' Dogs and children piled into the kitchen, and Patrick introduced them. Fiona, the eldest, was thin and beautiful like a nervous thoroughbred, with her father's fine bones and mane of dark silky hair; Samantha was a bouncy plump child with pigtails, and Marcus, a pale little boy with Patrick's gangly frame and his mother's pugnacious nose and fair hair. They all just stared at Kate in silence.

'I made some tea,' she said. 'I expect you're hungry.'

'Tea!' said the tall thin one scornfully. 'I never eat tea – much too fattening.'

Samantha, who had seized a sandwich, paused with it halfway to her mouth. 'What's in them?' she asked suspiciously.

'Marmite,' said the boy, throwing a half-eaten sandwich to one of the terriers. 'Urgh, I hate Marmite.'

'Pay no attention to him, he's been sick all the way home,' said Patrick.

'I thought everyone liked Marmite,' said Kate, determined not to be put down. 'All the children I know love it.'

'Well, we don't and we're not *all* children,' said Fiona loftily. 'We're Bray-Smiths.'

Kate glanced at Patrick in mock despair, expecting him to retrieve the situation, but he wasn't looking at her.

'They're not all Marmite,' she told them. 'Some are honey.' Samantha looked at the pile of sandwiches rather wistfully but quailed beneath her sister's watchful eye.

'Here, Sheba, catch.' Marcus threw another sandwich at the lurcher, who caught it neatly in midair and wolfed it down.

'Come on, Kate,' said Patrick, choosing discretion as the better part of valour. 'I'll show you to your room.' She followed him thankfully out of the kitchen. 'Do you have any luggage?' he asked dutifully.

'It's still in the car.'

He got her suitcase out of the car and led her upstairs without another word. It occurred to her then that he might have been more horrified than she at this arrangement of Deborah's. Her heart sank. She didn't think she could cope with all the difficulties that lay ahead if Patrick didn't want her.

'I'm afraid I didn't get off to a very good start,' she said as she followed him along a corridor to a room at the end.

'Don't worry – it's not your fault.' He pushed open the door and dumped her case down. 'Marcus was sick on the way back. The girls were upset seeing poor old Debs strung up like a chicken. We're all of us exhausted at the very thought of Christmas – ' he glanced down at her mischievously – 'thank God you've come!'

Suddenly everything was all right again. She burst out laughing. 'It really is the most incredible coincidence.'

'Incredible luck,' he said pulling her towards him. But she leant away from him.

'I didn't come here because of you,' she said. 'I came because the Colonel and his daughter wouldn't take no for an answer.'

'I know,' he said, shaking his head and laughing with her. 'They're a very overbearing family. Poor Kate, you had no choice. You know what they say – when rape's inevitable – only I don't have to rape you, do I, Kate?' He kissed her before she could stop him.

'Are you mad?' she said struggling free.

'I think I am a bit mad,' he said, suddenly serious. 'Do you know what I thought when Deborah told me? I thought she'd taken leave of her senses. But then, of course, she doesn't know. Or does she? Is she trying deliberately to throw us together? Is she trying to tell us something?'

'The only thing somebody is trying to tell me is that we'd better go down before anyone gets curious,' Kate said, not wanting to think what might happen if Deborah knew.

'Have it your own way,' he said. 'You needn't think I'll force my attentions on you, not if you don't want me to. But it won't be easy for me.' He leant forward to open the door for her. 'And I don't believe it'll be easy for you either, Kate my darling,' he whispered into her ear as she slid past him.

He was dead right there, she thought, as she fled down the corridor. Everything was going to be far, far more difficult than she had imagined. But exhilarating. Christmas, which she had been rather dreading when she thought she was going to spend it alone with the Colonel at The Court, had suddenly become as exciting a prospect as when she'd been an innocent child still believing in Father Christmas.

The children were all slumped in front of the television in a small cosy room off the hall. All Kate's plans for the next day were thrown into disarray when she discovered that they were all going hunting.

'Then I'll just have to do the shopping without you,' she said, trying to keep the disappointment from showing. 'You'll have to tell me what it is you like.'

'Oh we like anything,' said Fiona, fixing her with a nasty knowing look. 'Except fish pie.'

'You won't even get fish pie if we can't get hold of some eggs and milk from the farm,' said Kate, needled. 'Which one of you is going to go?'

'There isn't any milk, there aren't any cows. Daddy isn't that sort of farmer,' Samantha said with a triumphant smirk. 'He only grows corn.'

'Well then, it looks as if you'll all have to go supperless to bed,' snapped Kate, all her earlier resolutions put to rout.

They regarded her gravely. Marcus's face began to crumple. Feeling guilty, Kate left them and went to find Patrick. She reminded herself that she was here to make Christmas a happy one for them. It was no good losing her cool this early at the first hint of opposition.

Patrick was in the kitchen on the telephone. She busied herself peeling potatoes until he finished, then told him about the lack of milk and eggs.

'You don't really need milk and eggs for fish pie,' he said absently, as he dialled another number.

'Maybe not,' she retorted, 'but if you're going hunting tomorrow you'll want breakfast, I imagine. Can't you go and milk somebody's cow?' He sighed and dropped the telephone on to its cradle with a clatter.

'I suppose I can see what the village shop can produce. They'll be closed but I'll give them a call.' He redialled and soon he was sweet-talking somebody called Yvonne into helping him out.

'See if she's got any bacon,' hissed Kate.

'That's all right then,' he said, hanging up. 'She's going to open up for us if we send someone round straight away.' He grinned at Kate, pleased with himself. 'Anything else I can do for you or can I get on with my telephoning? There's a lot to arrange before we go out tomorrow.'

'You can go round and fetch the stuff from your friend Yvonne,' she said, putting the potatoes on to boil and trying not to let that mischievous smile of his weaken her resolve.

'I'll send one of the children round,' he said, getting to his feet.

'While you're at it, will you send one of them in here to lay up the table for supper?' she said. 'I don't know where anything lives and I want to get the pie in the oven.' He went out and she thought it was unfair that any man should look so good in jeans and an old sweater and moccasins.

Supper that evening was not a success. Kate tried to find out what they wanted to do with the holidays and began by asking them if they had lots of parties.

'We don't go to parties,' they said and Kate might have felt sorry for them except that she was left in no doubt that parties were for lesser mortals. But they did eat her fish pie, demolishing it without comment, squabbling and arguing among themselves and ignoring Kate completely. Patrick made no attempt to breach the silences, but sat with *Farmers Weekly* propped up in front of him, reading as he ate. Kate couldn't understand why the children were being so beastly to her and wondered uneasily if they knew about Patrick and her, or perhaps sensed something. Somehow she was going to have to keep him at bay and it wasn't going to be easy. She wondered if there was a lock on her door. As soon as supper was over and the washing up done, she escaped to her room, leaving the children watching television. She didn't think it was part of her duties to discipline them as well.

There was no lock on her door. She unpacked, had a bath, and resisted the urge to douse herself with scent. If she did that she would be admitting that she wanted him to come to her room and, of course, he would not dare come, not with the children at home, and if he did she would send him away. No question. All the same, she lay awake a long time listening for creeping footfalls, all her senses alive and kicking with excited anticipation. But he didn't come and she told herself she was relieved.

Next morning was like a theatre backstage before a first night. Kate, cooking bacon, eggs and fried bread in the kitchen, tried in vain to ignore the tension. Samantha and Marcus wolfed their breakfasts down but Fiona pushed her plate away almost untouched. Patrick was just as bad as everyone else, wandering round the kitchen with his plate in his hand, trying to eat his bacon and eggs standing. The telephone kept ringing, the children darted in and out with frenzied demands for safety pins and hairnets and help with hunting ties.

'You're useless!' shouted Fiona as Kate referred her to Patrick over her tie. Biting back a bitter retort Kate tried to stay calm and eat her breakfast but then the groom, Jenny, came rushing in to say they ought to be leaving, and one of the ponies wouldn't load. Kate found herself standing outside in her apron and sneakers with a freezing wind whistling through her and a whip in her hand while an angry pony stood at the bottom of the ramp refusing to go into the lorry.

'Give him a tweak, Kate,' shouted Patrick, standing at the pony's head. She touched the pony's rump lightly with the whip's lash. The pony lifted a hind leg menacingly and she backed away. 'Harder,' he shouted without the slightest compunction. Jenny, on the other side of the pony, brought her whip down with a sharp smack. Both legs shot out backwards as the pony bucked and let fly. Kate felt there was a real danger of her ending up beside Deborah in hospital. That would be poetic justice, she thought, nervously. But the pony went in at last and the lorry with its excitable cargo disappeared down the drive.

'Is it always like this on hunting mornings?' Kate asked, still shaking, as Jenny prepared to follow in the horsebox with the other two ponies.

'It's not so bad when Mrs Bray-Smith's here,' said Jenny. 'She's the one knows how to calm them all down and of course it's the children's first day hunting this holiday. They'll be better when they're into it again. Fiona's got a new horse – and it's quite a big step going from a pony to a horse. I expect she's a bit nervous.'

'Why are they made to do it if they're nervous – it's cruel.'

'It's not cruel,' said Jenny, smiling at Kate almost pityingly. 'Conquering your own fear is a wonderful thing to learn when you're young. Gives you confidence. You'll see, they'll be cock-a-hoop when they come back tonight.'

'*If* they come back,' said Kate, not at all convinced. 'They might end up in hospital like their mother.'

From inside the trailer came the sound of impatient stamping.

'I'd better get off,' said Jenny, climbing into the Land Rover. 'Don't worry. They'll be all right. Lightning never strikes twice.' She drove off and Kate watched her disappear round the corner of the house, the trailer swaying, and the horses leaning against each other to balance themselves. She hoped Jenny was right, but she remembered that troubles also never came singly.

Later that morning Kate found the tension in Waitrose almost as bad. She wandered up and down the packed aisles feeling helpless and indecisive, wishing she knew what the children would like and remembering the three scornful faces who had spurned all her best efforts the previous day. Then she remembered they had eaten her fish pie in the end. It was all just a ploy to make her feel inferior. She began filling her trolley with the sort of things her own family enjoyed. If the Bray-Smiths didn't like it, too bad. Let them starve, she thought. When she had enough to get through the next few days she joined the queue for the checkout and whiled away the waiting with her favourite pastime of studying the contents of everybody else's trolley. They had Christmas piled high. Kate panicked as she thought of things like mince pies, stuffings for the turkey, crackers, brandy butter. Only four more shopping days to go and she hadn't begun to get to grips with anything Christmassy. Did Deborah have Brussels sprouts out of the garden or did she buy them? Was there cranberry sauce amongst all those bottles in the larder? It wasn't until she got to the checkout that she realised she hadn't arranged with Patrick about housekeeping money. Oh well, she would just have to pay and get him to reimburse her.

At least Patrick wasn't like the Colonel. He wouldn't argue over every item of expenditure.

She got back to The Manor and staggered in and out of the kitchen unloading her boxes one by one. At some stage Sheba, the lurcher, bounded past covered in mud and threw herself down in front of the Aga. The groom must have come back to collect Patrick's second horse and left the dogs loose in the stable yard. Kate collapsed into a chair with a cup of coffee and a Mars bar.

'What have you come to, Kate?' she asked herself, unwrapping the chocolate with guilty delight. She hadn't eaten a Mars bar since she was a spotty teenager, but today she was in need of sugary comfort.

She looked about her at the untidy kitchen. The lurcher had left a great lake of mud in front of the Aga, the table was littered with boxes laden with food, the cat came and jumped into her lap, sniffing the Mars bar delicately before curling up into a ball of purring fluff. Kate was conscious of a creeping sense of irresponsibility. It doesn't matter, the siren call of sloth sang in her ear. It's not your problem. It's not your house. It doesn't matter if it's a mess. She closed her eyes and must have drifted off because when she opened them the clock above the dresser said half-past three.

Guiltily Kate scrambled out of her comfortable chair. If she didn't get rid of all this stuff before they came back from hunting she'd never manage. Putting it all away took time, particularly as Kate didn't know where Deborah kept things. When she was finished she wasn't much the wiser. Deborah isn't one for order and logic, thought Kate a little smugly. The pots and pans were dotted about in various cupboards, the drawers were filled with all kinds of non-essential trivia, there were glasses muddled up with china and baking dishes, all lumped together in one place. The kitchen may have looked like something out of *Ideal Home* but inside the cupboards was more like Steptoe and Son.

By four there was still no sign of them. Caroline was always back home by four. Kate began to worry. Who would be looking after the three children when Patrick was busy looking after the field? Marcus was very young and vulnerable still. And what about Patrick leading them all over those enormous fences? To distract her mind, she went out into the hall where the trunks still spilled their contents on to the floor. Systematically she began sorting out the worst of the mess and took a pile of dirty clothes to put in the washing machine.

It was dark by the time she heard the crunch of tyres on the gravel outside and saw the lorry, followed by the Land Rover and trailer, pulling into the stableyard. She rushed outside to ask how they were but they were too busy getting the horses out to notice. They all seemed to be in one piece, so she left them to it and went back inside to put the kettle on. She laid the cake she'd bought in the middle of the table and a large squashy white loaf of bread by the toaster. She didn't know what they had when they came home from hunting but she had a horrible feeling it was probably quite a lot. Anyway, she wasn't going to make the mistake of doing sandwiches again.

They came piling in through the back door, chattering and laughing, four barely recognisable figures plastered from head to toe in mud.

'Heavens,' she said, recoiling in shock, 'you're filthy.'

'I know,' Patrick grinned at her. 'All that spit and polish this morning and now it's all to do again. Come on, you lot – boots off, breeches in the washing machine. You can leave your coats until after tea.' They began pulling off boots, stripping off dirty coats and breeches.

'Some bloody fool's put the washing machine on. What are we going to do with our breeches?' said Fiona, staring at the washing machine merrily twirling soapy water. Guiltily Kate scuttled back into the kitchen. It didn't seem as if she could do anything right.

'Chuck 'em on the floor.' That sounded like Samantha. 'I'm starving. What have we got for tea, Kate?' Samantha asked, coming into the kitchen in her shirt and knickers.

'What would you like for tea?'

'Boiled eggs – that's what we always have. I say, what a smashing cake.'

'And a new tin of biscuits – mmmm.' They came into the kitchen and crowded about the table helping her – a different bunch from the panic-stricken mob who'd left that morning. Kate, listening to them reliving the day, was struck by the animation in their faces. Her own children were never like this.

'How did the new horse go?' Kate remembered to ask Fiona.

'Starlight's brilliant. I fell off once and got run away with twice,' said Fiona.

'Oh dear.' Kate wasn't sure whether she was supposed to be impressed or sympathetic. 'You weren't hurt?'

'Course not. I had a wonderful day,' Fiona informed her. 'He's the best I've ever ridden.'

'Did you kill any foxes?' Kate couldn't resist asking. They paused; looked at each other.

'Did we, Daddy?'

Patrick smiled at Kate. 'You see what a blood-thirsty lot they are. They don't even know. Yes, we killed one fox. The one who's had Mr Waite's chickens three days in a row. He was pleased as punch.'

As soon as tea was over they all put on jeans and disappeared to the stables to help Jenny with the horses. Kate thought it might be a good time to tackle Patrick about the trunks still in the hall, the undecorated Christmas tree and other problems, but he was on the telephone apologising to some farmer whose cattle had jumped out.

'Difficult old bugger,' he said hanging up. 'I'll have to go round there with a bottle of whisky tomorrow.' She opened her mouth to ask about the housekeeping money but he was already telephoning again. Giving up, she went to see how the washing was going and was relieved to see that it had finished its cycle. She hung it up on the pulleys in the wash room thinking that however unmethodical the kitchen cupboards were, the washing arrangements had been very carefully thought out.

Just as she had put the breeches, ties and string gloves on a half load, Jenny came in. 'I usually put these numnahs in with the breeches,' she said. 'Oh well, perhaps you could do them when the breeches are finished.' She dumped a pile of what looked like imitation saddles on the floor.

'Whatever are those?' asked Kate, appalled.

'It's what the horses wear under their saddles to stop them getting sore backs,' Jenny explained. 'They're full of sweat and mud and have to be washed. They'll never dry before next hunting day if we don't put them in the machine.'

'When's the next hunting day?' asked Kate faintly.

'Christmas Eve – then they'll all want to go out again on Boxing Day. It's quite a job getting everything cleaned up in time.'

They're mad, Kate thought, staggering back to the kitchen. And I'm mad to be here.

Patrick was off the telephone, his long legs stretched out in front of him, lazily regarding her.

'What's the matter, Kate?'

'I think it's Christmas that's the matter,' she said. 'I thought I'd come here to help you give the children a proper Christmas but it's only four days away and we don't seem to be making any headway at all.'

'Christmas is for people who don't have anything to get them through the winter,' he said. 'People who are truly content don't need festivals. The only thing that's going to spoil Christmas for this lot is the weather.'

'What am I doing here, then?' she demanded angrily. 'You don't need me – what you need is a bloody workhorse.'

He laughed, not in the least put out. 'Don't be like that, Kate. You don't usually swear – it doesn't suit you.' He stretched out a hand and caught hold of her as she passed, pulling her on to his knee. 'Relax,' he murmured trying to nibble her ear. 'It'll be all right, you'll see.'

'Why do men always tell women to relax when what they really mean is submit?' she said, scrambling off in a resentful fury. 'I bet your wife swears all the time,' she added accusingly.

'She does,' he grinned at her mischievously. 'That's why I find you so restful to be with.'

It was useless, Kate thought. He wasn't going to help her at all. All he was going to do was try and make love to her and she didn't need that, not now. What she needed from him now was some sort of support. The telephone began ringing again. He picked it up and she went back to the more immediate problem of getting supper.

# *Chapter 12*

That night Patrick came to Kate's room. She was asleep, exhausted by the day's exertions and so dead to the world that when he slipped into her bed and started kissing her, she kissed him back instinctively as in a dream. She came alive gradually as he explored her body with his tongue and fingers and lips, responding to him with a relaxed sensuous ardour as her body outraced her sleepy mind until she woke to find her arms around his waist, her nightie somewhere round her ankles, and desire coursing through her like a raging torrent.

'No!' she gasped as he rolled over on top of her. 'I can't, we mustn't.'

'Mustn't what, darling?' he murmured.

She tried to protest but how could she when he was busy kissing her with those wonderful fragrant world championship kisses which turned her dizzy with desire? Somehow Patrick never spoilt things by lying too heavily on top of her. He managed to use his body, hands and lips to cover all the most urgently clamouring parts of her other men couldn't reach without squeezing the breath out of her. Deftly he slipped inside her and it felt good. Bloody marvellous in fact. So wonderful that when they tumbled together headlong into momentary bliss, she had to bury her face in his neck to stifle the cry of spontaneous joy. Then it was over, the last gasps of ecstasy smothered in the pillow, and they were reduced to just two satiated, satisfied, slippery bodies, panting and pressed close together in the narrow bed. He didn't ask her, as Alan did, how it had been for her. He didn't have to.

'Mmmm – nice.' She could hear the satisfaction in his voice as he ran the tips of his fingers down her spine.

'Don't do that.' She was fully awake now and already beginning to feel resentful of how he had taken advantage of her.

'But you love being stroked – it's one of the things that turns you on – you're such a sensual little kitten.'

'You shouldn't be here. You shouldn't have caught me unawares like that, it wasn't fair.' She wriggled out from under him, tried to distance herself, but it wasn't easy in a little bed made for one.

'You loved it, darling – no good trying to pretend you didn't – and I loved it too. So stop being so silly.'

'Patrick, you must understand. This has got to stop.' She sat up, pushed his hands away.

'You were happy enough to do it before. What's got into you now?'

'We weren't hurting anybody then. We were just having a bit of fun once a year. Until Deborah found out. Now it's different. The rules have changed. I've met Deborah, and I know your children and your father-in-law. They're real people. I can't go on betraying them all like this.'

'I don't know what's got into you, Kate,' he grumbled, getting out of bed. 'Women – you're all the same. Bloody temperamental.'

She stretched out a hand to him. Irrationally she didn't want him to leave her. They had been so close a moment ago, locked into a physical union so complete it was as if they were one person. Now she couldn't see his face in the darkness, had no idea what he was feeling.

'I'd better go.' He tiptoed across the floor, opened the door a crack, stood listening to the silent house and crept away.

Kate lay on her back in the darkness feeling forlorn. He might at least have kissed her good night. She stretched languorously, trying to recapture the feeling of pure joy she had felt that moment before climax. Then guilt assailed her and with it resentment. She ought to have been able to stop him, would have stopped him if she hadn't been taken unawares, been so thoroughly aroused before she was awake. She had been betrayed by her own rebellious body, and by Patrick, of course, who wouldn't take her protestations seriously. Somehow I've got to convince Patrick that whatever it was between us is finished, she thought. Stop him taking my ready compliance for granted. She switched on the light and began resentfully straightening out the tangled bedclothes. What really annoyed her was that Patrick seemed to think she had planned it all along. That he was just doing what she wanted – arrogant bastard. The thought surprised her; she wasn't used to thinking ill of him. I ought to have put a chair against the door or something, she thought bitterly. Then he might believe that I'm not chasing after him, that I'm here by chance, a malevolent turn of fortune's wheel. He seemed to believe that he only had to raise a finger and she'd come running. Well, she always had in the past, she thought, fishing about at the bottom of the bed for her discarded nightdress. If only he wasn't so bloody attractive physically.

She struggled back into her nightie, cursing herself for a fool. She would never convince Patrick that it was over until she had succeeded in convincing herself.

On Christmas Eve Patrick and the children went to the hospital to visit Deborah. They had come back from hunting early as a gale was blowing and the scent was hopeless. Kate was left alone, happy to have the kitchen to herself with time to stuff the turkey, make the brandy butter and get well ahead so that Christmas Day would be fun for everybody. Somehow she seemed to have caught Christmas at last, even if it had been like running after a departing bus and hurling herself on it at the last possible moment. Without her knowing quite how, the Christmas tree had got decorated. The Christmas cake appeared, brought by Sue, and the school trunks vanished from the hall.

Sue was a treasure, married to Jack, one of Patrick's two farm men, and she had helped out at The Manor as nanny, cleaner and willing slave ever since the children were born. It was to Sue that Kate had confessed the difficulty she was having finding out how Deborah usually did things.

'Every family has its traditions at Christmas, its special way of doing things,' Kate confided. 'I just don't want to upset any of them by getting it wrong. But nobody seems to want to tell me what their traditions are.'

'Don't you worry about them, Kate.' Sue, on her hands and knees scrubbing the kitchen floor, had sat back on her ample haunches. 'Just you keep the food coming and the washing machine going and your sense of humour, and Christmas will look after itself.'

Kate had tried to take Sue's advice, although she found it difficult at first. She was used to having to find entertainment outside the home for her own children but the Bray-Smiths were busy all the time. At no stage did they ever say, 'We're bored, what can we do?' Kate began to understand why they didn't want parties. Hunting was all the social life they needed, all their friends hunted and the time they spent with each other on the hunting field was far longer than other children spent meeting at parties. When they weren't out hunting or in the stables with their ponies, they applied themselves to Christmas. Their shopping was done one afternoon on the way back from visiting their mother in hospital; but they spent hours threading holly leaves and ivy together and making long streamers which they hung in great loops down the staircase, and around the hall. Kate had been charmed to find that Christmas seemed to be a uniquely village affair, decorating the church, reading the lessons in the carol service, singing carols around the village with half the villagers while the other half stayed at home to listen. What seemed like the entire village population had ended up drinking mulled wine and wolfing mince pies in The Manor. It was all very different, very satisfying and she was at the hub of it.

Now Kate finished stuffing the turkey and sewed it up with neat deft stitches. Christmas wasn't the problem any longer, she thought, admiring her handiwork. The problem was that she was beginning to enjoy it all far too much, to forget that she wasn't mistress of this splendid house, to relish Jenny's friendly help, and depend on Sue's indefatigable labour, even to rearrange the cupboards so that they were more to her own way of doing things, for heaven's sake. The problem was she was beginning to feel as if she belonged here.

By the time Patrick got back with the children from the hospital Kate was ready and waiting for them. She'd got roast pheasant and treacle tart for dinner and planned to have it in the dining room in candlelight. She'd lit the log fire and laid the table with the best silver. She'd even had time to bath and wash her hair and put on a flared skirt of soft fawn suede and a black mohair jumper which set off her pale colouring to advantage.

'Wow!' exclaimed Fiona. 'That's a dreamy skirt. Can I have one like it, Daddy?'

'God, no. It looks far too expensive for the likes of me. You'll just have to be content with what Father Christmas sends you.'

'Daddy, don't be stupid.' Fiona was looking puzzled and it amused Kate to think that she still hadn't come to terms with her role in their lives. The children knew that Kate was not a servant, yet Fiona couldn't accept that she could be financially independent, perhaps with more money to spend on clothes than she herself had. Nobody was better off than the Bray-Smiths. It went without saying.

'Your father's quite right, Fiona,' Kate told her. 'It cost me a great deal of money and I've had it quite a long time already. I'm sure you wouldn't want to spend that sort of money on something you might be tired of in a week.'

'Fiona knows quite well that little horse of hers cost me a fortune.' Patrick didn't seem particularly grateful for Kate's support. 'And she has a very generous clothes allowance. What she chooses to do with it is her own affair.' Fiona was looking mulish and so Kate quickly asked how Deborah was.

'Poor Mummy, all alone and in bed for Christmas,' said Samantha tearfully. 'It isn't fair.' Kate tried her best to cheer everybody up but it was plain that they were depressed by the visit to the hospital. They wolfed down the wonderful dinner she had made for them, but there wasn't much Christmas cheer around the table. When she asked if anybody was going to church that night they all declared they were far too sleepy to stay up until midnight, and besides they wanted to watch *The Wizard of Oz* on the telly. Patrick, when appealed to, said they could all go to church on Christmas morning. It didn't seem to occur to him that Kate might not have time to go in the morning. She knew from past experience that on Christmas Day the hours between breakfast and noon would mysteriously vanish and that amid the general celebrations and present openings and animal husbandry, the turkey would not cook itself, nor the Christmas pudding miraculously boil for the requisite number of hours, and that unless she stayed at home and in control of the kitchen chaos would break out like bubonic plague. It was years since she'd been to church on Christmas morning. She liked to savour the spirituality of Christmas at night, when there was time to relax and listen to the Christmas message without her concentration being ruined by thoughts of birds being basted and oven temperatures being too high or too low and all the other myriad troubles a wife and mother's flesh is heir to on Christmas Day.

I too have my own special Christmas traditions, she thought stubbornly as she cleared away the debris of dinner. If nobody wants to go tonight I shall just have to go on my own.

Kate went upstairs to get ready for church in plenty of time, just in case Patrick might have a sudden change of heart. When she came down, well wrapped up in her warm calf-length coat and fur hood, the children were glued to the television, Patrick slumped in front of the fire, with the lurcher stretched out at his feet and one of the terriers curled up on his knee. He made no move to accompany her.

'Don't you think you ought to see they go to bed?' she admonished him. He grunted and she left him nodding off over his whisky. It wasn't her responsibility, after all. Let them stay there all night if they wanted. Disappointed, annoyed with him and even more with herself for being so, she set off for the church alone.

She hadn't realised it was so windy until she was outside the house. Walking quickly down the drive, she was buffeted by great gusts and could hardly hear the church bells above the roaring of the wind. In the wavering beam of her torch she could see that already some quite sizeable branches had come down in the drive and she looked up anxiously at the wildly thrashing trees above her head, praying that the Good Lord would not choose this moment to smite a sinner on her way to repentance. By the time she reached the church, thankful to have arrived safely, she was quite out of breath. The church was a twelfth-century Cotswold stone gem, small, compact and reassuringly solid. Tonight it was darkly mysterious, lit only by candles and the twinkling fairy lights on the Christmas tree beside the altar. Someone thrust a hymn book and service booklet into Kate's hand and she peered about her uncertainly, wondering where she should sit. She knew, from her occasional visits to the church in Little Riddleton, that there was a fiercely guarded precedence concerning everything in small country churches, all the more inviolable in that it was unwritten and explained. Villagers sat at the back, the squire's family at the front. Others less pigeon-holed socially settled for somewhere in between and usually managed to upset somebody before establishing their own squatters' rights to a pew. Tonight, however, Kate could see that anarchy had broken out and that numbers had conquered tradition. Strangers had strayed unwittingly into the Bray-Smiths' pew in the front and even if Kate had wanted to take advantage of her association with The Manor, there was no room for her there. So she crept round to the side transept where the last few pews still had a gap or two left, wondering what Patrick would have done had he been with her.

He might have come. The thought took her unawares, springing from her subconscious to pounce upon her carefully suppressed emotions. The church was so romantic in the candlelit dark. The congregation was hushed, expectant. The atmosphere was so charged with the elusive magic of Christmas Kate desperately needed someone to share it with. She knelt down to say her prayers, but she couldn't concentrate. If he had the slightest, teeniest scrap of feeling for me, he'd have come, she thought sadly. It had always been like this. She had been the one wanting commitment from him, he the one holding off. There was a pattern to every relationship and that pattern never changed, no matter how much circumstances altered.

'There's one who does the kissing and the other who holds the cheek.' Corny but true. With Patrick it's me who does the kissing, she thought with a pang, as she got up from her knees. But with Alan it's the other way round. I know where I am with Alan, which is why our marriage has been such a success. The thought of Alan made her feel guilty. She and Alan always went to Midnight Mass together on Christmas Eve and came away at peace and quietly mystified by the magic of it all. Were they missing her? she wondered. Had they got their presents? How were they celebrating Christmas in the heat and the dust of Saudi?

She tried to relax and feel holy but found it difficult to concentrate on the sermon. Why is it, she thought, trying to control her wandering thoughts, that the best sermons only seem to be delivered when two or three are gathered together? You would have thought that with the church filled to overflowing for about the only time in the year a priest might rise to the occasion and convince some of these people that it was worth coming more often. But they never seemed to. Perhaps priests too were worn out with the pressure from Christmas.

Communion took a long time. Kate, sitting waiting for her turn to join the queue of people at the altar, recognised several who lived in the village, but there were many more who plainly didn't. Some were dressed in jeans, others in evening dress, a few carried babies, one young couple were kissing and cuddling and had eyes only for each other, a severe case of Christmas fever. But although they didn't live in Puddleworth now, they clearly all had at some time and they had come back to the village with their wives or husbands or sweethearts to be with their families at Christmas. There was a sense of family pride about them all which made Kate feel the more alone. What am I doing here? she wondered as she knelt at the altar rail. Do I want to be Patrick's wife and live in his beautiful house and be part of this tightknit community? It was a question she only dared ask herself because confessing her sins – 'The remembrance of them is grievous unto us; The burden of them is intolerable' – had left her feeling exposed to His Wrath and Indignation. No good asking for God's mercy in triplicate and then not seeking after truth.

Of course I don't want to be married to Patrick, she thought, getting up from her knees and making her way back to her pew. I just want to belong too. I don't really belong in London, she thought suddenly. I don't miss our home in Fulham at all. I just put up with it all those years to please Alan. I'm good at putting up with things. It was why, she supposed, she was not more of a success.

Communion over, the congregation rose for the final carol.

O come all ye faithful
Joyful and triumphant
O come ye O come ye
To Bethlehem.

Kate sang it with none of the pleasure she usually felt at this part in the service. How many times had she heard that much-abused carol pumping out of supermarket and radio station and shopping mall? The familiar tune had been a kind of reproach which she'd come to dread. Christmas is coming and I'm not ready. Now it was being sung in churches all over the land proclaiming Christmas Day and it was the words which reproached her. 'O come all ye faithful.' But I haven't been faithful, thought Kate as guilt threatened to overwhelm her. I'm an imposter, masquerading as a ministering angel. I should be out in Saudi being a good wife and mother instead of trying to douse the flames of a rekindled romance.

The wind seemed stronger when they came out of church. People were standing about in little groups wishing each other Happy Christmas and worrying about the weather.

Kate didn't linger. The wind was frightening in its power. It was quite a struggle to walk the few hundred yards back to The Manor and she was relieved when she was safely back indoors again. The house was quiet, the dogs sleeping in their baskets in the kitchen. Even the cat was curled up beside the Aga. No living thing would be out in such a wind if it didn't have to be.

Kate turned out the lights. It would have been nice if Patrick had waited up for her – to wish her a Happy Christmas. Arrogant and selfish, she told herself firmly as she mounted the stairs. But perhaps he was waiting for her in her room. Asleep perhaps in her bed. Ever since that night when he'd caught her unawares she'd put a chair under the door handle. She wondered if Patrick knew about the door. He certainly had never said anything, although occasionally she had caught him looking at her in a knowing kind of way, amusement in his eyes. Had he tried it and given up, or having got what he wanted, had he had enough for a bit? She would love to know, but of course she was determined to resist him. She just didn't know how she was going to do it if she found him in her bed.

Patrick wasn't there. Kate got undressed and into bed and lay listening to the wind howling round the house. Every now and then it rose to a roar, like a great tidal wave racing down upon the poor puny little house from afar. Then The Manor would shake just a little and Kate would tremble in her warm bed. The wind was never like this in London. At some stage she realised she'd forgotten to put the chair against the door. It was too bad. She wasn't going to get out of bed now. She was just drifting off to sleep when she became aware of the door opening. She sat bolt upright in the dark and opened her mouth to tell Patrick to go away as a small pyjamaed figure crept into the room.

'Kate?' The young voice was a bit quavery. 'The house is shaking – do you think it's going to blow away, like the one in *The Wizard of Oz*?'

Marcus! She was out of bed in the instant.

'Of course not, darling,' she soothed, putting her arms around him. 'That was just a silly film.' As if to contradict her, there was a great roaring from the wind and the windows rattled alarmingly as the house shook. She hugged him tightly.

'Dorothy's house blew away and the Wicked Witch nearly got her,' he said.

'That was in America where they have tempests and hurricanes. This is just a little gale.'

'It feels just like a tempest,' Marcus said as the wind screeched in agreement outside the window. 'Can I stay with you until it's all over?'

'If you like,' she said. He snuggled down beside her and she wondered what she was going to do if Patrick decided to visit her. Thinking it unlikely she closed her eyes and tried to sleep, but then again the door was opening and behind the wavering beam of a torch she saw a familiar pair of muscular legs. Patrick!

'Here's Daddy come looking for you, Marcus,' she announced loudly, reaching out a hand to switch on the bedside light. 'The electricity's gone off,' she said, dismayed when nothing happened.

'I'm not frightened.' The small voice from beneath the blankets was muffled and uncertain. Patrick swept his torch quickly round the room and over the bed.

'Daddy, you're not frightened of the storm too, are you?' asked Marcus, venturing to poke his head out from beneath the bedclothes.

'Of course not. I just came to see if Kate was all right. She's not used to storms like we are here. But I see she's got you looking after her.' To give him his due he had plenty of presence of mind, she thought.

'You don't think a big tree will fall on the house and crush us all to pieces, do you?' Marcus asked.

'Of course not – there aren't any big trees near the house.'

Kate was relieved. It was something she had been worrying about for quite some time.

'Now come on, I'll take you back to bed. Kate's all right, aren't you, Kate, and there's not really room for two in that little bed.' He was grinning at her conspiratorially, but she couldn't be cross with him, not with Marcus listening to every word. He picked the child up in his arms.

'Stay with him until he goes to sleep,' Kate whispered. 'It's really very frightening, this wind.'

'If that's what you want,' he whispered back, and in spite of everything – her good resolutions, her disappointment in him, her guilt – she felt a surge of excitement. He had been coming to make love to her. God, it was going to be difficult not to give in again.

When Patrick had gone she groped about in the dark to find the chair to wedge under the door handle. Then, by this time shivering with cold and excitement, she jumped back into bed. But it was a long time before she finally fell asleep.

Kate awoke to a dark cold morning. The wind was still howling, the electricity was still off, and her bedroom was very cold. She peered at her watch and thought it said half-past nine. It couldn't be. She grabbed her dressing gown and slippers and hastily ran a comb through her hair. Outside in the corridor she paused to listen. Apart from the wind the house was very quiet. Were they all still sleeping? She remembered the happy family breakfast she had planned while they opened their presents before church. How could she have overslept on today of all days? She hurried downstairs filled with guilty alarm. In the hall she glanced at the Christmas tree. Without its twinkling lights, it looked rather forlorn. But at least the presents were still heaped up in a colourful pile at its foot. They hadn't started Christmas without her.

The kitchen was deserted but warm. The clock above the dresser also said half-past nine. Kate stood aimlessly warming herself in front of the Aga, wondering how she was going to get through Christmas without hot water, central heating, or electric lights. Surely there was something she ought to be doing about the crisis. Where were they all? In bed perhaps, staying out of the way until everything was back to normal? She picked up the telephone thinking there must be someone she could summon to their aid but the line was dead. Then she noticed that the kettle was warm and there was a mug of half-drunk coffee in the sink. Somebody must be up. Was it Patrick?

A woman suddenly appeared, walking into the kitchen from the back door. 'Good morning,' she said waving a Thermos. 'Happy Christmas. Do you think I could trouble you for some hot water for a cup of tea?'

'Of course,' stammered Kate. 'I'll put the kettle back on. It won't take long, it's only just boiled.'

'Aren't you lucky to have an Aga?' the woman said. 'Mine is an all-electric house, wonderfully labour-saving but hopeless in an emergency like this. I'm Jane Evering, by the way. I live in the house on the green.'

'Kate Hopegood,' murmured Kate.

'Oh, I know all about you,' Jane smiled, rather patronisingly, Kate thought. 'I think it's absolutely marvellous of you to come and look after them all while poor Deborah is in hospital.'

'Oh well,' said Kate vaguely, wondering what the woman would say if she knew the whole story.

'You don't mind, I hope, my barging in like this?' said Jane, sitting down at the kitchen table and making herself at home. 'I'm afraid I'm one of those people who just can't think until I've had my morning tea.'

'Not at all,' murmured Kate politely as the kettle came to the boil. 'Would you like a cup of tea to drink here and I can fill up your Thermos to take back with you for breakfast?'

'That would be very kind of you.' Kate made the tea and poured the woman a cup and then, not knowing what else to do, sat down at the table and poured one for herself.

'Such a terrible night,' Jane said, sipping tea. 'I was quite terrified and now here we are with no electricity and I don't know how we're to get our turkey cooked.' She looked meaningfully at Kate.

'Oh I expect they'll get it fixed soon,' said Kate.

'I very much doubt it, my dear.' The woman was quite adamant. 'The thing is that we who live in the country have to help each other out in crises like these. I remember one year not long after we came here we were cut off for a week with the snow piled up in roads so high nothing could get through. Patrick drove his tractor across the fields and brought a milk churn back. We were all queueing up with our little pitchers like medieval housewives.' The woman laughed, a little hysterically. Kate hoped Jane would feel better when she'd drunk her tea. 'Of course I don't expect you to understand coming as you do from London.'

'Well, I suppose in London it isn't often that a gale leaves everyone without electricity for more than an hour or two at the most,' conceded Kate.

'Here in the country the battle against nature is much closer to the front line,' the woman said, pouring herself another cup of tea. 'Survival is something we country dwellers learn to do for ourselves.'

Suddenly the children came bursting into the house. They were dressed in jeans and sweaters and gumboots and, from the bits and pieces of straw clinging to various parts of them, had obviously been in the stables.

'There you are,' Kate greeted them, relieved. 'I thought you were all still in bed.'

'We've been helping Jenny muck out,' said Fiona. 'Everything is all right at the stables, thank God, but there's a tree down in the village – it's right across the street. Daddy and the men are there now with the chain saw.'

Kate put the kettle on again and started making toast. Jane Evering was looking at her hopefully. Perhaps she ought to offer the woman breakfast. Jane got up and came to stand beside Kate.

'The thing is,' she said, almost confidentially, 'I was wondering whether I could bring my turkey round and pop it into your Aga. If you turn the heat up high it'll cook in the slow oven in plenty of time for tonight and you could use the hotter one for yours.' Kate was about to say that of course she didn't mind sharing the Aga, when she was forestalled by Samantha.

'What about Jack and Sue?' the child demanded. 'They haven't got an Aga. How are they going to get their Christmas dinner cooked?'

'And Jenny?' put in Marcus accusingly.

'And Stan and Iris?' added Fiona. It was turning into quite a litany.

'There must be quite a few people in the village wondering how they're going to cook their Christmas dinners today,' Kate mused not looking at Jane.

'Perhaps we ought to organise a rota,' said Fiona, standing by the Aga buttering toast in midair.

'Jolly good idea.' Marcus seized a piece of toast out of her hand and crammed it into his mouth.

Jane was looking decidedly glum. As well she might, thought Kate. She hops out of bed like an early bird and comes bursting in here hoping to catch me, the worm, and she would have done too if the children hadn't come back in the nick of time.

'If you'd like to go round and find out how many Agas there are in the village, Jane,' Kate suggested, 'one of the children will find out how many people want to share them.'

'I know there aren't more than three or four Agas,' snapped Jane.

'I dare say not everybody will be having their Christmas dinner at home,' Kate said, feeling magnanimous. It really was very gratifying watching someone else loosing their cool in a crisis.

'They may not be able to get out – not with so many trees down,' said Jane.

'Don't worry,' Fiona put in. 'Daddy and our farm men will clear them all eventually. They've almost finished with the one in the village.'

'I'm sure if we organised it properly we could manage to get everything cooked somehow,' said Kate. 'It'll be a bit like the two small loaves and five big fishes in the Bible – or was it two big loaves and five small fishes?'

'I don't see that our present predicament bears any relation to Christ's miracle in feeding the five thousand,' Jane replied huffily as she tried to put Kate in her place.

'I know what Kate means,' Marcus leapt to her defence. 'If we share everything out, the cooking and stuff, you'll be surprised at how it'll all go round.'

'We could make a fire out of the brushwood from the tree they've sawn up,' said Samantha. 'There's a whole pile of it on the village green. Couldn't we cook a few things on that?'

'I suppose if we could get a really good fire going we could boil the Christmas puddings over it, like we do at camp.' Jane, who was not a commissioner of the Girl Guides for nothing, was beginning to recover from her initial defeat. 'Well,' she said more briskly, 'we'd better get going if we're to get the first lot into the ovens before church.'

Kate ran upstairs to get dressed, wondering what to do about church. Should she make sure the children went? And what about Deborah lying in hospital, waiting to be visited by her loving family, and the presents lying unopened at the foot of the tree? The Christmas bus she'd hurled herself upon now seemed to be careering away out of control and all her carefully laid plans were falling by the wayside like so many discarded passengers. Oh well, organisation never had been her strong suit so better to leave it to the capable Evering woman and be a good little Girl Guide.

Patrick was in the kitchen when Kate came downstairs again, wolfing bread and butter and drinking coffee standing up. He was dirty and bits of wood shavings were clinging to his hair. His forehead was streaked with grease and his jaw covered in dark stubble as he hadn't shaved. Kate's heart did a triple somersault and landed somewhere above her stomach.

'What's all this I hear about you having arranged to cook Christmas dinner for the entire village?' he said, grinning at her.

'It wasn't me – it was your children,' she retorted. 'They seem to think they have a duty to see that everybody shares and shares alike. You should be proud of them.'

'I am proud of them,' he said. 'They've got the ever-ready Jane whipping in for them now, trying to get all the gooses cooked before the morning service.' He was staring at her in a rather unnerving way, as if he'd only just seen her for the first time. 'And I'm proud of you. Debs wouldn't have let them do this. She's too possessive, she hates sharing things.'

Dangerous ground. It was the first time he'd ever criticised his wife to her. 'Don't be,' Kate said. 'I only did it to spite that Evering person.'

'Debs can't stand the woman, she says she's always trying to boss her about.'

'You know it was remarkable how quickly Jane recovered once she was faced with an organisational challenge,' Kate said quickly, afraid of what he might be going to say next. 'And I'm quite happy to let her take charge. Organisation was never my strong point. I'm not nearly bossy enough.'

'Thank God. Maybe that's what I find so appealing about you, Kate.'

'Are you coming to church?' she asked, seizing the kettle and turning on the cold tap. 'If you are I'll boil up some water for you to shave.'

'Can't do it,' he said, gulping down the coffee. 'Make us a Thermos of coffee and a few sandwiches, there's a good girl. I've got to get the roads out of the village cleared and I don't know how long it's going to take. There's quite a few trees down, so we're told.'

'Surely you and Jack and Stan can't do it all by yourselves,' she said.

'If we don't do it nobody'll be able to get out and you'll have the entire village to feed. We can't have that. I want a proper Christmas dinner some time tonight so don't overload that Aga too much.' He grinned at her and disappeared as two women arrived heavily laden with roasting tins.

'I think we could manage one more,' Kate said, 'if we juggle them about a bit.'

She left the women arguing about which oven to put their tins in and hurriedly made sandwiches with the cold pheasant left over from the night before. Then she filled Thermoses with strong coffee, and took it all out to Patrick, busy loading up the Land Rover.

'You're a good girl, Kate,' he said, smacking her on her bottom appreciatively as he got into the Land Rover. 'See you tonight. Make sure the bath water's hot.'

'Some chance,' she shouted back at him as he drove off.

It was remarkable what fun Christmas could be once you abandoned all attempts at a carefully orchestrated Christmas dinner, Kate discovered. As people ran from house to house with their roasting tins and various pots and pans, juggling ovens, and roasting potatoes in the fire on the village green, it developed into a cross between a medieval fair and a crazy variation of a pancake race. Kate, supervising the cooking of several different joints in The Manor kitchen, swapping turkeys and sides of beef and pheasants between hot, medium and simmering ovens to try to get them all cooked somehow, became resigned to chaos. Instead of striving for perfection she was just trying to get by, and she was loving it. The children were having the time of their lives. Christmas had become a great adventure. They were happy to leave the presents all sitting unopened beneath the tree and go off to church in their jeans and wellingtons and thick sweaters and Barbours, and Kate went with them. It didn't matter that the water was cold and the Aga slowly dying and the house freezing, that they were groping about in the dark and spilling candle grease wherever they went, that when Patrick eventually got back, having cleared the roads round about, they sat down to their own Christmas dinner in the kitchen still in their jeans, unwashed, and with none of the trimmings necessary to turn an ordinary meal into a feast. None of it seemed to matter any more. They were tired out by the day's exertions but happy, united, triumphant. What mattered was the spirit of Christmas and that they had in abundance.

Afterwards they lit a huge fire in the hall and opened their presents by candlelight. Kate had bought them silly little things, not wanting to be too overtly generous. She had thought long and hard what to do about Patrick and decided that something impersonal and inexpensive was the only way to emphasise her resolve and not arouse Deborah's suspicions. So she got him three blue and white spotted cotton handkerchiefs. She was glad she had done. His present was a middling-sized bottle of Tweed eau de toilette. Just for a moment she felt totally disillusioned. If he thought she used a boring old-fashioned scent like Tweed he had no imagination whatsoever and precious little nose. What use all the trouble she took to knock him senseless with her fragrance if that was what he wanted her to smell like?

Her disappointment lasted until she opened the Colonel's little package. It was a small silver powder compact, engraved with flowers. Beautiful and useful and just right, not too personal yet something which he'd obviously taken a great deal of trouble to find. She was touched and grateful. The Colonel would have been in his element rising to the challenge of the crisis here in Puddleworth, Kate thought, and wondered how he was getting on in Caroline's perfect house in Arlington Crescent.

# *Chapter 13*

Caroline sat and watched her father peering suspiciously at the dish Josef was holding out to him. It was a very special sort of devilled tetrazzinni, something Angélique, Josef's wife, did supremely well; pasta with lots of bits of turkey and pheasant in a hot and highly spiced sauce, which was an excellent way of using up leftovers. But from the way the Colonel was poking about in it with the serving spoon, it might have been something served in a soup kitchen for the homeless.

Caroline sighed and gazed at the Christmas tree standing in one corner like an ethereal ghost with its silver and blue baubles, and wisps of imitation snow. She had taken a great deal of trouble with her beautiful decorations, which were all in silver and blue and white to match the deep blue wallpaper and curtains of the dining room, but especially with the tree. Everybody had thought it magically original – except her father. He couldn't see the point of spraying a perfectly healthy green tree white. 'Why bother to have a tree at all?' he'd asked with deadly logic. 'The whole point of a tree is that it is green surely?'

The Colonel finished helping himself to a minute amount of tetrazzinni and dropped the spoon carelessly back in the dish. It bounced off the edge and fell to the floor with a clatter before Josef could catch it.

'Bad luck,' said the Colonel, winking at Josef. The Filipino's face was a perfect mask of oriental inscrutability as he bent down effortlessly to retrieve the spoon from the floor, the dish delicately balanced above his head. The Colonel watched him fascinated, as if he'd been some sort of tumbling act, but John was drumming on the highly polished table with impatient fingers.

Caroline tried not to catch her husband's eye as Josef glided over to the sideboard to fetch a clean spoon. John found Christmas difficult at the best of times. With everybody on holiday for five whole days he was like a caged beast, unable to telephone or make deals, and with her father staying in the house he was finding it more difficult than ever. The Colonel was not above ordering the servants about as if they were his own, and disagreed with everything John said out of pure habit. In vain Caroline had told him not to mind, it was just the way Daddy was. But John did mind. He wasn't used to being disagreed with. Still, at least John hadn't tried to tackle Daddy about the holiday village. Not yet.

Caroline pushed the pieces of tagliatelle around her plate and tried to stifle her irritation. She had done everything she could think of to make this Christmas a happy one for her father, to make him feel at home and welcome. But it was so very difficult. He was always down too early, sitting at the dining-room table with far from resigned patience waiting for breakfast long before the servants had it ready. Then on Christmas morning he had driven her mad standing about in the hall hours before it was time to go to church, looking at his watch and demanding of anybody who would listen what time they were leaving for church parade. It wasn't as if there was any need for hurry and the time dragged interminably while the rest of the world caught up. His stamina was awe-inspiring. He hadn't seemed to mind all the parties they took him to and had been charming to the people she filled the house with on Christmas Day, although pretty scathing about them as soon as they were gone. She had kept the people coming and her father as busy as possible until tonight, the evening after Boxing Day. Tonight for the first time since she'd brought her father back with her, they were alone together just the three of them, and she was afraid that John would not fail to seize his opportunity.

With sinking heart Caroline watched Josef clearing the table and setting out the dessert. He padded silently round with the fruit and nuts and port glasses and set the port decanter in front of John, while they all watched as if he was about to perform a particularly intricate conjuring trick. He really was the most perfect manservant, thought Caroline, with appreciation. Not by one unnecessary gesture did Josef show that he was aware that he was the centre of attention. When he was satisfied with the table, he stayed hovering by the sideboard for a few moments. But then he slid quietly out of the room. Caroline wished she could keep him there, silently tidying until it was time for her father to go to bed, as John asked the Colonel how he was getting on with his campaign to fight the holiday village scheme. Caroline's heart sank.

'It's going very well.' The Colonel selected a walnut from the dish in front of him. 'We've raised £7,000 already. I should think we'll soon have enough to retain this solicitor friend of Kate's. You'd never believe the number of experts you need even for a little public inquiry like this one. It's a scandalous waste of tax-payers' money.'

'I agree, particularly as you're going to lose,' John told him, pouring port into his glass. Caroline winced. He might have been a little more gentle. John got up and carried the decanter round the table to Caroline.

'There is no way you can stand up to a big company like Meccarda and win.'

'If we lose, we'll go down all guns firing,' said the Colonel cheerfully. 'And you know what they say – God isn't on the side of the big battalions but of the best shots. This solicitor friend of Kate's sounds a pretty good shot. She's a bit of a specialist in this sort of thing apparently.'

'The clever move for you to make would be to sell out to the enemy,' John said filling up the Colonel's glass and leaving the decanter in front of him.

'Well, of course the house isn't mine to sell, as I expect you know.' John nodded gravely as he resumed his seat. 'It belongs to the two girls. I always thought I'd break my neck on the hunting field, which is why I put the house in their names so I could go on riding with a clear conscience.' The Colonel contemplated his port sadly. 'That's the dreadful thing about old age. It creeps up on you so quiet and slow you don't know it's there until you can't do a damn thing any more. You never think you're going to get to be too old even to break your neck.' He turned a little stiffly in his seat and fixed his daughter with a hard stare. 'You wouldn't put me out – would you, Caroline?'

'Of course not,' she mumbled not looking at John. 'Not if you didn't want to go.'

'Of course I don't want to go. I don't need to tell you that and I don't need to tell John either.'

'Look, AB, I don't think you've thought this thing through.' John put down his glass and leant towards his father-in-law the way Caroline imagined he did at board meetings when he wanted to carry a difficult director with him. 'Sooner or later you've got to face the future. You're not going to break your neck. You're hale and hearty and will be with us, we all hope, for a long time yet. But the house is falling down, the roof's in a dreadful state. The whole place needs about a hundred grand spending on it to bring it up to modern standards of living. Nobody'll want to buy it once the holiday village plan goes through – and believe me it will go through. You'll be living in the greatest possible discomfort in a white elephant nobody wants. Is that the legacy you want to leave to your daughters?'

The Colonel didn't answer, he just growled into his port and Caroline felt terribly sorry for him. She would have stopped John if she could but she'd given up trying to stop John long ago.

'You've got to think positive.' John was getting properly into his stride now. 'Instead of thinking of it as a disaster, you've got to see this scheme for what it is: the chance of a lifetime. All you have to do is get planning permission for your house and the fifteen acres of land, which with your contacts on the District Council shouldn't be too difficult. Then you do a deal with Meccarda. I'm sure they'd jump at the chance to buy you out at building land prices in return for your co-operation over this campaign. You'll be able to name your own price. Your daughters will be millionaires. Think of that.'

The Colonel gazed about him at the pictures, the silver on the table, the festoons of expensive silk hanging across the windows, the highly polished mahogany dining table. Then he picked up the antique silver nutcrackers.

'Haven't you got enough money already?' he asked, glaring at Caroline just as he used to do when she was a child.

'I don't want the money for myself,' she explained, determined not to let him browbeat her. 'But I'm sick of always having to work with committees, to be always asking my friends for money. It's not easy doing charitable work, believe me. There is so much more I could do if I only had the money. I'd like to start a chain of foster homes for children who've never had a chance of a decent start in life,' she glanced at him appealingly, 'like we had.'

But her father wasn't impressed. 'Just because you've never had any children of your own you want to go round encouraging the working classes to breed like rabbits by taking their offspring off their hands,' he said with a scornful sniff.

'You don't understand, you'll never understand, will you, Daddy?' she accused. 'All you want me to do is have children and go well out hunting. I can't do either but at least I can do a bit of good for other people. If you'd only listen to John and not be so damned obstinate about it all.'

'Deborah could be Joint Master of the Blazers,' John pointed out, reaching out for the decanter and filling the Colonel's glass. 'And Caroline could start her own charitable foundation just as she's always wanted to. You must see that it makes sense.'

'You want me to go back on my word?' demanded the Colonel, trying unsuccessfully to crack a walnut. 'Let a lot of people down? What about all the people in the area who are against the scheme? The people who've already subscribed to our fighting fund?'

'You'll have to give the money back, of course,' John agreed, taking the nut and the nutcrackers from the Colonel's fumbling fingers. 'But it shouldn't be too difficult if you've kept proper accounts. Better to give them the money back and pull out now than lose everything.' With a quick squeeze of the nutcrackers he broke open the nut. 'They'll thank you for that in the end. You're not going to win, AB. It's a foregone conclusion.' He put the broken pieces of walnut on the Colonel's plate.

'If it's such a foregone conclusion what makes you think Meccarda will pay through the nose for my house when they can get it for nothing by waiting until I die?' demanded the Colonel, swilling the port round and round in his glass.

'Nobody wants the cost of a public inquiry if they can help it,' replied John, 'least of all Meccarda. It was a clever move getting the District Council to turn down the planning application. It raises the stakes a little.'

'I'm not playing poker,' objected the Colonel. 'I'm trying to save the countryside from vandalism.'

'You go to Meccarda,' John went on, ignoring him, 'and propose you give up your opposition to their scheme if they'll take your house and fifteen acres at the going rate for building. It's an offer they can't refuse.'

'Let me get this quite straight,' said the Colonel quietly, putting down his empty glass. 'My daughters want to sell my house and my land to make a fat killing. They don't need my permission to do that. It's theirs to sell. But they do need me to persuade the Council to grant planning permission on The Court and the fifteen acres. Right, John?'

'You could put it like that.'

John was nothing if not ruthlessly unemotional when making a deal, thought Caroline uneasily. She'd always been rather proud of him, until now.

'You know all the planning committee,' John went on. 'You've served on it yourself in your time. In fact, I'd go so far as to say only you can get it through.'

He's trying to flatter him now, thought Caroline miserably. It won't work. He's never responded to flattery.

'You could even make it part of the deal. The Council would be delighted to get the scheme through without opposition.'

'I thought the Council had turned down the planning application for the scheme, John,' she said, annoyed with him. 'Are you saying they'll change their minds just so Daddy can make a killing?'

'The Council don't want this public inquiry – it's going to cost them thousands.'

'I'll see you in hell first!' The Colonel's voice was all the more deadly in that he didn't shout, but his face was turning an alarming red.

'Daddy, please!' Caroline tried to avert the scene she had been dreading ever since John had insisted she ask her father for Christmas. 'We don't want to make you do anything you don't want. It's for everybody's good – you must see that.'

'And what do you get out of it, John?' the Colonel suddenly demanded, ignoring her. 'It's my belief you knew about this plan all along.'

John said nothing, just went on cracking walnuts, but he had the grace to look a little uncomfortable.

Caroline was horrified. 'John?' she demanded, a nasty suspicion making her more annoyed than ever. He had been very persistent, very tenacious about this holiday village scheme. But he always was very persistent. Once he got hold of an idea he was always determined to see it through. It was what made him so successful as a banker.

'You're not on the Meccarda board, are you?' she asked him. 'It's not one of your non-executive directorships?'

'No, of course not.'

'Not yet,' said the Colonel, his moustache twitching alarmingly. 'But I bet it's part of the deal. I bet he's the bastard who's behind it.'

'Oh John, you should have told me,' Caroline wailed.

'We're advising on the takeover bid, for God's sake. I can't go talking about boardroom secrets. The head of Meccarda asked me what I thought of the site and I told him that Riddleton would be ideal. Why not? It is ideal, and if your father wasn't so pig-headed he'd realise what a lucky chap he was.'

'*Cui bono?*' muttered the Colonel. 'As they say in all the best crime detection, who stands to benefit the most?'

'Stop looking at me like that, Caroline.' John was beginning to lose his cool. 'I'm no criminal, for Christ's sake. I'm only trying to help. Not everybody has a chance to make a tax-free killing like you're going to make with this one if you just play your cards right.'

'Tax-free?' she asked. 'Surely not. Although The Court's in our names it's not our primary residence.'

'Yes, but your father's living in it rent free. I'm pretty sure you could claim dependent relative exemption.'

'Money!' The Colonel pushed back his chair and lurched awkwardly to his feet. 'It's all you two ever think about. You're rich but it's never enough. The more you have the more you need. You're so busy trying to turn every penny into a pound that you forget there are other sorts of values.' His face was almost purple now and his moustache was quivering dangerously. 'I'll not stay in this house any longer. I'm going home tonight.'

Caroline leapt up, laid a restraining hand on his arm. 'Daddy, please try not to be so judgemental. John was only trying to do his best for all of us.'

He thrust her aside. 'Tell me something. Does Debs know about this? Do Debs and Patrick want me to sell some of the best of the Monday country for building?'

'It's only fifteen acres, and it hasn't been the best of the Monday country ever since the gravel pits came,' she shouted at him.

He rounded on her savagely. 'When I put the house in your names I never thought it would come to this.'

'Daddy, please!' she said again, struggling for calm. 'It hasn't come to anything yet. John and I were just trying to point out some of the advantages and pitfalls, to stop you wasting everybody's time and money over this public inquiry business.' But he wouldn't listen. He stumped off out of the room, breathing fire and brimstone. Never had Caroline seen him in such a rage.

'Oh dear,' she said, sinking into a chair as he left the room. 'You don't think he'll do something silly, do you? Like slipping out of the house and trying to get back to The Court tonight?'

'Of course he won't,' John said coldly. 'Your father's an old campaigner. He's only bluffing. He can't get away tonight. He hasn't got his own car here, thank God, and there isn't much of a train service running at this time of evening. He'll simmer down when he's slept on it.'

The Colonel didn't leave and didn't refer to the subject again. When he came down to breakfast next morning he seemed much more fussed about getting through to The Court to find out what might have happened during the storm. Normally Caroline had her breakfast in bed whenever she could, and was never at her best until after eleven, but with her father in the house she felt she had to get up. John had left to go shooting and Caroline was relieved her father seemed to have forgotten the night before. The telephones in Gloucestershire all seemed to be still down and the Colonel was very anxious. For a moment Caroline was tempted to drive her father down there just to pass the time, but resisted the temptation. If the telephones were down and the electricity cut off, The Court was the last house to take someone of her father's age to. Besides, she had prevailed upon two of her neediest friends to come for lunch and bridge in the afternoon. The Colonel played bridge like he did everything else, erratically, selfishly, but with great enjoyment and just occasionally exceptional flair. It would at least stop him worrying about storm damage at home.

They managed to get through to Little Riddleton that evening.

'Right,' said the Colonel to Caroline, after a long, involved conversation with Murphy. 'No structural damage. Electricity's restored. A few trees down, but nothing serious. You'll no doubt want to hunt tomorrow. It's a good meet and the mare's bursting out of her skin, so Murphy says. You can take me home with you. Kate'll be back as soon as Deborah gets out of hospital and you'll be glad to get rid of me before New Year.'

She protested vigorously; now that the worst was over and the end was in sight she almost believed she would be sorry to see him go. But her father wasn't so easily fooled.

'No need to pretend, my dear,' he said. 'I've been a sore trial to you. Can't stand London, never have. You did your best, I know that, but I shall be glad to get back home. Even if it is falling down around my ears, I've been at The Court the best part of fifty years and I'm not really happy anywhere else.' He fixed her with a particularly meaningful stare which left Caroline in no doubt that he had absolutely no intention of ever leaving it quietly.

'I think you've got to go and talk to that sister of yours,' John said when she warned him that night as they were getting ready for bed. 'Persuade her to stop sitting on the fence, and support us in this.'

'Fat chance,' Caroline laughed uneasily. 'Debs has never supported me in anything. She prides herself on being Daddy's favourite although she does bugger all for him.'

'Don't be silly, Caroline. You're just being negative and self-indulgent. You've got to tackle Deborah and convince her that it's in her self-interest to support us.'

'I tried to,' Caroline protested, 'out hunting, several times, but she's always too busy concentrating on the hounds or that new horse of hers. Then she got kicked. It's not the sort of thing you can discuss with someone when they're lying in hospital in a public ward.'

'Well then, as soon as she's home, you go down there and see her. With that leg in plaster she'll be a captive audience. We've got to present a united front.' He got into bed while she was still taking off her make-up, and by the time she'd cleaned her teeth he was sound asleep.

Caroline got in beside him feeling depressed. Torn between her loyalty to her husband and her duty to her father she didn't see how she could possibly please both. And it was clear neither of them was going to give up easily.

Deborah left hospital on 30 December and Caroline went to visit her on New Year's Day. She and John never made much of New Year's Eve. John was always shooting next day and didn't want to be too hung over and Caroline usually went hunting. But she didn't mind missing it today. Anybody who had a horse with four legs would be out hunting today. The crowd would be terrific. When she arrived at The Manor it seemed deserted. Caroline hoped Deborah hadn't gone with somebody in a car following the hounds. Surely she couldn't be ready for that yet, not if she'd just got out of hospital? She tried the front door. It wasn't locked. Someone must be in. She pushed open the door and shouted a bit in the hall. No reply. Then she wandered into the kitchen. It was in its usual state of half-ordered chaos. There was a velvet cap and a hunting whip on the kitchen table beside a half-empty bottle of champagne. Odd! Could Patrick be back? But where were the children? Caroline began to be afraid there'd been another accident. Panicking, she rushed out to the stables to find the groom, but there was no one there. Then she noticed a strange horse tied up in one of the loose boxes, still saddled and bridled but with a day rug flung over it to keep it warm. Odder still.

She ran back to the house, still afraid that some sort of accident had overtaken somebody. Perhaps Jenny might know. She went into the kitchen to find Jenny's telephone number, which she knew Debs kept scribbled on a noticeboard above the fridge. Then she noticed a man's black hunting coat lying on a chair. A black coat. Patrick wore pink, and the velvet cap was a farmer's, not a master's. Curiouser and curiouser – surely Debs would never . . .

She wandered out of the kitchen and into the hall, paused at the bottom of the stairs. Should she go up and find out? Dare she? Is it any business of mine? she asked herself. Of course it was. If Debs was upstairs in bed with a man she was asking for trouble. Anybody could walk in and catch her at any moment. She must have taken leave of her senses. Caroline found herself creeping up the stairs, propelled by curiosity and a certain sense of outrage. On the landing she paused to listen. There was muffled laughter, a man's and a woman's, coming from the master bedroom. Caroline hesitated, not knowing what to do. Suddenly the bedroom door opened. Caroline turned and leapt down the stairs to seek refuge in the kitchen. How terrible to be caught spying.

A second later Ned Jones appeared at the kitchen door, dressed in breeches, stockinged feet, hunting shirt and tie. Just for a second he looked taken aback. Then with enormous *savoir-faire* he picked up his black coat from the back of the chair.

'Good morning, Mrs Kindersby,' he said. 'You not out hunting today?'

'No, my horse is a bit under the weather so I thought I'd come and see how my sister is,' she explained, feeling far more ill at ease than he appeared to be.

'Shame, they're having a great day – scent's breast high.' He looked genuinely sympathetic. 'My horse lost a shoe,' he told her. 'So I just popped in to ring for the lorry. Thought I'd visit Mrs Bray-Smith while I was waiting. See how she was. She seems to be getting on much better now she's back home with her family.' With which platitude he picked up his cap and his whip and walked out into the boot room.

Caroline was completely at a loss what to make of him. He was certainly an audacious rogue, the coolest customer she had ever met; either he was innocent or else absurdly practised in this sort of thing. She left him pulling on his muddy hunting boots and went back upstairs to confront her sister.

Deborah was lying in the middle of the big double bed, her leg in plaster, and the rest of her in very little else. The bedclothes were considerably disarrayed. One look at her convinced Caroline that her worst suspicions were the right ones.

'Debs, how could you – with Ned Jones of all people? He's nothing but a horse coper.'

'He's a wonderful fuck,' said Deborah, lying back on her pillows and smiling languidly at Caroline just like a cat that's consumed a whole bowlful of cream.

'Debs!' Caroline was seriously shocked. 'You're mad. Suppose it wasn't me but one of the children who walked in? Or Patrick even?'

'They wouldn't – they're out hunting. They're having a wonderful day – just as I am.' She was shamelessly unrepentant.

'Well, they might have come back early – suppose they lost a shoe like that Ned Jones?'

'Is that what he said?' She looked more pleased with herself than ever. 'How inventive. He's a very resourceful fellow.'

'Debs, stop lying there like a bitch in heat and pull yourself together. Think what you're about, for God's sake. Patrick! The children! You can't behave like this.'

'Why not? Other people do,' Deborah said a touch defiantly.

'But you're the Field Master's wife. If Patrick finds out he'll divorce you.'

'Of course he won't.' Deborah seemed remarkably unruffled. 'I know what I'm doing, Caroline, so just mind your own business, will you? What are you here for anyway?'

Suddenly Caroline remembered her difficult errand. It occurred to her that if Deborah wanted to be awkward she could apply a bit of pressure now, but she pushed the thought away as unworthy. She could not blackmail her own sister.

Deborah *was* difficult – very. She didn't at all like the idea of putting their father out of his house, nor of making him give up his great campaign.

'He's really got the bit between his teeth with this public inquiry thing,' she said. 'It's given him something to do, something to make him feel useful. You can't make him give it all up.'

'John says we should get at least a million each. Think what you could do with a million, Debs.'

'I don't know why you think we're always short of money,' grumbled Deborah, pulling a polo-necked jumper from under a pillow and struggling into it. 'Patrick's just as rich as John.'

'Probably richer.' Caroline was quite prepared to be conciliatory if it would help. 'But his money is all in land and buildings. The cash would come in pretty handy. You could be Joint Masters of the Blazers.'

'Don't be silly. The Duke's got plenty of money – he doesn't need any more masters.'

'Well, horses then. You don't need me to tell you how to spend money. You're the most extravagant person I know.'

Deborah looked doubtful. 'Where's Daddy going to live? What's he going to do?'

'Once we've sold the house we can buy him something more manageable in the middle of the Blazers. Centrally heated and labour saving, perhaps one of those nice sheltered housing places with a warden to keep an eye on him.'

'I'm not putting Daddy in an old folks' home – or sheltered housing either. It would kill him.'

'Debs, we've got to look ahead. If he was in sheltered housing I wouldn't have the perennial task of finding a minder for him – of having to go down on my bended knees to that frightful Mrs Murphy all the time.'

'Perhaps he'll marry Kate.'

'He's nearly eighty, for Christ's sake. Kate's got a perfectly good husband of her own, who's coming back in less than three months' time. Stop clinging to the idea that Daddy's some sort of Peter Pan in tweeds. He's old and very arthritic and has one foot in the grave and the other in the past.' All the pent-up frustrations she had suffered over Christmas came tumbling out of her like the pus from a burst boil. 'You've no idea how difficult he can be – it's like living with a dinosaur.'

'Kate seems pretty keen on him.' Deborah was fumbling about under the bedclothes. 'She was in an awful hurry to get back to look after him.

I tried to persuade her to stay on here for a day or two – but she was off the day after I got back. Said she didn't like him left alone to cope over New Year.'

'Well, it doesn't really matter.' Caroline sat down on the bed. It wasn't worth arguing with Debs over something so stupid. 'If he wants to marry Kate all the more reason for selling the house and setting them up in something more suitable.'

'Do you think you could help me on with my knickers?' said Deborah, coming up for air clasping a bundle of white. 'It really is awfully tiresome dressing and undressing with this wretched plaster.'

Caroline gave up then. If Deborah didn't want to face the truth it was hopeless trying to make her. Perhaps when she'd had time to think about all the money they would make she would come round to the idea – if she could think of anything other than the dreadful Ned Jones. Caroline couldn't imagine anybody letting a chance of a million slip through their fingers.

She picked up the two glasses by the bed. 'I'll take these downstairs for you. Try and be more careful in future, Debs. We don't want your little secret getting out, do we? You'd be the laughing stock of the whole hunt.'

Damn her, thought Deborah, collapsing on to her bed. Caroline had gone, promising to come again soon and proffering vague offers of help, but Deborah wasn't fooled. Her sister was very determined once she'd set her mind on something and she'd obviously set her mind on getting their father's affairs nicely tidied up once and for all. Poor old Daddy, she thought, he doesn't stand a chance.

Her leg was throbbing and her head ached from the after effects of the champagne. It was bad luck being caught by Caroline. I must have been mad, she thought ruefully, letting Ned carry me upstairs to bed like that, without a thought of the consequences. As always as soon as Ned was out of sight, reason was beginning to reassert itself. When she was with him he simply overwhelmed her; she was unable to deny him anything. It was a new feeling for her. Ned was so masterful, so daring, so outrageous, he put her in a permanent state of breathless excitement.

Deborah swung her legs over the bed and groped for her crutches. If it had been Patrick, not Caroline, who had caught her with Ned, would he have minded? she wondered, as painfully she stood up. Patrick's pride would have been hurt. She didn't care about that. She wanted his pride to be hurt. But she didn't want to be the laughing stock of the Blazers.

Slowly she made her way downstairs, sitting on her bottom with her leg stuck out in front of her and bumping like Winnie-the-Pooh from step to step. Why was it both her husband and her sister regarded Ned as some sort of bad joke? Was it because Ned was not their class? If he was good enough for the Duchess, thought Deborah, he's good enough for me. Damn the Duchess! She landed at the bottom of the stairs with a bump and pulled herself up on to her feet by the newel post. She'd asked Ned about the Duchess, when he visited her in hospital on Christmas Day.

Christmas Day itself had been really quite fun, with the doctors dressing up as Father Christmas and the surgeons carving the turkeys with breathtaking skill. Deborah wasn't ill, she was merely what hospitals euphemistically called uncomfortable. She could eat and she could enjoy being waited on, in fact it compared quite favourably to the frantic effort of Christmas at home, juggling so many balls in the air, doing presents and church and cooking turkey, and seeing to the horses and getting ready for hunting the next day. At least that's what she'd told Ned when he came to visit her, wanting him to think that she was very plucky to be so positive, and she thought she was really.

It was Ned who'd told her about the storm and the chaos it had caused with the telephone lines down and the electricity off. 'I thought I'd be safe coming to see you now. Your husband's out sawing up trees. There's no way any of them'll be able to be here today.'

Just thinking of poor Kate trying to cope with it all had made Deborah feel quite lucky to be lying in bed with her leg up, drinking champagne with Ned.

'Poor Patrick, wouldn't he be furious if he knew you were sitting here eating all the chocolates he brought me?'

Ned grinned at her. There was something about the way his blue eyes danced and his weatherbeaten chunky face crinkled when he smiled which turned her knees to water, even when she was lying down. Maybe it was the morphine, maybe it was lying on her back all the time, maybe it was his touch, the way his eyes held hers, the fact that they were alone and yet not alone, she didn't know what it was about him that drove her crazy with desire.

'He says you're a terrible Don Juan,' she persisted, watching him over the rim of her champagne glass. It was torture, but she must know.

'Me? Never. It's all talk. You know what hunting's like. The only knickers I'd want to get into are yours.'

'What about the Duchess – don't you go to bed with her?'

'The Duchess?' He looked shocked. 'You don't think she'd be so condescending? No, I look after her horses and I take good care of her. She's a bit windy, I egg her on a bit, give her confidence when she needs it. She's like all rich women, she likes her own private instructor by her side. Well, I'm good for that and I don't mind. The Duchess has been very good to me, but it's strictly business, I promise.'

She'd believed him because she'd wanted to, and because he'd been stripping her naked with his eyes. He looked about the small ward with exaggerated caution. There were only four beds in it and two of the inhabitants had been discharged for Christmas. Only the bed in the far corner was occupied and that by a post-operative emergency who was comatose.

He leant forward, took a sip of her champagne then swiftly kissed her. She opened her mouth and champagne trickled down her throat. It felt incredibly sexy and intimate. He kissed the last remaining trickle from the corner of her mouth.

'Nice?' he asked. Her whole body seemed to be on fire.

'This goddamned traction – I can't stand it,' she swore gazing up at him helplessly.

He laughed. 'Never mind – it'll be all the better for having had to wait.'

And it was, she thought now, hobbling painfully across the hall on her crutches. Quite, quite wonderful. So good that she couldn't wait to do it again. In the kitchen she caught sight of the bottle of champagne and poured herself a tumblerful. She would have to get rid of the bottle. The thing about crutches, it was impossible to carry anything and walk at the same time. She took a huge slurp of champagne. What did Caroline mean by that parting shot? Would she tell Daddy what she'd seen? Deborah took another defiant gulp of champagne. Daddy would be furious. And Patrick? There would be all hell to pay, if Patrick found out. He'd be bound to put a stop to it and she didn't want that – not yet. No, she definitely didn't want anybody finding out about her and Ned. She picked up the champagne bottle and carried it over to the bin, hopping with one crutch, a manoeuvre she certainly wouldn't have dared risk if she'd been sober. She didn't want to think of where it was all going to end. All she could think of was when it was going to start again.

# *Chapter 14*

Kate switched on the electric fire and the kettle and went back to bed taking her thermal underwear with her. She snuggled down beneath the blankets and listened to the rain drumming against the window, putting off the moment when she would have to get dressed. The thermal underwear had been a present from Alan, his Christmas present. It had been waiting for her when she got back to The Court after Deborah came home, with a loving card in Alan's own handwriting. Kate had been bitterly disappointed. She thought of the wonderful dressing gown she'd bought him, and how she'd pictured him strolling by his swimming pool looking like Noël Coward. What was she to do with a husband who envisaged her in passion killers like these? She wriggled out of her nightie and began struggling into the long-sleeved vest underneath the bedclothes. It was the way she used to dress when she was a child at home in those cold Scottish winters when the ice had formed on the inside of the windows in her bedroom. Her little flat above the stables at The Court was warmer than the main house but getting dressed still took a lot of facing up to. She supposed she should have been grateful to Alan for providing her with such an effective way of beating the cold.

The kettle began singing while she was still struggling. She pulled on the long woollen pants which reached to her ankles and leapt out of bed. She had come to an amicable arrangement whereby Mrs Murphy still got the Colonel his breakfast and Kate had hers in her own flat. Thereafter the kitchen and the Colonel were Kate's for the rest of the day. It was an arrangement which suited everybody, except the Colonel, who grumbled at being stuck with Mrs Murphy's cooking, but accepted it as the high price of devotion. He was good about things like that. But he hadn't been very good last night.

Kate took her coffee back to bed, trying to think how the argument had started. In the afternoon the Colonel had gone to Puddleworth to see Deborah and come back too late for his evening drink and the seven o'clock news. Kate had offered to delay supper until he'd had his drink but he didn't want that. He'd sat down rather tetchily and complained that his grilled chops were tough. She'd tried to distract him by asking how Deborah was managing to cope on her crutches.

'Not well,' he said, making a great play of cutting a large part of his chop in two and feeding it to his dogs. 'Poor old Deborah, all she can think about is how soon she'll be hunting again, but I'm afraid it looks like she's out for the season now. Of course I couldn't tell her that. Got to let her think she'll get a few days spring hunting in the hills.'

'You're all mad!' exclaimed Kate. 'How can you possibly want her to get back on a horse again? Isn't it enough for you that she's hopping about there with a broken leg and all of it totally unnecessary?'

'You could break a leg just crossing the street,' he told her, 'but it doesn't make you afraid to cross the road. Hunting is no more of a risk than life. Life's a risk. Deborah knows that.' He stared at her challengingly across the table.

'Only because you encourage her,' she argued, determined not to let him put her down. 'You should be hoping that an accident like that would put her off for good.'

'It doesn't, you know,' he said. 'What makes lions or cowards in the hunting field is the horse. A bold horse makes a man very brave across country.'

'So long as you've got enough courage to ride the thing in the first place,' said Kate with a shiver.

'Courage is something you can learn like anything else,' he said, scowling even more fiercely. 'It's no good pampering people. That's what's wrong with the country today. All this counselling and caring – it's turning us into a nation of wimps.'

Of course she wasn't going to let him get away with that. 'I don't believe you can make people brave by forcing them to do things they're terrified of – that only makes them hide their fear. It doesn't make them brave.'

'Of course it does. That's all courage is – the conquest of fear. Every time Deborah or Caroline fell off I made them get straight back on again. I can remember the first time I took Deborah hunting she didn't want to jump a bloody thing. But I told her if she didn't want to jump we'd turn round and go straight back home then and there. Of course she didn't want to lose face in front of her friends, so we got over the first two walls safe and sound and after that she was flying. Now she's the bravest little thruster in the Blazers.'

'With a broken leg to prove it,' Kate retorted nettled.

'Now then, Kate, don't get cross with us because we enjoy taking risks.'

'I'm not cross – you're the one who's cross,' she said without thinking.

'And if I am whose fault is that?' he exclaimed, pushing his plate away almost untouched. 'This dinner's disgusting.'

'Don't take your bad temper out on me,' she retorted. 'Just because you're upset to see Deborah on crutches. She didn't break her leg crossing the road or in a car accident, she broke it riding that dangerous horse you bought. It's her own fault and if you cared about her at all you wouldn't have bought her that horse.'

Immediately she'd said it she'd been sorry but he'd stormed out of the kitchen without bothering to finish his apple crumble, which was a particular favourite of his. It wasn't like him to take offence. He usually enjoyed a good robust argument with no holds barred.

Kate sipped her coffee slowly, feeling guilty. Of course he was right, she had been cross, but not because his family chose to take risks. She was cross because she was finding it so much harder to settle down again at The Court after spending Christmas with Patrick. The house was so cold, after The Manor. The Colonel was so much more difficult since Christmas. She knew she was probably being unfair. She wasn't making enough allowances. It wasn't the Colonel's fault that he was old and deaf and riddled with arthritis. It wasn't his fault that she was missing Patrick so much.

The room was warming up nicely. Soon it would be warm enough to get dressed. Kate finished her coffee wondering whether she ought to apologise to the Colonel. Then again perhaps it would be better to say nothing at all and hope he'd recovered his sense of humour this morning. He wasn't one to bear grudges. He lost his temper very quickly but never for very long. It was one of the things she had grown to like about him. She snuggled down further in the bed and began counting slowly to twenty. Then she heard someone calling her from down in the stables. She jumped out of bed, ran to open the door and peered down the steep stairs into the gloom below. It was Mrs Murphy. Kate's heart began to thump uncomfortably. Whatever could be the matter?

'Oh Kate – it's the Colonel, he's not right.'

'What's the matter with him, Ellen?' asked Kate, standing shivering at the top of the stairs in her long thermal underwear.

'He hasn't come down for his breakfast. Never been late in his life, so I goes up and knocks on his door, like, and he tells me to come in and so I go in and there he is struggling to put his socks on. "I can't seem to use my left arm, Mrs Murphy," he says. "Can you help me get dressed?" He looks sort of odd and his arm hanging useless, so I soon has him back in bed again – and the funny thing is he went. Now that's not like the Colonel.'

'Did you send for the doctor?' asked Kate, alarmed.

'No, I didn't like to. The Colonel hates a fuss.'

'I'll come right away – just let me get dressed.' Quickly she threw on warm clothes and ran through the rain to the house, into the study where she kept the doctor's number handy. It was barely nine o'clock. She wondered what to do if he wasn't there. Perhaps she should have dialled 999 straight away. Luckily the receptionist informed her the Colonel's own doctor had just come in. The surgery said he would come immediately. A little relieved, Kate went upstairs to see the Colonel, afraid of what she might find. He was still lying in bed but he didn't look too bad.

'I expect I've had a stroke,' he said, smiling at her a bit lopsided.

'Don't worry,' she said. 'The doctor's on his way.'

'I'm not worried,' he said quite calmly. 'This is the way I always hoped I'd go – if I couldn't do it on the hunting field.' That was courage, she thought, to face death so fair and square. It made her feel better. The Colonel, who fussed so much over small matters of punctuality, wasn't fussing now. She didn't have to pretend with him or panic if the doctor took his time.

'Do you think you could take the dogs out, Kate?' he said. 'It's long past their usual time, I expect.' The dogs slept in his room, curled up in their beanbags or sometimes, she guessed, actually in his bed. Since there was nothing to be done until the doctor came, she shooed them downstairs and out into the rain, where they stood by the back door shivering, their intelligent eyes full of reproach.

'The Colonel usually takes them out into the paddock first thing,' Mrs Murphy informed Kate. 'They won't do nothing, not on their own and in this wet, they won't.'

'Well, they'll just have to manage somehow this morning,' Kate replied, feeling threatened and all at sea, with the Colonel lying so quiet and good in bed upstairs. 'The doctor will be here at any moment.'

'Oh the poor Colonel – is he took very bad, do you think?' asked Mrs Murphy.

'No, I don't think so – it's probably just a little turn,' said Kate. She could see that Mrs Murphy was longing to sit down and revel in all the terrible trials and tribulations that might be about to befall the Colonel. But Kate could not face a detailed description down to the last dreadful gruesome detail of all the diseases that had carried off the various members of the Murphy family.

'You might as well get on with his study as usual, Ellen,' she said firmly, 'but I shouldn't bother to cook him any breakfast today, at least until after the doctor's been.'

The doctor was very efficient.

'It looks as if he may have had a minor thrombosis,' he told Kate when he came downstairs after examining the Colonel. 'I think we'd better send for an ambulance, get him into hospital and keep him under observation. The first twenty-four hours is the most critical time.' Feeling far from comforted, Kate went back upstairs to pack a bag for the Colonel.

'So they're carting me off to hospital, are they?' he said as she sat with him while waiting for the ambulance. 'I hope they're not going to start interfering with the natural course of things.'

'They're only taking you in for observation,' she said. 'The doctor says it's nothing. You're not going to die.'

He looked at her shrewdly. 'Damned fools, doctors. Never believe a word they tell you.' He fixed her with a hard stare. 'I don't want to be resuscitated or any of that nonsense. You make sure they understand that, Kate, won't you?'

She knew it wasn't quite as simple as that and was terrified he might try to wring some sort of promise out of her. 'It's not for me to say – it's for your own kith and kin. The doctors don't want Caroline or Deborah suing them for not doing everything they could to save you.'

'I doubt if they'd do that,' he muttered. 'Probably be delighted to be rid of me.'

She was so surprised she didn't know what to say, but then the ambulancemen arrived and took over. She could hardly bear to watch as they strapped the poor old Colonel on to a stretcher. He was such an indomitable fighter and he looked so helpless. But it was worse when they had him inside the ambulance. Spot and Fred suddenly jumped up into the ambulance to be with their master and had to be dragged out, whining miserably with their tails between their legs. Kate took them back with her into the house and by the time she'd got them shut safely in the kitchen the ambulance had driven away.

She sank down at the kitchen table trying to collect her scattered wits, wondering if she ought to have gone with him to the hospital. But the ambulancemen were very efficient and the Colonel was quite calm. It wasn't as if he was dangerously ill, just a minor thrombosis the doctor had said. Pray God he was right. She jumped up again. She ought to let his family know; which one ought she to ring? Caroline would be the easiest. She dialled Caroline's number but the manservant said she wouldn't be back until lunch time. Kate left a message for her to ring and hung up.

Spot was lying with his nose pressed against the closed kitchen door, whimpering softly. Fred came and put his head on her knee, gazing up at her questioningly. She tried to console them with bits of the Colonel's breakfast which Mrs Murphy, in defiance of her instructions, had left keeping warm on the side of the Aga. Then she took a deep breath and dialled Deborah's number.

Patrick answered.

'Kate!' She could tell by the wariness in his voice that he wasn't pleased. Perhaps Deborah was listening.

'Is your wife there?' she asked. It was the first time she'd spoken to him since she'd been looking after them all at Christmas.

'Deborah's in the stables.' He might sound a little more pleased to hear from me, she thought. Or is he still afraid I'm chasing after him? He ought to know better than that, after I was at such pains to hold him at arm's length, except for that once.

'Are you all alone then?' she asked to tease him just a little.

'For the moment.' She paused, waited for him to say something, to at least ask how she was. Nothing.

'I'm afraid the Colonel's been taken ill,' she said. 'He might have had a minor stroke. Could you tell Deborah? The doctor says he doesn't think there's much to worry about but they'll be keeping him in for observation.'

'Of course. I'll tell her.'

'She might like to go and visit him. He's in Bratchester Hospital.'

'That might not be such a good idea.' Patrick sounded more wary than ever.

'The doctor didn't say anything about not visiting, just that he's to be kept very quiet. They don't know yet whether this is just a minor hiccup or the precursor to something more serious. I'm sure Deborah will want to see him – he's quite himself. His speech isn't affected or anything.'

'It's not that, Kate.' He paused and she pictured him sprawling beside the kitchen table, his long lean body draped over the squashy armchair, the telephone cradled beneath his chin. It was less than a fortnight since she had been there, admired him rising to the challenge of the storm, shared that wonderfully dramatic, extraordinary and, in the end, magical Christmas with him, and here he was treating her like a perfect stranger. It made her feel very sad.

'Deborah had a bit of a row with AB when he came over to see her yesterday,' Patrick said. 'It was about this holiday village business. The girls want to sell the house and land to Meccarda. But, of course, first the Colonel's got to drop his campaign.'

'He'd never sell.' Kate was horrified.

'It's not his to sell. It belongs to the girls and they're agreed on this. They want to sell.'

'Put him out, you mean?' Kate was appalled. 'They wouldn't surely? He's their father. They can't do this to him.'

'Well, they can, of course, but they don't want to upset him. As a matter of fact that's what I thought you were ringing up about.'

'Oh my God!' Kate remembered how upset and cross the Colonel had been at dinner last night, and she'd been too wrapped up in her own problems to understand. 'We had a bit of a row last night too,' she told Patrick, overwhelmed with guilt. 'Poor old man, everybody against him. If I'd known I would never have said what I did.'

'Don't be silly, Kate. If it's anybody's fault it's Caroline and John's. They put the boot in at Christmas. Have you told them yet?'

'I tried to but she's out – the butler person is expecting her back for lunch, though.'

'Well, when you do get hold of her, could you try and stop her coming rushing down? She'll only make matters worse, I'm sure.' He didn't offer to tell Caroline himself, she noticed. 'I'll tell Debs. I expect she'll want to go and see him right away. I shall have to drive her, although I've got someone from the VAT people coming to see me in half an hour.' There was a pause and Kate wondered if she should hang up. 'I say, Kate,' he suddenly sounded much more friendly, almost conspiratorial, 'you wouldn't think of coming back to live with us while the Colonel's in hospital, would you?'

He'd got a nerve, she thought indignantly.

'Debs is finding it very hard not being able to drive, or anything. The poor girl's very low at times,' he went on when she said nothing, 'and I'm so busy with the farm and the hunting. You've no idea how difficult it is.'

'No,' she said, without a pang of remorse. She wasn't going to pull any chestnuts out of the fire for Deborah.

'I miss you, Kate – and so do the children. We had good times at Christmas, didn't we?' His voice was so warm it was almost like the old days. She remembered how her heart used to leap for joy when she heard his voice on the telephone after waiting for so many days and nights for him to ring. But that, of course, was when she'd been young and impressionable and very much in love.

'Don't even think of it,' she said, 'you must be mad,' and hung up angrily. Did he credit her with no principles, no feelings at all? Or was he perhaps so self-centred that he never even gave her a second thought?

Caroline rang at lunch time.

'Of course he'll have to give up this ridiculous campaign of his,' she said once she had been reassured by Kate that the Colonel was in no immediate danger and that it wasn't necessary for his daughter to come rushing down the motorway to visit him.

'I don't see why,' said Kate angrily. 'He'll need something to keep him interested when he gets out of hospital. If he can't drive or walk about much, all the more important to keep his brain active.'

'Look, Kate, be reasonable. There's a lot of money at stake.'

I wonder if she's going to try to buy me off, thought Kate.

'You know as well as I do that The Court is not a suitable house for an invalid. It's far too cold and quite impractical. Old people go downhill very fast once they get ill.'

'Well, of course if you decide to sell the house it's none of my business,' said Kate primly. 'But perhaps it would be better if you didn't try to bully your father into giving up his campaign until he's back home again. The doctor did say it was important that he should be kept quiet. I don't suppose you want him to have another stroke, do you?'

'Of course I do realise that he mustn't be upset,' Caroline said. By golly she must be thick-skinned. 'I just wanted to get you on our side, Kate. If you were to discourage him, tactfully, he might be really rather relieved to give it all up. My father thinks a lot of you, I know.'

'All I want is for him to be happy,' murmured Kate.

'That's what we all want,' Caroline told her and hung up.

Caroline wasn't going to try and bribe her after all. Kate couldn't help being disappointed. What a pity! It would have been fun telling her what to do with her money.

After that Kate wandered about the house aimlessly, not knowing what to do with herself. She would like to have gone to the hospital to see the Colonel, but she didn't want to bump into Deborah and Patrick. Deborah was very possessive, Patrick had said at Christmas. Kate didn't want Deborah to think she was usurping the family. But am I not? she asked herself. Of course not. At least only her husband, and not with any success. The wicked thought slipped into her mind and wouldn't go away.

The dogs were getting under her feet and followed her about miserably, so she decided to go for a long walk. She needed to think. It was cold and raw, a typical dark grey January day, but at least the rain had stopped. She set off across the fields at the back of the house, making for the water park, with the dogs running in front of her quartering the field, noses sniffing the air, ears and eyes alert to any sudden movement in case a hare got up. Nice to be a dog, thought Kate, and be able to forget one's cares so easily.

What would happen if the Colonel had a second stroke and died – or, worse, survived but was paralysed? She didn't think he would want to live unless he could recover the full use of his limbs. Either way, the campaign to save the village from the predatory hand of Meccarda was doomed. Without the Colonel the opposition to the holiday village would collapse. She was sure of that. She had reached a bit of high ground and turned to look back at the village lying so quiet and still with hardly a sign of life anywhere. Beyond she caught a glimpse of water, the tip of a brightly painted sail. Some mad enthusiast was actually windsurfing in a wet suit, even in this freezing weather. Before the gravel pits came it had been unspoilt grass and hedges. Now it was an attractive water park. Not much devastation there. Kate tried to imagine what it would look like all covered in nice neat little bungalows, and shuddered.

She walked on, thinking about the different strands in village life. There were those who came to escape from the hustle and bustle of modern life – the Jane Everings – who wanted to preserve the village as a haven of peace and tranquillity, and those who were the village – the Mrs Murphys – who wanted a shop and a pub and a school and cheap houses and jobs to bring it to life. Holding these two strands together were people like the Bray-Smiths, who provided jobs and, although they no longer owned every stick and stone any more, still had the feudal instinct to protect it in times of trouble. That's all the Colonel was trying to do – protect Little Riddleton from outside invasion. But if he succeeded, would he kill it off? Kate stood still and gazed at the far horizon. If only she had the Colonel's colossal certainties, his simple beliefs. Until now she had pretended she hadn't got a choice. She couldn't stop the campaign, it had a momentum of its own. But now she did have a choice. To side with his daughters against him, or support a stubborn old man defying the law of commercial realism in a doubtful cause.

The wind was cold, piercing Kate's warm winter coat. It was the beginning of January and in no time at all her six months would be up. She seemed to be no nearer finding herself than when she'd left home. All she'd found was an old flame she'd thought she'd extinguished. She [illegible] walking briskly as the forbidden thought she'd pushed down into [illegible] subconscious surfaced like a spider in an empty bath. Until now Patrick had been part of her past, a safety valve perhaps, a bit on the side. Now he was dangerous reality. But was it Patrick or was it his life that she found so enticing? Could she go back to her old life with Alan after all the excitement she'd found down here?

'I must,' she said to herself. 'It's a good marriage. I was happy.' Sheer madness to think of anything else. She tried to picture the man she'd been married to for over twenty years and was appalled to find she could not see his face at all. I need to know what he's feeling, if he misses me, she thought desperately. I've let all this get on top of me. Alan had been very quiet. Apart from his Christmas present, just one rather unsatisfactory telephone call after Christmas once the lines had been repaired. Perhaps he wasn't sulking, perhaps he'd lost interest. I've lost touch with my own family, she thought guiltily. If only they weren't all so far away, Alan in Saudi, Matt somewhere on his way to Australia, and Naomi in Edinburgh.

A man was walking towards her across the field, covering the ground easily with the confident grace of one whose muscles are used to being used. The dogs, who'd been investigating the hedge at the bottom of the fields, came bounding up to him, tails wagging furiously. Kate's heart gave a little jump like a frightened rabbit as she recognised Patrick. Then her first thought was that something had happened to the Colonel. She felt suddenly sick. She watched Patrick approach, convinced he must be the bearer of bad tidings.

'Ah, there you are, Kate. We've just come from the hospital.' He didn't look particularly upset.

'The Colonel?' she whispered, nearly speechless with fear.

'Holding court! Surrounded by visitors. Bad news travels fast.'

'I thought he was supposed to be kept quiet!' she exclaimed, relief making her indignant.

'The doctor says if he was going to have a second stroke he'd probably have had it by now.'

'Will he be very disabled?'

'There doesn't seem to be too much damage. His speech is OK, his brain as sharp as ever. His left hand is very weak and he's not very steady on his pins, but the doctor thinks that'll all come back.'

'How long will he be in hospital, do you think?'

'The doctor wouldn't say. A week or two at least, I shouldn't wonder. He's a good age and you can't be too careful. They'll start giving him some physio as soon as they think he's out of danger.'

'Poor Colonel,' she said. 'He'll hate not being able to do things for himself.'

'You don't need to worry about old AB,' Patrick reassured her. 'We left him ordering the nurses about, creating havoc. He gave Debs a list as long as your arm of things he wanted. She's busy getting them now.'

'I'd better get back then,' said Kate.

'There's no hurry, Mrs Murphy's helping her. She said you'd gone for a walk. I thought I might as well come and find you.'

Kate felt guilty for the little spurt of pleasure that ran through her. He'd actually sought her out. He was staring at her awkwardly and she got the impression he was looking for the right words to say something. This would never do.

'How are the children?' she asked brightly, beginning to walk back towards the house.

'They're fine. We left them at home. Jenny's looking after them. They're supposed to be packing their school trunks, but I expect they'll be in the stables cleaning tack. We thought it would be too much for the old man if we took them to the hospital.' He ran a hand through his hair and gave her his little-boy-lost look. 'It's pretty much pandemonium at the present. Debs is at her wits' end. Can't seem to get anything done on those damned crutches and the children go back to school the day after tomorrow.' She hoped he wasn't going to start asking her to come and help again. If he did she was damned if she was going to fall for it.

'Look, Kate,' he said suddenly. 'You've got to give up this campaign against the holiday village scheme. It's not going to work.'

So that was it. He'd been sent out to win her round. 'I thought you were against it too,' she said, rounding on him angrily. 'You're a wimp, Patrick Bray-Smith, changing sides at the first whiff of gunfire.'

'Don't be silly, Kate.' He tried to take her hand, but she had both of them firmly thrust into her pockets. 'What's happened to the Colonel changes things. You must see that.'

'All I can see is that you're trying to take advantage of him behind his back,' she retorted. 'When he comes home he's going to need something to keep him going.'

'You.' Patrick caught hold of her arm, swung her round to face him. 'He'll have you to keep him going. Nobody denies that you've done a wonderful job looking after him. But how much longer are you going to stay? I thought you were only here for the season. How long's he going to manage in that big house of his with only the Murphys and a succession of horse-mad girl Fridays to look after him? He needs to be warm and comfortable, Kate. Sometimes the right decision is the tough one. It's easy to be soft and sentimental but that's not always the best answer.'

Suddenly she'd had enough. She couldn't cope with any of it any more, least of all with him. She needed to get away. Edinburgh, she thought, that isn't so far away.

'I don't think I can handle this,' she said. 'It's not my family squabble – it's yours. I'm going to Edinburgh to see my daughter and you can tell the Colonel that whenever he wants to come home I'll be back to look after him.'

He grinned at her suddenly. 'So you're running away from me. Now who's the coward, Kate?'

'I'm doing no such thing,' she declared indignantly. 'I'm going to see my daughter because I wasn't there for her at Christmas. I have a loving husband and family of my own. Isn't it natural to want to know how they all are?'

'How will I know where to find you?' he asked.

'You don't need to find me,' she said firmly.

'I do, if only to send for you when AB is ready to come home,' he reminded her.

'I'll telephone when I get to Edinburgh,' she said. He promised to ring and tell her as soon as they knew when the Colonel would be coming home – or if he took a turn for the worse.

Kate knew she hadn't convinced Patrick that she wasn't running away, and he was right not to be convinced. But there were times, she told herself, when discretion was the better part of valour.

# *Chapter 15*

It was just after five when Kate arrived in Edinburgh the following evening. She had found a good hotel in a quiet square off Princes Street. When she'd booked in earlier, the receptionist hadn't seemed to mind when she'd said she didn't know how long she'd be staying. There wasn't much competition for rooms in January. Kate unpacked her few belongings, called The Manor to leave a telephone number, and took a long leisurely bath. The six-hour drive up the motorway had been quite exhausting. She lay back, letting the anxiety and strain of the journey soak away, thinking that six months ago she probably wouldn't have even attempted such a thing all on her own, not in the middle of winter with snow forecast. I've changed, she thought, surprised. I'm not the acquiescent housewife I was when I left London. I've learnt how to assert myself, gained confidence. For a while she lay frowning at the taps. But where was it all leading? It was a question she didn't know how to answer, so she got out of the bath quickly, wrapped herself in the hotel's fluffy white towelling robe and telephoned her daughter.

'Mum! You're here in Edinburgh, I can't believe it. What's happened? You haven't got the sack, have you?'

'Don't be silly.' Kate laughed but she wasn't terribly amused.

'Well, I'm sure it's an ill wind and all that,' Naomi said cheerfully, when Kate explained about the Colonel having been taken to hospital. 'It's lovely to have you here. I've missed you, we all have. Especially Dad.' Kate suddenly felt very much better. It was good to be loved and wanted.

'I'm longing to see you, darling,' she said. 'Can you come and have dinner with me? I'm in this really very nice hotel enjoying a quite ridiculously cheap bargain break. I expect you need feeding up.'

'Well, the thing is I'm a bit tied up tonight.' Naomi sounded guilty. 'I didn't know you were coming.'

'It's all right, darling,' Kate hastened to reassure her. 'You don't have to apologise.'

'Could I come round tomorrow?'

'Of course, darling. I'm sorry to bounce myself on you like this.'

'No, I'm glad you came, truly. It's just that I've met this wonderful guy. I'm seeing him tonight. I'll tell you all about it tomorrow. I can't wait for you to meet him.'

She rang off and Kate tried not to feel disappointed. She looked at her watch. It was only seven o'clock. What was she going to do with the rest of the evening? She didn't feel like dining all alone in the hotel's smart restaurant. She padded about the room in her bath robe, luxuriating in the hotel's all-embracing central heating and trying to do the same with her freedom. She noticed that her room had one of those little drinks cabinets complete with fridge. She examined it curiously. It was stocked with every kind of drink imaginable. It wasn't surprising that people who spent a lot of time alone in hotels took to the bottle, she thought, pouring a large slug of gin into a glass and topping it up with tonic from the fridge. Perhaps she could have supper here in her room. She took a sip of her drink and rang room service.

'Certainly, madam. What would madam like?'

Kate didn't know. Somehow faced with complete freedom and unlimited choice she didn't feel at all liberated. She ordered sandwiches and some fruit. Freedom without responsibility didn't seem what she'd been designed for. She sat down rather forlornly in a chair and eyed the television sceptically. She stupidly hadn't brought a good book to read. She sipped her drink wondering what she had been designed for.

Love! The answer came when she'd almost finished the gin and tonic. She snuggled deeper into her towelling robe and eyed the double bed sadly, thinking of Patrick. If only he'd been here with her, what fun they might have had! Oh dear, she wasn't supposed to have those sorts of thoughts any more. She got up and poured herself another drink. Patrick didn't love her. That was the trouble. Patrick never had loved her. Glass in hand she wandered restlessly about the room. Let's face it, Kate, my girl, you're making a great big fool of yourself if you think Patrick is going to leave his wife for you. She tried to drown the wicked thought with gin and tonic.

What about Alan? Kate put down her glass and gazed at herself critically in the mirror. Alan was what she needed. He loved her and she loved him – of course she did. But she wanted a little more than undying devotion and protection – a challenge, a little sparkle in her life. She peered at her reflection a little woozily. Was that too much to ask? The lights in the hotel bedroom were cruelly harsh. Kate noticed that her hair had outgrown its London chic. Well, that's something I can see to tomorrow, she thought, glad to have something positive to do. I'll do some shopping and explore the city, and in the evening Naomi and I'll test the restaurant out together. She was longing to see Naomi again, to find out how Christmas had gone and to hear all about Alan.

Naomi arrived the following evening. Kate, waiting for her in the lobby, watched her daughter come rushing round the hotel swing door muffled in layers of black: tight black leggings, a baggy sweater, an all-enveloping woollen shawl thing and a black woollen knitted cap pulled down over her ears, which Kate supposed kept her warm. She looked radiant. Kate hugged her enthusiastically.

'Don't you look wonderfully well and happy?' she said, as Naomi took off the woollen cap and shook out a mane of long dark hair. That's new, Kate thought. Her hair used to be mouse brown, like mine.

'And you look different too,' said Naomi, staring at Kate in surprise. 'Younger, prettier. You've done something to your hair.'

'I've just had it cut and highlighted a bit, that's all,' said Kate, pleased.

'Has Dad seen it like that?' Naomi asked. 'Does he like it?'

'He hasn't seen it. I had it done after he left for Saudi.' Kate didn't like the way her daughter was looking at her. 'I'm so proud of you, darling,' she hurried on. 'I can see university life suits you.'

'It must be love.' Naomi gave a little bounce like a miniature jump for joy. 'I feel as if the whole world's been suddenly reinvented just for me. Ever since I met William nothing else matters. I don't seem to mind about the cold, or my beastly old English tutor, or the lack of decent sanitation in hall.'

Kate smiled at her daughter. She knew exactly what Naomi meant. It had been like that for her when she met Patrick. As if a thousand-watt light bulb had been suddenly switched on inside her.

'And poetry!' Naomi sighed. 'Now I suddenly see what it all means.' Her face took on a faraway dreamy expression.

'Only our love hath no decay;
This, no tomorrow hath, nor yesterday,
Running it never runs from us away,
But truly keeps his first, last, everlasting day.'

'John Donne?' asked Kate. Naomi nodded happily. 'He's one of the best on love, the Dean. Probably because he was a priest.'

'Is that how it was for you when you met Dad?' Naomi asked.

'I can't really remember,' said Kate. 'It was all such a long time ago.'

'Mum?' Naomi suddenly swung round to peer at Kate anxiously. 'You do still love Dad, don't you?'

'Of course I do, darling,' said Kate, looking away. 'Why do you ask?'

Naomi took both of Kate's hands and held them. 'It's just that I can't help feeling there's something funny going on. Perhaps it's being in love makes me more intuitive.'

'It certainly makes one more emotional,' said Kate, giving her daughter's hands a squeeze. 'It's very poignant – first love.'

'First and only love,' Naomi said fervently. 'I just know that this is the real thing.'

'Everyone always thinks that first time around.'

'You mean Dad wasn't the first?' Naomi looked interested.

'Let's go and get something to eat,' Kate said quickly, tucking her daughter's arm through hers and leading her across the hall. 'The restaurant is horribly empty. I'm sure it must be dying for our custom.'

As soon as they were settled at a table and the waiter had taken their order, Naomi returned to the attack. 'Dad's doing ever so well. It wasn't easy for him at first but now he gets on brilliantly with the Arabs. He's got this great big house and swimming pool and servants and everything. You should go out there, Mum.'

'What would I do sitting by a swimming pool in Saudi being waited on hand and foot?' Kate pulled a face. 'I'm even at a bit of a loose end here in this hotel.'

'That's because you're all on your own. In Saudi you'd have Dad.' Kate watched the wine waiter opening the bottle of claret she'd ordered.

'We none of us can understand why you didn't come out for Christmas,' Naomi announced suddenly.

'I didn't come because your father didn't invite me,' snapped Kate, knowing it wasn't the whole truth but unable to bear the doubt in her daughter's eyes. 'I wanted to prove I wasn't dependent on him for everything.' She could see that Naomi wasn't impressed. 'Tell me all about Christmas,' she said, trying to sound normal. 'Did my presents arrive in time?'

'Yes, and they were lovely. Dad was so pleased with his dressing gown. You should see him lounging by the swimming pool looking just like Noël Coward. Wasn't he clever with yours, though, Mum? He put so much thought into it.'

'Thermal underwear!' exclaimed Kate. 'It wasn't very romantic.'

'Well, but Dad's not the romantic sort.' Naomi gazed at Kate accusingly. 'But he took so much trouble. In one of your letters you'd said how cold it was in this big country house you were in and so he wrote to me and asked me how people kept warm in a cold place like Edinburgh, and I found out about Damart and sent the catalogue out to him and everything, and he got it all there in time for Christmas. It was really very resourceful of him, especially stuck in a hot place like Saudi. He went to a lot of trouble.'

Kate felt suddenly ashamed. Of course Naomi was right and Alan's present had been a boon, she couldn't deny it. She'd been behaving like a silly teenager, mooning after the impossible instead of being happy with what she'd got. Perhaps she should pack it all in now and go back to her husband before she got into any more trouble.

'How's Matt?' Kate asked, changing the subject as the waiter brought their soup.

'Matt's fine. He's grown a beard and he's more confident. He's looking forward to getting to Australia. He seems to think he'll be able to do some sort of work there. He may even succeed,' Naomi laughed. 'He's not my baby brother any more, he's thinner and he seems taller. By the time he gets back I'll probably be quite proud to be seen with him.'

'Both my children doing so well. I'm so glad.' Kate smiled at her daughter fondly. 'Now tell me all about this young man of yours.'

'He's a third year, reading psychology. Not handsome but terribly sexy and very understanding. I know you'll love him.'

'He sounds nice,' said Kate, which wasn't what she thought. He sounded dangerous. 'I'll take you both out to dinner.' Naomi looked around the half-empty room and cast her eyes despairingly to the ceiling. 'Not here, somewhere cosy and romantic – I saw lots of lovely little restaurants when I was walking round the city today.'

'That'll be lovely.' If she'd hoped to head her daughter off she was disappointed.

Naomi studied Kate thoughtfully for a moment. 'Dad's lonely,' she said suddenly. 'He's missing you. A big conglomerate company may be going to offer him a two-year contract. But he's talking about turning it down.'

'I'm not surprised,' said Kate quickly. 'Who'd want to live in Saudi for two years?'

'I think Dad does,' said Naomi. 'It's the chance of a lifetime for him – wonderful job, really challenging. I think he's only turning it down because of you, Mum. He doesn't want to lose you.'

'Why hasn't he told me?' exclaimed Kate, exasperated. 'He could have consulted me.'

'Perhaps he would have done if you'd come out at Christmas,' muttered Naomi into her soup.

'Why does he never think I might have an opinion about anything?' demanded Kate angrily.

'Well, you know what Dad's like, he's not so sure of himself as you are. Maybe that's why he has this need to be the decision-maker all the time.'

Kate was stunned. It was a completely different view of Alan.

'You'll have to make the first move, Mum. If you do he'll welcome you back with open arms. He loves you, you know that.' Her daughter was looking at her anxiously. Kate watched the waiter pick up the wine as if it were the holy grail and reverently top up their nearly full glasses. Naomi was making her feel horribly guilty.

'You've got it all wrong, Naomi darling,' she said when the waiter had tiptoed away. 'I haven't left your father. We haven't had a row even. I've just been taking a little time out on my own trying to get to know myself better. And it's done me good. I'm stronger, more confident than I was before.'

'If that's what you want to believe, believe it.' Naomi began toying with her bread roll, crumbling it into little pieces on her plate. 'If you ask me, you seem to have become a sort of universal aunt. That's not finding your true self, that's just swapping one sort of dependency for another.'

Kate gave up. She had hoped that with Naomi's help she might find some easy answers but there were none, nor could she expect her daughter to understand when she didn't really understand herself.

It snowed in the night – just enough to turn the city into a Victorian Christmas card. Edinburgh was a city of cobbled streets, impressive monuments, royal splendour, sophisticated shops and international cuisine, expert in the art of satisfying the tourist, which it did year after year in August for the Festival. But in January, with snow on the ground it was quiet and empty, a place full of history and dark secrets, where the spirit of John Buchan lurked in the little cobbled courtyards and haunted the tall narrow houses.

Exploring on her own, Kate had plenty of time to think what her daughter had said about Alan needing to be the decision-maker to prove himself.

But I need to prove myself too, she thought. They all think I'm so useless. Patrick thinks I'm still chasing him; Naomi thinks I'm just a universal aunt; Shirley, that I'm unemployable. She stopped and stared up at the great craggy pile of Arthur's Seat dominating the city. She didn't really know what Alan thought of her any more, except he still loved her enough to go to all that trouble over her Christmas present. Patrick would never do that. I'm a fool, she thought, resuming her walk. I've got to stop it.

Perhaps the answer was to go to Saudi for two years. A clean break. Patrick would be out of reach and she could concentrate on putting some sparkle into her marriage. She walked on down an almost empty Princes Street, with its shops on one side covered in sale notices and the beautiful gardens on the other blanketed in white. If she wanted challenge she had to show Alan that she was worth challenging, prove to him that she could achieve something positive. If she could just defeat the holiday village scheme, that might show Alan that she was not as hopeless as he'd always thought.

She chose a friendly Italian restaurant with red and white checked tablecloths and candles stuck in wine bottles, to take the lovers to for dinner.

William, much to her relief, turned out to be a very nice young man. Both he and Naomi were obviously very much in love, holding hands, gazing into each other's eyes, laughing instantaneously at each other's jokes. It made Kate feel more alone than ever.

'Well, Mrs Hopegood, what do you think of Edinburgh?' asked William politely.

'I think it's probably a good place to be in love,' she said, 'but too full of secret trysting places and good little foreign restaurants to be alone in for long.' He looked so sorry for her that she added hastily, 'And I'd forgotten just how cold it could be in Scotland. That east wind, it's relentless.'

'Well then, why don't you go out to Saudi now?' Naomi was as single-minded as her father, thought Kate, amused. 'Dad would be thrilled to see you. Don't tell him you're coming, just turn up unannounced and take him by surprise.'

Perhaps that was the answer. To go – on the spur of the moment, just for a week. It wouldn't be an admission of defeat. She hadn't failed. She would be going on her own terms. And when she saw Alan again everything would fall into its rightful place.

'Suppose something were to happen to the Colonel, or they decided to send him home again suddenly?' she said, remembering her promise to Patrick. 'I don't think I dare go so far away. It's very important that I'm there for him when he wants to come home.'

'Well, if you're worried, why not ring the hospital?' Naomi suggested. 'Find out how he is, how long he's likely to be there. They must know by now.'

Of course! Why hadn't she thought of that herself? Perhaps if she was able to talk to the Colonel on the telephone, tell him what she intended to do, it would be easier to go. Then she could think about Saudi with a clear conscience. Her mind almost made up, Kate rang the hospital. She was told that the Colonel had been discharged, to a place called The Priory, which they understood to be some sort of nursing home.

Her heart sank. 'Has he had a turn for the worse?'

'Oh no, he's made a very good recovery. But we understand there is no one at home to look after him.'

'I see.' She asked for the name and address of the nursing home and hung up. Angry and filled with guilt, Kate threw herself on her bed. She'd let the poor old Colonel down. She got up and began to pace up and down the floor of her room wondering what she ought to do. If the Colonel was in a nursing home there was really no job for her at The Court. One of the family should have told me, she thought savagely. That shit Patrick! He had promised to ring her and he hadn't kept his promise. Patrick never kept his promises, surely she should have known that by now.

She poured herself a stiff drink and sat down on the bed again. Suppose the Colonel never got home again? Suppose the family sold the house and put the poor old boy into an old folks' home? She took another huge gulp of gin. She ought to stop them. But what about Alan? If Naomi was to be believed, Alan was about to turn down the job of a lifetime because of her, Kate. She couldn't let him do that. She ought to go out to Saudi and sort things out with Alan. There was nothing wrong between them except distance and a bit of hurt pride. Was there?

She stared into the glass in a panic. It's decision time, Kate, she told herself. You can't keep running away for ever. The glass, she was surprised to see, was empty. She poured herself another and telephoned her daughter. Naomi wasn't in. Kate left a message and went to run a bath. She took the drink and the telephone into the bathroom and looked at her watch. It was only six o'clock. I'm turning into an alcoholic, she thought, and took the glass back into the bedroom and left it on top of the drinks cabinet. Then she went to lie in the bath with her problem, hoping to steam some sort of decision out of herself.

Naomi rang while she was still steaming. 'We've managed to get tickets for that play you wanted to see,' she said, 'for tomorrow night.'

'I'm sorry, darling, I can't make it,' said Kate. 'I've got to go back down south. They've moved the poor old Colonel into a nursing home.'

'Well, that's fine. Now you can go and see Dad without worrying.'

'I can't, not until I've seen the Colonel. I don't like the sound of this nursing home. It's the thin edge of the wedge.' Kate explained about selling the house.

'It's like *King Lear*!' exclaimed Naomi, horrified. 'I hope you don't think you're going to do a Cordelia and go rushing down to rescue him with an army at your back.'

'No, darling. I just want to make sure he's all right, then I'll go off and see Dad.'

'It's not your fight, Mum. Better keep out of it.'

'That's what I thought when I came up here,' said Kate, studying her toes. 'But running away from trouble isn't really the answer. I've done too much of that in my life, I think. If I'd been there this would never have happened. I've got to see this thing through. Try to understand.'

'The only thing I can understand is that you've always got some sort of excuse for not going to see Dad.' Naomi sounded genuinely upset. Kate tried to reassure her daughter but she wasn't very successful – perhaps because Naomi had hit on the truth. Am I subconsciously avoiding him? she wondered. And if I am, is it because of Patrick? She lay in the bath feeling confused, guilty, unhappy with herself and furious with Patrick. Patrick had behaved abominably. He was unreliable, totally irresponsible and utterly self-centred. She couldn't still be in love with a shit like that.

The Priory was an attractive Cotswold stone country house about the same size as The Court. Approaching up the tree-lined drive the next day, Kate was pleasantly surprised by its stately air. It didn't look at all like a nursing home. She parked in the large tarmacked area for visitors' cars at the side and walked up to the front door. A light sprinkling of snow had been followed by a hard frost and everywhere was pretty as a picture in the setting sun. Spacious lawns, spreading cedars, artfully placed shrubs – it all looked very beautiful. Her spirits rose. Perhaps it wasn't going to be as bad as she'd expected.

The front door wasn't locked so she pushed it and entered a small porch. A second door led into a light airy hall, with a deep rose-coloured carpet, beautiful carved wooden staircase, and in the centre a polished table. It was just like a country house hotel. A well-dressed pleasant-looking woman of about Kate's age was sitting at the table behind a bowl of expensive white chrysanthemums.

'Oh yes, he's here,' she said when Kate asked for the Colonel. 'Do you want to have a wander round? He'll probably be sitting in one of the drawing rooms.' Kate thanked her and went in search of the Colonel. It really must have been a lovely old house at one time, she thought, strolling from room to room. Still was. The rooms were spacious, with finely carved ceilings and beautiful marble fireplaces. They were warm too and well lit, softly carpeted and prettily curtained. What depressed Kate to the bottom of her soul, were the little bundles of humanity sitting in lifeless heaps in winged armchairs or sofa or the occasional wheelchair. One of the rooms had a fine oak trestle table laid for what Kate guessed was supper, although it was only five o'clock, and already a few of the inhabitants were sitting at the table with the patient resignation of a herd of cattle awaiting their winter feed. Whatever it might euphemistically call itself there was no doubt in Kate's mind that The Priory was an old folks' home in everything but name.

There was no sign of the Colonel. A young nurse came bustling by. She was pink and pretty and blooming with youth. Beside the little grey bundles she looked absurdly alive. Kate asked where she might find the Colonel.

'He's in his room, number eight on the ground floor,' she told Kate, and it seemed to Kate she looked a bit flustered. 'You can go in. I've just got him up from his rest.'

Her heart beating a little faster, Kate found number eight and knocked on the door. There was no reply. Kate took a deep breath and opened the door.

'I've told you not to knock,' he shouted as she entered. 'No well-trained servant knocks on doors. It's bad form. Kate!'

'I've come to see you,' she said walking in and closing the door carefully behind her.

'It's about time,' the Colonel told her gruffly, but she could see that he was pleased. So pleased that she had difficulty controlling her voice, just for a moment. He was sitting in an armchair, neatly dressed and tidy, with a rug over his knees. Beside his chair there was one of those hospital bedtables on wheels on which was a copy of *Horse and Hound*, his spectacles, a glass of water and a little plastic cup with two pills in it. Kate felt so sad to see him reduced to such well-cared-for helplessness. It was like the horse Bella, all brushed and rugged up in her nice clean stall, with a full hay net and a fresh bucket of water and a manger full of feed. But Bella was only an animal. The Colonel was a human being in need of talk and love. He was watching her with the light of battle in his eye, and she knew it was no good trying to say something comforting.

'Have you been losing your temper with that poor little nurse just now?' she asked. 'She was pretty flustered. I met her flying down the corridor as if pursued by the devil himself.'

'She was trying to persuade me to go and have my "tea" in the communal dining room,' he grinned at her indignantly. '"Tea", I ask you. Why can't they call it supper and have it at a civilised hour?'

'Some people seem to like it early. There was quite a queue forming up when I went through.' He grunted and she had to force herself to be bracing, not to show pity. 'Do you hide away in here all by yourself all day then?' she asked.

He refused to meet her gaze. 'I can't stand it out there – the place is full of old people. Lot of old bores most of them – women mainly. The only man worth talking to is so deaf he can't hear a word I say. Served in the navy during the war and in the diplomatic service after. Been to some interesting places too. But he's got Alzheimer's and tends to wander away in the middle of a sentence.' There didn't seem to be much of an answer to that so she asked him how he was feeling.

'I'm not ill. Just broken down.' He moved restlessly in his chair. 'If I was a horse they'd shoot me. That's what we do with old hunters when they've outlived their usefulness. People think it's cruel. They give vast sums to pay for poor old horses to be turned out in the field, to be given a "home" until they finally succumb to rheumatism and all the pains and inconvenience of old age. What sort of life is that for a hunter who's been brought in during the winter and cosseted and fed and kept interested? So we shoot 'em. Quick end, painless. But we can't do that with people, more's the pity. Just look at all those little heaps of misery lying about this place waiting for death.'

'Do you want me to put a plastic bag over your head?' she asked, smiling at him.

He laughed. 'It's good to see you, Kate – I thought you'd abandoned me.'

'Is that what they told you? I was only having a bit of a holiday until you were ready to come home.'

'I'm ready to come home now,' he said, brightening immediately. It wasn't what she wanted to hear. Could she do it? Defy his formidable daughters, upset Patrick, hurt Alan? She had hoped that he wouldn't ask it of her. But she might have known that he was far too selfish to consider anybody except himself.

'I'll go and have a word with sister,' she said, grasping at straws.

'Kate!' he shouted after her as she whisked herself out of his room. 'Don't abandon me here!' He was nothing if not ruthless, she thought, as his voice echoed after her down the long narrow corridor. A necessary part of survival perhaps, when one was old and helpless.

The sister told Kate that there was no reason why the Colonel couldn't be looked after at home. 'He needs help dressing and undressing and going to the loo.' She looked at Kate very hard. 'Constant attention, in fact, but not nursing as such. I understood from his daughters that there was nobody at home who could fulfil such a role.'

'Yes, well, Deborah has a broken leg and children and a husband to look after and Caroline is only down here at weekends.' Why was she defending them, for heaven's sake? A natural instinct for not washing dirty linen in public perhaps? The sister was looking at her enquiringly.

'I was his temporary companion/housekeeper,' Kate explained. 'I wouldn't mind taking care of him for a while, until he's able to manage again on his own. Does the doctor think that's a possibility?'

'You'd have to ask him – but I doubt if he'd be able to tell you. We see a lot of strokes in here and the Colonel's is relatively minor. But of course he's quite an age. Recovery depends a great deal on the patient. If they're determined enough, have good regular physiotherapy, if they want to get their independence back – it's amazing what some of them achieve. One thing I do know: they don't make much progress when they're in here. They get institutionalised. They make much more effort in their own homes.'

Kate made up her mind. 'I'll take him home tomorrow,' she said. 'I'll have to make everything ready.'

'The district nurse will help you – I'll tell her to call.' She smiled at Kate warmly. 'I'm sure you're doing the right thing.'

# *Chapter 16*

The telephone at The Manor began to ring while Deborah was sitting on the floor in the wash room, stuffing dirty clothes into the washing machine. She made a grab for her crutches and as she did so, knocked over the packet of Persil. Ignoring the cascade of white powder pouring on to the floor, she levered herself up and scampered into the kitchen as quickly as her cumbersome plastered leg would allow. But the line went dead as she dropped her crutch and picked up the receiver.

'Shit!' she said.

She watched in helpless fury as the crutch she'd dropped knocked over a half-full mug of coffee abandoned by Patrick earlier, spilling a stream of coffee over the table and on to the floor.

'Shit! Shit! Fucking shit!' screamed Deborah, close to tears. She gazed at the telephone longingly. Had it been Ned trying to ring? She desperately wanted it to be Ned. Should she ring him, just in case? But she didn't dare. Ned didn't like her ringing him at the stables during the day. She stared in despair at the broken china lying in a little puddle of brown at her feet. The mess would have to be cleared up and Sue wasn't coming until Monday. Deborah reached out for the basket on a nearby chair and hung it by the strap attached to the handle over her head. Then she bent down awkwardly and started filling the basket with the broken pieces of china. Everything took so long and was such a damned nuisance when you were on crutches. She couldn't ride. She couldn't drive, which meant she couldn't leave the house unless someone drove her. She couldn't even carry a cup and saucer from the table to the sink without putting it in the basket round her neck first. Worst of all she couldn't keep tabs on Ned. She was utterly dependent on his sneaking a quick visit to see her when Patrick was out hunting and now with this hard frost there was no hunting and he couldn't even do that. All she had was the telephone and that was risky enough. She got up with the basket swinging from her neck like some stupid heroic St Bernard and hobbled on her crutches over to the bin. If only she wasn't so utterly besotted by Ned. If only she could believe that he was as desperate about her as she was about him. If only he wasn't such a one for the women. He swore he wasn't sleeping with anyone but her, and she believed him when he was with her. She'd have done anything at all then. She threw out the broken china, collected a damp cloth from the sink and went back to mop up the mess on the floor.

The trouble was she was with Ned hardly at all. Apart from that first time in bed when Caroline had caught them, there had been just one quickie in the corner of Ajax's stall, with the horse stamping about restlessly and Jenny about to come back from exercise at any moment. You wouldn't have thought it possible to achieve orgasm muffled up to the eyes in woollies and corduroy trousers standing on one leg in the back of a stable with Ned holding her balanced against the water bowl. But she had been so desperate for him and it had been so incredibly exciting Ned had managed it. He was brilliant at achieving the impossible. But apart from that time – nothing.

Deborah stared at the silent telephone, willing it to ring again. She had to speak to him. Unless she spoke to him on the telephone she didn't know how she was going to get through the rest of the day. There wasn't one single moment when she wasn't longing to be in his arms. She knew it was madness but she couldn't help it. She had never in her whole life been so out of control. It was more exhilarating than being run away with and jumping a line of huge hedges without being able to stop.

The telephone rang again. Deborah picked it up eagerly.

'Kate's kidnapped Daddy!' Caroline's voice screamed at her down the line. Deborah's heart sank. 'He's not in the nursing home any more. You'll have to do something.'

'I don't believe it!' exclaimed Deborah. 'Whatever for?'

'How should I know?' Caroline shouted. 'John says she wants to shame us into keeping the house.'

Deborah sat down carefully beside the telephone, her leg sticking out in front of her. This was obviously going to take some time. If only it had been Ned not Caroline on the telephone.

'Perhaps we could buy her off,' she suggested.

'Don't be silly. Kate's one of those people who thinks she doesn't care about money. She's never had much and what she's had she's not had to earn and so she can afford to think money doesn't matter.' Caroline paused for breath and Deborah tried to forget Ned and concentrate on this new crisis. 'The trouble with do-gooders like Kate is that they never think things through,' Caroline went on. 'What does she think is going to happen after they've won the campaign against the holiday village? She'll be off back to her husband when he comes home from Saudi and we'll be left with a house that isn't worth anything, holding the baby.'

She's missing the point, thought Deborah. She's obsessed by this holiday village thing.

'What are we going to do?' she said as soon as she could get a word in edgeways.

'John's trying to track down the husband.'

'How's he going to do that?'

'Kate sent some Christmas presents out to her husband in the Diplomatic Bag – John arranged it. He'll find him through the Foreign Office.'

Deborah couldn't help being impressed. John was terribly effective – not like Patrick.

'If the husband's a reasonable chap,' Caroline went on, 'he'll see what a mess Kate's making of everything and take her off back with him to Saudi.'

'If he wants her back,' said Deborah. 'If you ask me he's got tired of her and probably that's why he's run off to Saudi in the first place. All this is a ploy of Kate's to nobble Daddy and it seems to be succeeding. I told you Kate wants to marry him.'

'You may be right. I'd believe anything after this, though what she hopes to gain from it beats me. The Court must be terribly cold in this weather and Daddy's probably miserably uncomfortable and unhappy and wishing he was back in The Priory.'

'Haven't you been down there – haven't you even been down to ride Bella?' asked Deborah, unable to bear the thought of Caroline with a sound horse and two good legs, wasting all that lovely freedom sitting about in London.

'Of course I haven't,' snapped Caroline. 'The ground's frozen solid. You know as well as I do that hunting's off.'

'Couldn't you go and see him? I'd have thought you'd want to ride out at least,' moaned Deborah.

'It's better I stay out of it for the moment.' Caroline suddenly sounded rather sad. 'John and I are out of favour since Christmas. Get Patrick to drive you over to The Court. See if you can find out what Kate's up to.'

'I'll try, but it won't be easy. The girls are coming out from school tomorrow. Patrick's got to drive there and back twice in one day. He's not going to take kindly to driving all the way over to Riddleton as well, when we've got three fit hunters and three ponies all bouncing out of their skins and nowhere that isn't too hard to gallop them. They all have to be exercised and I can't do a damned thing to help when I'm on these bloody crutches.'

'Splendid!' Caroline sounded disgustingly bracing. 'You can take the children over to see Daddy tomorrow. What a perfect excuse!'

All very well for her, thought Deborah when Caroline had rung off, sitting in her snug house in London with all those servants to wait on her. She gazed longingly out of the window at the frozen garden. There were long icicles hanging from the gutter where it had been leaking. The pipes in the stables must be frozen solid. She wondered what they were going to do about getting water to the horses and felt her frustration mount. She longed to be out there seeing that everything was all right in the stables instead of here in the house with a pool of coffee still staining the floor at her feet. But it was slippery as hell out there and perishingly cold. Just getting from the house to the stables on her crutches was a problem. She couldn't risk falling. And what could she do when she got there? She couldn't carry buckets. What was Ned doing, she wondered? God, she must stop thinking about Ned and do something about Kate.

Resolutely, she picked up the telephone and rang her father's house. Kate answered. She sounded friendly and cheerful.

'Come for lunch tomorrow,' she said. 'He'd love to see you and the children.' Deborah accepted and hung up feeling upset.

'She sounds more and more like a wife,' Deborah said to Patrick when he came in later. 'I'm sure she's got designs on him.'

'Who has?' he asked, blowing on his fingers. 'God, it's cold out there today. It hasn't risen above freezing all day.'

'Kate. She's kidnapped Daddy from The Priory and has him holed up at The Court and now she's invited us to lunch there tomorrow so the girls can see their grandfather. She's got a bloody nerve.'

'Whatever would she want to go and do that for?' Patrick looked stunned.

'That's what I want to find out, which is why you'll have to drive us all over there tomorrow.'

'I can't.' He seemed quite put out and she didn't see why he should be. 'Christ, Deborah, I've got enough to do here just keeping the show on the road without spending half the day chatting up your father over lunch.' She might have known he wouldn't be any help, she thought in despair. Predictable, that's what Patrick was. She could always rely on him to pass the buck. He was never any good at solving problems.

'Can't you get Jenny to drive you?' he muttered.

'No I can't. I need you. This is a family crisis, Patrick. You've got to help me. Daddy's fond of you, he'll listen to what you have to say.'

'I'm not sure that I have anything to say,' he said, opening the fridge and peering inside it hopefully. 'Have we anything for lunch?'

'There's bread and cheese,' she said. 'What you have to tell Daddy is that he's got to abandon this campaign of his – it's doomed to disaster.'

'Are you sure you don't want me to tell him he's got to go back to The Priory?' he said, rather unfairly she thought.

'No, not if Kate's happy to look after him at The Court and he's being properly cared for – that's what we're going there to find out.'

'Haven't we got anything hot for lunch?' he said as he slammed the fridge shut.

'There's some soup in the larder.' He frowned. 'Sue's lentil soup. You liked it yesterday.' He was still looking unimpressed. With a sigh she started fumbling for her crutches.

'All right, all right, I'll get it.' He strode off in a resigned sort of way and she could tell that he was still cross by the way he came back and dumped the pan down on the side of the Aga. 'There's not much here,' he said, lifting the lid and staring at the contents as if they were something he'd just scraped off the floor of the stables with a shovel.

'I'm not having any.' She didn't see why he should be so cross when he'd had a nice invigorating ride on a perfectly marvellous horse and a wonderfully warm cosy kitchen to come home to. 'You can finish it all.'

He wrinkled his nose in disgust. 'I don't see how we can go and have lunch with your father tomorrow when there's so much to do here,' he said as he dropped the lid back on the pan. 'I suppose you know there's soap powder all over the floor out there?'

'For God's sake, Patrick, can't you stop thinking of yourself and try and help me for a change?' she shouted. 'It's my father Kate's stealing from me. My position as favoured daughter she's usurping. How do you think I feel?'

'OK, darling, don't take on so about it,' he said, putting the soup on to heat. 'I'll try and talk to Kate tomorrow. There must be some way of getting her to see reason.'

It wasn't very satisfactory, thought Deborah, not sure what good Patrick could possibly do talking to Kate. If only he were more like Ned. She tried to imagine what Ned would do in similar circumstances and failed completely. The utterly fascinating thing about Ned was that she never knew what he was going to do next. She only knew that whatever it was it always worked.

Kate decided on shepherd's pie for lunch. It was easy for the Colonel to eat with a fork and the children's favourite. Everybody loved shepherd's pie and she wanted something foolproof. Whatever had possessed her to ask them over for lunch? she thought, busy mashing a huge mound of potatoes on Sunday morning. I must be mad. But she knew it was the only thing to do. To pretend that everything was as normal as possible and then perhaps it just might turn out that way. All the same, she was dreading meeting Patrick again with Deborah in tow. If Deborah started shouting at her, would Patrick come to her rescue this time? It seemed unlikely. Kate wished she could hide in the kitchen throughout lunch as she had that first time. What a lot of water had passed under the bridge since that traumatic day, and it looked as if there were some quite turbulent rapids still to come.

Mrs Murphy stuck her head round the door. 'Shall I lay up in the dining room for you, Kate?' she asked.

'Yes please, Ellen.' Ellen Murphy was a real friend in need, thought Kate. Her devotion to the Colonel was single-minded and uncomplicated and nothing was too much trouble. They were completely united, Ellen and Kate, despite differences in age and background, bound together by their devotion to the Colonel. Kate piled the mashed potatoes on top of the cooked mince and put the pie in the top oven to brown. With the help of the Murphys, and regular visits from the district nurse, looking after the Colonel wasn't nearly so difficult as she'd expected, nor as embarrassing. He'd got over that fence very nicely the first time she had to help him undress.

'You're a married woman, Kate,' he'd said with a twinkle in his eye, 'so you'll be familiar with the geography.' And it had been matter-of-fact and jokey from then on. Her battles had been with the house and the cold, and the Colonel had been as helpful as he knew how. He didn't object to the drawing room being turned into a bedroom for him, and only put up a token fight over the central heating being left on day and night. Murphy came in every morning to lay and light the fires in the Colonel's makeshift bedroom and study and several times each day to fill the log baskets. There had been a small scene when the oil had run out because Kate hadn't thought to check the tank and the Colonel had been horrified at how fast it had gone down. The oil company had come very quickly but then the Aga had refused to start and Kate had to get the engineers out to it. For twenty-four hours Kate had wondered whether she was going to have to accept defeat and return the Colonel to The Priory but he'd been truly magnificent in adversity and quite determined not to go back to The Priory under any circumstances, and now all was well again.

The telephone rang while Kate was starting to make chocolate sauce but she went on putting butter and golden syrup in a pan to melt on the side of the Aga, knowing that the Colonel would answer it. The telephone rang constantly now that the Colonel was home again, and a steady stream of visitors came to the house to see him.

Mrs Murphy stuck her head round the door. 'The phone, Kate, for you.'

Kate picked up the receiver.

'Kate, darling. It's Alan.' Surprise, fear that something dreadful had happened, guilt and pleasure swept over her at the sound of his familiar voice.

'Alan! Where are you?' she asked, a little breathlessly.

'In Saudi.' There was a great clatter and Kate guessed that it was the Colonel dropping the receiver on to the hook in the study. The Colonel was no eavesdropper, he was making that quite plain. Kate tried to gather her wits together, to think what to say to her husband whom she hadn't spoken to for over three months – except for one unsatisfactory conversation at The Manor over Christmas, when Patrick and the children had been in the room.

'Darling, how are you?' she asked. 'Naomi said you're doing wonderfully well.'

'I think they may be going to ask me to stay on for two more years,' he said.

'Oh, darling, I'm so proud of you,' she said automatically. It seemed so extraordinary to be standing here in this huge old-fashioned kitchen talking to Alan as if he was in the next room. Kate simply could not bring herself to concentrate on what he was saying.

'If they do you'll have to make up your mind, Kate.' His voice sounded so familiar yet different. It wasn't her wonderful over-protective, loving husband, but a stranger pushing her up against the wall.

'When will you know for certain?' she asked, feeling threatened.

'Soon – within a month I should think.'

'If they do – you'll accept?'

'Of course. It's a very good job – the pay's three times what I'd get in England and I can save it all. Expenses are all paid out here.'

So he hadn't in the end decided to turn down the job because of her. 'Money's not everything, Alan,' she said.

'It's a fascinating challenge. Really stretches me. When I've finished here it'll make me much more marketable in the UK.'

'Why didn't you tell me this before?' she demanded.

'I'm telling you now, aren't I?' He sounded impatient.

Did he assume that she would just follow him wherever he chose to lead? Well, she always had – until now.

'Why didn't you discuss it with me, ask my advice?' she demanded, angry with him for making her feel so guilty. 'You can't just expect me to decide at a moment's notice.'

'You've had more than three months to decide what you want to do and it seems you've got yourself into a bit of a tangle. Perhaps you'd better come out here right away,' he said.

She was furious. 'Who told you? Was it Naomi? Naomi's young, idealistic, in the throes of her first big romance. She can't possibly understand.'

'I'm not sure that I understand, Kate.'

She was silent, thinking what Naomi had said about Alan needing to be the decision-maker to feel more sure of himself. Of course he was sure of himself. I'm the one who needs supporting, she thought, especially now.

'It wasn't Naomi who told me about the mess you're in now,' he said. 'It was John Kindersby. Interfering in other people's lives never pays. You'd better leave the family to sort it out and come out here.'

Kate was appalled. It was a mean trick getting Alan involved, definitely below the belt. But what could she possibly say to make Alan understand?

'I can't leave the Colonel, not just yet. Not now.' She tried to sound reasonable. 'He's so happy now he's back home. Already he's showing signs of improvement.'

'Are you sure you're not using the Colonel to prove something to yourself, Kate? Assuage past guilt? You weren't able to be there for your father and mother, remember. Are you perhaps trying to do for someone else's father what you couldn't do for your own?' Oh dear, Kate thought, darling Alan was always prepared to be so understanding. Only this time he was a little wide of the mark. It wasn't past guilt she was trying to assuage, it was current love.

'Kate are you still there?'

'Yes, I'm still here.'

'I do love you, Kate.' He paused and she knew what he was waiting for but somehow the words simply would not come. 'Well,' he said, 'I'll let you know as soon as I know for certain.' He hung up quickly and she knew he was hurt. She could visualise the expression on his face. It was one she knew well. She never had been able to resist that hurt, you-don't-really-love-me look. It was one of the reasons she always had given in to him in the past.

She went back to getting the lunch ready, feeling angry and confused and guilty. She ought to have been able to reassure Alan as he had reassured her. Except he hadn't. When she had rescued the Colonel she had thought she was doing the right thing. For once in her life she had been brave and she had been prepared to put up with the consequences. She supposed it was what Patrick had called making tough decisions. But Alan hadn't made it sound like that at all. All very well him saying he loved her, but she didn't feel loved, she felt she'd made a mess of things as usual. She added cocoa to the melted butter and syrup and stirred it furiously. 'Bubble, bubble, toil and trouble,' she muttered, wondering whether she ought to add a little syrup of figs just to get her own back. It was pretty mean using Alan against her like that. But that was what you got when you took on a tough opponent, she supposed. But if the Colonel's family were tough it was because he'd made them that way and he was still a match for the lot of them.

I just hope I don't get caught in the crossfire, she thought as she heard a car drive up.

They came into the dining room when lunch was ready like the last retreat from Moscow, the Colonel shuffling on his stick and Deborah on her crutches. Kate, busy ladling shepherd's pie on to plates at the sideboard, thought it would have been funny had the atmosphere been less strained. But there weren't any jokes being made this lunch time. The children were subdued, Patrick seemed to be sulking and Deborah cross and snappy. The Colonel tried to talk about hunting but since there hadn't been any for over a week nobody was very enthusiastic. Then he tried to interest the children in his physiotherapy – his PT as he called it. But they were embarrassed and applied themselves doggedly to their food. Everybody ate in silence until Patrick tried the weather, which brought them back to the dreary prospect of no hunting. When the Colonel began on some of the objections they were planning to bring up at the public inquiry Kate collected empty plates and escaped to the kitchen. Patrick followed her out.

'You've got to do something, Kate,' he whispered.

'Do what?' she demanded. 'I thought it was all going quite splendidly. The children haven't said a word and Deborah looks as if she's somewhere else most of time.'

'Sarcasm doesn't suit you, Kate.'

'Of course I expected her to be cross with me for interfering,' she said, dumping the plates in the sink, 'but I thought that when she saw how much better he was at home and how well he was managing she'd surely be pleased, that's why I was so glad when she rang and said she wanted to bring the children over.'

'Debs thinks you're doing all this because you've got designs on AB,' he said.

'Does she?' It was so ludicrous Kate wanted to laugh, but she saw from Patrick's face that he wasn't joking. 'It's a matter of human compassion,' she said, marching off to fetch ice cream from the deep freeze. 'I just couldn't leave him in that place, that's all.'

'Debs thinks you mean to marry him,' he persisted, following her out of the kitchen. 'Is that it?'

'Good heavens!' Kate was deeply hurt. How could he believe such a thing after all that had passed between them? 'I hope you told her that I'm already married and still in love with my husband,' she retorted.

'Are you, Kate?' he asked, examining her rather seriously.

'Of course I am.' She opened the deep freeze and took a long time searching for the ice cream. When she finally came up for air a large tub in her hands, he was smiling at her in a most unnerving way.

'Well, I'm relieved you've not got designs on the Colonel,' he said. 'I don't think I could stand having you as a mother-in-law.' She didn't know what to make of him and wasn't sure she wanted to.

'Alan may be staying in Saudi for another two years,' she said, hurrying back to the kitchen with the ice cream. 'He wants me out there with him.' She put the carton down on the table. Patrick said nothing. 'It's probably best if I go.'

'I'll miss you, Kate.'

Damn him, she thought, he might at least pretend to be sorry.

'Of course I shan't go until the Colonel's properly settled and the public inquiry's fought and won,' she told him defiantly. 'Fighting that is what's keeping him going, I'm sure of it.'

'God, Kate, you're so bloody obstinate,' he said, losing patience. 'When you win you'll have the satisfaction of doing us all out of millions. What then?'

'Then?' she said, glad that she had got under his skin for once. 'Why then I'll go back to my husband.'

'You bitch.'

She dipped a finger in the sauce, licked it thoughtfully, ignoring him.

'I never thought you had a vengeful nature, Kate,' he said somewhat sulkily. 'But you certainly know how to play rough.'

'And you don't think it was rough John getting hold of poor Alan in Saudi and telling him to whisk me away?' she retorted angrily.

'That wasn't my idea – I had nothing to do with it.' No, she thought, Patrick wouldn't be capable of anything quite so intentionally beastly. His sins were sins of omission, not commission. She began pouring the hot chocolate into the silver sauce boat while he stood frowning at her.

'We'd better be getting back to the dining room. Deborah should have had time to make it up with her father by now,' she said, smiling at him sweetly. 'If I bring the sauce can you bring the ice cream?'

If anything the atmosphere in the dining room was more frozen than the ice cream. The Colonel was scowling down at his plate, his face several shades darker and his moustache bristling; Deborah looked close to tears. The two girls were huddled at the end of the table murmuring amongst themselves. Oh dear, thought Kate, they've had a row and I did so want everything to be smoothed over. The rest of the meal was not a success. The children ate in subdued silence, Deborah pushed her plate away with the ice cream untouched, the Colonel had a second helping out of some sort of perverse determination to show that he was not in the least upset and Patrick kept him company saying it was the first proper lunch he'd had since Kate had left. That broke the ice. Deborah burst into tears, Fiona leapt to her mother's defence, and Patrick tried to pretend he'd only been joking.

'Quiet,' bellowed the Colonel in the midst of it all. 'I'm sick to death of the whole lot of you – ungrateful pack of bloodsuckers. Kate's done more for all of us than we have any right to expect and not one word of thanks does she get. Get out! Get out of my house and leave me alone. I've had enough.'

They went. The children fled, smothering relieved frightened giggles. Deborah, sobbing hysterically, groped for her crutches. Patrick, his face like thunder, helped his wife out of the room, while Kate bolted for the kitchen, utterly unable to cope with it any more.

She was washing up, worrying about the Colonel, lest the excitement brought on another stroke, wondering whether when he'd calmed down a little she might be able to persuade him to lie down and rest, when he came shuffling into the kitchen and sat at the table.

'Kate,' he said, 'we're not going on with this.'

'What do you mean? Not going on with what?'

'The campaign. I can't quarrel with my family. Lunch today was terrible. Let them sell the house, let them apply for planning permission. I can't stand in the way of millions of pounds. It's their inheritance.'

Kate was astounded. 'But the campaign? The people who've backed you, who've given money to fight – you can't let them down.'

'I'm letting my family down.' He shook his head sadly. 'Those kids – they're nice kids, good kids. I can't do them out of their future.'

Kate was stunned. 'Their future's the countryside as well,' she said, gathering her wits. 'Isn't it your duty to preserve it for them and others like them?'

'There's always two sides to every argument,' he sighed. 'I'm old and I'm tired. To win you have to be single-minded. I don't know how to be that any more, all I know is that blood is thicker than water. I've got to do my best for them.'

She sank down in a chair at his side and studied him anxiously. Perhaps he was weaker than she had realised. She'd never known him admit defeat before.

'We'll have to call the campaign off – do you think the others in the Amenity Society will agree?' she said quietly.

'Let them fight on if they like – we can tell them I'm too ill to continue.'

'Are you? Is that what all this is about? Because if you are I'll carry on for you. You don't need to worry about any of it.'

'Of course it's not.' Suddenly he brightened. 'I love a good fight – but not with my family. I've had a lot of time to think, stuck in a chair all day, and I know what I'm doing, Kate. Don't you worry. What we've got to do now is nobble that planning chap – what's his name – Evans? I wonder what it would take to get him to give us planning permission for The Court.'

She was appalled, unable to believe that he could change sides so readily. He was an old rascal all right – utterly without principle of any sort.

'I'm sure Derek Evans isn't the sort of man to accept a bribe,' she said, not bothering to hide her disapproval.

'I'm sure of that,' replied the Colonel, winking at her quite unrepentant. 'We'll go to work on that assistant of his. He's always been against me from the start. We'll let him believe that I'm applying for planning permission expecting to be turned down – so that I can use it as more ammunition in the case for the public inquiry. He won't believe that I'd give in. He may well grant it just to spite me.'

'Of course he won't, Derek Evans won't let him, not after all the trouble we've taken to have him eating out of your hand.'

'Then we'll have to do something to upset him. That shouldn't be too difficult,' retorted the Colonel, his good humour totally restored once again. 'The District Council's split. The chairman secretly hates my guts, I'm sure. Don't worry, Kate,' he said patting her hand, 'I've got a plan but I'm not going to tell you what it is. We may just be able to have our cake and eat it.'

Kate suddenly felt sorry for him and ashamed of her own disappointment. She had wanted victory not only for Riddleton but for her own personal triumph. She'd wanted him to be a hero to fight battles for her. She was forgetting he was an old man, and totally concerned with his own survival.

'And when it's all over and they've sold the house – what will you do then?' she asked, worried for him.

'Then, Kate? Why I'll walk out into the snow like Oates. I don't want to be a nuisance to anyone.'

Dear God, thought Kate, panic-stricken once more, now what does he mean by that?

# *Chapter 17*

Deborah's plaster came off on St Valentine's Day. She celebrated being able to drive again by going round to see Ned a week later when Patrick was out at a farmers' supper. As soon as Patrick had left she'd cleaned her teeth, washed her hair, dressed in tight jeans and her sexiest jumper and set off to surprise Ned. She drove into the yard at half-past seven when she calculated he would be just finishing evening stables. Nobody came out to greet her. She peered at herself in the car mirror feeling horribly unsure. All of a sudden she didn't feel very *femme fatale*. More like mutton dressed as lamb.

She got out of her car and walked into the stables, aware that she ought to have checked with him first, warned him that she was coming. She had been so excited at having her freedom again, so desperate to see Ned that she hadn't stopped to think he might not feel the same. She couldn't bear it if he wasn't here, or, worse, didn't want her. The stables were the old-fashioned kind like her father's at The Court, with indoor boxes down a long corridor on either side of a central arch. The lights were on and there was music coming from the far end. Obviously somebody was still at work. In the tack room Janie and Molly, Ned's two grooms, were finishing off the last of the tack and listening to Radio One. They looked at Deborah in surprise.

'I was wondering if Ned was about,' said Deborah, feeling foolish.

'I think he's up at the house,' Molly replied. The two of them exchanged meaningful glances and Deborah began to wish she'd never come. Desperately she searched her mind for some convincing reason why she might need to see Ned Jones at half-past seven in the evening. She couldn't think of anything other than the one she'd had in her mind ever since the doctor had decided to take her plaster off and nor, by the look on their faces, could Janie and Molly.

'Oh well, if he's not here . . .' she said, backing out of the tack room. She left the rest of the sentence, and a cloud of expensive scent, hanging in the air and wandered slowly back along the corridor, stopping to talk to the horses, trying to prolong her departure for as long as possible. But even the horses weren't interested in her this evening. They were far too busy eating their evening feeds. All except a beautiful chestnut in the end box, who lifted his head nervously to watch her. Deborah opened the box and went in. He left his manger and came to investigate her. She murmured to him quietly and he seemed friendly enough. He had a fine head and intelligent eyes. The rest of him was covered by his rugs and she was tempted to take them off and examine him more closely. He looked a very fine thoroughbred. She was just about to undo his roller when she heard a car door slam and the sound of cheerful whistling. Thank God, Ned was back. Her heart began banging against her ribs. Would Ned be pleased to see her, or would he be angry?

Ned came into the stables still whistling and she stood with her arms around the horse's neck, resting her cheek against his soft silky coat, waiting to be discovered.

'Hello, Mrs Bray-Smith,' he said. 'What are you doing here at this time of night?' His face was in shadow so she couldn't see his expression. Presumably he was calling her Mrs Bray-Smith for the benefit of the grooms. Or was anyone else with him?

'That's a nice chestnut you've got,' she said stroking the horse's nose. 'Is he new?'

'He's a failed steeplechaser the Duchess has just bought. She's going to run him in the point-to-point.'

'Are you riding him for her?' asked Deborah, hoping that that was what he'd been to see the Duchess at the house for.

'I might. If I can do the weight and if Garry Tree doesn't want the ride.' Garry Tree was one of a local farming family who bred point-to-pointers and all of whom rode like mad. Garry was the best and most experienced rider in the point-to-point business.

'You'll have to start dieting now,' she said. 'The point-to-point's only a couple of weeks away.'

He opened the stable door and came into the box. To her relief she saw he was alone. Just standing beside him in the dark shadowy stables made Deborah feel better.

'You haven't much time.'

'I know.' He stood looking down at her in the way she loved, stripping her naked with his eyes so that she could feel the moisture beginning between her legs. 'Your husband out tonight then?' he asked.

'He's at a hunt supper – for the farmers. He's taken my father with him. He won't be back for hours.'

He led her out of the box, closing the door carefully. 'Right then so what can I do for you, Mrs Bray-Smith?' he asked, swinging her round to face him.

'You know what you can do for me, Ned Jones,' she said, leaning against him, delirious with desire. He smelt of sweat and horses and cigarettes but she didn't mind. Tonight there was also a touch of whisky on his breath. He must have been drinking with the Duchess. She longed to ask him if that was all he'd been doing with the Duchess but she didn't dare.

'I see you've got rid of that plaster at last,' he said, grinning as he took hold of her arm and led her towards the centre archway. 'I'm glad I shan't have to carry you. The stairs up to my flat are a bit too steep and twisty.' Deborah's heart sang. It was going to be all right after all. She followed him with some difficulty to his flat above the stables. He was right, the stairs were very twisty. But she managed them.

The flat was little more than a bedsitter, with an alcove for the most basic cooking and washing facilities. Ned switched on the light and she rather wished he hadn't. The bed was unmade; there were half-filled ashtrays and empty coffee cups strewn about the place; the one sagging armchair was piled high with discarded clothes. She wondered whether she was one of several desperate females he had brought up to his lair or whether the untidiness was all his own. It was impossible to tell at a glance whether all the clothes on the chair were Ned's or if any of the mugs had lipstick on them.

He shut the door and locked it. She wondered who he thought might come wandering in but then she was in his arms and he was kissing her and she forgot about everything as she always did when she was with him. He was surprisingly tender for such a forceful man and very intuitive. He didn't say much, which she liked. It was easier to let her body do the talking. He knew so well how to feed her pent-up craving, how to use it to release her from the constraints of social position and marital status, how to make her shed her guilt and her fears as easily as her clothes. He rode her like a thoroughbred in a race, with control and pace and perfect timing so that as she passed the winning post she cried out in an ecstasy of passion, as breathless and triumphant as if she'd just won the Grand National.

Afterwards, lying spreadeagled beside him, she remembered the two girls in the tack room downstairs.

'What do you think Molly and Janie think we're up to?' she giggled.

'You don't need to worry about them,' he said. 'They're good girls. They won't talk.'

'Have they seen it all before?' she couldn't help asking.

'No, I've told you. Now shut up and let me sleep. I've had a hard day.'

'You can't go to sleep now. I've got to get back before Patrick gets home and finds I'm not there.'

'Go then, if you're going. I'm not stopping you.'

'God,' she shouted at him, shocked and hurt. 'You're not much of a gentleman, are you?'

'If you wanted a gentleman you wouldn't be here,' he laughed. 'You can't have it both ways. Now off you go back to that *gentleman* you're married to.' He gave her a slap on her bare bottom, pulled the duvet up to his chin and closed his eyes. She began to get dressed with a terrible sense of anticlimax. She longed to stay with him, to go to sleep and wake up with him beside her, not to have to pretend and snatch at these short forbidden moments.

'I bet you don't do this to the Duchess,' she said, hoping to goad him into some sort of response. But he went on pretending to be asleep. 'What's the Duchess got that I haven't?' she insisted. He pulled down the duvet, half propped himself on his elbows and regarded her thoughtfully.

'Money,' he said. She thought of the beautiful chestnut thoroughbred in the stall downstairs and wondered if he minded not knowing if he would ride it in the Blazers' point-to-point.

'Maybe I'll buy you a horse you could win the members' race on,' she said, thinking of her father's house and the letter he'd said he'd got from the planning people.

'I don't want to win races,' he said sleepily.

'What do you want then?' she persisted.

'A pack of hounds,' he said, suddenly reaching out and pulling her down beside him. 'If you could do that for me, Deborah love, I'd be yours for life.' He kissed her and she kissed him back, filled with excitement at a thought so wicked it frightened her.

'We can all dream,' she said as she pulled away from him quickly.

'You're all the same, you women,' he muttered. 'Put you at a real big fence and you run out every time.' She sat up and began pulling on her jeans. 'When will I see you again?' she asked.

'At your father's meet. I've got a young horse I'm teaching some manners. I'll see you there I expect.'

He knew she didn't mean that, but he never made assignations. He expected nothing from her and promised nothing in return. It was one of the reasons she was so utterly in his power. She finished dressing and he made no attempt to see her out. By the time she was ready to leave he was genuinely asleep, lying on his back and snoring peacefully. She wondered why he was quite so tired. Was it just the demanding physical life of a man who earned his living with horses, or had he already been in bed with the Duchess? How many performances could he do in a day? Deborah unlocked the door and peered downstairs. All seemed quiet below. No music coming from the tack room. No sign of the two grooms. Was Molly hiding somewhere, waiting to get into his bed for the second sitting? Gingerly Deborah descended the stairs, crept out of the stables, got into her car and drove away feeling miserable.

She couldn't bear leaving him there, not knowing what he was doing, or to whom. She was haunted by the thought of all those other women. Never had she felt so unhappy, or so alive. She didn't know what had come over her. All she knew was that she was out of control. She would run any risk just to be with him. If only she could get him away from the Duchess, from Molly. If only she could have him to herself for one whole night – or better still a weekend. She tried to imagine a dirty weekend with Ned in some romantic country hotel and failed utterly. No, that was not the answer. It was no good taking Ned out of his natural environment. What she loved about him was his fuck-you approach. You had to be very self-confident to be able to take it or leave it the way Ned did. But he was vulnerable too. Tonight she'd sensed it with the big chestnut steeplechaser. And he too could dream. It would be wonderful if she could make Ned Jones' dream come true.

* * *

Kate woke up with a start. Was there someone knocking at the door, or had she dreamt it? She had moved out of her little flat above the stables when she brought the Colonel back from the nursing home and now slept in the house to be with him in case he needed anything in the night. She was a light sleeper and he had a hunting horn which he used to summon her. She slept clad like Wee Willie Winkie in Alan's Christmas present, ready for a quick flit through the arctic corridors to the Colonel's bedside downstairs, and every time she did so she felt grateful for Alan's resourcefulness in having equipped her so suitably. She lay and listened for the sound of the hunting horn. All was quiet. Somehow she knew it wasn't the Colonel's call that had woken her this time. What then? There it was again. She got out of bed and ran to the window. The banging sound didn't seem to be coming from a door into the house but from the stables. Kate shivered and reached for her dressing gown. The moon was full, shining in and out of a bank of storm clouds. All was quiet again. Kate could see nothing in the courtyard below, although it was quite bright in the light of the moon. The stables cast long shadows across the paved yard. She ought to go down and investigate. She looked at her warm bed longingly. Perhaps she had just imagined it. Perhaps Bella had kicked her bucket over. But what if someone was trying to steal the mare? Kate knew she would have to go down. She couldn't sleep with such a possibility on her mind. Quickly she threw on a thick jersey and cords, ran downstairs in her bedsocks. Outside the drawing room she paused to listen. Should she wake the Colonel, tell him what she was doing, take the dogs with her for protection perhaps? There was no sound from the Colonel. The ferocious watchdogs who shared his bed were all too quiet. Useless poseurs, she thought fondly, much good you'd be at frightening off any intruder. She couldn't take the dogs without disturbing the Colonel and if she woke him he would probably insist on coming with her, and that would be adding guaranteed disaster to a faintly possible risk. It was probably all a wild-goose chase anyway. She hurried on into the back regions. In the boot room she collected wellingtons and a riding whip and unlocked the back door.

It was much darker outside than she'd expected. The yard was full of moving shadows. The moon was hiding now behind a big bank of cloud. A cold wind whipped her hair across her face as she peered about her anxiously. Her heart was racing. Then she heard it again – a muffled banging. She froze. Perhaps it would be better to fetch Murphy. She thought of the long dark drive she would have to walk down to Murphy's cottage and her courage failed her. Besides, in the time it took her to do that they might get the mare out of the stable and ride off with her. She couldn't let such a thing happen to Bella. Grasping the hunting whip more tightly, she ran across to the stables and groped for the light. The noise had stopped. All she could hear was her own heavy breathing as she fumbled about for the light switch. It seemed to take for ever to find it and all the time she was expecting a crippling blow from a blunt instrument to descend upon her unprotected head. At last she found the switch and turned it on. There was no one there. Nor any sign of the mare. Fearing the worst she ran to Bella's stall. The mare was lying on her back in her box her feet halfway up the wall.

Good heavens, thought Kate, a little less terrified. Whatever's the matter? She can't be having a foal, surely. The horse gave a grunt and began struggling to get up but all she could do was bang with her feet against the wall of her box. It was plain where the noise Kate had heard had come from.

'There, there, girl,' Kate soothed. 'It's all right, I'm here. Don't panic.' But Bella didn't seem to understand. She rolled her eyes and lay there like a beached whale looking at Kate as if to say, 'Don't just stand there – do something. I'm stuck.'

What to do? Kate looked at Bella's great steel-clad hooves waving in the air. Each one was a very lively blunt instrument which had already carved great grooves in the wooden wall of the box. Definitely time to fetch Murphy. She ran all the way to the cottage at the drive end.

She shouted and threw stones at the upstairs windows for quite some time before Murphy finally stuck his head out of the window. Kate explained the crisis to him but he didn't seem too worried.

'She'll be cast in her box like,' he said. 'I'll get a rope and come down directly.'

He appeared a moment later with an overall over his pyjamas and no teeth in.

'I'm sorry if I got you out of bed unnecessarily,' apologised Kate, relieved to have him with her. 'But she looks so helpless lying there.'

'You did right, madam,' said Murphy as they returned to the stables.

'Most times they gets up by theirselves but sometimes they don't and it's better not to let them kick away at the walls and do themselves a damage. Let's hope the poor old girl hasn't bruised herself with all that banging against the side of the box.' They reached the stables and found Bella lying where Kate had left her. When she heard Murphy's voice she nickered plaintively.

'There now, you silly old girl,' he said caressingly. 'Couldn't you manage to lay down a bit more careful, like, before today of all days?' He opened the door and the horse lay and looked at him expectantly. 'Now then, madam,' he said to Kate. 'If you'll just hold her head while I get this rope round her front legs we'll pull her over and have her up in a jiffy.'

Kate didn't like it but she didn't see how she could refuse. She had come this far and would have to see it through. He fumbled about breathing hard, trying to get the rope tied and she thought that his fingers were about as useless for intricate tasks as the Colonel's. The mare was very good. She just rested her head against Kate's shoulder, as if in gratitude. Kate pulled her velvety ears gently as she had seen Murphy do many times when Bella came back from hunting, murmuring to her sympathetically.

'Right,' said Murphy at last. 'Now, madam, if you'll just pull here on this rope, I'll look after the hind quarters. You'll have to look a bit sharp when we get her over – she'll probably get up in a hurry.' Oh my God, thought Kate, but the rope was in her hand and Murphy was making encouraging noises – so she pulled with all her might and Murphy darted about behind her and then with a huge grunt and a rather vulgar fart Bella rolled over. Kate dropped the rope and ran for the door while with a great flurry and scraping of hooves the mare struggled to her feet.

'Well done, madam,' said Murphy, bending down to untie the rope, while Bella stood panting a little with her rugs upside down and hanging round her neck like a child's giant bib. Kate ventured back into the box and Bella dropped her soft velvety nose into Kate's hand nuzzling expectantly. She seemed little the worse for her frightening experience.

'She'll do,' said Murphy, busy feeling the mare's legs. 'There's no harm done. It wouldn't do if she's not fit to hunt this morning. Miss Caroline'd be ever so disappointed not to be mounted at the Colonel's last meet.'

Kate gave a guilty start. The meet! Of course. She'd forgotten. The last meet of the hounds at The Court before it was sold. An emotional and difficult day lay ahead, and here she was in the stables in the middle of the night.

'Better get back to your bed, madam, and try and snatch a wink of sleep,' said Murphy, setting about the tangled rugs. 'It's going to be a busy day for all of us I shouldn't wonder, and thanks, madam. It's lucky for all of us you're such a light sleeper.'

Kate left him rugging the horse up again and went outside. She was worried about the Colonel and how he would cope on this most difficult of days. Up to now he'd borne up very well. He'd been thrilled when he'd got the letter from the Assistant Planning Officer.

'Bit of luck Derek Evans going on leave like that,' the Colonel had crowed. 'I don't think I'd have been able to twist *his* arm, got a lot of principles for a bureaucrat. But with this little bit of paper I think old John ought to be able to tempt Meccarda into making a bid.' Kate was afraid that the Colonel was so busy trying to get the better of the District Council that he hadn't thought about what it was going to mean. She hoped that when the realisation did finally hit him it wouldn't break his heart. She gazed up at the house, which looked all the more gothic in the bright, white light of the moon. It wasn't exactly a thing of beauty but it didn't deserve to be turned into a leisure centre. The banks of cloud were now massed behind the house and the shadows were just as long and dark and mysterious as before. Only now Kate was no longer afraid. She was filled with a strange unexpected exhilaration, as she stood listening to the mournful eerie sounds of the country at night, the hooting of an owl, the cry of a vixen calling for her mate. She wondered whether the dog fox, even now travelling across country in answer to the vixen's call, would be running for his life tomorrow. The thought no longer disturbed her too much. The Colonel had told her that all wild animals lived by fear. It was nature's way of protecting them from predators. Out here in the dark a great many creatures were preying on each other. It was part of the balance of nature which ensured the survival of the fittest and at the same time safeguarded the wellbeing of every species by preventing populations outstripping food supply.

Kate began walking back to the house, pleased that she'd been able to help Bella in her hour of need and filled with a thrilling sense of worth. Perhaps the Colonel was right. Perhaps fear sharpened the appetite and made the sauce of life more piquant. It was only humans who regarded fear as something to be eliminated from daily life and in so doing, according to the Colonel, made people less able to fend for themselves. It certainly made one appreciate a nice warm bed, thought Kate as she snuggled down beneath the covers again. But it didn't do much for helping one get to sleep. She tossed and turned restlessly for what was left of the night and awoke, to face all the difficulties of the day which lay ahead, unrefreshed.

The Colonel, however, seemed in fine fighting form. He ate his breakfast in his dressing gown, fussing about being ready in time, then he bawled out the poor district nurse for being late when she'd made a special effort to get there early. As soon as he was shaved and dressed he insisted on going outside to see that they were setting up the drinks in the right place. Kate, busy cutting fruit cake into finger-sized pieces in the kitchen, heard him tell the district nurse that he was quite capable of driving himself round in his Land Rover to the field at the back of the house where the meet was being held. Kate was about to drop everything and drive him herself when someone from the Amenity Society arrived and asked the Colonel if they could stage a small demonstration.

'Excellent idea,' he said. 'Pass the hat round, take a collection, you ought to be able to raise a bit more cash from the hunt. Nobody wants a damned holiday village on the best grass of the Monday country.'

Kate began to wonder if the idea of losing The Court was making the Colonel go a little mad. Surely he didn't think he could encourage the Amenity Society on one hand and apply for planning approval on the other. She was about to remonstrate but the telephone rang. She picked it up impatiently. It was Alan.

'Hello, darling, how are you?' she said, aware that the Colonel was setting off with the woman from the Amenity Society. She couldn't possibly let the Colonel drive himself. She'd have to take him.

'I'm fine,' said Alan. 'You don't sound very calm. Is anything the matter?'

'No, nothing. Everything's fine,' she said, frantically gesturing at the district nurse. She couldn't possibly ask him to ring back. He might think she didn't want to talk to him and she did.

Luckily, the district nurse rose to the occasion and offered to take the Colonel in her own small car.

'Alan,' Kate said, her latest crisis solved, 'I'm going to have to take it in another room, there's too much going on in here to talk properly.' She hung up and rushed into the Colonel's study, closing the door firmly behind her.

'We've got the meet here today,' she explained, picking up the receiver. 'The kitchen's like a mainline railway station in the middle of the rush hour, people running in and out every minute wanting the loo, the cake, the Colonel.'

'It sounds more like *Country Life* than a train station,' he said drily.

'Oh Alan, I wish you could be here to see it,' she said. 'The Colonel's been planning it like a major campaign for days. There's trestles from the village hall set up in the field behind the house and enough port and whisky to float the *Titanic*. The Aga's full of sausage rolls and there's an army of helpers rushing about.'

'You describe it very well,' he said.

'Do I? I wish you could see the village too, with the pond and the ducks and everything. It's all so unspoilt and beautiful.'

'You sound sad, Kate. What's the matter?'

'I just can't bear to think that it's all for the last time. The Colonel's given in, the planning permission's about to be granted, the battle's all but lost.'

'No battle's lost until it's over. Has the house been sold – the planning permission granted? It can't possibly have been that quick.'

'No, but the Colonel's got this letter from the Assistant Planning Officer saying it's more or less certain that the council will grant planning permission on The Court and its fifteen acres, especially if the public inquiry is abandoned, which it looks as if it will be. The backbone's gone out of the Amenity Society since the Colonel's been ill. They're all too frightened of the cost. So's the council. I think they all hoped that John Kindersby would pull something out of the bag. But now he's almost sure he can get Meccarda to buy The Court. He only seems to be interested in making money, not raising it to save the village.'

'I've told you before, Kate, it's not your fight.' Alan sounded even more distant than he was. 'I'm ringing you to tell you that I've been offered that two-year contract. Are you coming out or aren't you?'

She sat down in the Colonel's chair by the radio, took a deep breath, tried to marshal her thoughts. If only he hadn't rung today, in the middle of everything. It was so difficult to have a sensible conversation about the future when her mind was filled with a hundred different worries, most of them domestic.

'Kate, are you still there?'

'Yes, darling, I'm here. It's not something I can just decide over the phone. A few months ago I'd have said yes, of course. When I first came here, everything was so difficult, so strange, but I've learnt to cope with all kinds of things I never thought I could cope with before.' She paused, tried to grasp the feeling of exhilaration she had had in the night standing outside in the moonlight. How to explain to someone like Alan what it meant to conquer her fear of being afraid?

'There you are, you see, you'll find you can adapt in the same way here in Saudi.'

'Please, Alan, try to understand. I've only just learnt how to be brave, how to stand up for myself. Not to depend on you for everything any more.' She could almost hear him bristling over the telephone. She tried to make a joke of it. 'I just don't know how long my new-found confidence will last in a place like Saudi, where women are considered less important than camels.'

But he didn't laugh. 'I don't know what you think you're going to do if you don't come out here,' he said.

She didn't know either. All she knew was that she wasn't getting through to him. 'Oh Alan, it's so difficult trying to talk about this sort of thing over the telephone.'

'Well then, come out here,' he said. 'You're not giving me a fair chance, Kate. You haven't even seen the place.'

'I will come out, I promise.'

'When? I've got to give these people an answer pretty soon.'

'Just as soon as I can get everything sorted here.'

'For God's sake, Kate, stop making bloody excuses. First it's you can't leave the Colonel because he's in a nursing home. Well, he's out now, isn't he? You've made your point. So what's keeping you now? Don't say you've got to stay and nurse the old boy. He's got two daughters, some old retainers, and the National Health. His family are about to become millionaires, they can pay for a living-in housekeeper and nurse and God knows what if necessary.' She didn't know what to say. It wasn't like Alan to be so cross. He never lost his temper. 'It can't be the bloody campaign. You've lost that, haven't you?'

'Probably,' she said, determined to be fair. 'But if we have I'll have to give all the money back – it'll be quite complicated.'

'You just don't want to come out, do you, Kate? You don't even want to try.'

'I do. I am trying. Can't you give me a little more time, Alan, please?'

'You say you've become so strong and fearless after five months being bullied by this Colonel of yours but you haven't even got the courage to leave England and see a bit of the world. You're just burying your head in the sand like you always do. You wanted time to prove yourself and what have you proved? That you're not afraid of the dark? I'd hoped that this time on your own would have taught you to think before you rushed into things. Well, think of this. What are you going to do if you don't come out to Saudi?'

He hung up, leaving Kate trembling with shock and indignation. How could Alan, her Alan, be so unkind and cruel? Is it because I'm standing up for myself? she thought miserably. Is it that the only way Alan and I can be happy is if I'm a doormat? She replaced the receiver on its hook feeling deeply depressed. If that was what finding herself had done there didn't seem much point to it. She'd learnt to stand up to her husband and now maybe she'd lost him.

From outside came the sound of hounds baying. She got up and wandered over to the window. The kennel huntsman was unloading in the stable yard. Soon the Duke would be arriving. This was no time to be sitting huddled in the Colonel's chair feeling sorry for herself. Kate hurried back into the kitchen and began getting sausage rolls out of the Aga.

# *Chapter 18*

Deborah arrived at The Court a little later than she'd intended, and met Caroline coming back from the field behind the house carrying an empty tray.

'Need any help?' she asked, winding down her window.

'I don't think so. At least there's not much you can do with that bad leg of yours. Why don't you look after Daddy? He's wandering around out there somewhere and he's still not very steady on his pins.' Caroline rushed away leaving Deborah feeling more useless than ever, and she was feeling useless enough as it was, limping about without a horse.

She drove her car into the field and parked it beside a large oak tree where the hounds were waiting, all gathered up under the eagle eye of the first and second whips. Then she got out and walked over to say good morning to the Duke. The noise coming from the field, rising in decibels as the Colonel's army of willing helpers dispensed drinks, was like a particularly raucous cocktail party. She could see her father propped up against the side of the Land Rover holding court with a glass of whisky in his good hand and his weak one buried in his Barbour pocket out of sight. He seemed in high good form. She left the Duke talking to the Monday Field Master, and wandered off looking for Ned. There was no sign of him but she saw Patrick arriving, riding Ajax. The sight of her horse looking so eager with his ears pricked and his head tucked in, pointing his toes like a dressage champion as he did an extended trot across the field was almost more than Deborah could stand. She seized a glass of neat whisky from one of the helpers and threw it straight back. The Colonel, she saw, had abandoned his perch on the Land Rover and was tottering about regardless of the restless stamping horses, launching the tray bearers with a graphic use of his stick in the direction of anyone without a drink.

'Can't you keep better control of Daddy?' said Caroline, appearing with a tray of cake at Deborah's side. 'Someone's going to knock him down if he doesn't watch out.'

'What if they do?' Deborah said. 'It won't do him much harm to fall on the grass.' Caroline looked shocked but Deborah was damned if she was going to have Caroline telling her how to look after Daddy. 'It's no good treating him like a geriatric. He hates it. Let him enjoy his last meet at The Court in style. He certainly seems to be taking it all very well.' She caught sight of Ned at last, all by himself at the edge of the field riding a very fidgety grey that looked as if it was going to explode at any moment.

'Daddy's taking it all too well, John thinks,' said Caroline. 'He wouldn't be surprised if he's up to something.'

At the other side of the field, Ned's four-year-old exploded. It reared up waving both front legs in the air in an impressive imitation of something from the Spanish Riding School. Ned caught the horse a sharp blow between the ears with his whip and it returned smartly to earth. Deborah grinned appreciatively. Ned gave the horse another serious wallop on its quarters and both hind feet shot out behind in an athletic fly buck. But Ned remained glued to the saddle. He really was a very good nagsman, thought Deborah, filled with pride.

'Debs, you're not listening,' said Caroline. Deborah took a piece of cake from Caroline's tray and munched it absently, watching Kate come out of the house and make for the Colonel. He took Kate's arm and they walked slowly towards the Duke.

'That bloody woman, Kate!' she muttered. 'Why can't she leave poor Daddy in peace?' Caroline seemed about to protest. 'Where's her husband? You said John was trying to get hold of him.'

'John did and he said he'd sort it out. He sounded quite a nice chap so John said. Very willing to see reason. But I'm not sure that we don't need her here. You have to face it, Debs, she's doing a good job. I think we should encourage her to stay – just until the sale of the house goes through and everything's settled.'

'I simply can't see what Daddy sees in her,' said Deborah. The Colonel had finished talking to the Duke and was now among the hounds patting them on the head. Kate was standing decidedly warily on the edge of the pack. 'They've got absolutely nothing in common,' she added.

'She makes a good nurse,' said Caroline, 'and I suppose that's what he wants now.'

'Don't,' Deborah shuddered. 'I can't bear to think of him getting so old.'

'You've got to face up to it, Deborah. Ever since he had that stroke he's not what he was. I just don't think he realises what's happening half the time. John thinks we ought to try and get a power of attorney; he's terrified Daddy will somehow manage to screw things up.'

'Oh, I don't think we need do that,' said Deborah, feeling sorry for her father. Sometimes Caroline and John went too far. 'The house is ours, not his. He can't screw it up, surely? Isn't a power of attorney a bit unnecessary?'

Caroline picked up her tray of cake. 'Meccarda have put in a very good bid based on hope value.'

'Hope value?' snorted Deborah. 'It sounds like something Kate's got.'

'Hope value on possible building land is normally ten to twenty per cent of ordinary value,' explained Caroline patiently, 'but land is very scarce round here and Meccarda are very keen to extend the site for the holiday village. The Court would make a perfect reception area – properly converted, of course, with a restaurant, offices and all that sort of thing. They're so keen John thinks he could probably push them into paying fifty or sixty per cent of the building value, especially with the letter from the Assistant Planning Officer.'

Deborah watched the Duchess riding up to Ned. He lifted his hat and she rode on graciously. He must hate being so dependent on her, she thought.

'John says we're almost bound to get the planning. He's talked to the Ministry Inspector. He's very positive,' Caroline continued.

'Wouldn't we be better to wait until after the public inquiry then?' Deborah said. 'We might get more.'

'John thinks it's too risky. You never can tell with planning authorities. He thinks we've got to get the sale through quickly just in case Daddy throws a wobbly – or the Council does, or the public inquiry backs the Council after all.'

'How much does John think we might get?'

'About a million, maybe more.'

'As much as that?' Ned was now walking his restive four-year-old around at the bottom of the field, out of the way of everybody else and too far for Deborah to walk.

'That's what John thinks. He's doing everything he can for us. But it's not easy. We just can't allow Daddy to screw it up.'

'Poor Daddy,' said Deborah.

'I mean, those people protesting against the holiday village,' Caroline persisted. 'It wasn't very tactful letting them demonstrate at the meet today.'

'All the same, I wish I could believe that he doesn't mind our selling the house.'

'He'll come round if we get a lot of money for it. John says that he's just too old to be able to conceive how much it could all be worth. He still thinks in terms of five bob an hour for a blacksmith, for heaven's sake. If he can't accept decimalisation how can he understand getting millions for building land?'

The Colonel, Deborah saw, was now tottering across the field towards his Land Rover. Kate was nowhere to be seen. The Duke was looking at his watch.

'Hadn't you better be getting on Bella?' she said to her sister. 'The hounds look about ready to move off.'

'Oh I'm not in any hurry,' said Caroline. 'I'm going to get Daddy out of the way first. We don't want him being mown down in the rush.'

'I'll look after Daddy. I'm not a bloody cripple,' said Deborah annoyed. 'I suppose you're frightened the well-behaved Bella might put in a buck if you bring her straight out of her box into this mêlée. She'll be beside herself shut up in her stable listening to hounds in the paddock. You'd better sit tight when you do get on board. She just might forget her manners.'

'Not at all,' Caroline retorted indignantly. 'But I don't believe in asking too much of a horse – it isn't fair. Are you going to drive Daddy? I expect he'll like to follow for a bit.'

'Of course I am. I've brought sandwiches and coffee and a flask for him. We'll probably be out longer than you.'

'Well, don't tire him out,' warned Caroline as she walked away.

Deborah sat and seethed in silence. Bloody Caroline, bossing her about as usual. She couldn't bear watching them all riding off to enjoy themselves. Even baiting Caroline didn't seem to do any good. Deborah was stuck limping about on the ground, helpless and frustrated and thoroughly bad-tempered. She couldn't even go to talk to Ned Jones. He was keeping out of trouble far away in a corner of the field. It was too far for her to walk and she didn't dare drive. It would be far too obvious. Patrick would be bound to notice and the last thing she wanted was to arouse his suspicions. Once she would have been only too delighted to think that she could make him jealous. But now she didn't care. It was Ned she wanted to arouse. All she wanted from Patrick was to be left alone.

How horribly everything had changed, she thought. The Court to be sold, Daddy running after Kate, Patrick no longer quite the man she had once thought him. It was as if her known world was toppling. There were no certainties any more – nothing but change all around her and she didn't like any of it – least of all herself for her terrible obsession with Ned.

Kate, coming out of the kitchen with another plate of sausage rolls, encountered Caroline in the boot room pulling on her hunting boots.

'I want to thank you for rescuing Bella for me last night,' Caroline said. 'It was very brave.'

'I didn't feel at all brave,' Kate said, embarrassed.

'Maybe not but you did what had to be done,' said Caroline. 'It's not the first time you've done that here and I'm grateful to you.' She stamped her foot down hard on the stone-flagged floor and finished pulling on the boot.

Kate, feeling guilty and terrified of what might be coming next, wondered if she dared slip out with the sausage rolls, but Caroline was blocking the way.

'I'm sure you think that we're angry with you,' she said, fixing Kate with a rather headmistressy stare, 'and I admit that at first we were. We thought you were interfering, but now I see that you acted for the best. You've done a wonderful job with Daddy and you've shown me what can be done, I don't deny that.'

'He certainly seems to be accepting the sale of the house very well just now,' murmured Kate when she'd got over her surprise, 'but I'm afraid that may be because he's really not taken it in. Everything is happening so fast. It's difficult for him to adjust.'

Caroline put a booted foot up on the bench and began fixing her spurs. 'He seems very confused since his stroke. The other day he was talking about selling to a golf course or even turning The Court into an old folks' home. I do wish he'd leave everything to John. It's very difficult for him trying to get a deal with Meccarda when he doesn't know what my father's up to behind his back.

'What worries me,' said Kate, glad to have the chance to confide in his daughter, 'is what will happen when the house is sold. He doesn't want to be a nuisance to anybody. He said something to me about walking out into the snow, like Oates. You don't think he means to do something silly, do you, Caroline?'

'I've been thinking a lot about what to do with Daddy when The Court goes,' said Caroline, standing up. 'I think the time has come for John and I to move down to the country. With my share of the loot I'd buy a nice house somewhere hereabouts, convert some of it into a granny flat and then Daddy can come and live with us. I'd employ a housekeeper and perhaps a valet for him so that he can be independent. You've shown me how it can be done.'

Kate was stunned. 'What about Bella?' was all she could say.

'I've decided to give up hunting.' Caroline bent down and started fixing the other spur. 'It won't be the same once this place has gone. I thought Debs and Patrick might like to have Bella. She's such a reliable hunter. She would do Patrick beautifully as a spare and she's easily up to his weight.'

'Have you said anything of this yet to the Colonel?' Kate couldn't imagine what he might feel, but she had an uneasy suspicion that it wouldn't be relief.

'Well no, I haven't asked him yet.' Caroline started pulling on her gloves. 'I thought I'd wait until the house was sold and he'd had time to get used to the idea. I don't want to confuse him too much with too many new ideas.'

Kate was speechless. She couldn't think of anything safe to say so she just stood there hoping that she didn't look as dismayed as she felt.

'Well, I'd better be off,' Caroline said briskly, picking up her whip. 'Poor Bella will be in a terrible state by now. She probably thinks she's not going hunting today after all.' She marched out to the stables and Kate followed, trying to convince herself that this was exactly what she had wanted to happen when she'd rescued the Colonel from the nursing home.

Alan's right, she thought, making her way out to the field again. I never think anything through. The thought of Alan depressed her even more. She seemed to have got herself into a terrible muddle and she really didn't know how she was going to get out of it. If she left now she'd be leaving the Colonel in the lurch; if she didn't leave soon Alan might never forgive her.

There were plenty of people still left in the field. Once Kate had thought that hunting was only for the rich and socially ambitious but now she knew better. The people gathered in the field were representative of every part of country life, farmers, shopkeepers, craftsmen, builders, practically everybody who had a stake in the countryside. In a popular hunting country such as this, it was hunting which kept them all together and there was nothing they all enjoyed more than a chance for a good gossip outside in the open with plenty of liquor to loosen the tongue. The Colonel, Kate saw, was getting into the car with Deborah. They'd be out for the rest of the morning, if not the day, following the hunt.

She took some sausage rolls over to the Amenity Society people who looked as if they could do with some food.

'We took quite a bit of money this morning,' one of the men said, rattling his tin.

Kate looked at it in despair. What good was that little heap of money now? Soon she would have to give it all back again. She didn't know where she was going to start. 'I'm sorry,' she said. 'I'm afraid things aren't very good. It looks as if Meccarda are going to buy The Court. Since the Colonel's illness . . .'

'It's all right, Kate,' said a woman who lived in a charming house overlooking Little Riddleton village green. 'The Colonel's illness was a terrible blow – we all know that. And we all understand his position. We're wondering whether we can carry on fighting without him. Don't look so sad. We know it's not your fault. You've done your best.'

Kate wasn't comforted. If Alan was to be believed her best wasn't good enough. It wasn't enough to do what you could. Failure was failure.

In the distance she could see the Blazers spread out over the Colonel's fifteen acres of grass, jumping the small stone walls in line abreast, no doubt making the most of the last time they would be able to do it.

She didn't want to think about Alan, didn't want to remember that terrible end to the telephone conversation. 'What will you do if you don't come out here?' he'd said. Had he given her an ultimatum? She picked up a tray and began collecting empty glasses, going over the conversation she'd had with him in her head. Then she remembered something he'd said which gave her a crumb of comfort. 'I've got to give them my answer soon.' She had been too upset to take in the significance of the remark at the time, but she drew a little hope from it now. He hadn't accepted yet then. Perhaps if she were to write him a long letter trying to explain what she felt, he would reconsider. She would do it today, just as soon as everybody had gone and she'd finished clearing up.

But later, when she was alone in her room with pen and paper, Kate found that the more she tried to put her feelings into words the more unreasonable she realised she was being. Perhaps I should just pack it all in now and go out there, she thought, staring out of her little window at the beautiful unspoilt countryside, which soon might all be under the nose of the bulldozer. There must be something they could do to stop it. She stared at the half-written letter in front of her. Maybe Alan could think of a way. He was so clever. So resourceful. Everything Alan did was always successful.

She began to write quickly, describing the view from her window, the rolling peaceful acres and distant church towers. If she could only get Alan involved he might be able to understand her predicament better. If they could just save the village and its surroundings, The Court and its fifteen acres from becoming Meccarda's plaything, she told him, then she would happily spend the next two years in Saudi, learn to play bridge and tennis and to become a pampered bored wife. She finished her letter and walked into the village to post it before she had time to change her mind. It wasn't until it had gone that she remembered that she had been going to win this battle on her own, prove to Alan she could accomplish something without him. Well, that wasn't so important, what mattered was saving the village and the countryside from destruction. She knew in her heart that there was nothing Alan could do to stop Meccarda, but she thought that perhaps he might feel better if she pretended he could. At least it would give her a few more days before she had to come to a definite decision. If she waited a little longer perhaps things would just sort themselves out somehow. She knew she was being a coward. But if she went off to Saudi now and left the Colonel in the lurch she was also being a coward.

* * *

March came in like a lion, the wind roaring down the chimneys and making all the fires at The Court smoke most horribly. It wasn't so frightening or so damaging as the gale at Christmas, just tiring. The wind was a cold blustering bully, setting every ill-fitting window rattling and sending the draughts swirling through the gaps to mock the poor old central heating, which was burning money night and day and still failing to make much of an impact on the temperature. Kate worried more and more about the Colonel, whether he was warm enough, whether he was going to have another stroke, whether he was going downhill mentally if not physically, how to stop him trying to drive his car.

He fussed a lot about the sale of The Court and seemed terribly confused. Half the time he still seemed to think he was fighting the campaign against the holiday village, the rest of the time he couldn't wait to get the sale through. He kept ringing up John Kindersby at his office, asking how the sale of the house was going and then telling him that he'd had a wonderful offer from some completely fictitious body and asking John's advice. Kate didn't see how she could possibly leave him in his present condition. Caroline kept telling Kate that her father was losing his marbles and Kate was afraid that if she went away to Saudi now, the Colonel might be back at The Priory in no time in spite of all Caroline's good intentions. To add to her worries there was no word from Alan. Kate didn't know whether to be relieved or frightened and alternated between both.

The Blazers finished serious hunting after the point-to-point and went to the hills as spring arrived. When Kate looked out of her window in the mornings she could see tractors at work, harrowing the grass or busy planting spring barley. There were lambs gambolling in the fields and larks singing, daffodils just coming into bud in thick random clumps all down The Court drive, crocus adding splashes of colour in unsuspected corners and in the churchyard the grass was strewn with primroses. As Kate walked by everybody seemed to be busy in their gardens, planting or digging or pruning. But not at The Court.

John rang on 13 March to say the deal was done. Meccarda had completed in record time. The Court was sold. Although Kate knew it was inevitable she felt terribly sad. It was an awkward house, determined to resist all her best efforts to make it comfortable and convenient, but it had character and dignity and a mind of its own. Rather like its owner. A lot of money wisely spent could have made it a model Cotswold family home again. It seemed cruel to turn it into some pseudo-gothic leisure centre for refugees from the teeming cities.

In the meantime, John had been very clever and arranged with Meccarda for the Colonel to continue to live at The Court. It was an arrangement designed to suit both parties: the Colonel didn't have to find somewhere else to live, and Meccarda, who were allowing the Colonel's application for planning permission to reach a conclusion on their behalf, were only too pleased to have the house occupied at a nominal rent rather than standing empty and at risk from squatters and vandals. The Colonel seemed pleased with the arrangement and Kate couldn't help feeling that he still hadn't come to terms with the fact that his house was sold.

One morning about a week later, the Colonel, busy opening his post at the kitchen table over breakfast, gave a great shout.

'Tally-ho! Gone away!'

Kate came running from the boot room where she had her head in the deep freeze. 'What is it? What's the matter?'

'The planning permission for The Court has been turned down,' he cried, waving a letter in triumph. 'Derek Evans says the Assistant Planning Officer has been transferred to another job in the north. The Council has turned down our application.'

'But it's been sold – Meccarda paid sixty per cent of building land price for it,' said Kate, bewildered.

'I know.' The Colonel looked smug. 'John should have listened to me, tested the market more. But he's always in such a hurry, is John. Very impatient man. Afraid of missing the bus.'

So that's what he had been up to! thought Kate. Goading John into getting a quick sale before Derek Evans came back from his holiday and set about opposing the planning appeal. Letting them all think he was confused and losing his marbles. 'Now that's settled we've got to brief that friend of yours to take them on at the public inquiry. What's she called – Sheila – Susie?'

'You mean Shirley?' Kate said, groping for what was left of her wits. So he still meant to go on fighting the public inquiry. He wasn't confused at all, the devious old sod. 'I don't think we've got enough money yet,' she said doubtfully. 'We've rather back-peddled on the fund-raising recently.'

'We've got over £10,000. I thought your friend whatshername said she'd be interested in taking us on at that figure. The Council will pay its share – I have a promise here from Derek Evans.' He waved the letter under her nose triumphantly. 'Now, who can we get to stump up the rest?' Kate was feeling breathless – lost in awe at the diabolical cunning of it. 'I don't think Caroline – do you?' The Colonel winked at her mischievously. 'But we might try Debs. She's a millionaire now, thanks to John. I'm sure Debs won't mind doing her bit for the countryside. How much more do you think we need to get the ball rolling?'

He was happy as a skylark again, ready for battle and full of energy for the task ahead. Kate sank down at the kitchen table and poured herself another cup of coffee, feeling quite weak just contemplating the challenges that lay ahead.

'I'll drive over and tackle Debs tomorrow,' said the Colonel, eyes twinkling. 'She'll be at a bit of a loose end now hunting is finishing and Patrick's out all day on the land.'

'I'd better come with you,' she said. She didn't want to but she couldn't possibly let him go on his own.

'Good,' he said. 'I'll ring Debs now. I might just catch her before she goes out riding.' As he dialled the number, Kate marvelled at the way he had manipulated her into offering to take him. Trading on her fear of letting him drive himself, just as he had traded on John's fear of losing the sale of The Court to another bidder. It was all a bluff, probably, but it wasn't very nice of him to play on her good nature like that. She left the kitchen while he was talking to Patrick, remembering she'd left the deep freeze open when the Colonel had shouted.

When she came back he was looking rather shaken. 'What's happened, what's the matter?' she asked.

'Deborah's run off with that horse-coping fellow,' he said. 'Now that she's going to be a rich woman in her own right she can buy him a pack of hounds and go and live with him on some hillside in Wales.'

'I don't believe it!' said Kate, her mind in a whirl.

'Money, Kate,' he said sadly. 'It's the root of all evil. Coming into a lot of money never does anybody any good. It never makes them happy.' He sat staring down at the table in silence while Kate's thoughts went round and round in her head. If Deborah had gone, Patrick was free.

'I wish I could think of a way of bringing her back,' said the Colonel at length. 'I blame myself for not realising how desperate poor old Debs must have been for attention. Patrick's always too busy, too self-centred. And these last months I've had you to keep me company and this holiday village thing. But poor little Debs has been cooped up at home with that leg, not able to ride, not able to hunt. It's too bad. That fellow Jones is nothing but an opportunist and he's taken advantage of her when she's down.' He looked at Kate sadly. 'I wish I could think of some way of getting her back,' he repeated.

Kate blamed herself too. She had a horrible feeling that if Deborah hadn't caught Patrick out being unfaithful this would never have happened. We thought we were just having a bit of harmless fun, she thought, but there's no such thing as harmless fun if it's with someone else's husband, especially if you do it more than once. It becomes a habit, whether it's once a year or once a week, and habits are difficult to break.

All the same she couldn't help feeling excited. Patrick was free. The thought wouldn't go away. But though Patrick's free, I'm not, she told herself fiercely. I'm still married to Alan. Only she didn't know what Alan wanted any more, she thought in sudden panic. Alan still hadn't replied to her letter. Had he, like Deborah, found someone else? Had her indecision and – yes – lack of love, driven him into someone else's arms?

# *Chapter 19*

'Your father is an out-and-out bastard!' John came storming into the bedroom where Caroline was having her breakfast in bed.

'Why, what's he done now?'

'Only persuaded that Planning Officer he has in the palm of his hand to turn down the planning application for The Court and all the land.'

'Oh John, no!'

'And that's not all!' He came to stand at the foot of the bed and glowered at her unnervingly. 'AB's going on with the fight. He's briefed Balcock and Sims to represent them at the public inquiry and he's got the Council paying half the costs. I shall have to resign from Meccarda's board.' Caroline's heart sank. One thing John couldn't stand was being made to look a fool.

'It's not your fault,' she said. 'You were only trying to help.'

'I know that. But when things go wrong the chap at the top should accept the blame. The only decent thing I can do is resign.'

'Well, it won't much matter,' she said, trying to be comforting. 'You were only a non-executive director after all. You won't miss the money and it's not as if you were going to be there more than once a month.' He began to pace up and down and she knew by his furious expression that she hadn't succeeded. She put down her teacup and tried again. 'You probably wouldn't have enjoyed being on the board much anyway,' she said. 'It's going to be very uncomfortable for some of the people at Meccarda now they've been taken over by ABC.' His scowl deepened and she realised too late that she probably hadn't been very tactful. 'I know you only accepted that seat on the board because you wanted to look after our interests and those of the people of Little Riddleton, of course.'

'Don't be such a fool, Caroline,' he said. 'I was hoping for great things from Meccarda once the dust of the takeover had settled. But now your father's fucked everything up.' She was shocked. John hardly ever swore – only when he was really furious. He was slow to anger but when he did occasionally erupt he was like a volcano, spewing rocks and molten lava for miles around. It would be days before she would be able to get him to calm down.

'You'll have to go down there and sort out the mess,' he said, coming back to the foot of the bed.

'I don't know what I can do,' she said, carefully pouring tea.

'You can start by sacking Kate. This is all her doing. If it wasn't for her none of this would have happened.'

'Oh John, I can't do that,' Caroline pleaded. 'It would be too cruel. Father depends on her so, and the damage is done now, surely?'

'No, it's not too late,' he insisted. 'We'll appeal – of course. The whole thing can be dealt with at the public inquiry. I'll see if I can't bring some pressure to bear on the Minister. If the inspector overrules the Council and allows the planning we'll get our development in the end.'

'There you are, John, you see. You can't possibly resign.' Caroline smiled at him proudly. 'They still need you to sort it all out for them.' He looked a little mollified. At last she seemed to have said the right thing.

'What we can't have is your father rousing the whole countryside and fighting us,' he said, beginning to wander about the room again. 'It'll make the entire thing so damn costly. The whole point of Meccarda paying all that money for The Court was to get the scheme through without any opposition. You've got to go down and talk to him. Make him see sense.'

Caroline began spooning yoghurt on to her bowlful of bran. She didn't see how she could make her father do anything he didn't want to do.

'Perhaps I'll ring Debs,' she said, stirring it into a porridgey mess. 'She might be able to come up with something.'

John laughed, a short bitter sound. Caroline stared at him in surprise. 'No good ringing your sister Deborah,' he said. 'She's run off with the local gigolo apparently.'

'What!'

'Your father blames us, naturally. He says she never would have run off if she'd not had the money to do it.' Caroline dropped the spoon with a clatter, thinking of Ned Jones that day she'd caught him coming out of her sister's bedroom. Had Deborah gone out of her mind? She couldn't have gone off with a man like that. Not when she was married to someone like Patrick. It didn't make sense.

'Poor old Patrick,' she said. 'Is he taking it very badly?'

'Patrick blames us – Patrick will always blame somebody else for his problems – it's never his fault.' John was pacing up and down the room again, scowling furiously. 'You'll have to go down there. The whole place seems to be falling apart. Your father thinks he's got all the trump cards but he seems to have forgotten that his house has been sold and he's just double-crossed his landlord.' Caroline pushed aside her beautifully arranged tray in disgust, completely stunned by this latest crisis. John, having spoilt her breakfast, seemed more cheerful.

'Well,' he said, coming round the side of the bed, 'I must get off to the office. I'm late as it is.' He bent over to peck her on the cheek. 'I'll let you finish your breakfast in peace. I know I can rely on you, darling,' he added as he left the room.

She lay back against the pillows and thought sadly of how she had planned to spend a delightful day visiting estate agents and looking for possible country houses. But there didn't seem much point now. John would never agree to have the Colonel living with them, not after this. And if Deborah had run off he couldn't go there. God what a mess! Damon the whippet got out of his beanbag, stretched, yawned and approached the bed with careful circumspection. Caroline watched in loving silence, as the dog sat down gingerly and gazed at her with wistful longing.

'All right,' she said. 'You can come up. He's gone.' He jumped on to the bed with the graceful precision of a cat, settling himself down beside his mistress without endangering the breakfast tray.

It occurred to Caroline suddenly that she didn't need John's permission to buy a house in the country. She'd got her own money now. He couldn't stop her doing what she wanted with it. But of course she didn't want to upset John. She loved him. John was her whole life. He protected her from her family and she found her fulfilment in pleasing him. But now John would blame her, if she didn't do something. They all would, she felt sure. It really wasn't fair. She looked at the telephone beside her bed wondering where to start. Kate? But she'd tried Kate before. John was right. Kate was part of the trouble.

I should never have taken her on, thought Caroline in despair. It's all my fault. She stroked Damon's soft fur absently. All she had ever wanted to do was solve everybody's problems and now Deborah had run off, and Daddy was about to be made homeless, and Patrick was blaming everybody except himself, and she, Caroline, was expected to sort out the family once again. She stared accusingly at the telephone. Where on earth was Kate's husband? she wondered. John had been so confident that the husband would appear like the proverbial knight on a white charger to whisk Kate away from the battlefield. But where was he?

It was a question Kate too was asking herself that morning, as she collected the letters from the floor by the front door and sifted quickly through them, looking in vain for a Middle Eastern stamp. It was now over three weeks since Alan had telephoned and she hadn't heard a word from him. He must have got her letter by now. She picked up the letters and carried them into the kitchen where the Colonel was finishing his breakfast.

It wasn't like Alan to keep her waiting and his silence was beginning to frighten her. Never in her whole life had Alan been anything other than dependable, predictable and totally devoted. It was one of the reasons that she had been tempted by Patrick. But devotion she now discovered was like money or health, it was only something you really appreciated after you'd lost it. It was strange how much she remembered about Alan now that she was afraid he had forgotten her. The way his hair felt so thick and springy when she ran her fingers through it, the way the corners of his eyes crinkled when he smiled, the little tune he used to hum when he was happy. Several times she had stood in front of the coin-operated telephone in her flat and contemplated telephoning Saudi. She wanted to but she didn't dare. Once she even got as far as laying out the coins and Alan's telephone number, but her courage failed her at the last moment. She was too afraid that he might not want to hear from her. She could not bear it if he offered lame excuses, or sounded embarrassed, or worst of all told her he'd finally had enough.

'Right,' said the Colonel, suddenly interrupting her depressing train of thought, 'give me your shopping list and I'll be off.'

Kate sighed. If only he'd stop this nonsense about wanting to drive. She supposed it was all part of the desire for independence but it really was beginning to get on her nerves. Sometimes she was tempted to let him try driving his car, just to prove to him that it was quite impossible. But not this morning.

'It's no good your going into Bratchester for me,' she said. 'I've got to go there anyway to get my hair done.'

He looked at her roguishly. 'But you've just had it done. It looks very pretty.' She couldn't help smiling. He really was a very gallant old rascal. 'What excuse are you going to give me today then, Kate?' he asked, watching her like an eager bird waiting to catch a worm.

'I'm not giving you any excuses.' She took refuge in truth and the direct approach. 'I'm not letting you drive, that's all.'

He gave in gracefully. 'All right then. I'll go and write some letters. There's two more cheques in today, it's important to write and thank straight away.' He shuffled off to his study and she wondered whether the recipients were able to decipher the wavering scrawl he'd achieved with the aid of the physiotherapist. At least if they didn't it wouldn't much matter. The pen might be mightier than the sword but in the Colonel's restricted hands the car was by far the most lethal weapon. She left him under Ellen Murphy's watchful eye and sprinted away before he had time to change his mind.

Pushing her trolley round Waitrose a little later, Kate felt relieved just to be away from The Court and all its problems for a while, able to wander idly up and down, looking at the well-packed shelves with nothing more taxing than food on her mind.

She paused in front of the pasta, wondering whether she could persuade the Colonel to eat ravioli stuffed with ricotta and basil. Perhaps if she added cream and tomatoes, a little garlic even. It would be very easy for him to eat. Ought to slip down a treat as Ellen Murphy would say. A hand appeared over her shoulder and grabbed a packet from the shelf in front of her.

'Live dangerously, Kate,' whispered a familiar voice in her ear, 'go for the ones stuffed with smoked salmon.' She spun round in amazement.

'Patrick, what are you doing here?' she asked. He dropped the ravioli packet in her trolley and grinned at her cheerfully.

'Looking for you,' he said. He didn't seem to be taking his wife's desertion too much to heart, she thought, backing away warily. Heads, she noticed, were beginning to turn, women smiled at her enviously. It wasn't surprising, Kate thought, gratified in spite of herself. He looked so handsome and so vigorously male, even in his faded jeans and worn old sports coat, storming into such a female preserve as Waitrose on a Tuesday in the middle of the morning, rather like a splendid peacock straying into a cage of battery hens.

'If you've finished shopping let's go and have coffee somewhere,' he said. She hadn't finished but she knew she'd never be able to concentrate with him breathing down her neck and so she went with him to the checkout and took her place in the queue. While she waited her turn, he caused quite a sensation, darting up and down the aisles seizing things and adding them to her basket, accosting the various female assistants to help him find what he wanted, causing every female heart over thirty-five to flutter, creating such a stir that by the time he'd finished Kate felt she was in need of a pacemaker herself. She couldn't help feeling a little flattered that he'd come looking for her, in Waitrose of all places. But as she began taking things out of the basket and piling it on to the checkout counter, she realised that far from looking for her, what he'd in fact come into Waitrose for was instant dinners for one.

'Are you expecting the Colonel to pay for yours too?' she asked, piqued in spite of herself.

'Of course not, I'll pay for both,' he said, flashing his wallet and his pearly white teeth at the checkout girl. The effect on her was predictable. The girl blushed and dropped a melon she was trying to put in a bag. It rolled like a well-thrown bowl towards the edge of the desk and Patrick caught it with perfect reflexes as it hurled itself over. Kate avoided his triumphant smile and waited patiently for the girl to recover. Eventually all was bagged and paid for, the girl's day made, the shopping stacked in boxes. Patrick carried it out to Kate's car for her. Then taking her by the elbow he steered her off to the old wool market and into a low-beamed picturesque little bower redolent with the smell of freshly ground coffee.

The coffee house was almost empty. In the bow window one or two little grey-haired old ladies sat gossiping and drinking coffee. Patrick chose a table in the darkest corner at the back of the room and ordered coffee and walnut cake for two. He was being very macho and protective, Kate thought, and wondered what enormous favour he was about to ask her. It was too dark for her to see his expression but she could feel his thigh hard and sinewy brushing against hers.

'I'm so sorry about Deborah,' she said, inching away.

'Don't be,' he replied, taking her hand. 'I was angry at first but that's probably because my pride was hurt. Now I realise it's all for the best.'

'But the children,' she murmured, trying without success to remove her hand, 'won't they be terribly upset?'

'For a while, I expect they will,' he murmured. 'But they'll get over it. Lots of their friends' parents are divorced, it's quite common. The important thing is not to change the children's routine. Keep the continuity going. If they can still come home to their own bedrooms and their ponies, and everything is still the same, they'll get used to Debs not being there in time.' A large motherly woman arrived with their order and Patrick let go of Kate's hand. Kate took the opportunity to thrust both hands deep inside her coat pockets. Was Patrick about to offer her a job or something much more improper? she wondered as she watched the woman set out the two coffees frothing with whipped cream and two plates each with a slice of homemade cake.

'The Colonel's very sorry for Deborah,' she said, as soon as they were on their own again. 'He thinks she only did it because she was feeling lonely and neglected. He's trying to think of some way to get her back.'

'That's all balls,' Patrick said harshly and she realised he wasn't quite as detached about it as he'd tried to pretend. 'Debs went off with that fellow Jones because she couldn't bear to think of him screwing half Gloucestershire when he wasn't with her. She thinks she's got him on a short rein now but she'll know different when she catches him with his leg over some Welsh kennelmaid.' Kate stared down at the blobs of whipped cream sprinkled with little bits of chocolate floating on the top of her coffee as she remembered that terrible scene in the Imperial. She didn't think even a Welsh kennelmaid would stand much of a chance with Deborah. All the same, she couldn't help feeling guilty.

'You don't think, do you, Patrick, that she did it to pay you out for what we did?'

'No I don't,' he said quickly – too quickly almost. 'Oh, I daresay that's how it all started – but she'd never run off and leave me and the children unless she was out of her mind. It's all that money, it's gone to her head.' Kate was silent, absently sprinkling sugar on to the cream. The women in the window had their heads together busy passing on secrets.

Patrick moved closer so that his leg was touching hers again.

'You know, Kate,' he murmured, 'we've been lucky, you and I. It's not often people get a second chance in life.' She was afraid he was going to take her hand again so she picked up her coffee and held it firmly with both.

'We had a great thing going for us all those years ago,' he went on, putting his hand on her leg instead. 'And it's still there, that's the whole wonderful thing about it.' His hand was moving slowly up her thigh. Short of throwing the coffee over him there wasn't a great deal she could do about it. So instead she sipped her coffee and tried to ignore him. 'Kate,' he squeezed her thigh gently, 'will you marry me?' She almost dropped the coffee cup. As it was she spilt some of it down her flowered Laura Ashley blouse. He whipped out a blue and white spotted cotton handkerchief and began mopping her up.

She remembered with painful clarity how he had done the same thing all those years ago over lunch in the Imperial. Then she had been so overcome with lust she had been barely able to contain herself. Now she felt nothing but a huge sadness. Chemistry it seemed was no more reliable than electricity. One moment she was lighting up with desire every time Patrick touched her, the next moment, nothing, just as if someone had pulled the plug. And that someone was Alan. His desertion had reduced what she felt for Patrick to a low-voltage glow, not even enough to keep a greenhouse frostproof in winter. She became aware that Patrick was waiting somewhat impatiently for her answer.

'I can't marry you, Patrick, don't be silly,' she said. 'I'm married to Alan.'

'Of course. I'd forgotten. He's such a shadowy figure, your Alan.'

Kate removed his hand from her leg and pushed her chair away with a great scraping noise, so that the two old tabbies at the window table looked round in surprise. 'Well, I haven't forgotten him,' she declared firmly, 'and just as soon as you've found someone to take care of the Colonel I'm going out to join him in Saudi.'

'You don't expect me to believe that's really what you want, Kate darling,' he said, grabbing her hand and holding it tightly. 'You don't want to go out and waste yourself in a place like Saudi. What you want is to live here in Gloucestershire.' She tried to pull her hand away but he held on, grinning at her. 'With me, Kate.'

She sat still, feeling cornered. Somehow she had to make him understand that she wasn't still in love with him. But she doubted very much whether he was in the mood to believe anything she said. She didn't want to kick a man when he was down and she doubted whether his vanity would stand rejection from both his wife and his mistress at the same time. It wasn't Patrick's fault that the scales had at last fallen from her eyes. It was Alan's. Patrick was no different than he'd always been: a handsome shit, but weak, vulnerable, self-centred. It was Alan who had changed from being the ever-loving, dependable husband.

'Look, Patrick, let's leave it, shall we?' she said wearily. 'You don't really know what you want. It's far too soon for you to be rushing round asking people to marry you.'

'I'm not rushing round asking people to marry me,' he said, rather sulkily. 'I'm rushing to ask you, Kate, because it's what I should have done all those years ago, only I was in too much of a muddle after my father's death to think straight. Well, I'm not going to make that mistake again. I'm not going to let you go a second time.'

'You're not in a position to ask me now,' she prevaricated. 'You're still married to Deborah. Ask me again, if you must, when you're free. By that time I might know whether you really want me or just someone to keep house for you and the children in Deborah's place.' He looked so contrite she guessed that she had not been too wide of the mark. Feeling depressed she gathered up her coat and her bag. It was just as well the scales had fallen from her eyes otherwise she'd have been taken in by that proposal of his, she thought as they walked back in silence to her car. What a mess she'd have been in then.

But am I not in a mess now? she asked herself when she was driving back to The Court. If Alan doesn't want me, what am I going to do? It was the question which plagued her each night in that unrelenting time between darkness and dawn, when she lay awake, consumed by guilt and a nameless dread, unable to see any simple solutions and utterly bowed down by the impossibility of it all.

When Kate got home to The Court she heaved the box of shopping out of the car and carried it into the house, hoping to get it all put away before the Colonel realised she was back. But the dogs came rushing out to welcome her and no sooner had she dumped it all on the kitchen table than the Colonel came shuffling in after them to investigate.

'So you're back,' he said, consulting his watch. 'It's past twelve. What took you so long?'

'I don't know,' she replied. 'There were a lot of people in Waitrose today. I didn't know there was any hurry.' He glared at her, but she took no notice.

'The Murphy woman tackled me about what was going to happen to them when Meccarda take the place over,' he said, leaning on his stick and watching her unpacking her purchases. 'They're very worried.'

'What did you tell them?' asked Kate.

'I told her that the family would look after them, of course,' he said, sitting down at the kitchen table.

'I thought Ellen was hoping they could stay on in the cottage and act as caretakers,' she said cautiously. 'Although, of course, now the planning application has been turned down Meccarda may not want it.'

'I'm not worried about the Murphy woman – she'll be happy enough pensioned off. No, it's poor old Murphy I'm worried about. He's the kind that wants to work till they drop. It'd break his heart not to have horses to care for.' Kate deduced that Caroline had broken the news she meant to give up hunting. Murphy wasn't the only one who was silently breaking his heart at the thought of not having any horses around. Damn Ellen, thought Kate, putting the melon on the rack above the Aga to ripen, she might have had more tact. Up till now the Colonel had said nothing about what was going to happen after Meccarda had taken possession of The Court, but perhaps he too lay awake and worrying in that dreadful hour before dawn.

'Caroline was hoping you might like to set up house with her,' Kate said, thinking it might be better to get a few worries out into the open.

'Good God, no. I had enough of that at Christmas.'

'Not in London – in the country. She's got it all worked out. She wants to buy a house somewhere round here with an annexe she can convert for you. She means to employ a living-in couple who can look after you and the house as well.'

The Colonel was adamant. 'No, Kate. It wouldn't work.'

'You'll be quite independent. I expect she'll only be down at weekends. You'd be doing her a favour really.' He was sitting scowling at the remains of the shopping strewn over the table and she wondered whether he was thinking that Caroline might not want him now, not after he'd pulled the mat from John's feet so to speak.

'What's this rubbish?' The Colonel pounced on the packet of pink ravioli and held it up accusingly. 'You don't expect me to eat this foreign muck, do you?'

Kate laughed, relieved to be able to change the subject. 'I don't – but Patrick does. He thinks we don't live dangerously enough.'

'Don't we though.' The Colonel winked at her and she smiled back, glad that he seemed to have got over his depression. 'You've seen Patrick then?' he asked, tossing the packet of ravioli back in the box. Too late she regretted letting Patrick's name slip out.

'He was in Bratchester today, shopping in Waitrose,' she said making light of it. 'He seems to be taking it very well all things considered.' He was sitting staring at her rather fixedly.

'Do you want me to give this away to the Murphys?' she asked, rescuing the ravioli. She didn't want those shrewd old eyes of his seeing too much. 'I'm sure they'd love to try it for their tea.'

'No, of course not. We'll have to give it a go. Even if it plays havoc with my digestion. But don't you go wasting my money on such nonsense in future.'

'It wasn't your money, Patrick paid.'

'Did he now. That was good of him. I wonder what he wants from me.'

'He just wanted to be friendly, I imagine,' said Kate, wishing more than ever that she hadn't brought Patrick into the conversation.

'Patrick has no imagination,' said the Colonel studying Kate thoughtfully. 'That's what makes him such a fearless rider; he's brave because he never allows himself to think of the consequences.'

Kate pondered the Colonel's words as she took the empty box out to the woodshed for kindling. He was right, Patrick was another one who didn't think things through. Patrick was like her in that respect and now look at the mess they were both in. She should have left the Colonel in that nice nursing home and gone out to Saudi, then none of this would have happened. If only Alan would ring, I'd be on the next plane to Saudi, she thought longingly. She dumped the empty box down beside a pile of dry logs. Don't be such a wimp, she told herself fiercely. You started all this to prove that you could do things on your own. You can't go and leave the Colonel in the lurch now. Oh dear, it was all so very difficult.

The more she tried to help the worse everything became. She felt a wet nose against her hand. Spot had followed her out into the woodshed, hoping she was going to take him for a walk. She sat down on a pile of logs and put her arms round the dog's neck taking comfort from his warm soft body.

'I so wanted to show Alan I could succeed at something,' she poured her troubles into the dog's sympathetic ear. 'Now it looks as if all I've succeeded in doing is driving him away altogether.' Spot wagged his tail in token agreement. Perhaps what Alan was doing, she thought with a little spurt of optimism, was letting her prove herself. It wasn't much to cling to, but it was better than believing Alan didn't want her at all.

When Caroline telephoned that evening Kate was in the study with the Colonel listening to the six o'clock news on Radio Four. The Colonel was brusque and obstinate and refused to give up the fight against Meccarda. Caroline then asked to speak to Kate. With the Colonel sitting there all ears, Caroline asked Kate outright when she was going back to her husband.

'Just as soon as your father wants me to go,' Kate replied, stung.

Caroline didn't seem able to think of a suitable answer to that one and hung up after reminding Kate that soon her father wouldn't have a roof over his head. Meccarda could hardly be blamed if they were to give him notice to leave.

After that everything went very quiet. The Colonel seemed quite happy busy getting their case ready for the public inquiry. He seemed not to worry about where he was going to live if not with Caroline, nor who was going to clear out The Court ready to hand it over to Meccarda. With Deborah gone the task was bound to fall on Caroline and she was lying low. But the Colonel didn't seem to be worried and Kate, living in daily dread of an angry deputation from Meccarda demanding his immediate removal, began to wonder if he really had lost his marbles. Time seemed to be standing still, but it made Kate all the more uneasy. She felt this was just the calm before a very angry storm indeed.

# *Chapter 20*

Coming out of church on the last Sunday in March the vicar asked the Colonel in his bereavement counselling voice if it was true that the sale of The Court had fallen through.

'No, thank God,' said the Colonel breezily. 'The sale's all done, signed and sealed. They can't get out of that now, I'm glad to say. It's the planning permission that's not gone through.'

'Oh dear,' the vicar looked more nonplussed than ever. 'I'm so sorry to hear that. It would bring a bit of life to the place. Might even swell our congregations on a Sunday.' He gave a self-conscious smirk.

'Don't be sorry, Padre,' snapped the Colonel. 'It's what I've been praying for every Sunday I've been to church since I got out of hospital. Come on, Kate. Good morning, Padre.' Leaning heavily on her, he shuffled off through the churchyard, leaving the vicar looking decidedly put out. Kate wondered whether he had been praying for a whole new congregation and thought it must be very difficult for God if He listened to the prayers in English country villages every Sunday. It wasn't surprising really that He didn't answer very many.

'What have we got for lunch?' the Colonel asked, once she'd helped him safely into the car and they were on their way home.

'Roast chicken and plum tart,' replied Kate, hoping he wasn't going to start being contrary about it. She didn't feel up to an argument about food, not so soon after church. The peace of God which passeth all understanding ought to keep at least until lunch time.

'That's good.' For once the Colonel seemed prepared to agree with her. He didn't attempt to interfere as she drove slowly out of the village, nor to warn her to give old Haygate a wide berth as he was deaf as a post and liable to wander into the middle of the road at any moment, or to point out, as he invariably did, that there were two ducks across the road from the pond who might be about to take it into their heads to cross.

They had reached the T-junction at the end of the village when he said: 'I've asked poor old Patrick over to lunch. He'll be in need of a square meal I expect.' Kate was so disconcerted she forgot to brake before turning left. 'Look out!' shouted the Colonel as a car appeared in front of them. Kate jammed on the brakes and the car whizzed by on its way unscathed. 'Sure you wouldn't like me to drive?' teased the Colonel, totally undeterred. 'You don't seem very safe to me.'

'I'm better than you,' Kate told him firmly. 'I just wasn't concentrating – that's all.'

'Women drivers,' he muttered, pleased to have caught her napping. 'Always thinking of something else – never got your mind on the matter in hand.'

'It's all very well for men,' she told him as they turned into The Court's drive, 'you can concentrate on one thing at a time because you only have to do one thing at a time. It's different for us women. We have to cook and entertain you and drive and think about the cooking and the children and goodness knows how many other different things at once.'

Delighted to have succeeded in getting a rise out of her, he got out of the car chuckling happily and went away to his study saying that if she found it that difficult to do more than one thing at a time he would leave her to get on with lunch in peace.

She was relieved. She needed time to prepare herself. She didn't think Patrick would be able to renew his proposals of marriage with the Colonel there, but he might try to get her alone and if he did so she would have to be very firm, convince him once and for all that she was not interested in anything he had to offer. All the same, she didn't feel ready for another confrontation with Patrick quite so soon and so she laid the lunch in the kitchen instead of the dining room, thinking that there would be less opportunity for Patrick to catch her on her own. If the Colonel objected she'd tell him it was cosier in the kitchen. But the Colonel seemed quite happy with the arrangement.

Patrick arrived at one o'clock full of apparent good spirits. He carved the chicken while Kate dished up and the Colonel sat at the kitchen table happily recounting to Patrick the progress they were making in fighting the holiday village application.

'We've sent all the stuff to this girl – what's her name – Susan, Sharon?'

'Shirley,' said Kate, putting his plate down in front of him.

'I knew it was something like that,' the Colonel nodded, pleased with himself. 'She's ready to start briefing the experts now. We'll have to go to London, I expect, to meet them. You might like to come with us, Patrick.'

'Have you raised enough money yet?' asked Patrick as he piled his plate high and sat down beside Kate.

'The Duke's promised to help us once we raise enough to brief this hot-shot solicitor friend of Kate's,' the Colonel said, spearing a piece of the chicken Patrick had cut up for him and smearing it with bread sauce. 'I think we need to bring up the big guns.' He raised the fork carefully to his mouth. 'The Duke must be good for at least a thousand. What do you think, Patrick?'

'Don't you think it might be better to wait a bit?' Patrick mumbled.

'Wait!' the Colonel shouted through a mouthful of food, so that little specks of chicken and bread sauce shot out in a fine spray and clung to his moustache like snowflakes. 'We can't afford to wait – not now. The public inquiry's due some time in the spring. We've waited long enough as it is. I'll telephone the Duke after lunch – Sunday's a good day to catch him at home. If he's free you can drive me over, Patrick. It'd be better if we saw him together.'

'I'm afraid I can't this afternoon.' Patrick had his head down busily dissecting a chicken wing. 'Sorry, AB.' He didn't attempt to give any excuses, probably because he had none. The Colonel was now attacking a rather crisp roast potato with his fork and failing to break its resistance. Kate blamed herself for not having cut it up for him.

'All right then,' the Colonel said with a deeply cunning smile. 'I'll just have to drive over there myself.' Patrick threw Kate an appealing glance.

'Don't fall for it,' she whispered as she got up. 'He's only bluffing. He's found it's a wonderful way to make people do what he wants.' She cut the Colonel's potatoes in half for him and went back to her seat. The Colonel munched in silence for a while, occasionally shooting glances at Patrick from beneath his bushy eyebrows. It was meant to be unnerving but Patrick didn't seem unnerved. Kate, who had finished, sipped her wine pensively.

'Have you heard from Caroline at all?' Patrick asked, getting up to help himself to more chicken.

'No. I don't think they're speaking to me at the moment – I can't say that I blame them. I've made John look an awful fool. Egg all over his face.'

'Yes, well, serve him right I suppose for pushing the thing through so quick. If he hadn't been in such a hurry to get the money Debs wouldn't have done a bunk like that.'

'No good blaming poor old John for that,' said the Colonel. 'He may be unable to resist a chance to make money but if Debs went off with that fellow what's his name – Smith? Jones? – it was because you weren't keeping her on a tight enough rein. Debs has always been a bit of a one for kicking over the traces if she wasn't ridden into her bit. You've been slack, Patrick my boy. But she'll be back presently. That chap she's run off with is using her like he used the Duchess. Soon as some other bored wife comes along with money to spare he'll be at his tricks again and poor old Debs will be back home a sadder and wiser woman.'

'I doubt if it's quite as simple as that, AB,' said Patrick looking uncomfortable.

'Of course it's not simple.' The Colonel pushed his plate away. 'Marriage isn't simple. We all know that marriage is as full of pitfalls as a German bloody minefield, which is why you might as well go through it with the devil you know, because it doesn't get any easier if you change partners, isn't that right, Kate?'

Kate didn't dare look at Patrick. How much did the Colonel know? How much had he guessed? What was he up to now?

She got up and started clearing plates, stacking them in the sink and scraping the leftovers into the dogs' dish. But when she came back with the pudding plates the Colonel was still looking at her speculatively. She searched about in her mind for a safe topic of conversation.

'What about Bella?' she asked as she got the plum tart out of the bottom of the Aga. 'Are you going to have Bella, Patrick, now that Caroline's giving up hunting?' The subject of horses always seemed a useful safe harbour when the conversation was getting into troubled waters, Kate had noticed.

'I don't know. Isn't Bella a bit old?' Patrick said.

'Old she may be but she's led an easy life,' the Colonel replied. 'The way Caroline rides her she's done very little over the years. Back in the stable by two most days.'

'I can't say I've ever seen her in action.' Patrick didn't seem to be very keen. 'Caroline keeps her so far back I don't even know whether the horse can perform.'

'She's a good hunter,' the Colonel told him. 'Sound, reliable. She's got a great pop in her given half a chance, so Murphy says. She'd do you well, Patrick, I should think, and with the job you've got to do you can't look a gift horse in the mouth. Tell you what,' he added, as Kate put the pie on the table, 'we'll go and have a look at Bella after lunch. She's out in the field during the day now. We'll take some tack with us and you can have a sit on her if you like.'

'All right,' Patrick agreed.

Kate, doling out plum tart, was relieved that the Colonel seemed to have abandoned his former plan of driving over to visit the Duke of Blazeborough.

'Well, that takes care of Bella,' said the Colonel, tucking into his plum tart with obvious enjoyment. 'But what about me? I don't suppose Caroline will want me to come and live with her, not now I've behaved so disgracefully. More than flesh and blood can stand, I dare say?' Kate's heart sank. There didn't seem to be any certain refuges for her today.

'What are you going to do, if Meccarda want you out straight away now?' she asked, unable to feel sorry for him when he was looking so smug. 'You're not going to try and sit it out, I hope?'

'No, I wouldn't do that – too undignified. Staged sit-ins are for the lower classes and *Guardian* readers. I thought I'd come and live with you, Patrick.'

'Live with me!' Patrick looked just like the loser in a game of pass the parcel, left holding the brown paper bundle when the music stops.

'Can't have a good-looking chap like you living all by yourself,' insisted the Colonel. 'You'll not be on your own for long, if I don't watch out. He's got to have someone to keep an eye on him until Deborah decides to come back, isn't that right, Kate?'

Kate got up to make the coffee, unable to meet that penetrating gaze. Having hit Patrick with his first barrel, the Colonel delivered his second.

'I don't suppose you'd come too, would you, Kate?' he asked.

'No!' she exclaimed, glad she had her back to them both as she put the kettle on.

'We could bring the Murphys as well.' The Colonel went on talking to Patrick impervious of any opposition. 'He can supervise the stables – that girl groom of yours needs an experienced eye on her, especially now Debs isn't there to keep her up to the mark – and Ellen can give a hand to that tractor driver's wife you've got working in the house.' He'd really got it all worked out, thought Kate, impressed at the sheer audacity of the man.

'Must keep the show on the road until Deborah discovers her hero's got feet of clay,' the Colonel told his son-in-law.

Kate began to laugh. It was really too ridiculous the way he thought he could manipulate everybody to suit himself.

'What are you laughing at, Kate? I'm quite serious.'

'I know you are,' she said. 'That's what's so funny. You really can't go arranging everybody's lives to suit you, you know.'

'Why not? It seems that the trouble with all you young people is that you don't know what you want out of life. You think you do but half the time you're so busy chasing around looking for happiness you can't see it when it's right under your nose.'

He was quite impossible, she thought, pouring boiled water on to the coffee. All he wanted was for her to keep Patrick and him happy until Deborah returned. Well, she wasn't going to be made use of like that. The Colonel was watching her as she placed his coffee in front of him, the expression on his face half mischievous, half wistful. In spite of everything Kate couldn't help smiling at him. He was such an indomitable fighter, so tetchy one minute, so full of humour the next. She admired him so much, for the way he refused to be beaten by age, by infirmity, by family disloyalty, for the way his spirit never flinched. He gave no quarter and expected none, but for all that he was capable of inspiring great affection. It wouldn't be easy to refuse him. But of course what he wanted was nonsense – it couldn't possibly work.

'Why not?' asked Patrick when the Colonel had gone for his rest and they were alone together washing up. 'I can't think of anything nicer than having you back at The Manor with the old boy as chaperone. Though I'm not sure I don't draw the line at Ellen Murphy and there won't be much for Murphy to do once the horses are all out at grass.'

'Will you stop taking me for granted and listen just for once?' she said, knowing that the time had come for her to be firm, and keep him at arm's length, although it wasn't easy with her hands encased in rubber gloves and plunged in hot soapy water. 'I'm not the least little bit in love with you any more, Patrick Bray-Smith, so why would I want to come and slave for you and your father-in-law?'

'It wouldn't be slaving. You'd have Sue coming in three days a week as usual and Ellen to do the rough and me to carry the logs and lay and light the fires.' He came to stand behind her and cupped her breasts in his hands, pulling her against him. 'The only seriously hard work you'd have to do would be at night in bed after the Colonel goes to sleep,' he murmured kissing her neck.

'Patrick, don't be silly,' she said, swirling the dishcloth over what was left of the Colonel's best china with little regard for its fate. 'I've said no. How many times do I have to say it to convince you?'

He ran a finger down her spine. 'You might even get paid. I dare say the Colonel would agree to keep you on at whatever he's paying you now. It's an ideal arrangement. Don't be a spoilsport, Kate.'

'Of course it's not an ideal arrangement. It's bloody selfish of the pair of you. I'm not going to be used and that's it.' She took her hands out of the water and pushed him away.

'I know, I know, I know. Of course it's not ideal. I was just joking. But don't you see – it gives us time.'

'I don't need time. I know what I want.'

He tried to take hold of her hands and ended up with water dripping down his shirt front. 'For God's sake, I can't have a serious conversation with you over the kitchen sink,' he said. 'Take those bloody silly rubber gloves off.'

'It won't make any difference. I'm going to Saudi to be with Alan. You've got to understand that, Patrick.'

'I understand you need to get out of here,' he said, dragging her away from the sink. 'Come on, we'll go and look at Bella. The dogs are dying for a run, aren't you, fellows? Walkies, Fred – walkies, Spot. Shall we go and find a hare?' Immediately there was pandemonium as both dogs leapt up from where they'd been quite contentedly sleeping in front of the Aga and began rushing to the window barking excitedly.

It wasn't fair. Kate was tempted to tell him to go and look at the horse by himself but it sounded so petulant. She didn't want to sound anything other than totally indifferent. So instead she peeled off her rubber gloves and untied her apron.

'All right,' she said, giving in graciously. 'I'll just go and get the Colonel.

He'd hate to be left behind.' Patrick's face fell as she went off in triumph to the study to fetch her chaperone.

The Colonel, since his stroke, always had a nap in the afternoons. He'd agreed to go off to his room, although he refused to go to bed. He'd just have forty winks in his chair, he'd said, then come out with them to look at Bella. When Kate went to wake him he was sleeping peacefully in his favourite armchair, so dead to the world, it seemed a shame to wake him. There didn't seem much harm in going to look at a horse in a field. So she got her wellingtons and borrowed an old Barbour jacket of the Colonel's and joined Patrick outside in the bracing cold of a blustery March wind.

The mare didn't think much of being disturbed in the middle of her Sunday afternoon. The dogs burst into the field and set off full of hopeful expectation towards the far distant hedge. Bella gave a quick start, but soon had her head down again, making the most of the spring grass like a condemned prisoner eating his last meal before the morning of execution. Kate called and waved Polos but the mare remained where she was in the middle of the field unmoved. Patrick, encumbered with saddle and bridle, shouted instructions to Kate but the mare had her measure. She waited until Kate was within an inch of her head collar, then threw her head up and pranced away. Bella captive in her stable was a completely different animal from the free spirit with a whole field to graze in at her leisure. In the end Patrick gave Kate the tack to carry and caught Bella himself. It looked so easy when he did it. Bella didn't even attempt to evade him. She just stood looking resigned and patient while he saddled her up and jumped on her.

He walked, trotted and cantered the mare around the field while the dogs abandoned hunting in the hedge and chased Bella instead. Kate wandered about the field, admiring the way Patrick rode. Under his vigorous heels Bella had been transformed once again into an eager black beauty. Then to her horror Patrick cantered Bella purposefully towards the hedge at the bottom of the field. The mare seemed a bit surprised but he whacked her hard once on each side of her round shiny black rump and she gathered herself together and disappeared over the hedge with a great heave of her powerful hind quarters. Kate let her breath out in a long sigh of relief. Patrick turned Bella and aimed her at the hedge again. This time she sailed over in fine style.

'Well done, Bella,' Kate cried out loud. 'You've probably just jumped into a good home and a lot of hard work for years to come.' Patrick looked pleased as he walked the mare over to Kate and pulled her up.

'She'll do,' he said, slapping Bella on the side of the neck. 'AB's quite right – she's got a great pop in her. She's been wasted on Caroline all these years.' Bella was panting and nosing Kate hopefully, leaving grassy slobber down the front of the Barbour. Kate fished in her pocket and produced the now popular Polos.

'Might as well ride her back to the stable,' said Patrick. 'It'll save old Murphy having to come out and catch her again later on.' Kate stretched out her hand with the Polo on the palm and Bella snaffled it up. 'Do you think you could bring the head collar?'

It occurred to Kate as she followed Bella and Patrick out of the field that she could go back to the house to see if the Colonel was awake, that there was no need for her to go with Patrick to the stables, that if she just walked off and left him it would show him more clearly than any words could that she simply wasn't interested any more. Then she looked at the leather head collar she held in her hand. What should she do with it? Murphy would need it, surely, when he came to do the mare that evening. Without really meaning to, she found herself trailing after Patrick towards the stables.

'Just hang on to her for me, will you, Kate?' said Patrick, jumping down in the stable yard. 'I'd better sponge her off.' He removed his coat and Bella's saddle and went off to get a bucket of water.

Standing in the stableyard holding the steaming black horse, she looked like an advertisement for country living. So it was that Alan, coming out of the house in search of his wife, first caught sight of her. He stared at the woman he had once promised to love, honour and cherish until death. He'd kept that promise without too much difficulty for more than twenty years. It was his duty to take care of her and Kate so obviously needed looking after. But until that moment it had never once occurred to him that some other man might want to take her away from him, and that it might not be death that parted them.

Patrick appeared carrying a bucket of water and began sponging the horse down. Alan wondered who he was. He looked too well bred and handsome for a groom. Neither of them seemed aware of his presence. As he stood watching in perplexity, Alan noticed that Kate's hair was different.

She looked younger, prettier. He felt suddenly wary. He had thought she had just got herself into one of her muddles as usual and didn't know how to get out of it. That was why he was here: to sort out the mess she was in. But looking at her standing there in her muddy wellingtons and long shapeless green coat, holding the horse so confidently, she didn't look like a woman in need of rescue. She looked completely at home.

He began to walk towards her feeling unaccountably at a loss. Suddenly two shaggy dogs appeared, racing towards him, barking ferociously. She turned and saw him.

'Alan!' Kate let go the horse and came running across the cobbled yard to meet him. 'How lovely to see you.' She kissed him quickly on the cheek. He kissed her back and she ducked her head just as she always did, pulling back just a fraction so that instead of getting her mouth he got her cheek. Was she glad to see him? He took her hand and peered into her face, trying to read there what it was that had kept her from him for so long.

'I've missed you, Kate,' he said.

'Oh Alan, and I've missed you too,' she said, gazing at him lovingly. Nothing wrong there, he thought, feeling slightly better. He became aware of the handsome fellow who'd been washing down the horse, staring at him rather belligerently. As Kate performed the introductions, Alan tried to think where he'd heard the name Bray-Smith before.

'I just can't believe you're actually here, Alan,' Kate said wonderingly.

'Nor can I,' said Patrick. 'I sometimes wondered whether Kate really had a husband at all. You must be very sure of her to go off to Saudi and leave her running loose in the countryside.'

'Kate and I have always been able to trust each other,' Alan replied rather stiffly and wondered, even as he said it, if it were true. Sometimes he was aware that there was a part of herself that Kate kept a secret, a small corner he never seemed to reach.

'Alan, what are you doing here?' Kate asked. 'It's so unexpected. There's nothing the matter, is there?' She seemed embarrassed, he thought and he didn't like it, not one bit. This wasn't at all how he'd expected her to be.

'I came home because I'm not prepared to live without you.' He blurted it out fiercely. It was not what he'd intended to say, but all his fighting instincts were aroused.

'I'll just put a rug on the mare and then I'll be with you,' said Patrick, cool as you like. 'Kate, could you hold her for me?'

Bastard, thought Alan, watching Patrick stalk off into the stables as Kate obediently took hold of the horse's bridle.

'I'm sorry, Alan.' Kate looked more embarrassed than ever. 'You mustn't mind Patrick, he's such a tease. But it doesn't mean anything. His wife's just run off and left him, he's much more upset about it than he pretends.' Then Alan remembered. Patrick Bray-Smith. He was the shit who'd dumped Kate so unceremoniously all those years ago.

'Did the Colonel send you out here?' asked Kate.

'No, there was no one about when I arrived. I just wandered out.'

'I just can't believe you're here,' she said, and he hoped she was pleased. 'How did you know where to find me?'

'John Kindersby told me where you were.'

She had the grace to look a little guilty.

'John?' Patrick came strolling back carrying a rug. 'What's poor old John been up to now?' He threw the rug over the horse. 'Don't tell me! He sent for you to come and haul Kate off to Saudi. He thinks all this is Kate's fault, I suppose. Well, let me tell you it's not. Kate has been an absolute angel. The Colonel will tell you that. We couldn't possibly manage without her. None of us could.'

Alan took a firm hold of his temper. No good losing control of himself just because this arrogant bastard was acting all masterful and protective towards Kate. Patrick finished rugging up the horse and took the bridle from Kate.

'Alan, please don't be angry with me,' Kate said as Patrick led the horse into the stables. 'I am coming to live with you in Saudi, truly I am. I wanted to tell you but you didn't write and you didn't ring and I was afraid perhaps you didn't really want me out there after all.' The look on her face made him want to take her in his arms, but Patrick was coming out of the stables again. Alan decided it was time to play his trump card.

'Look, Kate,' he said, 'I think I can help. That letter you wrote. I realise how much it all meant to you. The company in Saudi who offered me the job – it's Allied Brownstone Conglomerates, the company that's taken over Meccarda. When I got your letter I asked them if perhaps they might reconsider this holiday village plan and I think I've persuaded them. It's very expensive, especially with all this opposition, and Meccarda are very overstretched at the moment.' She was looking at him just as she always used to look, full of pride and gratitude for his cleverness. 'Kate,' he took hold of her hands. 'They agreed to drop the scheme and build the holiday village somewhere else, if I agree to work for them – in Saudi.'

'Oh Alan! Did you accept?'

'I said I'd have to ask my wife first. I'd turn it down, Kate, if you don't want to go out there with me.' Kate looked stunned.

'Then they'll drop the public inquiry? Can they do that?' demanded Patrick.

'I don't see why not. The Government will be delighted to save money. Public inquiries cost a lot.'

Patrick didn't like it, thought Alan. His nose was doubtless put out of joint. Good.

'What about The Court?' said Patrick. 'Meccarda have bought The Court. They've paid a huge amount of money for it.'

'That'll be John Kindersby's problem,' said Alan. He looked at his wife. 'It's up to Kate really.' He wondered if he were being fair forcing her into a corner like that. He had been prepared to give up his career and come home, if that is what she wanted. But with that fellow standing there so possessively and Kate looking so desirable with her new hairstyle and healthy pink cheeks, he didn't feel like being fair or reasonable. All's fair in love and war, he thought grimly.

'Let's go and tell the Colonel,' said Kate, linking her arm through his. 'He'll be so happy, won't he, Patrick? It's like a miracle really.'

Patrick didn't look so terribly pleased with himself now, thought Alan, gripping Kate's arm tightly.

'The Colonel's probably still asleep in his chair. Let's go and wake him. It's the most wonderful news.'

The Colonel wasn't asleep and he wasn't in his study. Kate turned to Patrick, a worried look on her face.

'The car,' she said. 'I left it in the drive when we got back from church. You don't think he could have gone off to see the Duke of Blazeborough as he threatened to do?'

'There was a Subaru parked there when I arrived,' said Alan.

'That's mine,' said Patrick. 'Was there not an old Volvo estate?'

'No – nothing.'

'Oh my God.' Kate had turned very white. 'Try the garage, Patrick,' she said. 'Maybe Murphy's come up and put it away without our knowing.'

'Maybe, but where's the Colonel then?' Patrick seemed too stunned to think.

'I don't know. You look in the garage, I'll search the house.' She rushed out of the study, closely followed by Patrick. Alan stood in the hall wondering what all the fuss was about. When Kate came rushing back, he tried to find out, but she was in too much of a state to be able to enlighten him.

'He's not anywhere in the house,' she said, 'and the car's nowhere to be seen. I'm sorry, darling, we've got to find him before he comes to any harm. He's always going on and on about driving again, but I never believed he would actually do it. He's not fit to drive. I should have taken the keys out of the car. Oh my God, I do hope nothing has happened to him.' She ran out of the house to join Patrick, who was already getting into his Subaru parked outside. Alan sprinted after her. He wasn't going to stand by and let the two of them go off on some wild-goose chase together. He'd not come all this way to rescue his wife only to have her run off from under his nose in the first five minutes.

# *Chapter 21*

Kate found herself sitting in the front of Patrick's Subaru without knowing quite how she got there. Her mind seemed to be divided into two quite separate compartments. Half of it was trying to grapple with Alan's sudden unexpected appearance, the other half was totally taken up with the Colonel's fate. Neither side seemed capable of making any sense at all. Dimly she was aware of Alan leaping into the car as Patrick started the engine. 'We'll assume he went to see the Duke,' said Patrick, setting off at gravel-scattering speed.

'Wouldn't it be more sensible to ring the police?' said Alan, pulling the door shut with some difficulty, as the car shot down the drive.

'Good God no!' Patrick sounded shocked. 'We must keep the police out of it if we can. The old man isn't fit to drive. We've got to find him before he kills someone.'

I ought to be sitting in the back with Alan, Kate thought. What's he doing here? He's so calm. All very well for him to be calm. He's not emotionally involved. Dear God, don't let the Colonel do anything dreadful.

'Better slow down a bit through the village then,' said Alan as Patrick took the turn into the road on three wheels. 'We don't want to kill someone too.'

Kate felt sick. This can't be happening, she thought. Oh dear God, let it be all right.

'No sign of him in the village,' said Patrick, accelerating again once they were past the pond, tearing along the road to Great Riddleton, changing gear a lot on the bends and making the tyres squeal.

There really wasn't any need for Patrick to make quite such a car chase out of it, thought Kate, sure he was only doing it to impress. She twisted round in her seat. Poor Alan, what must he think of us all? she thought, trying to catch her husband's eye. But Patrick was putting his foot down as he came out of another corner and she was flung against the door.

'Better put your seat belt on, Kate,' said Alan. She grabbed the belt and braced herself against the back of the seat, fumbling for the clasp as they roared down a straight bit of road like the getaway car in some second-rate cops and robbers film. It was lucky that it was Sunday afternoon and the roads were deserted.

'Hang on a minute,' shouted Alan. 'There's a hole in the wall back there. It looks as if someone's gone through.' Patrick slammed on the brakes and Kate, still fumbling, very nearly went through the windscreen. Patrick threw the car into reverse. Thank God Alan still had his wits about him, thought Kate, clinging tightly to the unfastened belt, as they roared backwards.

'Oh my God!'

The road had a wide grass verge on either side, ending in a dry stone wall, then on one side it fell away down a grassy slope. In the middle of the long straight stretch of road the verge was deeply and freshly scarred by marks of tyres; there was a gaping hole in the wall and down below in the field beyond was the Colonel's ancient Volvo estate lying on its side.

Patrick was first out of the car. He vaulted the wall while Alan was still helping Kate, whose legs seemed to have turned to water.

'You'd better stay here, darling,' said Alan as Patrick went leaping down the sloping bank. 'I'll go and give Bray-Smith a hand.' He scrambled through the gap in the wall after Patrick while Kate leant against the car, numb with shock. As if in a dream she watched Patrick and Alan peering into the Colonel's upturned car, unable to believe that all her worst fears had been realised. The car looked strangely unreal, with its underbelly exposed like that and its wheels in the air. It reminded Kate of the horse Bella when she'd been lying cast in her box. Then Patrick came running back up the hill, white and grim, and she forced herself to go and meet him.

'He's still alive and he's conscious. We'll have to see if we can get him out. But it's going to be difficult with the car lying on its side like that. Lucky it's on Joe Gorse's land. I'll nip up there and get Joe to bring his tractor down.'

'What we need is the ambulance and the fire brigade,' said Alan, following Patrick more slowly up the hill. 'And the police, of course. They'll have to know now.'

'Fire brigade nonsense!' said Patrick. 'A tractor'll get that car right side up in a jiffy.'

'This isn't the time for do-it-yourself first aid,' said Alan. 'That old man in there is badly injured. What we need is the professionals and as quick as you can get them. Do you want me to go or will you?' Patrick glared at Alan and Kate, coming out of her trance, realised he was still trying to get the better of Alan. They were like two stags rutting on the hill, but this was not the time for male rites of passage.

'You go, Patrick,' she urged. 'You know the way to the nearest telephone and it's your car. You'll be quicker than either of us, but get the lot – ambulance, doctor, fire brigade – and hurry.'

He looked relieved, she thought, as if he couldn't get away from the scene quick enough. He sprinted away like a greyhound, leaping back into his car and setting off down the road in a cloud of exhaust fumes as he accelerated sharply. A very macho figure, full of courage and physical strength, ready to leap into the breach and shed his blood with any man. But that wasn't what was needed now. What was needed was a cool head, and someone to bring comfort to the Colonel until help came. She began scrambling over the wall which the Colonel's car had reduced to great shards of stones. But Alan caught hold of her.

'I must go and stay with him until the ambulance comes,' she said, pushing him away.

'Better not, darling. You'll be too upset. Let me.'

But she shook her head. 'No, Alan, it's all right. I have to do it. If he's conscious I must be with him. Help him.' There wasn't time for more elaborate explanations but Alan seemed to understand at once, because he didn't try to stop her.

'Brave girl,' he said, giving her a reassuring squeeze as he helped her into the field. 'I'd better just go and check that there isn't another casualty lying anywhere,' he added. 'It's odd that he should have gone off the road like that right in the middle of a long straight stretch.'

'Oh Alan, no!' she said, horrified at the thought of a body lying in a ditch somewhere.

'It's all right, leave it to me. I'll come and join you in the car as soon as I can.'

As she ran down the hill to the wrecked car, Kate wondered what Alan thought of the mess she'd got herself into this time. The poor darling, it wasn't much of a welcome home for him. All the same, it was a tremendous relief to have him here helping.

Judging by the marks in the field the car must have rolled over several times before finally coming to rest against a sturdy gorse bush. The Colonel was lying trapped in his seat, hanging by his seatbelt. There was blood and crushed metal everywhere. He looked very bad, covered in blood and there was a grey-greenish tinge to his face. Kate longed to turn and run. To wait on the road for the ambulance as Alan had urged. But she couldn't. She had seen the Colonel through so much already. She had to see him through this last agonising finale. The front passenger door was buckled and jammed immovably, but the rear door looked as if it might respond to some brute force. The car was firmly imbedded in the gorse bush and didn't seem likely to move. She began trying to prise open the rear door.

'Kate – is that you?' said the Colonel as she was struggling to get it open. His voice was quite strong, she was relieved to discover – and calm.

'Yes, it's me. The ambulance and the doctor are on their way,' she said. 'We'll have you out of there in no time.' She yanked open the door and crawled into the back of the car. She didn't know what to say or do. But he reassured her.

'I can't feel much – shock, you know.' His breathing sounded alarmingly fast. 'Don't worry, Kate.' She wished she could think of some way she could help him, but she was terrified of moving him in case she made matters worse.

'You were quite right – you said I couldn't drive the damn thing.'

'It doesn't matter,' she murmured. 'I'm here now. We'll have you out and into a nice warm bed in no time.' If only it were true. He smiled and closed his eyes. Maybe he believed her. What to do? Dimly she remembered stories of trapped victims being kept talking, that you had to keep people conscious, make them make an effort. The Colonel looked as if he might slip away at any minute. Perhaps it was better to let him go. She eased herself forward a little, trying to get nearer to him without getting impaled on the jagged edges of crumpled metal.

'I was a stupid old bugger,' he said.

'Never mind,' she soothed, reaching out and taking hold of his hand hanging limp and useless by the gear lever.

'My foot got stuck on the accelerator. I couldn't seem to move it. Bloody useless thing.' He paused as he struggled for breath. 'I was in the middle of the road when I got round the bend and the car was racing away with me.' He paused again and she wondered if she should try and stop him talking when every word seemed to be such an effort. 'There was this fox . . . running down the middle of the road . . . coming straight towards me.' He waited, panting hard, as if he'd been in a five-mile race. 'I had to go for the wall,' he went on at length. 'You do see, don't you, Kate? I had to. I couldn't run over Charlie.'

How absurd, she thought. How utterly tragically absurd! His eyes were closing again, the effort to talk had been too much. His hand was cold and sticky with blood. Where was the ambulance? Would it never come?

Alan's face appeared in the window. 'No sign of any other casualties,' he said. 'He must have had a blackout or something.'

Impossible to explain to Alan that the Colonel had been trying to avoid killing a fox! He would never understand.

'Oh Alan,' she whispered, 'I don't know what to do, whether to keep him talking or let him rest. Is Patrick not back yet?'

'It's all right, darling. You're doing fine. They'll be here in a minute. Just keep him quiet – that's all you can do. Stop him from worrying too much if you can.'

The Colonel doesn't need me for that, she thought. He's not worried. A tremor ran through him and the hand she held clenched hers tightly. Was he in great pain?'

'Alan's here, my husband,' she said to distract him a little.

'That's good,' he said. 'You'll need someone to look after . . .' his breath rattled rather horrifyingly, 'when I'm gone.'

'Don't be silly,' she said. 'You're not going to die yet. Where's your fighting spirit?' Dear God, would the ambulance never come? His eyes were closing again. She couldn't bear it if he were to die without knowing that his campaign to save the countryside from Meccarda had been victorious.

'Alan's got such good news about the holiday village.' She gave the hand she held a little shake. 'It's not going to be built after all. Alan's fixed it. We've won.' She wasn't sure whether he understood. Then he opened his eyes, looked at her quite lucidly.

'"The strife is o'er – the battle won,"' he said and she thought she could detect a glint in his eyes of something which might have been triumph, or amusement or may have just been pain. 'How does it go? The rest of it.'

She couldn't think what he meant.

'The hymn, woman, the hymn,' he muttered impatiently. 'How does it go?' Desperately she searched her poor distraught brain, but couldn't even think which hymn he was quoting from. Was it 'Fight the Good Fight'? 'Fight the good fight with all thy might.' She tried desperately to remember the words but her mind was like one of those little kaleidoscope things, give it a shake and it formed a pattern, give it another shake and a different pattern emerged. She noticed that Alan was still at the window waiting patiently and drew comfort from the sight of him.

'Any sign of them yet, Alan?' she whispered.

'No, not yet. But I'm sure they'll not be long.'

She looked back at the Colonel. He seemed to be getting more restless. Was the shock wearing off? He must be in terrible pain. 'Alan,' she said, '"Fight the Good Fight". How does it go?' He looked surprised. 'You know? The hymn?' She began to sing softly. '"Fight the good fight with all thy might . . ."'

'"Christ is thy Strength, and Christ thy Right",' Alan stuck his head through the smashed window and rose to the challenge. '"Lay hold on life, and it shall be/Thy joy and crown eternally."'

'That's it! Oh Alan, I'm so glad you're here.' Kate repeated it in triumph to the Colonel, but he didn't seem to hear her.

She wriggled forward so she was hanging over what was left of the front seat, trying to get closer to him. His eyes were closed and he'd gone a very funny colour. Perhaps she ought to be doing mouth-to-mouth resuscitation. If only she'd done one of those first-aid courses she might be able to help him more.

'Don't worry, Kate,' the Colonel murmured, almost as if he read her thoughts. 'This is how I always wanted to go. With a bang. I didn't manage it on the hunting field but this is better than sitting about waiting to die.' She lifted his cold hand up and held it against her breast to warm it a little. His eyes flickered open and he gave her the ghost of a smile. 'You'll have to let me go in peace now.' He was very breathless, pausing between each word, struggling to get enough air into his lungs. Suddenly he smiled. '"The strife is o'er, the battle done;/Now is the Victor's triumph won;/O let the song of praise be sung. Alleluia!" That's it, Kate. You got the wrong hymn.' She couldn't bear it. Even in extremis he was able to tease her.

Patrick suddenly appeared and stuck his head in through the smashed window. 'Are you all right in there, Kate? Help is on its way. It won't be long.'

The Colonel's eyes were closing again and she thought he might be going to slip into unconsciousness. She gripped his hand and held on to it tightly.

'Do you think we should undo his seat belt?' Patrick asked. 'It might be a bit easier for him.' Kate looked at the Colonel suspended above the steering wheel, the crushed metal entangled with his body, and thought Alan was right.

'Much better wait for the professionals,' she said.

Patrick's head disappeared and she heard him talking outside to Alan. The Colonel began to ramble a bit – about the gravel pits coming and the best grass of the Monday country being spoilt. She wondered if he had understood at all what she'd been trying to tell him about the holiday village. Perhaps it no longer mattered to him. He was slipping back into the past, talking about people and places she didn't know. Once or twice he called her Charmian, which was his first wife's name. 'Warren gorse,' he said suddenly, gripping her hand with surprising strength. 'That was a great ride. A ten-mile point and only five of us left at the death.' He seemed happy reliving the best moments of his long and eventful life.

Then Alan stuck his head through the window again. 'The doctor's here – I think you'd better come out now, Kate.'

She gave the cold limp hand she still held in hers a final squeeze.

'I'm going to hand you over to the doctor now, Colonel dear,' she said. 'You'll be all right with him.' He opened his eyes and looked at her, the gleam back.

'"Faint not nor fear, His Arms are near,"' he took a lungful of air. '"He changeth not, and thou art dear." You're right, Kate. It's a good hymn.' His breathing seemed to be a little better but his normally red face was very grey. '"Fight the Good Fight".' He winked at her. 'Once I knew it all off by heart. We used to sing it as we went into battle.' He smiled and closed his eyes again. She could see the doctor beckoning to her through the window. Kate put the cold hand she held to her lips and eased herself backwards. The Colonel didn't seem to notice her any more.

Alan and Patrick helped her out of the car between them. The doctor, she was relieved to see, was the Colonel's own GP. At least he had someone he knew and trusted with him. She hoped the doctor would give him a shot of something to help him through the next terrible ordeal.

'What I can't understand,' said Patrick, as they stood shivering in the cold March wind while the professionals set about extracting the Colonel from his crushed and battered car, 'is how he came off the road in the middle of a perfectly straight stretch.'

'He was trying to avoid killing a fox,' whispered Kate, trying not to watch as the ambulancemen and the fire brigade went about their gruelling task with impressive efficiency.

'Ridiculous!' Alan put his arm round her and held her tight. 'Ironic too, considering he's spent his whole life killing the damn things.'

'Not at all!' said Patrick indignantly. 'That's not the way hunting people see foxes – we love them almost as much as we love our horses and dogs. That's what you town people can't seem to understand. The fox is a worthy adversary, respected, cherished even.' He glared at Alan angrily. Kate couldn't bear it. They were still sparring and she supposed it was her fault. She wanted to tell Alan it was all right, he had nothing to fear from Patrick; to tell Patrick to stop being so childish. But her throat was choked with unshed tears. So she leant against Alan's shoulder, drawing strength and comfort from his arm around her, hoping that he would draw comfort too, from her silent submission. It was all she could do to reassure him. The rest of her was totally dedicated to helping the Colonel.

They were bringing him out of the car, strapping him to a stretcher, hovering round him with hypodermics and drips and all the high-tech paraphernalia of their trade. The ambulancemen picked up the stretcher and started up the hill to the road.

'How is he, Dr Ferguson?' asked Patrick.

'He's unconscious, but he'll do. It may not be as bad as it looks. He's a tough old devil and doesn't frighten easily. Makes a great deal of difference in cases like this. You'd be surprised what some old people can take. His sort have had a great deal of practice in the art of survival.'

'Then you think he might make it? He's not going to die?'

But the doctor wasn't prepared to commit himself so far. 'I'd better be off. I've got to get on the telephone and see if I can haul some senior consultant off the golf course. Sunday evening's no time to land up in a casualty ward in a critical condition. We don't want the Colonel at the mercy of some junior houseman, now do we?' He sprinted off in the wake of the ambulancemen.

'Can't I go with him in the ambulance?' asked Kate, breaking away from Alan and setting off in pursuit.

'Better not,' said Patrick, catching hold of her. 'They'll be busy keeping him going in there. They don't want weepy females getting in the way.'

'You did what you could when it mattered,' Alan said. She smiled at him gratefully as she disengaged herself from Patrick.

'Come on, Kate,' Patrick interrupted impatiently. 'I'll take you to the hospital.'

'Alan, do you mind? I must see it through.'

'Of course you must.' His brown eyes, so full of warmth a moment ago, became harder as he looked at Patrick. 'Come on, we'll all go.'

The hospital they took the Colonel to was the Princess of Wales at Crickendon, just off the M4, the one where they took all the motorway crashes. It was large and impersonal and impressively efficient, Alan noted with relief. The Colonel had been whisked away on his stretcher before they arrived, even though Patrick had driven with quite unnecessary bravado to keep pace with the ambulance. There was nothing for the three of them to do but wait in the cold unwelcoming corridor of the hospital's casualty department. Kate looked just about done in, he thought, and wondered if he could lure her away to find a cup of coffee, or perhaps send Patrick to find some. She had been terrifically brave all through what must have been a terrible ordeal for her; she had shown an inner strength he didn't know she possessed and he was terribly proud of her, but now he expected her to go to pieces and he wanted to be able to comfort her without that handsome devil Bray-Smith getting in his way. But Kate to Alan's surprise didn't break down. Nor did she seem to need his support. She seemed to have forgotten his existence entirely.

'You'll have to ring Caroline, Patrick,' she said. 'And Deborah. She's got to be told.' Patrick looked at Kate in amazement as if she'd committed some terrible social gaffe.

'I can't ring Deborah – I've no idea where she is.'

'Well, you can find out surely?' she insisted. 'She'll never forgive us if we don't send for her.' He stood staring at her sulkily but she didn't relent. Alan watched his wife, astonished. The shy little woman he had been married to all these years had suddenly come out of her shell. He couldn't believe it. Here she was ordering Patrick around with a familiarity Alan found decidedly worrying.

'I suppose the police could find her,' Patrick conceded at last.

Alan was appalled. 'Not the police. Do you want to frighten the poor girl silly?' he said. Really the man was unbelievably insensitive. Perhaps if Patrick had taken better care of his wife she wouldn't have left him, he thought. Out loud he said: 'Can't you get hold of this man she's run off with? If you can get hold of him, he can break it to her. It's going to come as a terrible shock. She'll need someone to drive her down.'

'Debs can take it – you've no idea how tough Debs is,' Kate muttered.

'Tough she may be but she's going to feel pretty guilty if her father dies and she knows nothing about it because she's run off into the blue.' Alan rounded on Kate angrily and she had the grace to look ashamed. He was aware that there were undercurrents here that needed to be carefully navigated if they weren't all going to end up in a sea of emotional recrimination. He didn't know what this fellow Patrick's obvious interest in Kate meant and perhaps it was better if he never found out. She was his wife, to have and to hold, and that's exactly what he was going to do – hold her against all comers. In the meantime all he could do was support her as best he could until they knew what was to become of this Colonel of hers.

Dr Ferguson had done his job well and managed to conjure up a consultant who appeared enormously capable and confidence-inspiring.

'Well, there's hope, I think,' he said when Dr Ferguson brought him to meet them, not much later. 'Colonel Beamish has been very lucky. He doesn't appear to have done anything irreparable. There's broken ribs and neck injuries, some damage to the shoulder where the seat belt did its work – but remarkable really, all things considered.'

'Then he's going to be all right? He's not going to die?' asked Patrick.

'I hope not.' The doctor was very bracing. 'We're going to have to operate immediately. There's internal bleeding, I'm afraid. Probably the broken ribs have severed an artery or a blood vessel. We'll have to go in through the front. It just depends how he comes through the operation. But Dr Ferguson assures me he's a very tough customer.'

'And if he does survive the operation?' asked Kate, her face white and set. 'How long will it take for all his other injuries to heal?'

'Well, of course I can't really say. He's old and pretty arthritic, so Dr Ferguson tells me. The old don't heal as quickly as the young. We'll have to put him in a straitjacket for a time.'

'How long is he to be in this straitjacket?' asked Kate.

'Three months perhaps, maybe more. I can't tell. Not yet. First we've got to stop the internal bleeding. So if you'll excuse me . . .'

'No,' said Kate, and Alan marvelled at the steel in her voice. 'No operation. He wouldn't want it.'

'I'm sorry,' the surgeon explained impatiently. 'I thought I made myself clear. If we don't operate now – immediately – he will die for certain.'

'I know.' Kate was quite calm. So calm Alan thought maybe she was suffering from delayed shock. It was what some people did in a crisis – became frozen into immobility. But the doctor was right. This was no time for keeping calm. Time wasn't on the Colonel's side. 'He doesn't want to be resuscitated or carved up or put through agonies of post-operative trauma so he can survive three months in a straitjacket.' Kate was becoming agitated now. 'What he wants to do is die in peace.'

'Kate, please.' Alan took her hand, tried to draw her into his arms. 'Let the doctors get on with it. They know what they're doing.'

But she shook him off. 'And I know what I'm doing,' she declared rounding on the surgeon. 'You're not to operate. The Colonel doesn't want it. You can't operate without his permission, surely?'

'We can if the patient isn't in a condition to give it,' snapped the surgeon.

'But I *know* he doesn't want it,' she pleaded. 'He told me – in the car he said, "Let me go in peace." And that time when he had his stroke he said he didn't want doctors interfering in the course of nature. He didn't want to be resuscitated. You can't operate on him, doctor. He's old, he's had his life, he's got to die one day. Don't make him suffer unnecessarily.'

'Are you his next of kin?' demanded the surgeon, clearly rattled.

'No, I'm not, but his daughter is on her way from London now. She should be here within the hour and we're trying to trace the other daughter now. Can't you wait until one of them gets here?'

'It may be too late by then.'

'That's in God's hands then,' she said. 'We'll wait until Caroline gets here. Fill him up with morphine if necessary. Just ease him out.'

The surgeon looked disappointed, thought Alan. He'd obviously been looking forward to exercising his skill in the operating theatre, to battling against the perpetual enemy death, to dragging one more victim back from the brink even though it was Sunday evening, a time when lesser mortals were contentedly watching the dramas of life and death being enacted on their television screens.

'Where is the Colonel?' demanded Kate. 'Where have you taken him? I must see him.' Obviously she didn't trust the look of disappointment on the surgeon's face.

'They're getting him ready for theatre. He can't have visitors now.'

Kate drew herself up to her full height, looking the surgeon, who was not a tall man, full in the eye. 'Take me to him,' she said. Alan had never felt prouder of his wife. She might have been a grand dame in some drawing-room comedy, she was so imperious. The surgeon too was impressed.

'Very well,' he said, 'but I must warn you he doesn't look good.'

'I'll go with her,' said Alan to Patrick. 'You stay and wait for Mrs Kindersby. Explain things to her if you can. It's only right she should be the one to take the final decision.'

The Colonel was in a private room, nicely decorated in pastel pink, with en suite bathroom, television and an expensive-looking menu lying on the bed trolley they'd pushed against the wall. All these things Kate noticed because she was afraid to look at the limp figure lying on the bed. The surgeon was right. He didn't look good. They had washed the blood off him and dressed him in a white theatre gown and he lay on his back in the middle of the bed with his eyes shut just like a corpse. They had taken his teeth out and his bold moustache, no longer bristling, covered his mouth like autumn debris over a sunken ditch. His face was the colour of the spotless white pillowcase and he looked so shrunken and old and helpless Kate could hardly restrain the tears. But she must. She had to be brave this one more time, for his sake. She had to keep the well-meaning angels of mercy at bay. She sat down at the side of the bed and took the Colonel's limp cold hand in hers once more.

'I'm here,' she whispered. 'It's me – Kate. Trust me.' From the still face there was no flicker of recognition. The hand in hers was limp and cold.

'He's unconscious,' said the nurse who had been busy getting him ready. 'He's had his pre-med all ready for theatre.'

Kate ignored her. 'Don't worry,' she told the Colonel. 'I won't let them do it – not if you don't want them to.' The face was impassive, his breathing a loud moaning sound, terrible to hear.

'Why don't you wait outside in the corridor – you and your husband?' the nurse said kindly. 'It would be less distressing for you.'

'But not for him,' retorted Kate.

'He feels nothing, knows nothing. He's not in any pain.' The nurse was adamant.

How did they know, thought Kate, how did anyone know what went on in the human mind when it was not conscious? How could they be so sure, these people who thought that life, any kind of life, was so infinitely preferable to what lay beyond? She began talking to him quietly, even though he still showed no sign of having heard a word she said. Alan, she saw, was still there, standing with his back to her, looking out of the window. When she told the Colonel about what Alan had managed to do to the holiday village scheme, how he had persuaded ABC to scupper the scheme, Alan turned round and smiled at her. It warmed her heart.

'So you see, Colonel dear,' she said, 'we've beaten them, you and I. We did it, with a little bit of help from our friends. We kept the enemy at bay and now Alan's come in the nick of time just like the Americans during the war and we're going to win.' Just for a moment she thought she felt a light pressure from his hand, a brief rustle of his moustache which might have been the ghost of a smile or one last tortured breath, a tiny sigh, and then nothing. The nurse laid her hand on Kate's shoulder, leant over to look at the still figure on the bed.

'I'm afraid he's gone,' she said.

'May he rest in peace,' whispered Kate, knowing that he would.

# *Chapter 22*

The Colonel's funeral took place in St Saviour's, Greater Riddleton. The church was a fine fourteenth-century tribute to the fortunes made out of the medieval wool trade. It could hold over three hundred people and was far too large for the two or three who gathered together Sunday after Sunday. But for the Colonel's funeral it wasn't big enough. Half an hour before the funeral was due to start there were people queueing to get in and with fifteen minutes still to go every available seat was taken.

When Kate arrived with Alan and saw the long snake of people waiting patiently to give their names at the church door a great wave of emotion threatened to overwhelm her. Until that moment she hadn't felt sad. She was sure the Colonel was at peace now and happy. This was a celebration, not a defeat. The old man had got his own way right until the very last and he had gone out with dignity. But seeing all these people crammed into every nook and cranny of the spacious old church and standing three deep at the back, completely threw her. She clung tightly to Alan's arm as they entered the packed church and walked together down the aisle to their reserved pew, terrified that she would break down and cry. But it wasn't sorrow that brought the tears to her eyes; it was pride for him – the gallant old sod.

Alan pressed her arm against his side in silent sympathy and it made her feel more emotional than ever. He understood. It was wonderful to have him here, supporting her through this last final ordeal. Alan had been such a tower of strength. It was Alan who'd taken charge at the hospital on that dreadful day. Alan, not Patrick, had dealt with the police and the doctors and tracked down Ned Jones. Patrick had seemed incapable of taking decisions. Kate had been disappointed. She had discovered that Patrick was selfish and vain and full of unfulfilled promises, but she hadn't expected him to be useless in a crisis. It was only a little disappointment. Compared to the huge, numbing, appalling disappointment of the Colonel's death it was nothing. But to Kate, teetering on the verge of emotional meltdown, it was the final straw. It was as if the rose-tinted spectacles she had always clung to when looking at Patrick had been whipped from her nose and she saw him like the Emperor in his suit of magic new clothes, without a shred of romance to cover his nakedness. Romance wasn't what she'd had with Patrick. It was more than a bunch of red roses. It couldn't be conjured up by moonlight or music or champagne or flowers. But it could transform a frog into a prince with just one kiss. Romance, she thought with a sudden overwhelming sense of loss, was what she'd had with the Colonel.

It was Alan who'd had to break the news to Caroline when she'd arrived too late at the hospital. Caroline had been very subdued at first. She hadn't wept or questioned the doctors or blamed Kate in any way. But once she'd got over the initial shock she'd taken charge. Alan then had offered to let Kate stay and help Caroline with the arrangements for the funeral and Caroline had accepted gratefully. That was when Kate realised she had some quick decisions to make. With the Colonel's death her job was finished. Alan had offered her a choice between Saudi or their old life back in London. He had shown that he was willing to give up a lot for her sake, but of course she could never accept such a sacrifice. Besides, if she did and Alan didn't accept the job ABC were offering, then the Company might not scrap the holiday village scheme after all. She couldn't let the Colonel down.

So much for her bid for independence. But what was independence compared with love? Alan loved her and she loved him, she knew that now. Just seeing Patrick and Alan together made Kate realise what a silly little fool she'd been to come so close to throwing away everything she and Alan had for someone like Patrick. No, it wasn't difficult choosing Alan rather than Patrick. Alan had a gift for loving, something which Kate suspected Patrick had never learnt, and Alan had never been more loving and protective than he was with her in the difficult days at The Court after the Colonel's death.

Caroline had moved into The Court and set about planning her father's funeral with breathtaking efficiency. Kate had been amazed at the scale of the arrangements and afraid that guilt was making Caroline go over the top, especially when she had a marquee erected on the lawn, with a full bar and a long tea table and all the local flower club ladies doing huge arrangements in the church and the marquee and the house. It was more like a wedding really than a funeral, Kate had thought, except that they had no idea of numbers. Caroline had ordered four hundred printed hymn sheets and Kate had gone on making sandwiches and cakes to keep herself busy and Caroline happy, but had privately wondered what they were going to do with so much food, especially when the farmers' wives started arriving with cakes and things. She couldn't believe that it would all be needed.

'It seems so strange,' she'd said to Alan. 'I've always thought funerals were something to be got over as swiftly and painlessly as possible. I can't understand why she wants to make such a big thing of it.'

'She's rich and she's feeling guilty, I expect,' Alan had said. 'Perhaps this is to show everybody how much she cared.'

Kate watched Caroline walking into church with John. She was dressed in a tailored black calf-length coat and large black hat. She looked stylish, rich and very composed. The same could certainly not be said for Deborah, who looked quite dumpy in her mink. Her blonde hair was scraped back from her face with a black velvet Alice band, and her eyes were red from recent weeping. Deborah had refused to come back until now, and as Patrick ushered his wife into the front pew, his face impassive, Kate remembered the Colonel's words. 'If only I could think of some way to bring her back.' Deborah was back now. A shiver ran down Kate's spine. Was the old manipulator even in death still trying to get what he wanted? Did he walk out into the snow? Was it an accident or was it intentional? Nobody would ever know – that was something between the Colonel and the Almighty now. The congregation was getting to its feet. The service was about to begin.

The vicar read the opening sentences. 'I am the resurrection and the life . . . he that believeth in me, though he were dead, yet shall he live.' The congregation cleared its throat and settled down for a good burial. It was going to be quite a show, thought Kate. Caroline had seen to that. She felt quite calm again now. She had herself well in hand as the music of Sibelius' *Finlandia* filled the church.

Be still, my soul: the Lord is on your side;
bear patiently the cross of grief and pain;
leave to your God to order and provide;
in every change he faithful will remain.
Be still, my soul: your best, your heav'nly friend
through thorny ways leads to a joyful end.

Kate failed to sing a single solitary note. Caroline had asked Kate to choose the first hymn and Kate, touched and terribly conscious that it was important to get it right, had spent a long time with the hymn book. She had been pleased with her choice. The music was inspirational and the words equally so. But the trouble was, she realised now, it was too good. At funerals you didn't want moving hymns which stirred the soul. Nothing which might turn on the tap of emotion, or release the unshed tears which were kept back like a lake behind the great dam of proper behaviour. At English funerals what was needed was good rousing cheer, which is why people had the sort of things they sang at weddings. No good plucking at the heart strings, she could almost hear the Colonel's voice admonishing her. People don't want to let the side down. Give them something nice and easy – like 'Jerusalem' and 'Dear Lord and Father of Mankind'. Well, they were having both those later. Deborah had chosen them.

Kate gave up trying to sing and let the tears slide down her cheeks unchecked. Alan took her hand and squeezed it. She looked up at him gratefully. Love's pure joy restored there, as the hymn said, thank God, and in the nick of time. She had made her choice. Her bags were packed, her bridges burnt. Two seats were booked on the plane to Saudi tomorrow and as soon as the wake was over they were leaving.

Through a mist of tears Kate examined Patrick's erect pinstriped back and sleek dark head. How she once had lusted after him. She remembered that first time when they'd lain in bed together at the Imperial, discussing the future. How they'd sworn to each other that their marriages must come first. How they'd devised their plan for the perfectly safe affair. There's no such thing as a safe affair, she thought miserably. But I've been very, very lucky, much luckier than Patrick. Deborah was fumbling in her handbag for a hanky and Patrick gave her his. Would the Colonel's death bring them back together again? Difficult for a man so good-looking as Patrick to accept that his wife had not only been unfaithful but had run off with another man much less handsome or well born. Would Patrick ever be able to get over the slight to his manhood? Would he be too proud to take her back?

John was walking up to the lectern for the first reading. '"Death is nothing at all . . . I have only slipped away into the next room . . . I am I and you are you . . . whatever we were to each other, that we are still ."' The fashionable choice at funerals. Kate supposed it was because so many people were afraid of too much religion. For religion to be a comfort you needed faith and plenty of practice. People who couldn't believe in an afterlife wanted to keep people alive, and when they couldn't do that they wanted something more solid to cling to, like the idea that the dead were still around. But the Colonel had gone. She felt it. When they were planning his funeral, arguing about what he would have wanted, Kate had a sudden vivid impression of him young and laughing. He didn't care what they did at his funeral, she thought in surprise. He was leaping through the firmament swift and eager for new adventure, riding on clouds of glory, hunting through all eternity. The conviction had comforted her so much she had been able to get through the difficult days of waiting without feeling sad at all, until now.

'Fight the good Fight with all thy might!' The rousing opening bars of the next hymn brought the congregation to its feet once more. Kate hadn't wanted that one. She knew she would never be able to get through it dry-eyed. But they had to have it. Everybody had agreed. She clung to Alan's hand and thought of the Colonel, young and strong, singing as he rode into battle. He must be knocking all kinds of shit out of the heavenly host she thought. He would never forgive her if she couldn't get through it somehow. She stared at the coffin heaped with flowers, and willed herself not to let him down.

'Faint not nor fear,' she sang, managing the last verse quite well. It's all just an exercise in waste disposal, she told herself firmly. He's gone. He's happy. He's won.

Now the Duke of Blazeborough was climbing into the pulpit. The congregation sat down with a rustle of expectancy. A difficult task – an impossible task – to do justice to someone like the Colonel. The Duke avoided all the pitfalls. He didn't attempt to steal the vicar's thunder and bring religion in, nor did he attempt an obituary. All he did was tell stories about the Colonel and soon he had a relieved congregation laughing. All that pent up emotion which it wasn't done to show was released in laughter, and with the laughter and the stories he brought the Colonel to life.

They finished with 'Jerusalem', which the congregation sang lustily. Three hundred and fifty voices belting out the words so many knew off by heart while the organist pulled out all the stops. When the service was done and the vicar had pronounced the church's final blessing, hunting took over. The Duke blew Gone Away on his hunting horn and they carried out the coffin to 'Do Ye Ken John Peel'. The galloping notes, more suited to a bugle than the organ had the poor organist all at sea once or twice and certainly the bearers of the coffin found it impossible to keep up with the pace. Kate knew the Colonel wouldn't have been impressed. Not much of a show – it was almost as if he was at her shoulder. Silly buggers can't keep in step to a tune like that. Ought to have stuck to Handel's Largo. Obviously the heavenly host hadn't robbed him of his sense of humour, she thought, smiling in spite of herself. She hadn't expected to feel him all around her like this. She walked out of church with Alan almost as if there were three of them. It was disconcerting but at the same time comforting. 'I have only slipped away into the next room . . .' Perhaps she'd been wrong. The Colonel hadn't gone, or perhaps only his spirit had gone. His presence was still here.

Back at The Court it was more like a wedding than ever. The sun was shining on the red and white striped awning of the marquee and the daffodils lining the long drive were nodding their heads jauntily in the stiff March breeze. By the time Kate and Alan got back from the church there was already a queue of cars waiting to park in the paddock where only a few short weeks ago they'd held the meet.

'I must say I never thought so many people would come back just for tea,' said Kate, wriggling out of her coat and throwing her black beret on to the back seat. 'You'd better drop me off at the end of the drive. We'll need all the hands we've got just to get the tea poured for this lot.'

'OK, darling. I'll come and give you a hand as soon as I've parked.' She leapt out and sprinted up the long drive, relieved to have to shake off the emotional stress and grapple with the more practical problem of getting tea. In the kitchen everything was under control, Caroline's meticulous planning bearing fruit. The two large electric boilers from the village halls of both Riddletons were simmering nicely and a bevy of sturdy farmers' wives were filling the huge kettles with tea and carrying them off to the marquee in the paddock.

'Everything all right?' asked Kate, impressed at their expertise. 'I came as soon as I could to give you a hand but you seem to have everything under control.'

'So far so good,' said one farmer's wife. 'We've done it all before many a time for the puppy show. It'll get a bit frantic for the next half hour or so, but if we just make sure the urns are kept topped up constant so they don't have too much cold water to heat up at once, we'll manage.' Kate left them and went out into the tent to see how things were going at the sharp end.

Caroline had been right after all, she thought amazed by the number of people pouring into the tent. Half Gloucestershire seemed to be milling round the tables in busy ant-like clusters, descending on the teacups laid out in one corner and crowding round the tables laid with food, which were dotted about the marquee. At the far end the bar was already doing brisk business. Emotional stress was thirsty work. Kate seized a kettle brought in by one of the women from the house and started pouring tea. By God, it was heavy. She filled a row of cups and rested the kettle on the edge of the table. No wonder country women had fat arms, she thought. They needed the muscle.

'Here – let me do that for you.' Alan suddenly appeared at her side. 'The sandwiches are running out. Have you any more?'

'Plenty. I must have made enough to feed the five thousand.'

'Good girl.' He picked up the kettle and began filling cups. She darted away thinking how good Alan was at popping up at her elbow whenever she needed him. She was kept busy for quite some while keeping the food tables replenished and the milk jugs topped up. The women had been right – the first half-hour was frantic. People kept pouring into the tent until it seemed as if there wasn't an inch of space left. Just getting about with the trays of sandwiches and cakes was fraught with difficulty. She could see Alan was making himself useful in an unobtrusive but effective way and she was pleased he'd managed to fit in. After all, he knew nobody here, or virtually nobody, and it was a completely alien environment for him, yet he seemed to be getting on remarkably well. When she saw him go up to John Kindersby, she felt a prickle of alarm. John wasn't going to be very pleased with Alan over the holiday village débâcle. Ought she to go to his rescue? She caught his eye, and he smiled reassuringly at her. There was no need to worry, Alan was quite capable of looking after himself.

'What a lovely party!' Jane Evering loomed in front of Kate as she was making for the kitchen with an empty tray. 'The Colonel would have loved it – what a pity he's not here too.'

'Yes, it's a pity he had to die before the party,' said Kate and was pleased when Jane looked shocked. She wondered what Jane was doing here since she couldn't have known the Colonel very well, but then she supposed that was the difference between a funeral and a wedding – you didn't have to be invited to a funeral.

'So brave of Deborah to come back alone and face all these people she knows so well.' Jane's inquisitive eyes fixed on Kate's face as if trying to prise the truth out of her.

'I don't see how she could very well not,' said Kate with a shrug. 'It wouldn't have been very tactful to have brought the lover.'

Jane pursed her lips disapprovingly. Perhaps she has designs on Patrick, thought Kate, amused since it didn't matter now. 'I do hope Deborah and Patrick can get it together,' Jane said. 'She was hanging on to him in church I noticed.'

Kate wondered if the lady protested too much. 'I daresay she's feeling the loss of her father very much,' she said. 'She was his favourite, I believe. I expect poor Deborah's feeling very at sea.'

'She doesn't look lost now,' said Jane, staring across the tent. 'She looks remarkably sexy. The horse dealer must be doing his stuff.'

Kate followed her gaze and saw that Deborah had discarded her mink and was wearing a black dress that was just a little too tight and a little too short and very low in front. She looked a real hot number and was being befriended by Alan. Perhaps I ought to get a sexy dress like Deborah's, she thought as she picked up her tray and went off to the kitchen for more supplies. Alan certainly seemed to be enjoying looking down that cleavage. But she knew that it wasn't necessary. Their sex life was better than it had ever been, more fun, less restrained. In the past she had always had a little corner of herself reserved for Patrick but that corner was swept out now, and Alan, instead of trying to get it right, was being much more demanding. Perhaps before he'd been as bored as she had been and now he saw her not just as his wife and the mother of his children but as a woman in her own right. She didn't need a sexy new dress to inflame him when she'd got a whole new personality, she thought with elation. But would he give her the chance to be herself when she was no longer at The Court and being treated as indispensable by the formidable Caroline Kindersby?

Deborah had bought the black dress as an act of defiance, and also to impress Ned. She'd hoped that they would come to the funeral together but he had thought it better if he stayed away. 'It won't be easy for you going back so soon,' he'd said, 'but it'll be a whole lot more difficult if I'm there with you. The whole hunting world and his wife will be there to see your dad put away. If you and I turn up together it's like rubbing their noses in it. It don't do to make people look foolish.' She'd argued with him right up until the moment of leaving, but he'd put a stop to that, drawing her to him and kissing her roughly so that soon she couldn't think of anything except wanting him so badly she thought she would burst.

'You'll be all right without me, love,' he'd said, straddling her. 'We're the winners now – you and me. We've got what we want.' He made love to her then with brilliant speed. 'That's one to remember me by – a quickie.' He'd grinned at her cheekily, while she was still gasping with delight and she'd set off full of elation. He was hers. She had given him what he wanted and he gave her everything she hadn't had with Patrick. Confidence, courage and constant sex. She didn't have to try hard to please him or be good with the village, or struggle to keep the show on the road. All she had to be with Ned was herself. If she behaved badly Ned scolded her, spanked her sometimes even, but she didn't mind. With Ned she never felt guilty or cross, just constantly challenged. He took the decisions, and the risks and the blame. All she had to do was try and keep up. It was enormously stimulating and at the same time reassuring.

But today Ned was a hundred and fifty miles away, halfway up a Welsh mountain and without him she didn't feel brave, she felt desperately alone. It wasn't as if anybody had said anything. Everybody had been so incredibly kind, even Patrick. Not one word of condemnation or criticism. It was as if her father's death had turned her into an invalid again. People weren't unkind to invalids; invalids were too delicate to be burdened with the truth; what people did with invalids was humour them until they were strong enough to return to reality. But where was reality? Certainly not here. Her father was dead, her old home would soon be gone. Patrick was a bore. She didn't belong here any more. Reality was Ned.

'Are you all right, darling?' Suddenly Patrick appeared at her side. 'You look as if you could do with a drink.' She was dying for a drink so she let him steer her towards the bar at the far side of the marquee. Sooner or later she was going to have to talk to Patrick and she'd find it easier with a drink in her hand.

'It's a good show,' he said when he'd brought her drink. 'It's such a shame poor old AB can't be here; so many hunting people from all over the country. He'd have had a ball.' She supposed he meant it kindly but she didn't want to think about her father. All she wanted to do was get through this difficult day and escape back to the simple life with Ned.

'It's all so unreal. I can't seem to accept that he's gone.' She took a deep slug of whisky, feeling terribly sad. 'It feels so strange, all these people at The Court and him not here. I can't get used to it at all.'

'You should have come back before,' he said, putting the boot in with amazing complacency. 'Maybe if you'd been at the hospital – or even helped a bit with the funeral it would seem more real. Kate and Caroline have worked so hard. It must be difficult for you not being a part of it all.'

If only Ned were here. She clung to the thought of Ned, unable to think of anything to say to Patrick that wouldn't be catastrophic.

'You mustn't feel guilty that you weren't there,' Patrick went on. 'Kate was with him when he died.'

If he was still trying to be kind he was making a real mess of it, she thought miserably. But then that was the trouble with Patrick, he was totally insensitive.

'I don't feel guilty,' she told him defiantly, 'not unless you make me.' He looked surprised and she gazed helplessly round for a way of escape. But Patrick had her backed against the canvas wall at the end of the bar and the others had drawn away, tactfully ignoring them. They're leaving us alone to make it up, she thought. Oh God!

'I hope you don't think we should have got the children out of school?' Patrick said presently. 'Perhaps they should have been here. It's a great occasion. It might help them to know how well respected and loved their grandfather was.'

'No, you were quite right – much better leave them out of it. They're too young for all this.'

'They'd have enjoyed the wake and I thought perhaps you'd like to have seen them.'

She took another swig of whisky to give herself courage. 'I have seen the children.'

His face fell and she could see she'd taken him completely by surprise.

'Ned and I have been to see them, at their schools – to explain things.' It had been Ned's idea. He'd made her do it and she was glad now, seeing Patrick's dismay, that she had.

'You've got a bloody nerve!' he exclaimed.

'What's the matter, Patrick? Did you think I was going to leave you to tell my children that I'd abandoned them – that I didn't love them any more?'

He glared at her. 'How did they take it?'

'I think they'll come round to it in the end. When they realise that they can have ponies and hunting and all the things they love with me as well as with you.'

'Are you trying to steal the children from me?' he demanded.

'No, Patrick – you can have custody.' She took another restoring gulp from her glass. 'It's better that they stay with you. It's their home, after all. I just didn't want them to think I didn't love them any more.' She threw back the remains of the whisky.

'But how am I going to manage, for Christ's sake?'

'You managed all right at Christmas. Perhaps you can get Kate to come and live with you.' It was a mean jibe she knew, but he was being so helpless. She wasn't going to fall for his little-boy-lost act any more.

'Kate's off back to Saudi tomorrow,' he said suddenly looking so shifty that she wondered whether she had in fact stumbled on something. 'Her husband's turned up. He's here with her now.'

'I always thought she was after Daddy, but perhaps I was wrong,' she said, watching him curiously.

His face gave nothing away. 'I don't know what Kate's relationship with your father was,' he said. 'They wanted to operate to stop the bleeding but Kate wouldn't let them. Did you know?'

'Does it matter? He's dead now.' She didn't want to think about how he died or what could have been done to save him. She didn't want to think of her father at all. It was too painful. She looked about her desperately. All she wanted to do now was escape. Kate was cruising past carrying a tray of sandwiches. She tried to catch Kate's eye but Kate kept her head down. She's like everybody else, thought Deborah in panic. She's leaving Patrick and me alone to heal our differences.

She tried to ease out from her corner but Patrick caught hold of her arm. 'Deborah, come back and live with me. We'll start all over again,' he pleaded. The moment she'd been dreading had arrived and she couldn't bear it. 'We can make it work – for the sake of the children.'

'No, Patrick.'

'For your father's sake then. It's what he wanted. That day he drove off on his own, he was trying to persuade me to have him living with me. He wanted to keep an eye on me until you came back. He always knew you would.'

'Patrick, stop it.'

'It's true – ask Kate.' He let her go so suddenly she almost fell against the canvas wall of the tent. Bewildered she watched him dash across the room and seize hold of Kate, dragging her back by the arm. 'Tell Deborah what her father said,' he demanded. Kate stared at him blankly. 'You know, that last day at lunch,' Patrick urged impatiently. 'He wanted to come and live with me to keep me out of mischief until Debs came back. Tell her,' Patrick insisted. 'It's true, isn't it? Tell her.'

'Of course your father wanted you back,' Kate said, smiling at Deborah apologetically. 'It's only natural. You're his favourite daughter after all.'

She's humouring me too, thought Deborah. Is it because she's had it off with my husband? She was pretty in a fragile kind of a way and had a very sweet smile. Funny, she'd never noticed Kate properly before. Was it Ned, she wondered who'd made her so much more aware of ordinary people? If she was having it off with Patrick it's my own fault for having thrown them together, thought Deborah, surprised that she didn't feel jealous.

'Your father was a wonderful man. I was very proud to have known him,' Kate said gently.

Deborah suddenly felt a great weight of sadness descending on her like a suffocating blanket. 'You were with him at the end, weren't you?' she said to Kate. 'Did he say anything about me?'

Kate was looking concerned. 'Your father died happy,' she said. 'He was reliving his best moments out hunting.'

The blanket was weighing Deborah down, threatening to engulf her.

'I don't think he suffered – hardly at all.'

The weight of sadness was so heavy Deborah could hardly breathe. She knew if she didn't get away now, she would break down and cry. Kate smiled a kind understanding smile and made a move towards her. Deborah was afraid she was going to put her arms around her. If Kate did that she'd be finished. She mustn't break down in front of all these people, mustn't cry in public. Daddy would be so ashamed. She had to get out, get away. She didn't want sympathy or kindness from anyone – all she wanted was to get home to Ned.

'Debs, you look all in.' Deborah felt Patrick's hand on her shoulder. There was genuine concern on his face. She couldn't bear it. 'I don't think you're in a fit state to go back tonight. Why don't you come home with me? You'll feel better after a good night's sleep.'

'Fuck off!' she shouted, pushing him away. 'I'm all right. I don't need you. Leave me alone.'

Kate watched Deborah running through the crowded marquee and wished she could do something to help her.

'It must be terribly difficult for her,' she said, turning to Patrick. 'She was his favourite and she wasn't there for him at the end.'

'She doesn't feel guilty – she told me so,' he muttered.

'Of course she feels guilty – she's just bottling it all up. She's got to get through the day somehow. You'll have to be patient with her – give her time.'

'What makes you think I want her back?' he demanded defiantly.

'I don't think you know what you do want, Patrick,' she said, trying to be fair. 'A few days ago you were trying to persuade me to marry you.'

He looked at her sadly. 'I know I was. But I thought you'd forgotten.'

She felt sorry for him and ashamed of herself and most of all relieved that she was cured of him for ever. 'No, Patrick, I haven't forgotten. I haven't forgotten any of it. All the times we had when we were young, or those wonderful once-yearly meetings at the Imperial or last Christmas with you at The Manor. It was all quite magical. It's just that I think I've grown up at last. I've realised that it's no good day-dreaming my life away.'

She caught sight of Alan bearing down with a plate of cakes in his hand, his face purposeful, his mouth grim, coming to separate her from Patrick. But there was no need now for Alan to worry. All these years she had been harbouring a secret fantasy but she was like the pools winner who wins a million and finds, when she gets what she's always wanted, that she wants what she already has.

'Here, Patrick.' Alan thrust the plate of cakes into Patrick's hand. 'You know all these people better than I. You'd better go round with these.' Patrick looked stunned. Nobody had ever treated him like a waiter before. 'I'm going to take my wife outside for a breath of fresh air. She looks all washed up.'

'It's been a difficult day for all of us,' muttered Patrick, turning his back on them in disgust.

'Poor Patrick – I feel rather sorry for him,' said Kate, watching Patrick dump the plate of cakes on the bar and accept another drink from a group of farmers.

'The one I feel sorry for is that poor wife of his. Deborah,' said Alan.

'She'll survive,' said Kate. 'She's tough.'

'Poor little Deborah, trying to look like a *femme fatale*.'

Kate raised her eyebrows at him.

'Deborah's not tough,' he went on. 'Oh, she may be brave physically – that's because her father's brought her up to it – but she's also been spoilt. Her father was a strong man and her husband's weak – that's why she ran off with someone like Ned Jones. She wanted protection, a strong man to lean on. Nobody could lean on Patrick for long.'

'Did you get all this amateur psychology from looking down Deborah's ample cleavage?' asked Kate scornfully.

'I've walked round and I've listened to the gossip,' he said, taking her arm and steering her outside. 'Handing round sandwiches is a very good camouflage, you know. Nobody here knows me and they're all gossiping away like mad. I've learnt a lot of interesting things this afternoon.'

Kate felt suddenly cold wondering if perhaps he might have heard too much.

'You're the one who's tough,' he announced with a slightly rueful smile.

'Me!' Kate was stunned. It wasn't how she saw herself at all.

'I suppose I should have realised it before, but love is blind so they say.'

Panic swept through her. What was he saying? Had Alan finally fallen out of love with her just when she was beginning to appreciate him properly?

'All these years I've been so busy protecting you and trying to make you into the sort of wife I thought I wanted I couldn't see the real woman behind the waif I fell in love with. You should hear what they've been saying about you. Everybody's singing your praises.' Kate opened her mouth to protest but he went on quickly, 'I've been a selfish fool, Kate my darling.' He put his arm around her shoulders. 'I was afraid to let you be yourself in case I couldn't keep up.'

'I got so used to depending on you for everything,' said Kate, relief making her incautious. 'I just sort of switched off. Marriage makes people blind too. It dulls the expectations. We were stuck in a rut and we didn't know it.'

'Then I suppose I just got too immersed in the job. I didn't notice you that much any more.'

'Until I woke up one morning and found I'd become a non-person.'

'It wasn't until you got away from me that you were able to blossom. I can't forgive myself for that.'

'Oh Alan, that's not true. It wasn't your fault. I was a hopeless little wimp until the Colonel whipped me into shape.'

He laughed then and kissed her. 'From all that I've heard of this Colonel of yours today, there isn't another woman who'd have lasted half as long as you did, let alone done everything you did. It makes me very proud.'

'Really, Alan? You're proud of me? After I've behaved so badly?'

He held her tight. 'In what way badly?' he asked.

It was on the tip of her tongue to tell him about Patrick but his face suddenly became guarded and she knew whatever he might suspect he would never want to know the truth.

'Kidnapping the Colonel from The Priory, encouraging him with the holiday village thing when his children were selling to the enemy – causing mayhem – interfering in people's lives.' She couldn't resist a quick dig at him – he'd been so very hard on her over the telephone.

'I'm sorry, Kate. I've been a pompous prig at times. You'll have to take me in hand. I just haven't got your rebellious nature.'

She laughed. 'I learnt it from the Colonel.' He was looking at her with such pride she felt warm all over. 'I shall be a model of propriety in Saudi – you'll see. I'll walk three paces behind you and carry all the luggage on my head like the well-behaved Arab wife should.'

He laughed. 'It's not as bad as that.' He suddenly looked concerned. 'All the same, it's going to be pretty boring for you at times, don't think I don't realise that. Maybe we needn't stay in Saudi all the time. Perhaps I can do a deal with the company, see if I can't do some of it from London – or at least come home once a month.'

'The question is,' said Kate, looking wistfully at The Court, 'where's home? I thought our house in London was still let.'

'Well, the people there are happy to stay on, but if you want it back you've only to say so. I can tell them we've changed our minds.'

'No, don't do that. I have a better idea. We'll buy a country cottage somewhere. We can afford it, can't we?' He looked a bit taken aback. 'If our house is let and we're living free in Saudi,' she added persuasively.

'Perhaps we could afford it.' He still looked dubious. 'But what would you do in the country?'

'What would I do in London? I'm not a career girl – I've learnt that at least. Shirley says I'm unemployable and she's right about that. The holiday village protest wasn't a great success. I realise that now. We weren't nearly effective enough. We were nowhere until you came along and saved it.' He relaxed and she saw that although success had made him more sure of himself, he still needed to be depended upon.

'Is that what you'd really like?' he asked. 'To live in the country?'

'Not permanently.' She put her arm through his, squeezed it gently. 'I'm like Ruth – whither thou goest I will go. I can see you're going places and instead of being left behind like so many wives whose husbands get on I'm going with you. But wouldn't it be fun to have a little bolt hole to run to? We can put down proper roots, somewhere to retire to in our old age. You've no idea how many friends I've made just in the few short months I've been here. Village life is much more timeless, more community-spirited. I'd like to start getting stuck in now.'

'Maybe you could help Caroline with her latest project,' he said, looking suddenly thoughtful. 'She's going to turn The Court into a foster home. Something she's always wanted to do, apparently.' Kate was amazed. 'She sees a lot of life, being a magistrate, a lot of hopelessness, a lot of despair. All the persistent offenders seem to be children who've been chucked out of the family home by the stepfather or mother's new boyfriend. Nobody wants them. What Caroline wants to do is set up a home for some of them here. Meccarda have agreed to let her have the house at a nominal rent. I think they're probably delighted to have the excuse to write the loss off as charity. Be good for PR.'

'What a wonderful idea!' Kate was thrilled. 'The Court needs to be full of children and it's such a peaceful, happy place. I'm sure it'll do wonders for children who have never known love or security.'

'She'd have made a good businesswoman, that Caroline,' Alan said. 'She's a brilliant organiser and she's got the money now to get real results. She told me she intends to have a chain of homes in the end – if this one works.'

'Beneath that rather aloof exterior she's quite a decent sort,' said Kate. 'I've always got on rather well with her – in spite of all the trouble with Meccarda. She never took it out on me personally.'

'Perhaps you could help her. There'd be plenty of scope for your caring skills.'

Kate's heart sank. 'No, Alan. Stop trying to organise my life for me. I thought you'd promised not to any more.'

'Sorry, darling, it's a bad habit. Twenty years of it, it'll take some getting rid of.' He was looking at her a little too patronisingly, thought Kate. She'd better start standing up for herself straight away.

'I thought I might start a catering business,' she said. 'Nothing big. Just stuff for deep freezes. All these people who hunt are so busy they don't have time to cook properly, yet it's when they're hunting that the social life is at its peak.' He frowned but she wasn't going to be put off. 'Or perhaps I might even produce a cookery book – recipes for dinner parties that can be prepared in advance. I might call it *After Eight*. Get those peppermint people to back me.'

'My God, Kate, you don't waste time. I thought you said you weren't a career girl. Aren't you being a bit ambitious?'

'You've got to aim high. The Colonel taught me that – amongst a lot of things. Reach for the ceiling, he once said, and you may land on the mantelpiece but if you only reach for the mantelpiece you'll end up on the floor.'

She reached up and kissed him. He was looking a bit stunned and she could see that she would have to go a little more slowly with him until he had time to get used to his new assertive wife. It wasn't going to be easy holding her own with someone like Alan, not nearly as easy as standing up to the Colonel. With Alan she would have to let him think he was the decision-maker all the time, and let him help her every now and then. But with Alan's help there was no end to what she could achieve. All it needed was for her not to be faint-hearted. She had learnt that she wasn't a wimp, and whenever her courage failed her, all she need do was think of the Colonel and reach for the sky.